DRACULA'S DAUGHTER

BOOK 1 OF THE ALISTAR KAIN SAGA

ANDREAUS WHITEFYRE

DEDICATION

To all of you that thought this couldn't be done, I say with all love... Bite Me. (Vampire Joke)

With that said, I have Several people I'd like to thank for making this all possible.

First, My mentors, Rachel Carr, and Rick Gualtieri who took all of my questions in stride and took me under their wings to walk with me down this path of Authorship.

Next, My Editing team. Lori, Nicole, Marissa, Brady, it has been a wild ride. You've cried with me, screamed with me, scolded me. Begged me for more to read. And yes, I know I've put you through Hell, and yet you all helped me make this book what it is.

My Beta readers are next. Without these folks, I and my team would not know what we needed to fix to make this go from a good book, to a great book.

Melissa Levine... What can I say? You started as one of my

Beta readers and just decided to edit and help me on a professional editing level, even though I wasn't able to pay you what you are worth... Yet.
(https://www.redpenediting.net)

Finally we get to the last but MOST important person in all this... My Witch. Babe, you pushed me through this, you were brutally honest in what you thought about it, both on the good, AND the bad. When I wanted to quit, you wouldn't let me. When I disappeared into writing for weeks at a time, you took it in stride. The best part was when you'd let me read you to sleep. Love you. Forever and Always.

PROLOGUE

A young girl of sixteen years, dressed in sackcloth and ashes, is dragged by two burly men toward a metal stake on a metal grate set deep into a concrete pad in front of a large crowd of people. She screams and struggles, calling out for her brother. "Please! I'm not a witch! You are making a mistake! " The men tie her to the stake as a man dressed in cardinal's robes steps forward. He looks sternly at the girl and nods to one of the men who strikes the girl, silencing her.

"Sophia Kain! You are accused of being a witch, of having the ability of Sight without the guidance of the church! You stand accused of witchcraft and heresy and for that you are condemned to die in the holy cleansing flames of heaven's wrath!"

Sophia raises her eyes and looks pleadingly at an older man standing at the front of the crowd held between two other men. He is in his thirties and looks at her with shame and anguish. "You said they would cure me! You promised!" she screams.

"And so we shall! For you will be cleansed by heaven's fire and reborn anew, a holy creature, untainted by the darkness that now infests your soul!" the cardinal responds vehemently.

He nods again and one of the men lights a torch before throwing it at Sophia's feet. The gas under her ignites with a woosh and she screams as her clothing burns.

"Alistar!" Sophia's cry spurs the man in the front of the crowd and he breaks free from those holding him, rushing toward her. Three men, dressed similarly to him, step into his path. He kicks out, crushing in the nose of one man. A punch to the chest stops the heart of a second, and a roundhouse kick snaps the neck of a third. He leaps on one of the men holding the girl and wrenches his neck around breaking it with a sickening crunch. Five more men tackle him to the ground, kicking and beating him as others join them. The ferocity of their attacks overwhelm even his skills, and all he can do is look at the girl with despair in his eyes as she burns.

"You see the powers of the witch?! She holds sway over even one of our own! Clouding his mind to get him to save her from this holy cleansing!" the cardinal shouts over the girl's increasing screams. One of the men holding the man down looks towards the cardinal and after receiving a nod, strikes the man, knocking him unconscious.

1

The man woke with a start to the chill of the night air and his breath rushed forth in a steamy cloud. The fire he had set earlier had burned down to embers, its warmth fleeting and useless against the cold. He checked his old military-grade kinetic watch, its faded glowing numbers telling him the time is 2:30 AM on March 18, 2142. Off in the distance the sounds of an animal struggling clued him in to what woke him and he slowly rose to his feet, grabbing his heavy cloak he had been using as a blanket, and throwing it over his shoulders to ward off the low temperatures.

Picking up his knife and pistol, he slowly made his way through the dark woods of Romania's Carpathian Mountains. He walked down an animal trail that was lit by dappled moonlight passing through the branches of the evergreen trees overhead. As he got closer to the noise he slowed, his footsteps becoming almost inaudible.

Maybe it's a deer and you might actually eat well for a few days, Alistar. Alas his hopes for roast venison disappeared as he entered the edge of a small clearing and saw a great white wolf with its leg caught in the vicious teeth of a hunter's live trap. He stopped when the animal noticed him and growled low in its throat. Something about the wolf suggests that it was female.

She noticed the man as he stepped into the moonlight and growled low in her throat, her eyes wary and mistrustful. Her leg was badly wounded and she still chided herself for not sensing the trap before she stepped into it.

"Easy there lady," Alistar said, raising both hands with palms facing outward. He stepped forward and stopped just outside the limit of the chain as the wolf's growl deepened and she lunged at him. "Hey now, I bet you'd like to be free." Reaching slowly into his pack, he pulled out a small piece of dried meat and tore off a strip, tossing it near the wolf.

"Go on, eat it." Alistar crouched down. Based on the range of the chain, he knew he was safe where he was.

Who was this man? Most humans would have run when confronted by something my size and so dangerous. When the man threw a strip of beef at her feet, she looked down at it, sniffed it and then looked up at the man.

Taking the other strip of beef, Alistar bit a piece off, and chewed thoughtfully. "It's not poisoned, if that's what you're thinking." He kept his voice soft, not wanting to spook the wolf any more than it already was. Most dogs could understand body language and voice inflection when a human spoke and he trusted that this wolf understood him as well.

The wolf continued to look at the human before snapping up the strip of meat and chewing twice. This human was strange. She could sense his fearlessness and unthreatening nature even though most humans would try to exterminate one such as her on sight.

Alistar pulled out another piece of meat and held it out to the wolf. When she didn't take it, he placed it on the ground and scooted a little closer. The wolf growled at him again. "Easy now," He slowly spoke in a soft tone. "I just want to get this off your leg." He reached toward the trapped paw intent on freeing the animal from its condition.

The wolf lunged at him, her jaws closing on his gloved left hand. Only the glove prevented her from drawing blood. The man froze and after a moment the wolf let go and the man grabbed the jaws of the live trap. "Look, this may hurt and I am sorry for that, but we gotta get this off your leg." Alistar slowly pried the jaws of the trap open.

The wolf snarled and at this point the man knew if she wanted to kill him, there was nothing he could do.

The man intrigued the wolf and she lay there watching him. She understood perfectly what the man was saying.

With a click, the trap opened and Alistar set it to the side, examining the injured wolf's leg. The damage wasn't as bad as he had thought. Pulling a red western-style handkerchief out of his pocket, he gently tied it around the wolf's leg and then quietly sat there making no further moves away or toward the creature.

The wolf rose to stand on all four legs. She could kill this man easily, but she decided not to. She inched closer until she was nose to nose with him and inhaled, breathing in his scent, putting his smell into her memory. After a few seconds, she slinked into the dark woods, turning one last time, her eyes glowing in the moonlight.

Alistar studied the teeth of the trap as the wolf moved away. *Now who would line the teeth of a live trap with silver? What were they hunting, werewolves?*

He took his knife and disabled the trap, walked over to a nearby lake, and tossed it far out into the water before making his way back to his campsite. He stoked the fire to life, piling on more wood to ward off the night's chill and wrapped himself back in his blankets.

From deep in the woods, the white wolf watched him

for a bit before deciding this human was most certainly not a threat. Five great wolves approached her and she looked at them. *"Do that one no harm."* Her telepathic command issued forth to them before she turned tail and loped up the mountainside toward a large imposing castle, easily covering that distance in an hour despite her injured leg.

Crossing through the front gate, her form shifted, smoke and fur blending impossibly. Where once a large white she-wolf stood, now was a tall, pale, naked woman with elfin features and long black hair. A man, gray in hair, but strong in body, approached her, He wrapped a cloak around her svelte body.

"Have a good hunt Mistress?" He walked beside her, noticing her injury but not saying anything about it.

"Yes, Richter, but there is a human on my lands." the woman replied, looking at her injured leg. She couldn't see the injury, wrapped as it was in the man's red handkerchief, but to her it felt better.

"Did you kill him?" Richter asked, concerned that there might be a dangerous interloper that he might have to deal with.

"No, he freed me from a trap that I was unfortunate to be caught in." The woman's long strides quickly carried her inside the castle building proper.

"Well that's interesting." Richter's eyebrows rose in surprise.

"Yes, it is. He wasn't afraid of me at all. He is intriguing-: that much is to be sure. Bring me some blood. I wish to eat before I retire for the day." The woman made her way up a long winding stairway to a tower. The stairs were cold stone, and the stairwell itself was lit with gas sconces, lighting her way as she ascended. The bedroom she entered was somewhat opulent with wall hangings covering every wall, and a four-post canopy bed made of dark mahogany along one side. Against one wall sat a large armoire, its doors partially open revealing multitudes of gowns and outfits, many of which she had not worn in ages.

"Yes, Mistress," Richter replied before hurrying off.

The woman stared out the window. Off in the distance, her eyes picked up the small glow in the woods that marked the location of the man's camp. This human intrigued her, but from what she had seen, he was transient and not likely a local.

"I have brought you one of the finest vintages of blood from the cellar. I believe it is from 1968." Richter walked up behind her.

Reaching back for the the dull golden, jewel encrusted chalice, she took a long drink, savoring the cow's blood as she swirled it around her mouth. The blood had hints of herbs almost like it were a spiced wine. "Thank you Richter. This will do. You may leave."

"As you wish." Richter bowed and left the room, leaving her to her quiet contemplation as she sipped the blood from the chalice like a fine wine. Hours later, as the sun came up, she closed the curtains and lay on her bed. *I wonder how fast the man can travel.* Closing her eyes, she slipped into a deep slumber.

2

As the sun rose, Alistar woke and started packing his belongings. After he finished, he kicked dirt on the fire, before pouring water over the ashes and stirring them to make sure it was truly out. He didn't want to start a forest fire in this beautiful wilderness.

Picking up his pack, he opened a map and pulled out a compass. Checking the map and taking a heading, he gazed around one last time, then walked in a northern direction to the city of Brasov. There he could get a hot meal and maybe a bath and bed for cash he had in his pocket. With only two thousand Romanian leu to his name, he had to be careful.

He walked with quick measured paces, but numerous trees filled the forest. The mix of evergreens, and beech trees grew close together. They forced him to stop many times to reassess his direction as the overhead canopy blocked most of the sun. The hills and valleys made the going just as rough and he slipped, twisting his ankle and hindering his pace even further. He rechecked his map, and found a small town just a few miles up the road. Gazing up at the sun's position, the man realized that more than half the day had passed and he would have to stop there, losing the other half of the day to rest. Taking out his knife, he cut down a small sapling and striped its branches, turning it into a makeshift walking stick.

Dusk began to fall as he entered the town. The people gave him side eye glances as he approached a small tavern. The tavern appeared to be well built out of stone and timber, made to look rustic, but from the cracks and peeling stucco, he could tell it would have been a modern building in the pre-war days. A cool wind blew through the town as he limped inside and over to the bar where the tavern wench slowly stocked the evening's supplies. "Excuse me, Miss, would this town perhaps have a room I could rent?" He looked down at his leg. "And perhaps a healer? I twisted my ankle on the way here."

The comely woman looked over at him. "We might. Where might ye be heading?" she asked with a lilt.

"Brasov. I figure it's another forty kilometers," Alistar said, pulling out a chair at a table and sitting. He threw back the hood of his cloak, revealing a weathered, sun tanned face with a scar running down one side.

"Aye, it is. You won't make it there before the end of tomorrow. The room here is not much, just a sleeping area in the loft on some straw, but it's warm and dry." The woman smiled slightly and headed behind the small bar. "Say twenty-five for the room, another ten for a hot meal?"

Alistar nodded. "That seems fair." He pulled out a small wad of bills and set the money down on the table. The tavern wench walked over and picked it up after drawing him a beer from a nearby keg and setting it on the table in front of him.

"Marcus, run and fetch the doctor," she called to the back. "This man is injured." The young man nodded and rushed out the back door and down the street while Alistar took a long pull of his beer.

~

The woman opened her eyes suddenly, going from sleep to instant wakefulness. Opening the blackout curtains, she wrapped herself in a black cloak, and looked out her bedroom window, and felt a faint warmth on her cheeks as the sun's fading light caressed her face. Stretching her leg, she remembered last night's event. The man must have moved on by now.

Walking down the tower steps, she entered the castle's main hall and Richter made his way quickly towards her.

"My Mistress, I did not expect you up at this hour. My apologies; I will fetch your meal immediately," he said bowing.

"Quite alright Richter, and no need," She waved away her servant's apology. "I feel like going for a run around my lands. I'll take down a deer or rabbit while I am out and feed then."

"Very good Mistress." He removed the cloak off her shoulders and, in mere seconds she transformed. The large white she-wolf now stood where the human had been. Her leg was healed after a night's rest and she loped off down the castle hall and out the door into the fading light.

~

The door to the tavern opened and Marcus entered, followed by an old, withered man who spoke to the bartender. His head swiveled to the man sitting at the table. "Is this my patient?" She nodded and the old man headed in that direction. "What seems to be the problem, sir?"

Alistar looked up at the healer. The old man had snow white hair and cracked spectacles set in a withered, but kind face, tanned by years of living. "I've been traveling cross country and I twisted my ankle pretty bad." He slowly removed his boot in obvious pain. The old doctor tugged over a chair and propped the man's foot in his lap, feeling along Alistar's ankle until he winced.

"Yes, a good sprain you have there. Lucky for you, nothing is broken. A night's rest should help you recover. Just make sure you wrap it tightly before you set off again in the morning," the old doctor said before pulling out a glass bottle of pills. "Take these before you sleep; they should help with the pain."

Alistar held out his hand and the old doctor dumped two pills. "What do I owe you?"

"Ten leu." The old doctor began packing up his belongings. Alistar handed over the bills as the tavern wench brought him a steaming bowl of stew. He nodded at the woman as the doctor pocketed the money and left.

"Enjoy the meal. When you're ready to retire for the night, you will need to go outside and up the backstairs." the wench said as she pushed some strands of faded red hair away from her comely face and behind her right ear. "If you need anything, don't hesitate to ask."

The white wolf easily moved through the dark forest, occasionally stopping to sniff the air. The man's scent floated along in the slight breeze which meant that he was still within reach of the castle. How strange; she figured he would have made further progress. Had something happened to him? The faint scent led her to the small town of Calia, to people under her protection. She or her wolves dealt with any other creature hunting there.

Shifting back into her human form, she grabbed a frock hanging on a line in the back of a town folk's yard and put it on. She made a note to return it before she left, and headed into town, keeping her head down so as not to draw too much attention. The man's scent brought her to the small no-name tavern in the town's center, and she peeked through the window and listened to the conversation inside. Her supernatural hearing picked up the conversation through the tavern walls. After the man had injured himself, he had stopped here to rest for the night.

A deliberate scrape of a boot on the gravel path behind her signaled she was not alone. She spun around to see three burly tough-looking thugs. "You look lost, pretty lady. You looking for a good time?" One of them, who had an ugly scar down his left cheek, sneered.

Bandits. She neglected to check on Calia as often as she should, and did not realize that these thugs had moved in. Otherwise they would have been drained and tossed into the forest for the wolves.

"Hey, lady, the boss is talking to you," one of the other thugs spoke, his evil grin missing more than one tooth. "There's a tax in this town and everyone's got to pay one way... or another." They took a step toward her and she took a step back, bumping into the tavern wall. She really didn't want to fight here in the open where townsfolk might see her. But she had no other choice. Her eyes turned red and her fangs and nails lengthened... The tavern door opened.

~

"Thank you for the meal and the room." Alistar said to the tavern wench as he stepped outside. He looked up, reading the scene. A woman waited outside, alone and versus three men. He knew a bad situation when he saw one and this was bad. Two of the men had rusty old knives in their hands and had evil leers on their faces and glints in their eyes. That info alone told him they wanted to harm this woman.

The door closed behind him as the bartender's shouted words of "Don't forget to stop in and have breakfast before heading to Brasov!" floated out behind him.

Well shit. He quickly stepped over in front of the woman and shoved her back toward the still slightly open door. "Hey fellas, you look like you're about to do something really stupid."

It is him, and again he's saving me! the woman thought to herself as the man stepped in front of her to block the thugs. *I could rip these bandits in half in mere seconds, but all he sees is someone in need of help.* The thoughts echoed through her mind as her temper cooled and her eyes, fangs and nails returned to normal.

"Nah. We were just going to have a little fun with the lady here. There's a tax in this town and everyone's gotta pay." one of the thugs said with a smile.

"A tax you say… Hmm I don't think that's it. I think you're a bunch of thugs preying on the locals," Alistar said grimly as his stance widened for more stability.

"Yeah, so what? What are you gonna do to the three of us? We've got numbers on ye." another thug said with scorn.

"Numbers? Sure. But I have an equalizer." Reaching behind him, Alistar pulled out what he had holstered there. The pistol whipped up in his black gloved hand, pointed straight at the men. "Do you know what this is? It's a Vietnam era Colt nineteen eleven, bored out to four sixty Rowland. Back where I'm from, people use it to put down wild hogs, and from where I'm standing, all I see is three little pigs in front of me. Now leave this woman alone, and leave this town, or I will put holes in you the size of teacups." Alistar's glare darkened and stilled to a completely deadpan look.

One of the thugs pulled out a rusty knife, and in a flash Alistar moved his aim slightly and fired. The gun roared, and all that remained of the thug's cheap metal weapon was a broken hilt and half a blade.

"Shit!" The ruffians backpedaled in surprise and then turned tail and ran. This man was no easy mark to be swindled. Alistar waited to be sure they didn't return then regretfully reholstered his weapon with a sigh.

Damned ammo is so hard to come by this far from home. But at least that trick shot scared them off. Walking over he picked up the spent brass off the ground before turning back to the woman.

"Go home miss. I don't think those three will be coming back anytime... soon..." The woman had disappeared. *"Hmm, she must have run off. Smart lady."* Heading around the back of the tavern and up the stairs to the loft he entered, laying his pack down and spreading out his cloak on some straw. Lying down he pondered the strange woman whom he just saved.

~

High atop her perch on the tavern's roof, the not so helpless woman was lost in her thoughts. Again, the man's actions confused her. The beast inside her growled, reminding her that she still had not eaten. That small expenditure of her powers left her feeling empty. But she could not feed here. She jumped from rooftop to rooftop until she made it back to the edge of town where she got the frock. She sniffed the air and easily picked up the scent of the bandits. Hanging the dress back on the line she transformed into the great white wolf and raced off toward the fear laden scent.

From her vantage point deep in the forest shadows she carefully studied the small camp set up on the outskirts of town. Taking her role of protector seriously, she vowed they would not live to prey on her helpless people— even one more night.

She listened to the men talking about the strange man and his even stranger handheld cannon as they sat around the camp. Taking advantage of their distraction, she swiftly moved among them, her gracefulness like a ballet dancer. She lashed out, slicing open the jugular of one bandit with the tips of her diamond-hard nails. He died with a gurgle on his lips. She easily disemboweled the next one. She left the leader for last, sweeping up behind him before he knew of the danger.

"That man may have let you live tonight, but I shall not. You prey on my people, hurt them, and steal from them. This I can't allow." She murmured, her needle-like teeth laying along his carotid artery. She could feel the wild jump in his pulse and her lips curled in a wicked grin. The bandit leader let loose one gasp before her fangs sunk deep into his neck. His blood was tainted and tasted stale, but still she drank. His body twitched and his heart beat faster and faster. It didn't take long for the beats to grow fewer and farther between until it finally stopped cold. Satiated, she dropped the body to the ground and sent a telepathic call. Five great wolves silently appeared on the edge of the fire-light.

"Take these bodies deep into the woods and feast; leave no remains behind." With those words said, she turned and walked through the woods at a leisurely pace heading back towards the castle. Tomorrow night she would head to Brasov and try to find the man again.

3

Leaving the town of Calia after a hearty breakfast, Alistar headed out once again, his twisted ankle still bothering him slightly and slowing him down. A few hours later, a splatter of water hit his face and he glanced up to see rain falling. Lightly at first, then harder and harder as the hours lengthened. Although he moved as fast as he could, the pace was still slow, and night had more than fallen by the time he reached the city of Brasov.

∼

As the day turned into evening, the woman's eyes opened. Richter stood by her bed with another chalice of blood. "Your breakfast, Mistress." He holds out the same chalice as before. She gently withdrew it from his hands.

"Thank you Richter. I shall be going out tonight." She drained the contents.

"As you wish, Mistress. Will you be running wild?" he asked, taking the chalice.

"No, saddle up Midnight for me. I am riding to

Brasov." The woman stood and walked over to a large armoire and looked inside.

"I shall do so post haste." Richter bowed before leaving the room heading to perform his assigned task.

Hmm... I need to visit Francois at some point and see about having him make me some new clothes. These are so last century. Picking out a black shirt, riding breeches and a set of black knee length riding boots, the woman dressed and strapped a short sword to her waist. She didn't need it. Over the years she had come to find that having a blade at one's side persuaded ne'er do wells that she was a tougher prospect to rob than someone else on the street. Finally she picked up the red handkerchief off the bedside table, looking at it deep in thought before smiling and tying it about her neck giving her just a splash of color to her otherwise black outfit.

Her swift steps carried her down the stairs, through the main castle halls, and out into the courtyard where Richter waited with her pitch-black mare saddled up and ready. The rain pelted on her as she put her foot in the stirrup, threw her leg over the saddle, and sat.

"Go Midnight, carry me swiftly to Brasov!" she commanded her horse who sprinted swiftly out the front gate and down the road. Through the woods she rode, her eyesight helping her guide her mount in the darkness far better than any human could in the fading light. She bursts out of the woods onto a road leading north toward her destination. The road had seen better days, broken and in disrepair, its concrete long since passed seeing the wheels of cars on a daily basis.

Midnight's hooves clattered against the broken pavement, and splashed through the developing puddles, carrying her rider onward. Soon the city of Brasov came into sight. The lady climbed off her mount and released the reins.

"Wait for me here my friend. I shall call on you should I need you," she whispered in the horse's ear. Midnight nickered softly in response, nudged her rider, and moved into a nearby field to eat grass.

The lady had been to Brasov before and knew that only one inn would accept strangers this late at night. Quickly she moved into the city taking shortcuts down back alleyways and across the rooftops where necessary. Pausing on top of a two story building, she sniffed the air as the wind blew in from the south, catching the faintest hint of the man's scent. Turning in that direction, she leapt from rooftop to rooftop following the scent trail along the wind, the rain not hindering her sense of smell.

~

Alistar entered the city through the south gates, moving down the roads, looking for the cheapest-looking place available. He knew what to look for having stayed at many such places before. Unfortunately, one by one, each place he came to refused him. Finally, one of the innkeepers told him about a place called "the Old Rams Inn" and how they would have late-night lodging. With that information, he trudged deeper into the city.

~

There! The lady's mental shout when she spotted the man would have woken the dead had it been expressed verbally. He turned down a main street and headed quickly toward the Old Ram's Inn.

~

Alistar trudged on, not knowing that the lady on the rooftop followed him. Shoving open the door to the tavern attached to the inn, he stepped inside. The place went quiet as he gauged the crowd. Everyone stared back at him as water from his cloak dripped on the floor. He slowly walked toward the bar and placed a hand on the counter. "Do you have any rooms available, and perhaps a meal and a hot shower?"

The innkeeper eyed him up and down. "For you, five hundred leu... for the room. The bath is another hundred and the meal fifty," he replied in a gruff voice.

Damn that's highway robbery! Alistar knew he had no choice. If he didn't get out of these wet clothes and warmed up soon, he would likely become sick.

"Fine," Reaching into his pouch, Alistar tugged out an old wallet. He drew out the requested cash and slid it across the bar.

The innkeeper quickly snatched the money and pointed at a door off to the side. "Up the stairs next door, last room on the left. The bath is at the end of the hall. However hot the water comes out is however hot the water is. Deal with it. You can eat here afterward."

Alistar nodded and disappeared through the door.

The lady watched and listened to the whole exchange from the dark shadows by the door where she had entered unnoticed. After the man went through the door she stepped up to the bar and glared at the innkeeper.

"You took advantage of that man!" she hissed under her breath, loud enough for the innkeeper to hear.

"So what, lady, he's obviously too tired to argue and I like money." The innkeeper sneered at her.

The lady looked him dead in the eyes and pushed with

her will. "You will refund him half his payment when he comes back down. You had a mix-up in the math. You charged him too much."

The man's eyes blanked for a moment. "I had a mix-up in the math. I charged him too much." His vision cleared and he noticed the money in his hand. "Aww geez. I charged that guy too much. Well, he'll be back down and I can correct it then."

The woman slipped away among the wait staff, but this time not unnoticed. A girl in the bar's back corner watched her. After the woman exited the bar, the girl walked over to a table with four guards and said something to them. Quickly, they all get up and gathered their things.

The woman looked up to the roof as she stepped outside before glancing around. Seeing no one else on the street, she lept, landing feather light on the inn's roof. She moved around to the back side where she located the man's room. Leaning over the roof's edge, she grasped the side of the building, her palms and boots sticking to the side through supernatural force as she scaled over to his window.

He had the window opened slightly and she silently watched him as he placed his pack on the bed, unpacking the things he needed to clean up. Miserably he shivered in his cold wet gear, completely soaked to the bone as he took off his cloak, hanging it on a peg on the wall. He moved to the bed and sitting down, unfastened his boots one at a time. The one on his injured ankle gave him trouble and caused him to wince. Standing again, he unbuttoned his shirt, revealing a massive burn scar, along with scars from being whipped across his back and shoulders.

The woman hissed in a sharp breath, and scooted back away from the window as the man turned to look outside.

~

Alistar pushed open the grime-covered glass pane a little bit more and leaned out. He breathed in the night air, not knowing that two feet to his right, one of the most dangerous creatures in the world hid in the shadows of the overhang, watching him. Or maybe he did. His head rotated until he peered into the dark shadows searching.

The woman gathered the shadows about her as he opened the window. *You don't see me.* The words echoed in her head as his gaze stared at where she hid. His dark brown eyes locked with her crystal gray ones and she knew he had found her. *Damn. You do see me. But how?* The alarming thought went through her mind. No mortal had ever been able to pierce her shadow veil before.

Alistar's gaze drew upward and his eyes locked with two glimmering gray ones set in a face he had seen just the night before. Below that face, his eyes caught on a familiar red handkerchief tied about her neck, and he leaned back in surprise, seconds before a light shined in his face from the street below.

"There! On the side of the building!" The shout came from the street.

4

"Go. Now!" Alistar's voice issued out in a hiss and the woman leapt east across the street to another building. He watched her leave, the men on the ground chasing after her, and then spun around, throwing his clothes back on.

Alistar, you are one dumb motherfucker. This may get you killed. He set his pistol at full cock and puts the safety on before sliding it into his holster. Wrapping his cloak back around his shoulders he reached into his pack and grabbed a small black cylinder before he rushed out of the room, leaving his pack behind. He would come back for it later if possible. He slid down the banister, rushed out the door, and headed east down the street.

"Damn. Damn. Damn." he muttered to himself with each step his foot hit the ground. Why did that woman follow him? He didn't know, but if she died, then he'd never find out. He could see the woman on the rooftops and the men following her close behind from the street.

～

The woman leapt from roof to roof, not bothering to lighten her steps. Roof tiles clattered to the streets below whenever she landed. Turning, she headed south, leaping toward the outer edge of town where not all the street lights were lit, trying to find places to hide. If she could get far enough away, she could lose them.

~

Alistar saw the woman turn south, and watched the men skid on the wet street, one even falling. He was thankful they were only town guards and not actual Hunters, meaning they didn't have the pursuit skills actual Hunters had. Leaping up, he planted one foot against the wall and shoved off, hopping off the other wall, and moving back and forth, wincing as he did so.

He managed to scrabble up onto the roof-top and took off after the woman, doing his best not to fall to the street below.

Hearing the shouts, he dared a glance back to discover the guards following his trail. Dropping down to the street, he shoved a stack of wooden crates over, blocking the alleyway the guards were running down. "Heh. Have fun taking the long way around, assholes," he muttered as he raced east again after the woman.

Alistar stopped at an intersection, trying to see where the woman had gone. Something hit him from behind, knocking him to the ground. He rolled to the side, brought up his pistol, and found himself staring into the same fair elfin face of the very woman he was looking for. Only this time her eyes were blood red and filled with rage, and her fangs were out.

"Whoa! Whoa! Wait!" he shouted.

The woman knocked her prey to the ground and he

rolled away from her. She found herself staring down the barrel of a gun. Behind that gun was the face of the man she had been watching. Again, he did not seem afraid. Her anger cooled and her fangs retracted. She backed away a step as the man slowly lowered his weapon and climbed to his feet.

Alistar hesitated. He knew what this woman was, but he also knew she could have attacked him whenever she wished in the past few days but hadn't. "I've slowed the guards down, but we don't have much time. I don't know you, and you sure as hell don't know me from Adam, but if you want to escape, follow me. It won't be long before the rest of the town-guards are checking every street and every building," he said, holstering his gun, leaving his hands empty as a show of trust.

The woman cocked her head to the side. "Why would you help me?" she asked quietly in a heavily Romanian accent. She tilted her head further to the side in interest.

"I don't know. Maybe it's the fact you could have killed me twice now and you didn't. Maybe it's the fact you seem to be following me, and I want to know why. Or maybe I'm just a dumbass with a death wish." Alistar shrugged in response. "What I do know is we have about two minutes before this town is swarming with more guards, and I think if you were going to fight, you would have stood your ground rather than run."

The woman paused for a second then smiled mischievously. "What makes you so sure I won't just eat you the first chance I get?"

Alistar looked skyward with a *heaven help me with this one* look. "Again, IF you were going to do that, you'd have done it the last time I saved your ass from those thugs in Calia, or you could have just slipped into my room back there while I undressed and taken me out then."

The man's tone and manner showed that he clearly did not know or care who he was talking to. It amused the woman greatly and she smiled, showing a bit of fang. "You make valid points."

The shouting behind them grew louder. "Damn, they found their way around that blockade quicker than I thought." He cursed and turned away. "Look, you have a choice to make. Either trust me, or don't, but I'm heading in the opposite direction of them." He pointed back down the street, where lights could now be seen moving.

The woman made up her mind in that instant and nodded before taking his warm hand in her cool one. "Very well." This surprised Alistar for a moment as he clearly had not expected this, but a second later, he nodded back and the two ran, heading south. He calculated the search pattern of the guards in his head and aimed down a dark alley, and then down another. They were quickly running out of space and needed a place to hide or a way over the wall.

"There!" He spotted a cathedral up ahead on the edge of town. He did not expect the woman stopping hard and his arm being nearly pulled from its socket. "What the fuck?" He gave a questioning look.

"I can't go in there. It's a church." she hissed at him.

"Yes, you damn well can."

"No I can't. Churches have crosses and holy relics that will hurt me," the woman said quickly, fear in her eyes.

Alistar sighed and closed his eyes for a second. Opening them he gripped the woman's face in his hands looking into her eyes. "No. They won't. Not if you don't directly touch them. It takes the faith of whoever is behind a holy object to make it project that faith as a weapon. Otherwise, it's just an inanimate object with a bit of an aura."

The woman's eyes go wide. *He touched me! How dare he!* For a second, anger flashed across her face but quickly cooled as she realized he was only trying to assuage her fear.

Alistar saw anger fill the woman's face and he thought he may have gone too far. *Way to go. dumbass. You just laid hands on a vampire.* Then the look passed and her composure returned to normal. "Well I guess she's not going to eat you... at least not right now anyway."

"Eat you? I've followed you for two days because I am curious about you. Why would I eat you?" Alistar realized he had said those last words out loud.

"That... was not supposed to come out of my mouth. Clearly my filters are not working, and I suddenly realize I just touched you like any other human," he said sheepishly, then he coughed. "Look, I gave you my word. You will be okay here, just uncomfortable. Don't touch any crosses and nothing will burn you."

The woman nodded and they pushed open the great wooden doors of the cathedral together. Walking inside she shivered and scrutinized the interior. He noticed this as he closed the doors and slid a pew in front of them. "You okay?"

"I feel like ants are running under my skin. I don't like this place!" The woman snapped back clearly irritated by the holy energy permeating the building.

"If that's all that's happening, I think you'll be fine. Just remember, touch nothing." Alistar shoved another pew in front of the door and then added a third one, stacking them on top of each other. "There. That should hold for a while. I think we will be safe enough to take a breather." He undid his cloak, draping it around the woman's shoulders.

"I am not cold. Vampires do not feel the cold." The woman stared at him with a questioning look.

"Sorry, it's just a habit. I'll take it back if you don't want it," Alistar replied, holding out his hand.

"Umm no. I will keep it. Thank you." The woman tugged the cloak tighter about her body, positioning the hood over her head as if to shield herself from the cross behind the altar and then sat on one of the pews. The man dropped his hand and gave a small smile before walking to one of the tall candelabras and snapping it off at the base.

"I see. Get me alone and you can stake me by yourself," the woman said dryly but still stayed sitting.

"Nope. Not at all." Alistar snapped off the top, leaving him with a four-foot staff with one broken end. "I only have so many bullets and eventually those guards will come for us, so I need another weapon. I'm not looking to kill anyone unless I absolutely need to do so." He spun the makeshift staff around his body in a display of martial arts before slamming the butt onto the stone floor, the metal butt cap striking sparks against the small specks of flint in the cobblestone.

The woman raised a well-defined eyebrow. "You are a curious one. You are clearly not afraid of me, you can fight, and yet you do not wish to kill unless you must do so to survive."

The man sat next to the woman. "Yep. I'm a conundrum, wrapped in confusion."

"Well mister conundrum, what do I call you? I can not call you man, or human, forever."

The man held out his hand. "I'm Alistar... Alistar Kain."

The woman considered Alistar's hand for a moment before taking it in her own and giving it a firm shake. Usually people would bow before her, not offer a handshake. "I am Elzibeth."

"Well, Miss Elzibeth, it's a pleasure to meet you." Alistar smiled slightly.

A loud force pounded against the cathedral doors, rattling the pews stacked against them.

"Well, that didn't take them long." Alistar commented dryly.

5

"Well, I guess it is time for us to fight," Elzibeth said, standing up, Alistar doing likewise.

"Nope. It's time for you to go up to the second level, smash out the stained glass window and escape. It's time for me to stay here and give these guards an old-fashioned ass whoopin' while you get away," he replied, cracking his neck.

"But they could kill you!"

"Nah, I'll be fine. I've been through worse than this and I'm still here." Alistar's grin made him seem almost boyish in the darkness of the cathedral.

A loud bang sounded on the door again with voices outside. "They must be in here! The door is barricaded! Come on, men! Push!" Slowly inch by inch, the pews started to scoot back.

This man is either a great fighter or overconfident in his skills. "And just how many fights with armed people have you walked away from?" she asked haughtily.

"Not including this one?" Alistar thought for a

moment. "Twenty… at least. The ones I can remember anyways."

The doors slid further inward with another bang and Alistar glanced at them. "Look Miss Elzibeth, you'd best move along. Another hit like that and those doors will be open far enough to let the guards in." Sure enough another bang sounded and one of the pews fell with a crash allowing entry. Ten guards came pouring into the church. Noticing some of them were carrying crossbows, Alistar stepped in front of Elzibeth, putting his own body in the line of fire.

"Get outta here Elzibeth, I'll be fine. I'm sure you will track me down later on if you wish." he said just loud enough for the vampiress behind him to hear. He stepped forward and the guards noticed.

"You! Surrender!" the one wearing a captain's golden helmet shouted.

"As if! But, if you wish to surrender to me? I'm cool with that. It's a far less painful option than me beating your asses inside a church," Alistar quipped.

The guards all laughed. "There are ten of us here and only one of you." The captain positioned himself in front of his men and drew his sword.

"Well I hate to tell you this, but you ain't got enough boys." Alistar's mirth suddenly dropped and his demeanor turned cold and calculating. "Because the vampire in this cathedral is not the monster you should be worrying about."

OK Alistar, old boy, they see you are armed, so they will go with crossbows first. Then close in with swords rather than reload. Alistar closes his eyes.

Five crossbowmen spread out around their captain and knelt to aim better. "Stand down or we will open fire!" the captain shouted at Alistar.

"Bring it on," Alistar replied, opening his eyes. Within

them was a resolve of cold steel. Years of fighting helped to focus his vision and hearing. A fly buzzed above his head.

The captain dropped his arm and five crossbows released their bolts with audible *thwangs*. Alistar spun his makeshift staff as the hail of arrows crossed the distance. One arrow managed to graze his cheek, but the others were easily deflected or simply smashed in two. He swiveled, taking a step to the left, and facing the guards once again.

～

He is saying that he is a monster and yet everything I have observed tells me that he has a good soul and is a good person. Why does he call himself a monster? Elzibeth watched as Alistar deflected and destroyed all but one arrow, her keen eyesight picking up the cut on his cheek. She saw the years of skill in his stance and his grim determination. But as more guards poured through the door, she somehow knew that if she did not help him, he would die.

～

Alistar was outnumbered but intended to buy Elzibeth time to escape. The captain and five guards drew their swords and rushed him. He spun, swinging the staff, sweeping low, taking out the legs from under two guards. He then brought the staff back up in time to parry a sword blow from the captain. He spun again, and cracked the captain across the side of the helmet with the other end of the staff, causing the man to stagger back. Shoving the staff backward, he caught another guard in the stomach with the butt end, knocking the wind out of the man and slamming him back against the wall. The other guards quickly take steps back out of reach.

The captain removed his helmet and threw it to the ground. "You might want to put that back on. I would hate for you to get a concussion," Alistar said.

"Fuck you!" The captain spit blood on the floor.

"No thanks. You are clearly not my type. I think I would rather take my chances with the vampire." Alistar's words came out a biting retort, making the captain even angrier as more men poured in through the door, totaling about twenty people. Alistar couldn't fight this many at once if they rushed him. He shifted back.

~

Elzibeth steeled her resolve. These were just human guards. They were not Hunters. She didn't have much to fear, especially if she got in close enough that they couldn't use their crossbows. She dove off the second floor balcony, landing in front of Alistar and lashed out with one clawed hand, slashing open the throat of the captain. Her next swipe slashed the cheek of the nearby guard. She opened her mouth and hissed loudly, showing full fangs and glowing blood-red eyes.

"I told you to leave!" he yells at her, surprised when she landed in front of him and killed the captain and another guard.

"Neither of us will make it out of here if we don't work together!" she hissed back as she downed another guard in a flash of claws. The rest of the guards started backing away in a panic from the whirling dervish in front of them. Some dropped their crossbows and scrambled to leave the cathedral, giving Alistar and Elzibeth a brief rest.

The respite would not last long. Alistar hauled the small black cylinder from his pocket and pulled a pin on it.

"What is that?" Elzibeth asked.

"Homemade flash-bang grenade with a little extra added in," Alistar replied as he bounced the grenade off a wall and out the open door. Turning, he grabbed Elzibeth and spun her around so they faced away from the door. They were met with a loud crack and a bright flash and the sound of coughing men outside. Grabbing Elzibeth's hand, Alistar led her up the stairs and to the great stained-glass window behind the cross. Rearing back he slammed his elbow into the glass, grunting in pain.

Elzibeth put her hand on his shoulder, stopping him, then she struck the glass hard, shattering it with her palm. She stepped out onto the ledge overlooking the city wall and beyond, the fields where farmers grew their crops. With one glance back at Alistar, she leapt to the ground.

6

Alistar watched as Elzibeth jumped twenty feet like it was only five, landing lightly on her feet.

"Well, in for a penny and all that." He jumped, and immediately knew more regret waited in his future. Sure enough his weight came fully down on his injured right ankle. He both felt and heard the sickening crunch as his bones broke. He bit back a cry of pain and tried to get to his feet, stumbling.

"Even I heard that." Elzibeth said from his side. She gently felt his leg until he winced in pain. "Your ankle is broken."

"Well damn. Guess you're gonna have to shoot me like a wounded horse. Get outta here before those guards show up. I'll make it on my own." Alistar again tried to get to his feet. Elzibeth put his right arm around her neck.

"'Umm, what are you doing?" Alistar asked.

"I'm helping you, and you don't get any choice in the matter. I will not leave you to the mercy of those guards." she replied testily. Alistar took a step and Elzibeth walked with him as they made their way out into the fields, and soon they were hidden by the tall stalks of corn. "There, I think we can take an easier pace. Those guards will not see us surrounded by all this corn."

"Look, at this point if they can, I'm just gonna lie down and let them take me in... That was a joke," Alistar replied at Elzibeth's alarmed expression..

"Well, it was not a very good one," Elzibeth glared at him. Mentally she reached out, finding the mind of her horse a field away. *"Come to me Midnight. I need you."* She sensed her mount heading their way.

"Yeah, well, I never said I could tell good jokes.. Especially when I'm in pain."

A horse's black head poked its way through the rows of corn and nickered softly. "Midnight, there you are my friend. Thank you for being so swift." Elzibeth pat her horse's nose. "Can you carry two, my friend? Good."

"Umm, yeah... One problem. I've never learned how to ride a horse," Alistar scratched his head.

"Really? Where do you hail from?" Elzibeth asked incredulously.

"Bethlehem, Pennsylvania... and we didn't have any horses growing up. I learned to drive a motorcycle by age fifteen, and a car by sixteen."

Pennsylvania? That's in the United States. This man is far away from his home. But now is not the time for questions. "Well, riding a horse shouldn't be much different. Especially since all you will be doing is holding on so you don't fall off." She turned, bent down and cupped her hands.

"Put your hand on Midnight's saddle and your good foot in my hands and I shall help you up." Elzibeth said with a tilt of her head.

Alistar paused, filled with uncertainty. "Umm, okay. I feel bad about muddying your hands with my boot, though, just so you know," Alistar stepped into her offered hands. It felt like stepping onto concrete. Such was her strength that she didn't move an inch under his weight and she easily lifted him so he could swing his other leg over the saddle. He settled in. "I've got ten leu that says I'm going to fall off at some point," He joked again.

Elzibeth ignored his joke and surprised him by swinging up behind him, wrapping one arm around his waist to hold him in the saddle and taking the reins in her right hand. "No, you won't. I won't let you." She snapped the reins once.

"Home, Midnight! Swiftly!" Elzibeth commanded her mount, and the horse galloped off through the fields.

Well, this is awkward. Alistar mused to himself. *Then again, it's kinda nice.-* Thankfully, this time, his musings stayed inside his head.

Midnight's hooves clopped against the dirt, throwing up clods of earth behind her and her riders.

They traveled through the dark, leaving the city of Brasov behind.

"You said that guard was not your type and you'd rather take your chances with me. What exactly did you mean by that?" Elzibeth asked in Alistar's ear, her breath soft.

"Huh? Oh, I, umm, mean that he was trying really hard to kill me, and you so far have not, so, umm, my chances were better with you." The small smile forming on Elzibeth's face remained hidden from him.

"You said you were from the states. Why are you so far from home, Alistar?" She again poked him with another question as they rode.

Alistar stiffened. "There was nothing left for me there. So I left and started wandering the world. It's not something I want to talk about. Sorry." He shut down Elzibeth's question for fear of what topic it might lead to.

"That's quite alright. We all have parts of our past we don't wish to visit." Concern filled Elzibeth's voice. *Parts of his past could mean trouble for me, but I guess we will talk about this more later.*

A castle sat high on a mountaintop off in the distance, silhouetted by the rising moon. The castle appeared somewhat run down and even from this distance, one of the towers was partially crumbled. Alistar looked to the west with concern as a howl floated through the night.

"Those are wolves," Alistar said, his voice betraying his concern. His gaze roamed the landscape as others joined the first howl.

"Yes, those are my guardians welcoming me back home. They roam throughout this land which my family has owned for eons. The creatures of the night are mine to command," Elzibeth said with a soft chuckle as she remembered meeting Alistar for the first time in her wolf form.

"Oh right. I have a question that's been nagging at me. That red bandanna around your neck, I recognize the half burnt corner. The last time I saw it, I tied it about the injured leg of a great white wolf. How…"

"How did I get it?" Elzibeth questioned.

"Yes." Alistar started to nod but stopped, not wanting to headbutt the vampire sitting behind him. The landscape continued to flash past them as Midnight carried them onward in the castle's direction.

"It should be obvious if you think about it." Elzibeth smiled and leaned close to Alistar's ear. "I was the wolf."

Alistar startled just a bit then settled again. He turned his head catching the mirth on Elzibeth's face.

"Huh. So I guess your guardians must have reported a strange human on your land and you just had to take a look?" he tossed another question at her.

"That would be correct. I was simply seeing what kind of threat you might be. It turns out that you were no threat, but a kind and caring man. So I left you be and told my guardians to do the same," Elzibeth replied while looking around, her eyes sparkling in the night.

The howls got closer and Alistar found four great big shaggy wolves running up alongside them. "Well it seems we have an escort."

"That we do. And no, you can not eat him. And no, he is not dinner for me either." Elzibeth laughed.

Alistar's eyes widened in alarm and he tensed up again.

"Calm yourself. My guardians were just asking questions. They think you look delicious." Elzibeth laughed again. *Although, I cannot disagree with them.* She muses. *Alistar did look good on the eyes.*

7

After another hour the pair trotted up the long winding road and into the castle's courtyard. As Elzibeth climbed off her horse's back and helped Alistar down, Richter came running out of the castle proper.

"Mistress, you are back. Oh, I see you brought company... for dinner?" he said, raising his eyebrows.

"No, he is not to be harmed." Richter nods at her words, as Alistar inspected his surroundings, confused.

Elzibeth turned on her heel. "Alistar Kain, I grant you the Accords of Hospitality of my castle under the old laws. This means that under pain of death, no one will harm you."

"That's cool and all, but does this pain of death thing apply to yourself?" Alistar asked with one raised eyebrow as he tried to take a step forward. His weight came down on his broken ankle, still unable to bear the weight.

"Well, no. But then, as you yourself have said on more than one occasion..." Elzibeth glided toward him like a breeze and grabbed his arm to steady him as he was about to fall. "If I wanted you dead, I could have just killed you within our first three meetings."

"True." Alistar tilted his head down in a nod to the right. "Very well. I too... umm... bind myself to the accords to... umm... do no harm to my host or her people." He actually knew the proper saying of the reply to the Accords of Hospitality, thanks to having been granted such hospitality in the past but he felt it safer hiding just how much he knew of such things for now.

"Close enough." Elzibeth once again put his arm over her neck, but, this time, Richter got on his other side and both helped him walk into the castle proper, where they brought him into a bedroom and set him on a bed.

"Thank you." Alistar began to say before Elzibeth put a finger to his lips, silencing him.

"Don't thank me yet Alistar. Your bones need to be set and that is going to be quite painful. Richter, go down into the cellars, I believe we have some Tuica that is from an old vintage of Father's. Fetch it for me."

Richter bowed "Right away, Mistress." Unlike Elzibeth, his accent spoke of British origins. He turned smartly and headed out of the room. Elzibeth sat on the edge of the bed and began unlacing Alistar's boot on his injured leg.

Alistar reached out to stop her and she pushed away his hands. "Part of being a good host is taking care of your guests when they need help," Elzibeth chided him. He folded his hands together and watched her intently as she moved to pull the boot off. "This is going to hurt slightly," she said, looking Alistar in his eyes and he nodded.

Slowly Elzibeth pulled off the boot revealing a well-worn black hiking sock. "You, sir, need a bath," She wrinkled her nose.

"Well, I was going to take one before a certain vampiric peeping tom was caught peeking through my window." Alistar replied with a laugh. Then he bolted upright. "Aww fuck. My pack! It's still back at the inn. Unless the guards have taken it." He flopped back down. "Damnit!"

"I can have Richter go fetch it after he helps me with your bone setting. He's very good at getting into places unseen where he's not supposed to." Elzibeth placed a hand on Alistar's leg in a calming gesture. She could see he had something in his pack that was of great value to him.

"I… I thank you," Alistar said softly and looked down at his lap. Elzibeth's eyes filled with kindness for a moment. Richter arrived with an old, glass bottle covered in dust along with two sticks and some long strips of cloth.

"This Tuica is so old it might actually kill him with its potency." He opened the bottle and the smell of fermented plums reached Alistar's nose. Richter handed him the bottle and Alistar took a long sniff and then coughed.

"Yep, that's some strong stuff!"

"Good. I want you to drink some of it. It will help to deaden the pain," Elzibeth said.

Alistar peered at the bottle before taking a long pull from it and immediately went into a coughing fit. "Fuck me, that's some strong stuff!" But even with those words, he took another pull, and then another, before handing it back as the warmth spread over him.

Elzibeth waited a few moments before she stood up and leaned over Alistar. She reached across and behind him, feeling for the snap to the holster under his coat and carefully pulled the large, heavy pistol out. She set it on the bedside table.

"You will not need this while you are here but I shall leave it by the bed. I know it will bring you comfort to have it near." Then she placed one hand on his leg and the other on his chest pinning him to the bed. "Richter will set your leg. I'm going to hold you down so you don't move while he does so." Alistar nodded at her words.

"Do it. I'm tougher than you may realize. I've broken bones in the—" Richter yanked hard on his foot. The bones snapped back into place with a crunch. "Past," Alistar gasped. He closed his eyes for a moment and Elzibeth stepped back.

Exhaustion clouded his eyes. "We shall leave you now." She walked over to an armoire and opened it, rummaging inside. "Ah! This should work!" She tossed a jerkin and some drawstring pants onto the bed. "They may be a little loose fitting but I want to burn what you are wearing. Later on, we can get you a proper bath."

She motioned Richter out of the room before turning back to Alistar, wrapping the cloth around his leg and tying the sticks, immobilizing it. "Should you need anything, just ring the bell on the bedside table. And you, for the most part, have free run of the castle while you are here, but I would be careful of going into the lower levels as many parts of them are in disrepair. And you are forbidden to go up into the north tower."

"Undershtood. No going into the norsh tower." Alistar slurred his words, the alcohol taking effect. Elzibeth smiled slightly, seeing him so vulnerable.

"And at some point we will have a talk about your past, Alistar," she muttered, turning around to leave the room. The soft sound of snoring commenced behind her, signaling that the human named Alistar had fallen asleep.

"Richter, go to the Old Rams Inn in Brasov and search the back left room for a pack and other belongings. Bring everything back here."

"Yes Mistress, I assume they are his?"

"Yes, oh, and get five hundred leu from the innkeeper. The shady old man tried to rip off our friend there just because it was late and he was a stranger." Elzibeth gave a curt nod.

"Understood Mistress. Everything in the room plus five hundred leu is to be brought back here. I shall depart post haste." Richter left for the stables, saddled up his horse and headed out into the night.

Elzibeth poured herself a chalice of blood and headed towards the stairs up to her room. She paused outside Alistar's room listening to him. Hearing him softly cry out in his sleep, Elzibeth stepped inside and saw that he was shivering. She gently covered him with a comforter and noticed a tear slipping down his cheek.

The poor soul must be having nightmares. What happened in your past, dear man? She gently wiped the tear off his cheek and slipped back out the door after seeing he had calmed down. She gracefully climbed the stairs to her room high atop the north tower and sat down in front of the window as she drank her chalice of blood. She stayed there until the sun started to rise in the east. Richter came riding back into the castle with a well-worn pack slung across the back of his horse.

8

Alistar woke with a start, dazed and confused. "How did I get... Oh right. Vampire, castle." He sat up, looked down, flipping the comforter off himself and stared at his splinted leg. "Broken ankle." He sighed and flopped back onto the bed. "Well, fuck, you are certainly in a situation, Alistar." Resting a little longer, he sat up again and looked around the room. A pair of crutches leaned against the wall by the bed within easy reach, and across the room laid his bag. "She kept her word on my belongings. Huh."

He moved to the edge of the bed and grabbed the crutches, shoving one under each arm. Sliding off the bed, he tried to put most of his weight on his good leg and hobbled over to his pack. "*Hmm*, now how do I get you to the bed?" He pondered the problem for a moment before picking up the pack and attempting to toss it onto the bed. He succeeded in doing so; however, he put weight on his broken ankle and the sharp spike of pain made him stumble before falling to the floor.

"Well fuck," Alistar muttered under his breath. Crawling to the bed he pulled himself up to a standing position and plopped onto the bed next to his pack. Opening it he felt for the hidden compartment sewn carefully into the bottom. A sigh of relief issued forth.

Feeling over the compartment, he started to panic. *Where did it go?!* Then a glint of metal drew his attention to the bedside table where he found a small, woman's heart shaped locket. He carefully opened it. On one side a picture of a young girl smiled out, and on the other a young boy glowered. He held it tight to his chest.

"I figured you might want that." Richter's voice startled him and he looked up to see the man standing at the door.

"Yes. Thank you," Alistar responded, wiping away a tear.

"Who is she?" Richter asked as he picked up the crutches on the floor and leaned them against the bed within Alistar's reach.

"She is… *was* my sister. She died a long time ago." Alistar closed the locket and puts the chain around his neck.

"My condolences." Richter gave Alistar a moment of silence, truly feeling bad for the man if only for a few seconds. "Now, you have slept all day and I bet you are hungry. My mistress will be up soon. I have prepared a meal for you both."

The mention of food sent Alistar's stomach grumbling in need. "Umm, yeah, I am kinda hungry."

"Good. Then come to the kitchen when you are ready. When you leave this room, go left and down two halls, then take a right at the second hall to the end." Richter explained before he left Alistar to get himself up and ambulatory.

Alistar glanced over at the 1911 on the bedside table and remembered Elzibeth's vow of hospitality and her words about him not needing it while he healed in the castle. "She's proven trustworthy so far. No reason to believe she won't continue to do so. Besides, it's not like you could do anything to her without special ammo."

With that thought passing through his head, he reached into the pack and jerked out an old windbreaker. Inside the pockets were his MP3 player and a set of earbuds. He then grabbed a pencil, an old notebook, and his pocket knife and shoved them into the back pocket of his jeans. Picking up the crutches he slowly makes his way out into the hallway.

"Now he said left from here and was it two hallways down and to the right, or was it three hallways down and to the right? Next time, dumbass, maybe you should pay attention," he muttered under his breath.

He hobbled down the hallway. The crutches, while modern, were old and the padding worn off and so were very uncomfortable to use. He passed one hallway, and reached the second. Stopping, he heard the clattering of plates from the right and the sound of a feminine voice scolding someone. *Hmm, must be two hallways and not three.*

～

Elzibeth was already in the kitchen taking her first sip of blood when Richter came back. "Good evening Richter, Where is Alistar?"

"Good evening, Mistress Tepes. He is slowly making his way here, I assume," Richter replied, matter of factly.

"And you didn't help him?! Richter, he is injured!" Elzibeth scolded her servant and got to her feet to help Alistar.

"Mistress, some men don't take well to being helped all the time. He is one of them. I can tell!" Richter snapped back, something he rarely did. "He's been on his own for many years."

"Still, he's under the Accords of Hospitality. We are obligated to help him." Elzibeth turned and nearly bumped into Alistar as he found his way into the kitchen.

～

The voices grew in volume the closer Alistar got, leaving him to wonder if Richter was none too pleased with him being here. *That's okay; I'll move on as soon as my leg is well enough to walk on. Don't want to be a burden.* Stepping into the kitchen, he nearly collided with Elzibeth. "Umm, good morning, Elzibeth."

"It's Mistress Tepes, not Elzibeth. And it's night-time so it's *good evening*, not good morning." Richter chided Alistar, causing a flash of annoyance to cross Elzibeth's face.

Elzibeth stepped backward and smiled. "Good morning, Alistar. I hope you slept well," she said, although she knew he hadn't.

"He is a guest, Richter. He does not have to follow the exact protocols that you do. And considering morning is when one usually wakes up, to him it's morning!"

"You are the daughter of Vlad Tepes, the Impaler, the Dragon. Proper decorum should be followed by all who are in your presence," Richter retorted.

Alistar'sgaze switched between the two of them. "Umm what?" Both Elzibeth and Richter paused in their argument and looked at him. "What did Richter just say? Who's your father?"

Elzibeth pursed her lips then helped Alistar to a seat at the table before sitting beside him. "My father was Vlad the Impaler. Also known as Dracula."

Alistar raised an eyebrow. "So you are literally..."

"Dracula's Daughter? Yes. My full name and title are Voda Elzibeth Tepes. But just to annoy Richter, you may call me Elle." She smiled and Alistar leaned forward in his chair, resting his head on the table as he took in this new information.

"Oh, holy fuck," he whispered.

Elzibeth patted him on the back. "Take a moment. I know it's a lot to process." Her smile widened as Alistar sat back in his chair and looked at her quizzically.

"You know you could have just opened with that line. Hi, I'm Elzibeth. I'm a vampire, and, oh, I'm also the daughter of Dracula," he said sarcastically.

"Yes, but it tends to drive everyone away." Elzibeth laughed in response as Richter set a bowl of stew in front of Alistar and refilled her chalice.

Alistar gazed down and nodded slightly before picking up a spoon and tucking in to the food in front of him. He ate fast, in military fashion, barely tasting the stew before swallowing. Elzibeth watched him with great interest as she sipped from her chalice of blood.

He paused in his eating and stared at her chalice. "Umm… Is that…?"

"Blood?" Elzibeth set the chalice down. "Yes."

"No, I mean, is it human?" Alistar continued with his question.

"No, it is cow's blood. I don't drink from humans anymore unless I am forced to in order to survive. Less mess and less questions from the authorities." Elzibeth smiled and Alistar slowly nodded.

"Okay." Leaning on the table he used it to push himself to stand. "Thank you for the meal, but I'd like to be alone for a bit. I'll be out in the courtyard should you have need of me." With those words said he grabbed the crutches and hobbled out of the kitchen toward the front of the castle leaving Elzibeth wondering if she had said anything wrong.

"Richter, did I say anything to set him off?"

"No, Mistress. I get the feeling that he is a man who's been used to being alone for so long that he's not quite used to being around anyone," Richter said calmly. "After all, you did find him camping out in the woods when a town full of people was only twenty kilometers away. I also sense he has a heavy burden on his shoulders. However, I don't believe he is a threat... to us anyway."

"Well, keep me informed about what else you sense."

9

Alistar seemed to struggle less with the crutches once he got in the open night air of the court-yard. The moon shone down, illuminating the courtyard as if it were midday rather than late at night. On the other side of the gate, three large wolves lifted their heads to glance his way from where they rested on the ground. He stopped, considering the situation, and then moved a little closer to the gate, testing to see what the wolves would do. The largest wolf stood and growled slightly.

"Okay, I guess that's a no-go. Not that I'd make it far with my leg like this. Elle or Richter could catch up to me just by walking even if you didn't try to eat me first." When he backed away, the large wolf lay down again but still watched him.

"What are you even doing out here Alistar?" he questioned himself as he looked around. In the corner of the courtyard, he spotted a chopping block with a stool next to it, a pile of partially chopped wood, and an ax. "Well, I guess I can get a bit of a workout."

Hobbling over to the chopping block he set the

crutches aside and sat on the stool, looking at the splint on his broken ankle. "*Hmm...* Not much I can do about you." A slight breeze filled the cool night air, and cricket sounds came from the forest beyond the castle. Grabbing a piece of cord-wood in one hand, he used the other to lift the ax high near the head and started billeting it carefully into smaller pieces. After a while he sighed, wiping his brow and still feeling the itch to do something. Brushing off his jeans, he picked up the crutches and rose, walking over to a set of steps that lead up the courtyard wall to the battlements, and carefully started climbing them.

From a window, Elzibeth watched Alistar limp around the courtyard and then head to the wood-cutting station. He spent a good couple of hours cutting firewood down into pieces that would easily fit into the kitchen stove. When he stood from that task and made his way up the steps to the battlements on the courtyard's wall, she tilted her head. "What are you doing now, Alistar Kain?" she muttered as she dipped a finger into her chalice of blood and stirred it. She continued to watch as Alistar sat on the wall between the crenulations and pulled out a notebook and pencil. After a moment of looking around he spotted Elzibeth through a castle window.

Watching her for a moment his hand moved and he started to draw. In a matter of moments he had a rough sketch which he filled in with details, his tongue sticking out of the corner of his mouth.

Is he... drawing me? Elzibeth thought as she watched Alistar put a pencil to paper. Just in case, she froze in place, not wanting to ruin his art even as her curiosity grew. *He's adorably cute with his tongue out like that.* After another thirty minutes or so, he seemed satisfied and he set the notebook and pencil down before leaning back and looking at the sky. He pulled a device out of his pocket and shoved two items into his ears. Standing, she opened the window and jumped down into the courtyard, walking slowly toward him. As she got closer she realizes she could hear music. Climbing the steps, she continued until her shadow fell on him.

~

Alistar sat staring at the sky listening to old music on the MP3 player. It had at least a 75 percent charge left and with the small solar brick in his pack he could recharge it. A shadow covered him and he looked over to see Elzibeth. He removed an ear-bud and held it up to her.

Fascinated, Elzibeth took the small device and positioned it beside her ear. The music came from it. "Stick it in your left ear."

"How?"

"This device in my hand is a media player. It wirelessly projects the music to the ear-buds, one of which you have held up to your ear."

"Fascinating. I need to get out more it seems. I did not realize technology had gotten this advanced. How much music is on your device?" Elzibeth asked as she sat against the battlement next to Alistar.

"Oh, about three hundred songs from various ages. And it can hold more, but it's hard to find a computer out here to grab music from," Alistar mused out loud and heard Elzibeth's sharp intake of breath. She reached over and grabbed the MP3 player from his hand.

"How does it work? Can I change songs?" She sounded like an excited school girl.

"Well, the buttons on the right side scroll through the song list on the screen, and the two on the other side adjust the volume. It's not a very complicated model." Alistar smiled, seeing the delight on her face. He heard the clicks as she scrolled through the list of songs and then another click as she found and pressed the play button.

He recognized the song. "That's *Love Exists* by an artist named Amy Lee. I believe it was recorded sometime in 2017. She's got a real set of pipes."

Elzibeth looked confused. "Pipes?"

"Means she has a fantastic voice." Alistar chuckled.

"I see. I have to agree. Some of my kind would take her in an instant just to preserve that voice." Elzibeth leaned back and let the music wash over her.

"And you? Would you take her?".

"No. I will not turn a human against their will. That was a rule of my father's, and it is one that I respect."

When the song finished Alistar heard more clicking as Elzibeth scrolled through more songs and then the click as she again pressed play. They focused on the music for a couple more hours as she found various songs from his eclectic library to listen to. She closed her eyes and smiles, her head swaying with the music as she leaned against him. More clicking sounds in his ears as the last song ended and she searched for another one. A final click sounded in his ear as Elzibeth pressed play. He recognized this song all too well and scrambled to snatch the player from her hand.

"Elle, I'm gonna need that back now," he said with a bit of panic in his voice. He managed to snatch the player from her hand and fumbled to turn it off. "Sorry, the battery is dying."

Elzibeth perceived the panic in his voice from the song's beginning lyrics. She heard his lie for what it had been. Glancing down at the device's screen, she saw the title scroll past. "If I Surrender" by some band called Citizen Soldier. She climbed to her feet.

"Alistar, is something wrong?" she asked softly.

Alistar glanced out over the wall toward the woods as he hurriedly shoved the MP3 player into his pocket. "I'm fine, Elle. Just suddenly tired," he sighed.

That too had been a lie and Elzibeth could read it on his face. He was ashamed that he had even said it. Something bothered him but he clearly did not want to talk about it.

"Very well then. Let's get you inside." She smiled but she would have to peel him apart like an onion if she ever wanted to learn about the real man. And that kind of work meant patience.

Alistar pocketed the player. "Sorry, I didn't mean to snap at you like that."

"Quite alright. I'm not going to eat you for it. Everyone has their moments," Elzibeth said comfortingly as she grasped his arm and helped him stand. Her gaze traveled upward as she did so and she realized that the sun would be up in only a few hours. She had spent the better half of the night watching him and sitting with him.

"Wait! My notebook!" Elzibeth looked behind them and saw the notebook and pencil sitting on the edge of the battlements where Alistar had dropped it. Bending down she picked them up and studied the picture. She gasped at the details.

"Alistar... this is beautiful."

He just lied to her, and snapped at her and here she was taking it in stride and complimenting him on his artwork. "You may have it if you wish."

The next thing he knew, Elzibeth was hugging him tightly. "Thank you. It is a gift I shall cherish." Then still hugging him she stepped off the battlements to the courtyard below, softening the landing for him rather than letting him walk down the steep steps with his injured leg.

10

Alistar walked with Elzibeth back into the castle proper and to his room."Again, thank you, and again, I am sorry I snapped at you."

Elzibeth smiled. "All is forgiven." She aimed for the door but stopped. "I'm willing to draw you a hot bath if you want one?" She arched an eyebrow questioningly.

"You know, for once, I think that and a stiff drink are something I could use," Alistar said, sighing and closing his eyes. He ran a hand through his hair and sat on the bed, shrugging off his jacket and removing the bracing sticks tied to his injured leg.

"Very well." Elzibeth nodded and headed into the next room. To Alistar's surprise he heard running water.

"Wait, you have running water here?"

"Both hot and cold! I may be an eternal creature of the night, but something is to be said for a nice hot bath." Elzibeth laughed back.

As Alistar struggled to get his pants off, he heard the water stop behind him and then Elzibeth's footsteps as she stepped into view. "Having trouble?" Alistar held up his thumb and pointer finger in the universal sign for just a little bit.

Kneeling Elzibeth helped him pull off his boot and tugged on the hem of his pants. Alistar coughed.

"Umm... Elle, this is—"

"What? Embarrassing? Mister Kain, you are going to be here for at least six weeks for that ankle to heal and you will need my help. You just have to get used to awkward situations like this," Elzibeth chided him and he scooted out of his jeans leaving him in tattered briefs.

Elzibeth wrinkled her nose. "Oh these are most certainly getting burned. And then I would toss the ashes into the lake, but I am afraid I might poison the fish." She threw the pants onto a nearby chair and gathered some towels out of the armoire, tossing them on the chair by the bathing chamber door while Alistar unbuttoned his shirt but didn't take it off.

Elzibeth just stared at him. "Well?" She raised an eyebrow.

Alistar grabbed a towel and wrapped it around his shoulders, covering his back as he took off his shirt. He felt the towel pulled down and Elzibeth's soft fingers tracing the scars and burns on his back. He shivered under her touch and closed his eyes.

When she next spoke her voice sounded soft and full of sorrow. "Take your bath, Alistar, but I know you are not fine. Something weighs heavily on both your mind and soul, and I am sure it's connected to these scars, and the fact that you always have your left hand covered by that long black glove. You will want to talk, and when you do, I will listen."

"Thank you." Alistar's voice came out momentarily choked up. He hadn't experienced kindness like this for the longest time that he honestly forgot what it felt like.

Elzibeth helped him to the bathing chambers. "The

rest you want to do yourself, I am sure. The rest of the towels are by the door," she said, stepping back out. Then she quietly reached into the pocket of the windbreaker laying on the bed, pulled out the MP3 player and earbuds, and slipped out of the room.

~

Alistar removed his briefs and slipped into the hot bath water. When he finally got out the water was cold and very gray. He toweled himself off and slipped into the bed just as a storm started to brew outside. He tossed and turned as nightmare-filled dreams took him in his sleep.

~

Elzibeth sprinted to her room as Alistar bathed. She quickly shut the door, sure he would realize his missing device. But no angered yell met her ears, no sounds of a human with a broken ankle trying to climb the stairs to her tower. Walking over she sat down on the bed and opened her hand, revealing the earbuds. She placed them in her ears, then pulled them out because they did not feel right. Then she noticed the L and R engraved on them. She put the one labeled R in her right ear and it felt better so she did the same for the other one. Scrolling through the songs she tried to find "If I Surrender," but before she did, she came across a song titled "To Big Brother" and hit play.

She listened intently as the song played, the look on her face dropping more and more as she realized it's not a song, but a recorded message. The girl in the recording cried.

"Big Brother, I need you! I'm scared! The sight has come upon me and I don't know what to do. I have visions I can't

control! I'm scared the church will burn me as a witch! I don't want to die! Big Brother, please come find me at our old hiding spot!"

The message stopped there. A bloody tear slipped down her cheek. "Oh Alistar, how much pain have you been through?" she whispered. "What hell did you experience back home?"

She found the song after searching for a few moments through others that made her feel even worse for Alistar, and she hit play. As the song ends tears rolled down her face.

She now understood that he didn't fear death; he wanted it. She thought back to him helping her as a wolf, and how easily she could have ended him then. Her next thought went to the fight with the thugs. If she hadn't been there, he never would have pulled his gun and he would have fought them. And the church... He knew that he wasn't going to make it, and he hadn't cared.

Was he now biding his time, waiting for her to drain him one night when hunger took over? Scrolling through the songs once more, she found one called "Right Here" by the band Ashes Remain.

With shaking hands she pushed play expecting another heart ripping song that might reveal more about Alistar. Much to her surprise, it did. The words of the song gave her hope that she could help him. "Yes, Alistar Kain, I will show you how to live again. And I will help you heal the brokenness within you," she promised under her breath.

Thunder crackled outside and she looked up with anger at a world that would dare hurt such a being as him. "I will give him a reason to live again!"

11

"Alistar, this is the seventh walk we have gone on tonight. I'm starting to get tired."

Alistar looked at Elzibeth quizzically. "Elle, you're a vampire. You don't get tired." He chuckled.

"You… you know what I mean mister!" she scolded him but, there was a bit of mirth in her voice.

In the short weeks after stealing his MP3 player and listening to the songs and the message, she did everything to increase her friendship with him as quickly as possible. So far the situation had improved. He had become less shy about asking for help. He was more open to her casual touches, even allowing her to lay her head on his shoulder whenever they sat or walked together, and cracking a joke. Smiling seemed easier for him, and he wasn't always walking on eggshells around her. He walked with more weight on his injured ankle.

This last part worried her, though, because tonight though would be a breaking point. Either their friendship would be stronger and he'd open up to her more about his past, or he would attempt to leave to avoid the subject.

She honestly liked him and the thought of him leaving saddened her.

But before she could say anything one of her wolves nudged her hand. She gazed down at the creature. Their talk would have to wait, it seemed. "We have visitors."

"Oh?" Alistar raised an eyebrow. The calm night held nary a cloud in the sky, and the moon brightly shone upon the land.

"Yes. It seems two young lovebirds are down by the lake having a swim." Elzibeth smiled at the thought.

"Well, let's go pay them a visit?" Alistar said as he looked down towards the lake through the trees that bordered the forest path south of the castle.

They walked down the heavily wooded path toward the mountain lake. The going was slow since even though he no longer needed the crutches, Alistar's ankle still caused him pain if he moved too quickly. Up ahead they heard splashing and carefree laughter. As they rounded the bend they saw a campfire flickering and two figures in the moonlit lake just offshore.

"Well they seem like they are having fun." Alistar remarked dryly with a smirk, as he watched the lovers splash each other.

"It does indeed." Elzibeth laughed. The splashing suddenly stopped as the lovers came ashore and wrapped themselves in blankets, falling into each other's arms.

"Best let me go first, Elle. They might get frightened of the scary vampire if you come out first." He nudged her lightly in the ribs, chuckling.

"You ass." Alistar gaped at her words and she gave him a slight shove. Elzibeth tried her best to look angry at him, but he could see the laughter in her eyes as they sparkled in the moonlight. "That's not going to happen. You are healing and can walk a bit, but you still need someone to lean on to walk for any significant distance if you don't have your crutches. I shall help you to the edge of the woods and let you walk the last few feet yourself."

Alistar shrugged and held out his arm. "Ain't that the truth. Okay, fine, let's go together." He smiled at Elzibeth and she stopped as he stepped out into the small clearing around the lake, limping towards the couple.

"Ahem," Alistar cleared his throat, startling the two lovers. They looked up at him in shock and quickly covered themselves more.

"You know, being out here this late at night is a bit dangerous. Especially when you're trespassing on someone's land." One of Elzibeth's guardian wolves stood off to the left, this one male, and trotted out into the clearing, then growled. Alistar raised a hand and the wolf lay down. Elzibeth had trained him with some hand signals, and they were told to follow his commands as if they were from her.

"We are sorry, my lord. We did not know this was your land," the girl said, lowering her head and hiding her face.

Alistar walked carefully over to the fire by the boy and put a few logs on it. "Not my land." He gazed back to Elzibeth waiting in the shadows. "Hers."

Elzibeth stepped out into the direct moonlight. It revealed the paleness of her skin and the two lovers gasped.

"Vampire!" the girl gasped as the moonlight made Elzibeth's pale skin glow slightly. The boy ruffled through their belongings and pulled out a crude wooden cross made from two pieces of wood tied together, holding it up in shaking hands. Elzibeth stopped suddenly.

Alistar calmly reached over and plucked the cross out of the boy's hand. As he did so, he noticed that the boy was the one that had brought the doctor to him a few weeks earlier in Calia.

"Kid, if she wanted you dead, you would be. Your faith isn't strong enough to make this an effective weapon against her kind." He snapped the cross in two and tossed it on the fire.

Fear shone within the lovers eyes. Alistar just raised an eyebrow in response. "Go ahead, shout, scream, get it out. Or you could just relax and enjoy your night. She's not hunting and even if she were, she doesn't feed on humans."

The lovers looked shocked and glanced over at Elzibeth. "She doesn't? Well then, what does she feed on?"

"Why don't you ask her yourself? She's standing right there, and you're being rude to her on her land after all. You can see she hasn't done anything to harm you two in the past couple of minutes. Maaaybe you should invite her to sit instead of asking me all these questions." Alistar's mild rebuke had an edge of humor to it.

The girl glanced at her lover and stood, wrapping a blanket around herself. She curtsied to Elzibeth as best as she could. "Ple-please join us, My Lady," She said, clearly nervous and wary.

Elzibeth glided over and sat down. The large wolf came over and lay down behind her, giving her something to lean against.

"Good evening," she said, smiling sweetly.

"Umm… Good… good evening, My-my Lady," the boy stammered back.

"I am Elzibeth Tepes, and my friend is right. This land is mine," Elzibeth inclined her head at the boy's broken greeting.

"La- Lady Tepes… we di-did not know," Elzibeth held up her hand, silencing him.

"It's quite alright. I don't have any wandering guards to tell you where you can and can't go, and the land certainly is not posted. Besides, it's refreshing to see two such as yourself enjoying my lands." At her words the wolf behind her lifted its head and licked her cheek. She scratched him under the chin. "Well not any human guards anyway. The wolves will not bother you. They are merely here to keep brigands and poachers away."

"So they won't eat us?" the girl blurted. Elzibeth laughed.

"No child, and neither will I. As my good friend Alistar says, I don't drink from humans unless forced into a very specific situation, and even then, I don't drink from children."

Annoyance crossed the girl's face at being called a child. "I'm sixteen, and Marcus here is seventeen. We are hardly children!"

Alistar laughed at the girl's words. "And I'm thirty-nine. Even compared to me, you two are still very much children, or at the most, young adults."

"Alistar. Be nice," Elzibeth chided him and he fell silent with a small wry smile.

The boy and girl also grew silent for a moment. "So is it okay that we're out here on your land Lady Tepes?" Marcus asked.

Elizabeth smiled and waved her hand in the air. "Of course dear boy. At least it means it will get more use than just Alistar and I walking through it. Feel free to hunt, fish, pick berries off the bushes and fruit from the trees. Your people did so in the past during my father's reign, so why not now? You may even visit the castle should you wish."

The girl perked up. "The castle? Really?"

Alistar snorted. "Yes girl. The gate is never locked."

"Indeed you may. Just remember that once you enter castle ground, you are under the Accords of Hospitality of the Old Accords. No one will harm you but in return, you may not harm anyone else."

"Umm… what happens *if* we harm someone at the castle?" Marcus asked nervously.

"Oh, I'm sure you can figure that part out," Elzibeth said, locking his gaze with hers.

Alistar stood. "Anyways folks, we just dropped by to say hey, and welcome you to the neighborhood, so to speak."

He nodded at Elzibeth. "Elle, I think it's time we let these two get back to what they were doing." Elzibeth rose as he turned away but then spun back, digging into his pocket. From his wallet, he removed a thick silver square, tossing it in the boy's lap. "I'm sure you know how to use that, and if you don't, you two can figure it out together."

Elzibeth took his arm and they walked back to the castle. "Did you just give that boy a condom?"

"Yes... Yes I did. Protection is very important." Alistar said so matter of factly that Elzibeth giggled and buried her face in his shoulder in tears of laughter.

They continued along through the woods.

"Alistar, we need to talk," she said, stopping suddenly as they got within sight of the castle.

"Yes?" Alistar leaned against a tree to rest.

"This is yours. I took it trying to understand you better and why you did all the things you have done." Elzibeth held out the MP3 Player. Alistar looked down at it, then back to her.

"Huh." He scratched his head. "I'll be honest, I knew you took it the night you left my room. I was just wondering if I'd ever get it back."

"So you're not mad?" Elzibeth softly questioned.

"Oh I'm madder than a bull seeing red." He shrugged. "But there's no use being mad at your curiosity, and I was less than forthcoming with any information. He sighed and sat on a nearby stump. Elzibeth positioned herself on the grass next to him.

Alistar put his hands between his knees and then focused on the bright, full moon. He sighed again. "This is gonna hurt," he whispered. "What do you want to know? Mind you, you're not going to like all of it and in the end we might become enemies."

Elzibeth put her hand on his arm, sliding it down till she wrapped her fingers around his, giving him support. "Anything you've hidden from me has been because you were not ready to tell me. Yes, I want to know everything because I want to know you better. I will not judge you for whatever is in your past before we met. I, too, have done some horrible things."

Alistar nodded slowly. "You've seen the locket, and I'm sure you've heard the message."

"Yes. The girl is your sister," Elzibeth said, studying his face.

"At sixteen she developed the Sight as you heard her say in the message. She was turned into them, and they burned her in the center of town as a witch. I tried to save her and was taken down and beaten unconscious. Then they used me as an example and whipped and burned me to cleanse me of the witch's taint," Alistar replied, choking up.

"Oh, Alistar that's..." Elzibeth started to speak but Alistar held up a hand.

"There's more, Elle."

He paused, gathering both breath and strength. The next breath he inhaled sounded shaky and broken. "The person that turned her in... was me. I turned in my own sister hoping that the church would make her a seeker. It's what they told us so many times before they would do if a family member ever became blessed."

"Why would they tell you that? The hunters who come here on occasion always kill anyone with the Sight. What would make your sister so different that you would turn her in?" Elzibeth's shock and confusion rung out in her voice.

Alistar disentangled his fingers from hers and slowly pulled off the black leather glove covering his left hand and wrist.

Elzibeth's eyes grew wide and red, and her fangs extended at the mark on his wrist. It was the mark of the Hunters. Slowly she stood and backed away.

"Because, Elle... I was a Hunter."

12

Elzibeth stared at the tattoo on Alistar's wrist, the symbol of the enemy.

Alistar stayed sitting, making no sudden moves. "I was a Hunter. Keyword Elle, WAS. I told you you may not like what you found out."

Elzibeth circled him like a wounded animal. Her urge to rip out his throat for being a Hunter, conflicted with the love and friendship developing between them in the short time she had come to know him.

"Look, Elle, if you'd give me a chance, there's more."

"What's to explain Alistar? You hunted my kind. How many?" Elzibeth asked plaintively.

"Fifteen vampires, two witches, and one werewolf pack. I took them all down without mercy. But they weren't like you. They killed people indiscriminately. And still, each one weighs heavily on my mind, every... day." Alistar tried to explain himself, but Elzibeth's claws surrounded his throat, just barely indenting the skin, her eyes and fanged mouth inches from his cheek.

"So this is where our friendship ends, eh, Elle? Nevermind that I've never attacked or hurt you, and I've saved you on more than one occasion. That's fine. I'd like to think I'll see my sister in heaven, but we both know that's not where I'm headed." Alistar's voice, soft and calm broke through the blood haze and rage running through Elzibeth's mind. She turned away, transformed into the white wolf, and ran north.

"Elle wait!" Alistar called after her, his hand raising but she had already disappeared into the woods. He let his hand drop to his side and limped back to the castle's courtyard, wincing with each slow step.

"Quite a mess you've gotten yourself into there." Richter's voice brought Alistar around to face him where he sat on the wall with a knife in hand.

"So I've gotta fight you now, Richter?" Alistar asked, reaching behind him for his pistol.

"Oh this?" Richter looked at the folding knife in his hand. "No, I was just eating an apple." He clicked it shut and stowed it in a pocket as he hopped off the wall.

Alistar paced the courtyard, his ankle shooting spikes of pain up his leg. "Fuck! I told her that she wouldn't like what she heard. I should have just kept it all locked inside."

"And if you did, what then? What happens when more Hunters show up at our walls? Surely one of them would recognize you eventually. Then what?" Richter asked, placing a hand on Alistar's shoulder. "She asked for the truth, and you gave it to her. Now the question is, what are you going to do about it?"

"I guess I'll wait for her to cool off and come back to either talk or kill me," Alistar said with a heavy sigh.

"That may not be an option, boy. There are Hunters in Brasov. Seems like your last escapade stirred up a bit of a hornets nest. And Brasov is right where she's headed,"

Richter said, walking over to an old ramshackle barn in the corner of the courtyard, opening the doors, and stepping inside.

"How do you know that Richter? And how do you know I am... well... *was* a Hunter?" Alistar asked, suddenly suspicious.

"Like knows like, Alistar. Besides, I keep tabs on my mistress. The spider gem broach she wears is also a tracking device."

"Like knows like?" Alistar said shocked and he grabbed Richters wrist, looking for the Hunter tattoo.

"You won't find one. Back in my day, we didn't have them." Richter's voice held amusement. "But still, I can spot another Hunter a mile away. The way we walk, the way we act, the wariness and how we immediately identify the exits in case we must leave in a hurry. Those kinds of things."

Alistar's confusion showed clearly on his face. "So how?"

"Dracula saved me. I hunted him for years before tracking him down one cold and rainy night. We fought on that very wall where I was just sitting. I was good, but he was better. By all rights, I should be dead twice over." Richter reached through the straw on the barn's floor and pulled up a long trap door. A gentle wood ramp led underground and Richter stepped into the darkness and flipped a switch.

Alistar stopped at the top of the ramp. "Then why did he spare you?"

Richter moved back into view. "I ask myself that question every day and still don't know the answer. What I do know is his wife Anna tended my wounds, and every night he would come to my room with an old chess board. We would play each other to a stalemate. Like you and my mistress, a friendship blossomed. By the time I was healed enough to leave, I found myself not wanting to go. I was tired of the hunt, tired of the chase, and I realized that not all so-called monsters were what they appeared on the outside. So I stayed." He vanished back into the shadows before reappearing pushing an old Soviet Ural motorcycle. He shoved it up the ramp.

"I've maintained this, and I think this will get you farther, faster than you can walk. You did say you knew how to ride one of these." Richter raised a questioning eyebrow.

Alistar nodded. "Yeah, but that still doesn't fix my leg."

"I might have something for that as well," Richter said, heading back down into the darkness, before coming back up carrying a large wooden crate. Opening it he moved aside.

Inside the crate was all manner of hunter gear. Alistar raised his eyebrows in surprise. "Where did you get this?"

"As I said, we occasionally get Hunters." Alistar started rummaging through the crate as Richter spoke. "I deal with them and collect their stuff. I store it in the back." He tugged out leather pants designed with buckles and straps to hold the multitude of items that a Hunter would need along with a vest designed to do the same. Completing the ensemble he held up an old leather duster. He quickly donned them on and, digging further he pulled out a small red case.

"No way," he said under his breath. Richter came up alongside him. "It's a class three medical support boot for Hunters who break a leg. You were not kidding when you said you might have something."

Alistar opened the red case, setting what looked like the bottom half of a shoe with two clamshell halves attached to each side on the ground and stepping into it.

The device unfolded, snapping the halves up and around his leg and solidified in place looking like a full knee-length boot.

"Will it help?" Richter asked.

"Oh hell yes. With this I can fight and move at ninety-five percent efficiency and not worry about breaking my ankle." Alistar says.

"Well good, then might I suggest the sawn-off shotgun to go with the ass-kicking boot?" He held up an old lever-action shotgun.

Alistar wrestled out a black backpack from the crate. "Yea, that will do." He started loading it up with magazines and shells. "This will be useful," he said, strapping a grapple launcher onto his left wrist. Lastly he slung the backpack onto the back of the Ural and strapped it down before mounting the bike. Taking the shotgun, he slid it into a scabbard on his back along with an old Japanese World War Two katana.

"You will need these." Richter handed him a small black box with a screen, and his credentials.

"That's a T-78 tracking device. Nice... And that's my creds." He had thought he'd hidden it in his backpack's compartment in his room. "You went through my stuff." Alistar grinned grimly.

"Don't be so surprised. I'm a nosey old man. Now, it will be sunrise soon Alistar. Elzibeth will have to find a place to spend the day and you and I both know how weak and vulnerable she will be then. Keep her safe and bring her home. Remind her that her father once showed mercy to a Hunter and everything worked out." Richter placed a hand on the other man's shoulder.

"You have my word, Richter. I'll bring her home, or die trying." With those words, Alistar peeled out of the courtyard on the Ural like a bat out of hell.

"Alistar… she hasn't fed tonight!" Richter shouted after him.

"I know, and that's what worries me," Alistar muttered as the trees flashed past along the sides of the road.

13

E lzibeth ran through the forest as quickly as her four legs could carry her, not stopping until she reached the edge of Brasov. She could sense the sun coming up soon and she needed to find a place to hide for the day. She slipped into an abandoned building and found shelter behind some old broken storage crates.

He did warn you, Elle. He warned you that you would not like part of his past. You promised him you would not judge him and yet still, you nearly killed him because of that tattoo. You should be ashamed of yourself. And ashamed she was. She wrapped her cloak tightly about her and scooted further back into the shadows, waiting for dawn to break. Her intent was on staying awake throughout the day and heading back to the castle when night falls. If she were lucky, Alistar might still be there and she could ask for his forgiveness.

～

Alistar drove on, taking the treacherous road at full speed. He couldn't ride a horse worth shit, but motorcycles were a whole different breed of animal, and no one else could ride them like him. His bike rode as close to the ground as he could get it without wrecking as he slid through the next turn, skidding on the gravel and almost going off the cliff, but he continued northward along the road. Even with a broken speedometer, he could tell he drove eighty kilometers per hour. Soon he sighted the city just as the first light of dawn started to hit the mountaintops to the east.

～

In her shadowy corner, Elzibeth felt the effects of the sun making her sleepy, and having not fed this night, the effects were more intense. She shook her head, turning this way and that. A rat nibbled at a bag of grain and she lashed out, grabbing it and quickly breaking its neck before draining it dry. What little blood its tiny body held, helped her stave off hunger pangs, but it wouldn't last long. Outside her shadowed shelter, the city started to rouse. People moved about, shops began opening and the world opened its eyes.

～

Alistar parked the motorcycle next to the Old Rams Inn and jerked out the tracker. Normally it kept track of a team of Hunters but on occasion if they tagged an entity, they could use it to track said prey. He flipped it on and the screen went fuzzy. He smacked it a few times with his hand before the screen stabilized and showed nothing. He frowned in response and slid it into his pocket before opening the door to the tavern side of the inn and stepping inside. All eyes turned to him and whispering started as he walked up to the bartender and put his hand on the counter.

"What are you doing back?" the bartender asked. Alistar reached out and grabbed the front of the man's shirt, wrenching him over the bar until they were face to face. When he next spoke, his voice was sinister as he dropped back into his old ways.

"You tried to rip me off last time I was here, so now you owe me. I'm looking for a woman. Six feet tall, pale skin, elegant, long shoulder length black hair." He lets the bartender go and the man had fear in his eyes.

"That one. She's rumored to be a vampire!" he replied nervously.

"I know. That's why I'm looking for her." Alistar said, peeling back the black glove just enough to show the tattoo on his left wrist. The bartender's eyes widened.

"Ah so you'd be with them then?" The bartender pointed to a group of five people dressed similarly to him. Three men and two women. One had a double-headed axe strapped across his back, while another had at least fifteen knives positioned across various parts of her body. The third sported two short swords at his waist, and the last man had a very large auto-loading crossbow. The last member, a young girl, looked to be about fourteen. She carried no weapons. Being a Seeker made his job more difficult.

"No. I'm not," Alistar said as he turned away from the bartender and walked to the group. He yanked out a chair, sat, and put his feet up on the table, surprising the others in the middle of their conversation.

"So what are we talking about folks?" he asked nonchalantly.

"And just who the fuck do you think you are then?" the one with the ax asked with a mouthful of cheese. He appeared the youngest of the actual Hunters with more brawn than brains.

Reaching over Alistar took a piece of the cheese off the table and popped it into his own mouth, chewing thoughtfully. "I'm the man telling you to stand down and go home. I claim this area."

"Do ye now? And what makes you think ye have the right to do that, ye cheeky bastard?!" the woman exclaimed.

"I don't know, maybe the tattoo on my wrist, or the creds in my pocket," Alistar replied, holding out his gloved hand. The woman grabbed his wrist and pulled back the glove.

"Well, I'll be fooked! They didn't say there was a class five roaming around the area," The woman said, dropping his wrist. He slid his glove back on.

The young hunter with the ax got in Alistar's face. "No! You need to back off! We were here first. This vamp is ours!"

Alistar raised an eyebrow. "Nope' I've been here for five months, and you guys rolled in. What? Last night, three days ago at most? Kill's mine."

"How about this, you damn shit. How about we beat yer ass so bad you can't move and then we take the kill? There's four of us and only one of you," Mr. No Brains said.

Alistar motioned with two fingers on his left hand for the man to come closer. "Can you say that a little louder in my left ear? I'm slightly deaf in the other one." The no-brains Hunter fell for the trap and leaned closer.

"I said…"

Alistar seized the man by the back of the neck, slammed his head against the table, whipped out his pistol with his right hand and placed the barrel against the side of the man's head, cocking the hammer. The rest of the man's party reached for their weapons, but Alistar stopped them with a glare.

"All of you seem to be forgetting your rank." He studied the man. "You. You're only a rank one. Your attitude and lack of caution tells me you are still wet behind the ears. You probably have one kill to your name... at most." He lifted the man's head and shoved him into a chair.

Examining the others, his gaze landed on the man with the crossbow. "You are more cautious and quiet, but still probably only a rank two."

His gaze next moved to the woman. "Rank two. It takes skill to use nothing but knives. But you are still a bit too cocky."

The last man holding the short swords, had yet to say a word. "You're the leader. Rank three, I bet." The man nodded back at him and with a slight smile. He had enjoyed watching his team get schooled by what he considered an old-timer.

Alistar stood. "None of you are ready for this one. She's different. I've been chasing her across this god-forsaken country and, believe me, she's led me on a merry chase. The church sent you on a suicide mission."

The woman with the knives watched him. "You say they sent us. Didn't they send you as well?"

"No... I was on sabbatical when this bitch showed up on my radar." Alistar started walking toward the door. "Again.... go home. You're not ready, and you won't survive trying to punch above your weight class."

The man with the swords stepped forward. "Just who are you?"

Alistar looked over his shoulder. "I'm Alistar Kain. Don't be here when I get back."

14

Elzibeth dropped the drained body of her third rat to the wooden floor. The sun's light now streamed through various cracks in the ceiling, illuminating all the dust in the room floating through the air. Thankfully none of the rays were close to her hiding spot. The day sleep weighed heavily on her and her eyelids drooped and then snapped back open.

Stay awake Elle. You must stay awake. Children's laughter sounded downstairs. Her eyes widened with fear at the sounds of small shoes on the wooden floor of the room below hers.

"No. No. No. Please don't come up here," she whispered to the children below.

~

Alistar stepped out of the tavern, hoping his words and actions would cause the other Hunters to quickly leave town. Searching for Elzibeth would be easier without having to worry about them. Walking down the street he pulled out the tracking device and smacked it again. The screen fritzed and stabilized, and the device gave a soft beep. He stopped and slowly turned.

"Beep." He swiveled away and back again. *"Beep"* *Hmm... west it is then.* Walking slowly down the street, he occasionally checked the tracker. Every so often it beeped, leading him further westward. After an hour it let out one final *beep,* then died in a frazzle of sparks and a low whine.

"Well fuck. Now how am I going to find her?" Alistar muttered as the wind picked up. An old newspaper blew down the street getting caught against his leg. Picking it up he glanced at it. The date was 2050, and the headline read *"War Against Supernatural Evil Continues! United States Launches Nukes!"* Crumpling it up he tossed it behind him.

～

The wind blew through the old building, making it creak and moan, but upon the wind a familiar scent tingled in Elzibeth's nose and her eyelids popped open from their half-close position. *Alistar?* The scent gave her hope and, closing her eyes again, she reached out with her senses and mentally tried to contact him. *"Alistar. Help."* Her cry was as weak as she was and she lacked hope that it would reach him. Locked in her mental cry, she did not hear the sound of small footsteps running up the stairs toward her room.

～

"Alistar. Help." Alistar stopped as a soft mental cry echoed in his brain.

"Elle, I'm here." he whispered, wishing he could talk to her, mind to mind. Vampire telepathy could only reach so far. He scanned the area full of ramshackle, run-down buildings. Perfect for a fleeing vampire to hide in. "Damn.

We should have headed here last time. Would have taken the guards forever to find us."

~

Children's voices rose, snapping Elzibeth out of attempting further mental contact as the door slammed open and two boys and a girl came running into the room. The boys are tried to take a small doll away from the girl and she fought back.

"Give it to us!"

"No, it's mine!"

One of the boys shoved the girl and she fell, landing next to Elzibeth, skinning her knee. She cried out in pain. Feeling anger, Elzibeth rose and glared at them. They backed away, and once they reached the door, they turned and ran screaming down the stairs. Elzibeth's hunger began rising as the smell of the blood from the girl's scraped knee reached her nose.

No Elle, this one is not food. Fight it. She kneeled, meeting the child eye to eye, trying to project calm, and noting that the girl looked like the twin of one of the boys who had run away. "There, there, child. Tis just a scrape." Looking for something to bind the girl's knee, her hand landed upon the red handkerchief around her neck. She untied it and wrapped it around the wound, cinching it tight. "There now, child, run along. It's not safe for you here," she said, pulling the young girl to her feet.

The little girl gazed up at her and then hugged her. "Thanks lady." With those words, the girl ran over, picked up her doll from the floor, and rushed down the stairs, outside. The door at the top of the stairs closed halfway behind her.

Elzibeth sunk back to the floor, weaker than before, and started shaking.

～

The sounds of kids screaming up the street grabbed Alistar's attention. Two boys were running away from the worst of the run-down buildings. Shortly after, a little girl ran happily out of the same building. On her leg a familiar red handkerchief had been tied. "Lord, thank you."

He quickly approached the little girl and bent down. "Little one, where did you get that?" he asked, pointing at the handkerchief.

The girl considered him and he smiled. "The sick lady in thewe gived it to me. I falled down and huwted my knee. She helped me get dolly back. She was nice. Am I in twuble?" she continued in a quieter voice. "Mommy says we are no s'pposed to play thewe cause we can get owwies."

"No child, you are not in trouble, but your mother is right. It's not safe for you in there. Now run along and enjoy your day." Alistar gave the girl ten leu from his pocket. "Go buy yourself a treat." His first step into the building caused the wood boards to creak under his weight and he stopped. Centering himself, he listened for sounds that a scared, hiding vampire might make, fully aware that Elzibeth may be under bloodlust and hunting him.

He searched the first floor as quickly as possible before moving up the stairs to the second and slowly pushing the door open from its half-closed position. "Elle?" he said calmly.

～

The creak of a board below alerted Elzibeth that. She listened as whoever searched the floor below made their way up the stairs. The door pushed open. "Elle?" The soft voice brought hope to her and she cried out.

"Alistar?" He rushed to her side. "Alistar, I'm sorry." A blood red tear slipped down her cheek but he put a finger to her lips, shushing her.

"It's fine Elle. Don't worry about it." She was weak and near bloodlust. If that happened, she would feed indiscriminately until satiated. Looking around he saw the drained bodies of rats next to her. *Clever girl*

"You need blood Elle." He took her face in his hands. She pulled away and shook her head.

A look of annoyance crossed Alistar's face and he pulled out his knife, slashing his left wrist open with a small cut. Blood flowed freely as he offered it to her. Again she shook her head, trying to back away but the wall stopped her from doing so.

"Elle, I know you won't hurt me, but you NEED to feed. Otherwise this whole town is at risk. The adults... and the children." His words were a harsh rebuke that struck through her brain and touched the logical side of her. Grabbing his wrist she bit down, and sucked hard. Waves of pain and pleasure ran through him as she fed. The scrape of a boot behind him and Elzibeth's widening eyes clued him that they were not alone. She dropped his wrist and scuttled back as he stood and turned around.

"Well isn't this cute? It's the great Hunter and his vampire bitch." The female Hunter he had encountered at the tavern only an hour before sneered as her companions fanned out around her.

15

Alistar stared at the four Hunters. "I told you to leave. You have no idea what's going on here," His voice was low and full of anger. He noticed the slight blue glow of the woman's eyes signaling her use of a certain drug he knew all too well.

"Right, I think we understand exactly what's going on here. Ye found yourself a little vampire snatch and decided that was worth more than your duty to the church," The woman sneered back.

The young seeker appeared at the top of the steps. "Get out of there now! I looked him up! He really is a class five! Furthermore the church regards him as an extreme danger! Avoid at all costs and call in backup!"

Alistar looked at the floor and chuckled with an evil tone. "So... my past really has caught up to me after all." He glanced up, his expression cold and dead. "Does it list my kills? Fifteen vampires, two witches, and one werewolf pack? By. My. Self. And let's not forget the five level-four Hunters I killed after my sister was burned at the stake for being a witch. They had taken her innocent life all because —like you—she developed The Sight." His gaze flashed over to the young Seeker, causing her to shrink. Even the other hunters took a step back at his gaze.

"Because the one behind me abhors unnecessary taking of life, I WILL offer you one last chance to stand down and walk away. After that, though, I offer no further mercy. You will NOT take my friend." He stepped forward.

He called me his friend! Elzibeth thought, feeling warmth and happiness flow through her body.

Three of the hunters moved further away, but the one with the crossbow raised his weapon and fired. The bolt streaked toward Alistar who reached up and caught it out of the air inches from his face, the point just barely touching his forehead. He casually tossed it to the ground.

"Oh shit," the female hunter muttered. She pivoted to the Seeker behind her. "What else does it say?"

The seeker scrolled through Alistars bio. "Trained in multiple hand-to-hand combat skills, honed his body beyond the point of needing serum. And, oh fuck, oh fuck. He was slated to become the Godhammer!"

Elzibeth stayed behind the crates listening to the exchange. *The Godhammer?! This man protecting her was slated to become the most powerful living weapon the church could level against the supernatural world?* Her eyes went wide and she started to stand.

"Stay down, Elle. This will be unpleasant." Alistar's command forced her to sit back down.

He cracked his neck, looking cold and dispassionately at the hunters before him as he spit on the ground. The tension in the room felt so thick that anyone could cut it with a knife, and that was exactly what happened next.

The female hunter threw three daggers in one fluid motion, and just as fast in one smooth motion, Alistar freed the katana from its sheath on his back with his right hand and knocked them aside. His left hand tugged out his own military-grade combat blade and hurled it across the room in an underhanded throw, impaling the woman straight through the heart. She dropped to the floor with a gurgle.

"Next."

Elzibeth's eyes widened. The skill that Alistar had just shown in those two actions made him a very dangerous individual indeed.

The Hunters regarded each other and then Mr. No-Brains raised his big ax and charged. Alistar observed him for a moment. *He's top-heavy.* At the last second, he side-stepped and stuck out his foot. Mr. No-Brain Hunter tripped and crashed to the floor face first. With an impassionate expression, Alistar switched the katana to his left hand and calmly removed his pistol, shooting the man in the head without even looking at him. The loud bang caused Elzibeth to jump slightly. Putting his gun in the holster, Alistar switched the katana back to his right hand and tilted his head.

"And two were left. If you can't even beat me, how do you expect to beat her when she's at full power? I told you that you were punching above your weight class, but you didn't listen. Unfortunately, some mistakes you don't live to learn from."

Elzibeth shrunk back at the casual slaughter. *He just executed that man without hesitation. And his face! It's like he doesn't even care. He's clearly more powerful than they are, but he shows no mercy.* This was not the Alistar she knew. This Alistar scared her very much.

The Hunter with the crossbow fired as fast as he could pull the trigger, and Alistar deflected each bolt. *Twang.* The crossbow dry-fired, its seven-bolt magazine empty. Alistar advanced and the Hunter turned tail and ran.

Alistar punched his left wrist forward and pushed a thumb stud. The grappling launcher fired, and Alistar watched with a satisfied look as the hooks deployed, sending its payload through the meaty part of the Hunter's right leg. The hunter tumbled forward and Alistar yanked back hard, pulling the hunter halfway across the wood floor. The hunter flipped onto his back, his face full of fear and he scrabbled halfway to his feet. Alistar smiled an evil smile and resheathed the katana.

No. I don't like this Alistar one bit. Elzibeth watched as Alistar bent down and grabbed the ax of the lifeless second hunter. Picking it up he weighed its heft before lifting it over his head with both hands and sending it spinning end over end. It hit the fleeing hunter between the shoulder blades with a sickening crunch.

The Hunter's leader turned to leave and Alistar shook his head. "Don't make me chase you. You'll only die tired." The Hunter resolved himself to his fate and pulled out his short swords. "I tell you what; I'll make this fair. No tricks, no guns. Just this katana. One sword versus two," Alistar commented nonchalantly. Reaching back he unholstered his pistol and held it up. Setting it on the ground he kicked it backwards.

The leader dropped into a wide stance with both swords held at his side in front of Alistar, who stood there as if he hadn't a care in the world. The Hunter dashed forward striking seven times, each strike being knocked away with the ringing of steel on steel as Alistar easily deflected them.

The leader jumped back after Alistar swung once across his chest, the blow cutting a small slit in the man's leather armor.

Both men circled each other. "Why do you go against the church?" the leader questioned. "They raised you!"

Alistars eyes narrowed. "They brainwashed me!"

The leader kept moving, trying to force Alistar off

balance but Alistar's turn to follow was smooth. "The church was your family!" the leader said.

"THE CHURCH *KILLED* MY FAMILY!" Alistar shouted. Both the leader and Elzibeth could see that he had struck a nerve. Seeing this the leader knew he had found a possible chink in Alistar's proverbial armor that he could attempt to use to his advantage.

"Oh right, they burned your sister for the witch she was. I remember hearing about you now. She died the way she deserved to."

Alistar roared and charged the man. The leader waited and at the last second lept, intending to flip over Alistar, but Alistar stabbed upwards with the katana, catching the leader in the stomach. The man fell on top of him with blood dripping out of his mouth. Letting the man roll off his shoulder and onto the floor, Alistar retrieved his combat knife from the female Hunter's chest before turning around.

He walked back to the lead hunter and knelt, lifting the man's head. The Hunter tried to talk, but only a gurgle emitted. Alistar leaned close to the man's ear.

"I will destroy the church for that one day. I will kill every Hunter that stands in my path or hurts those I care about," he whispered before shoving the dagger up through the bottom of the man's chin and into his brain. Twisting it, Alistar pulled the knife free, wiping it on his pants, and put it back in its sheath. Dislodging the katana, he flicked the blade. Crimson drops of blood flew off and splattered the crates nearby. Wiping the blade on the shirt of the dead leader, he resheathed it over his right shoulder.

The Seeker crouched in the corner, shaking at the display of savagery. Kneeling, Alistar clasped her face, brushing a gloved thumb across her cheek, revealing a bruise as his thumb wiped away the makeup foundation. For a moment he said nothing. "Get out while you can.

Go to another city, or even another country. Just get out before the church decides that Seekers are no better than witches." His soft voice held none of the sinister edge it had moments before.

The Seeker stood to rush out of the room. "Wait," Alistar said. The girl paused and looked at him. "If you bring more Hunters down upon us, I will find them, I will kill them, and then I'm coming after you. This is your one chance. Do we have an understanding?" Even though his voice was still soft, it held a slight growl.

"Yes. Yes sir," The young Seeker squeaked out. Alistar nodded and motioned for her to leave. "Why did you kill them but are letting me leave?" Alistar eyed her over his shoulder.

"You weren't given any choice in this. Everyone else in this fight made their decision when they signed up, even me. But you... you only had two choices since the church does not abide a witch unless that witch is serving them. If I told them no eighteen years ago, that would have been the end of it. But had you said *no*, they would have sent someone like me to execute you. So you get a pass today. This is your second chance. Use it well."

Standing he looked at the bodies on the ground. Then something caught his attention.... Elzibeth had his own gun pointed at him, fear in her eyes, and he sighed. He knew what he had just done, and how he must look to her, all covered in blood, hair askew, a totally different man than the one she had befriended. He peered around at the bodies and bloody floor before looking back at the vampiress in the corner.

"Elle." he said with kindness.

16

Alistar advanced and the gun wobbled in Elzibeth's hands. The lack of blood made her weaker than she appeared if she couldn't even hold up a 1.3 kg gun.

"Well… if you're going to shoot, you're going to want to take the safety off first. Then I'd suggest you aim for the center mass." He tapped his chest. "After that, you just have to commit and pull the trigger. But before you do, remember that taking a life changes you. You and I both know that sometimes you have to kill in combat, but it's a different experience taking one outside the heat of battle and it changes you more."

After a few more moments Elzibeth lowered the gun. Picking up the Seekers data-pad, Alistar walked over and sat next to her. He gently confiscated the gun and holstered it, then leaned against the wall with a tired sigh. "If you didn't run away, I would have explained all of this to you so that you'd have some sort of warning the first time I had to kill. What you saw is the monster the church made. Everything that the Seeker said is true."

Alistar handed her the data-pad and continued to talk

while she read it. "My parents died in a house fire, and my sister who was only two at the time was taken in by my aunt and uncle. Because of my age and other things, they sent me to the church. The church made me a killer of the supernatural, groomed me from the age of eighteen to be the best weapon they could have because of my natural ability. And I was the best. I quickly rose through the ranks, surviving mission after mission, many times being the only one left of an entire team. I'd come out covered in blood, my task done, and my friends gone. They'd shove me to a new team and send me out for it to happen all over again. And the thing is, I didn't mind. I knew the risks. They knew the risks." As he talked, Elzibeth creeped out from where she sat, moving towards the fallen lead hunter with hunger in her eyes.

Alistar placed a hand on her shoulder and pulled her back next to him. "Don't. Their blood is poisonous to you." He held out his wrist again.

Elzibeth shook her head with fear in her eyes. "No, if I start to feed again, I won't stop until I drain you."

Alistar sighed before continuing. "That was my life, hunt after hunt. Day after day, month after month. I rarely got to see my sister. Sure, we talked on the phone once a week, but the church monitored those calls, and the only time I ever got to see her was on my birthday... and hers. Killing and loneliness are all I've ever known until I met you."

Elzibeth gaped at him. "Not even love?"

"Especially not love. Sure your team was supposed to be your family, but almost every one of them would turn you into the church at the first sign of heresy. Love wasn't a luxury anyone could afford," Alistar replied, his eyes closing at the memories of his past.

Elzibeth reached up and touched his cheek. "Alistar?"

"Hmm?"

"Can we go home?" Elzibeth wiped a tear from his cheek and leaned against him.

"Sure princess. I promised Richter I'd keep you safe, and I still intend to do that. Just give me a moment to clean things up and figure out how I'm gonna get you outta here." Alistar chuckled but leaned into her touch.

Princess? Did he just give me a pet name? Elzibeth blinked, not knowing what to say.

Standing, Alistar examined the bodies on the floor again. He stripped them of anything useful and piled it on the floor. All the money they had went into his pocket along with their creds. "I'll be right back; I just need to get our transportation," he said before heading outside.

He left for a few minutes before Elzibeth heard an engine outside, and then his footsteps clomped back up the stairs. When the door reopened, he carried a pack with him, which he used for the Hunters' weapons and gear. As he searched through their things again, he discovered on each of them two blue vials that he pocketed quickly, but not before Elzibeth noticed.

"What… are those?" she asked, weaker than before.

"Serum." He headed back downstairs with the bag after zipping it closed but came back a minute later. Pulling a large canvas tarp off a stack of crates, he laid it on the floor. Walking over to Elzibeth, he picked her up in his strong arms and positioned her on top.

"I'm going to wrap you tightly in this to keep the sun off. It's going to be uncomfortable, but it's better than bursting into flames." He wrapped the tarp tightly around her and picked her up again.

"Alistar?".

"Yes?"

"This tarp smells like rat piss."

"Sorry. It's all I had on hand." A small smile crossed Alistar's face. He could feel her weak heartbeat against his chest and knew he didn't have much time. Mounting up on the bike, he set Elzibeth in front of him, side-saddle Using some rope, he strapped her to his body before taking off down the street headed for the south road. People stared at him as he passed, but not one questioned him.

Alistar raced out of Brasov and down the old road at a good pace, but not quite as fast as he had when searching for Elzibeth hours before. His life wasn't the only one on the bike now. Elzibeth's heartbeat against his chest slowed even further and as the castle came into sight he picked up speed on the straight parts of the road to gain time.

The bike sailed through the gates and Alistar rode it up the steps and into the great hall. He could catch shrift for that later. Right now he didn't care. Richter ran up to him.

"Cut the ropes. We have to get blood into her now. I gave her some of my blood, but the Hunters interrupted us before I could give her enough." Richter snapped open the sharp knife blade and sliced through the ropes and then the canvas and let it fall to the floor, leaving Elzibeth lying unconscious in Alistar's arms as he dismounted. She appeared paler and skinnier than when he'd found her. This fact told him her body is quickly using up what little blood he had given her.

"She needs blood faster than we can make her drink it. Richter, go into all that Hunter gear and look for a medical kit, and bring it to Elle's room... and hope there's a transfusion kit in it." Alistar rushed through the halls and up to the north tower without even waiting for a reply from Richter.

Kicking open the door to Elle's room, he laid her on the bed. Thankfully the heavy curtains were already closed, blocking out the sun's rays.

Stripping off his jacket and throwing it on a nearby chair, Alistar did the same with his shirt as Richter ran into the room holding a large soft-sided red bag with a white cross on it.

"Perfect," Alistar said as he rummaged through the bag and pulled out a coiled plastic tube with a needle on each end and a rolling clamp in the middle.

"Do you know what you are doing?" Richter asked, concerned.

"It's called a direct person-to-person blood transfusion. I've done it twice before on other Hunters, but I've never done it on a vampire. So... maybe." Alistar's reply was curt as he tied a rubber band around his right arm and slapped it to make the arteries and veins appear. Finding the one he wanted he uncapped one needle and making sure the roller flow controller clamp was set to stop the blood flow, slid the needle into his arm.

"Take that roll of medical tape and rip me off a three-inch piece," Richter did so and placed it on Alistars arm, taping the needle in place. "Good. Do another one for the tubing, just for extra support, and then prep two more pieces."

Climbing onto the bed, Alistar lay next to Elzibeth and slid the other needle into a vein in her arm. Seeing what he had done, Richter came over and taped the needle and tubing just like he had for Alistar.

Alistar grabbed Richters arm and looked at him solemnly. "I don't know what's going to happen. If this kills me, don't let her hate herself over it. None of this is her fault." Richter nodded and Alistar opened the roller on the clamp, watching his blood flow down the tube and into Elzibeth's arm.

"Based on the average blood flow rate in the human body, there should be three milliliters of blood flowing into Elle every minute. So by those calculations, in eleven hours I'll almost be drained. Check on me every two hours and shut this roller off at ten if she hasn't woken up by then. If she wakes before then, well, you know what to do."

Richter nodded at Alistars words. "Mistress Tepes would not want you to die so I will endeavor to keep you in this mortal coil."

"Good," Alistar said as he laid his head on the pillow and stared at the ceiling, reviewing all his past events. Richter quietly checked on him and Elzibeth every couple hours. At some point, his eyes closed and he fell into a deep nightmare-filled slumber.

17

Elle woke with a start in her room. Alistar lay shirtless and unconscious on the bed beside her. In a panic she checked him for bite marks.

"Oh lords Elle, you didn't. Please no." she whispered to herself. A creak signaled that they were not alone in the room. Richter increased the gas on the small lamp by the bed.

"He is okay, My Mistress." Richter said as he reached over her and stopped the flow of Alistars blood like he had promised.. Elle noticed and her eyes followed the tubing from her arm to Alistar's.

"He gave me a transfusion?" She had done it before during the Second World War as a night shift nurse. Only it was much cruder back then.

"Yes Mistress. Very skilled at it too. No hesitation on his part whatsoever." Richter smiled grimly.

"How much has he given?"

"Around two liters. He told me to stop the blood flow at the ten hour mark, and it has been about nine. I have been checking on him every two hours before deciding to sit here and read a book. He's in no danger. I think he may be stronger than anyone in this whole world." Richter said offhandedly.

Elzibeth checked Alistar's neck for a pulse and sighed. It was there, slow but strong. He would be okay.

Pulling the needle out of her arm, Elzibeth climbed carefully off the bed, not wanting to disturb the sleeping man. Rummaging through the medical bag, she found some cotton and the tape from earlier and carefully removed the needle from Alistar's arm before taping a piece of cotton over the needle mark to stop the blood.

"He is Richter. He is because he feels he has to be." She looked over at her servant and friend. "I watched him slaughter four hunters with no effort just because they were after me, and then he let a young Seeker go, giving her another chance at life." She sat on the bed next to Alistar and brushed the hair away from his face, looking at him. "Richter? Did you know what he was when you allowed him to cross the threshold into this castle?" she asked with a slight edge to her voice.

"I did. But I also saw how he treated you, and sensed something more about him. I used my best judgment, but was always ready to kill him if need be. I did not tell you because you would have killed him on the spot." Richter replied, knowing his mistress was on edge.

"*Mmm..* You made the right call. Thank you." Elzibeth's voice no longer held an edge.

Alistar muttered something in his sleep that only Elzibeth's keen hearing could make out. "Sophia... Elle." And then he rolled over onto his side. Elzibeth pulled a comforter over him and stood.

"He's going to be out for a while. We should let him rest," she said, making her way to the door. Richter nodded and followed her out of the room.

∾

A few hours later, well after darkness, Alistar awakes with a start to find himself still in Elzibeth's bed, alone. "Well I guess she's okay... Good," he said to himself before swinging his legs over the bed and standing. When a wave of dizziness hit him, he collapsed back on the bed. He tried again, standing much slower and walked to the door. Leaning against the wall for support, he made his way down the stairs, nearly falling more than once. As he reached the bottom, he caught sight of Elzibeth and smiled.

"Hey there princess. I see you're better."

Elzibeth's head whipped around and she was at his side in an instant thanks to her vampiric speed. "Yes, thanks to you, but you should not be out of bed," she scolded him as she helped him to a chair just as his stomach rumbled.

"I just gave you two liters of blood. I'm starving." Alistar said with a sideway glance at her.

"Yes, well, let's see about getting you fed then. "Elzibeth laughed. Just then Richter entered and set a bowl of broth in front of Alistar.

"It's a soup made of dandelions, wild garlic, and bone broth. It may not taste the best, but it will help you regain your energy," he said to Alistar before turning to Elzibeth.

"Mistress Tepes, there are two children here. Looking to be around sixteen. They said that you and Alistar invited them?"

Alistar paused while drinking his soup. "Sounds like those two from the lake, Elle."

"I agree. Richter, bring them in here so that Alistar may continue eating," she said sitting in a chair next to him.

Richter brought in the girl and boy from last night. The girl carried a basket, but stopped to curtsy while the boy bowed. "Lady Tepes, thank you for allowing us to visit your beautiful castle," she said and the boy nodded.

Elzibeth snorted. "You are laying it on quite thick girl. Most of the castle is still intact, but there are areas of great disrepair. As for addressing me formally, you are neither vampires, nor are you servants so you can stop that right now. It's just Elzibeth to you. But... I thank you for the respect. Welcome to my home. We are meeting in the kitchen because Alistar needs to eat." She inclined her head to the man at the table.

She motioned to two chairs across from Alistar and he kicked them out for the young couple, who seemed nervous. "The lady said sit... so sit. She's not going to bite you. I already told you that last night."

After another moment the two sat across from Alistar and the girl set the basket on the table. "We brought gifts. There's not much but we didn't want to come here empty-handed."

Elzibeth smiled. "Gifts are not needed, but thank you anyways. It was thoughtful of you." Alistar meanwhile finished off the soup and set the bowl aside. "You two certainly are polite. I give you that. By the way, we never really got your names." Elzibeth nodded at his words.

"I am Evelyn," the girl said, speaking up first.

"And I am Marcus,"

Elzibeth inclined her head in a nod. "Very nice to meet both of you." Alistar just nodded and smiled.

"So Evelyn, Marcus, I assume you come from Calia, yes?" Elzibeth asked. Both children inclined their heads. "What do you two do there? Do you have jobs? What is your life like? Is it good?"

"No Lady Tep... I mean no Miss Elzibeth," Evelyn replied. Elzibeth raised an eyebrow questioningly so Evelyn continued. "As you can probably guess, Marcus is my boyfriend. Ever since my mother died, I have been living with him and his sick mother. This morning, the church came through the town to collect tithes and we

could not pay. So they took his mother's inn in payment."
Evelyn hung her head and Marcus rubbed the toe of his
shoe on the stone castle floor.

"Welp, that's it. I'm getting my gun. Or maybe
Richter has a rocket launcher." Alistar muttered and
started to stand but Elzibeth placed a hand onto his shoulder, easily holding him in the chair in his weakened state.

"Wait, Alistar. You are neither in any physical condition to solve this problem, nor do I think your version of
solving it will help," she said before tapping her teeth with
one long fingernail. After a moment she stopped. "Do
either of you have a job in the town?"

"No ma'am," Marcus said. "We've been taking care of
my mother. I was working a bit at the inn, but mostly our
sustenance comes from the forests around town. I am a
fairly good hunter and Evelyn knows where the best plants
grow. Between the two of us we can usually trade in deer
hides and mushrooms for anything we need."

Elzibeth frowned. *These children should be out enjoying
their lives and each other, not having to worry about putting
food on the table and taking care of a sick parent.* Looking
over to Alistar she saw he was thinking the same thing. "I
have an offer for you both. Richter can no longer take care
of the castle by himself so what if you two worked for me?
I could use a good housekeeper, Evelyn, and I'm sure that
you, Marcus, could help Richter in the castle's upkeep. I
will pay you each one thousand Leu each a week and, on
top of that, I will use my coffers to take care of all your
basic needs. In addition you will live here and Marcus'
mother may live here too where she will be taken care of.
No one will feed upon you. I promise you that." Elzibeth
leaned back in her chair, waiting for an answer.

Tears began flowing from Evelyn's eyes and Marcus
put his arm around her. "Dear child, whatever is wrong?"
Elzibeth asked kindly.

"We were so unsure of what would happen when we came here. We honestly considered offering our blood in exchange for you healing my mother," Marcus said.

Elzibeth frowns again. "Marcus, I know that my blood could heal your mother, but she'd possibly end up a vampire like me, forever thirsting for blood," Elzibeth said with even more kindness than before. "Forever unable to go out into the sunlight, and forever worrying about someone trying to drive a stake through her heart. She would watch you grow up, grow old, and then die

while she forever remains frozen in time." Standing, she walked over and hugged both children.

"That is not to say that I won't try. But first we have to get you all here and settled in." A smile crossed her face and she handed Evelyn a white lace handkerchief and the girl wiped her eyes and moved to hand it back.

"Keep it, I have a few dozen in my room. I won't miss one." Elzibeth laughed.

"Will Master Alistar be staying here too?" Marcus asks.

The question shocked Elzibeth and her eyelashes fluttered. She was hoping he would, but she hadn't yet asked him.

Alistar suddenly stood. "I'm no one's master. Please excuse me." And with that he left and headed down the hallway to his room.

"Did I say something wrong, Miss Elzibeth?" Marcus asked.

"No child, I don't think you did. Alistar has a lot on his mind right now. Let me go check on him."

18

Alistar headed into the washroom. Filling the sink basin with cold water, he plunged his head under and held it there for a few moments before coming back up. He pushed the hair out of his face and stared at himself in the mirror. A well-weathered, tanned face with a thick uneven beard stared back at him. Not being good at shaving with a knife, he'd just hack it off as best he could when it grew too long. His dark brown eyes were haunted and deep, full of pain, and his long black hair showed gray.

Sighing he dunked his head under one more time and shivered as the cold water dripped down his chest and back, puddling on the floor.

"Alistar?" Elzibeth's voice sounded from the bedroom.

"In here, Elle." He noted her reflection in the mirror, and glanced over at her, still shivering.

"Alistar, what's wrong? Are you okay?" Elle asked, picking up a towel and wrapping it around his shoulders.

"I looked at Evelyn and all I saw was my sister. Something inside me just flipped and I had to get out of that room. It didn't happen the other night because her face was half hidden with the blanket and I was paying more attention to Marcus. So no, I am NOT okay." Alistar shook his head as if trying to clear the vision.

Elzibeth held Alistar in her arms as tears suddenly flowed from his eyes. He stepped away a couple minutes later and dried his face with the corner of the towel, then perched on the edge of the tub.

"Elle, there is so much locked inside this head of mine. You saw my darker side yesterday. You know my moods can flip in an instant. There is stuff in here I've been fighting against for the last five years, and I managed to lock it away behind a wall. But now the memories are coming back whether I want them to or not, and I don't know how much more I can take."

Compassion shown in Elzibeth's face. "Then we shall fight them and figure them out together. That's what people who *care* about each other do right?" She almost said "Love" but she felt unsure how he would take that.

"You can't help me with the monsters in my head, Elle. It's not like you can dive in there and start kicking their asses like I did to those guards a few weeks back. And now that the church might know I'm alive, they may start coming more frequently and in greater numbers, and I don't know how long we can last. Right now I am the biggest danger to you, and those kids in there. It might be best for me to leave and face them on my own," he said with pain in his voice. He actually liked it here, and he liked her, so thinking about leaving hurts like hell.

"No. You are wrong, Alistar. There is greater strength in numbers no matter the battles that are fought." Elzibeth crouched in front of him and lifted his chin, forcing him to look her in the eyes. He tried to look away but her gaze grabbed his and held it fast.

"You are a broken man taught to kill whatever the church pointed at. And yet you managed to break free of that. You've wandered the world alone for five years surviving because you had to, and then you faced down humans to save a vampire that had you met her in the past, you would have tried to kill just because you felt it was the right thing to do. You've shown that vampire that good people in this world still exist. And, Mister Kain, I promise you that THIS vampire is going to show you that life is worth living, and that you can fight anything so long as you have good people by your side. And if that's a community we have to build together around this castle then we shall do so."

She rose and extended her hand. "What I am saying is I'm not leaving you alone in this dark world to face your fears. I'll be right here with you if you let me."

Alistar breathed in a shaky breath, grasped her hand and she pulled him to his feet. Again she looked him in the eyes, putting every ounce of her soul into the gaze. "I know you are not okay, but together we will do our best to make at least some days better than others." Tugging him to her she hugged him tightly and, to her surprise he hugged her back.

"Thank you," he whispered.

"Do not think anything of it my friend." Stepping away, the corners of her mouth turned upward. "Now we left some very confused children waiting in the kitchen. It's best we check on them before Richter starts teaching them how to play poker," she said with mirth, her eyes twinkling.

"Why? Is he good?" Alistar asked, smiling slightly.

"Gods no. The man can't keep a good face to save his life." A laugh burst from Elzibeth and Alistar couldn't help but laugh with her. Together they walked back to the kitchen.. where Evelyn and Marcus were still waiting.

"Sorry kids, I had a call of nature and then a bit of a dizzy spell," Alistar said sheepishly.

Elzibeth gently pushed Alistar into a chair and looked at the children with a critical eye. "So now, we will need to get you three proper outfits. I guess I'll have to send a message to Francois and have him come here to get you all fitted. In the meantime, I shall send Richter with you to bring your mother and any personal belongings back here. Your first night here starts now. Now run along," Elzibeth said matter of factly, and Evelyn and Marcus rushed off towards the castle entrance.

Alistar grinned at her words. Then she turned to him. "And you... Alistar, will give Richter a list of anything you need to do your job as my guardian. Richter will help you clear out as many armory rooms as you need to have for your station." *Guardian?* he hadn't even thought of that as an idea, but he realized it fit him. "You're going to regret those words, Elle." Alistar's grin widened.

"Alistar I am six hundred and eighty-six years old. I probably have more money below this castle than in your United States and the entirety of Eastern Europe and Russia." Elzibeth tilted her head and eyed him from the corner of her eye.

Alistar shrugged. "Well in that case, I'm gonna need the entire US Naval fleet, and about ten thousand troops. No? Well, darn, I tried. I guess I'll just settle for the tools of my old trade... with some modifications of course. Wait... Six hundred and eighty-six? I could have sworn you were only two hundred."

Elzibeth smiled. "Sweet talker," she purred.

19

"So, umm, I'm gonna go find this armory you speak of. And umm, I forgot to mention that I may have parked a two hundred and fifty-kilogram motorcycle in the middle of your castle the other night," he said sheepishly as he slowly walked out of the kitchen, searching for the stairs to the castle's lower levels.

"You mean in the middle of the courtyard, right?" Elzibeth followed him and raised an eyebrow.

"Umm... not... exactly. I'm pretty sure it's on the entrance hall rug unless Richter moved it." Alistar winced.

Elzibeth sighed. "Stay... here." She let out a small growl, pointed at her feet and aimed for the entrance hall. A clear look of annoyance covered her face on her way back. Alistar swallowed hard.

"Did you have to park it on my favorite rug?" Elzibeth asked, raising an eyebrow.

Alistar's back straightened. "Well, it was in the mission to save your life, so,umm, I figured at the time it was worth risking getting eaten over."

Elzibeth looked at him deadpan for a moment and then patted his cheek. "Very well, you get to live, but you

WILL be cleaning the oil stain out. Come, I will show you the lower levels."

She linked her arm with his and they walked down the hallway, making a left and then a right, before descending some steep stairs. They took another right and then another, stopping at a thick wooden door at the end of a long hallway. Reaching for the door handle, Alistar found it locked.

"I don't suppose you have a key?" He raised both eyebrows.

"If I do, I don't know where it would be." Richter came walking down the hallway minutes later and Elzibeth pointed at the door.

"Yes Mistress," He knelt and pulled out a set of old lock-picking tools. His forehead furrowed in concentration and then he stopped. "The lock is rusted shut."

Alistar thought for a moment. "Hey Richter, did you see any C4 in all that Hunter stuff you collected? Would have looked like grey blocks of dough with some little round metal tubes and wires attached to them."

Richter gazed up at the ceiling in thought. "Yes, I do recall two blocks of such substance in one of the crates."

"What is C4?" Elzibeth asked, getting a worried look on her face.

"Oh, you know, just a few chemicals in the proper proportions." Alistar's face showed nothing but nonchalance.

"You mean like that flash grenade you used on those guards? You are not going to destroy my castle, are you, Alistar?" Elzibeth narrowed her eyes at him.

"Yes, kinda like that. Only soldiers use it for blowing holes in stuff," Alistar said with an evil grin.

"Oh, no. You are not blowing stuff up in my castle, Alistar." Elzibeth's voice was stern before she sauntered up to the door and knocked it off the hinges with two well-placed kicks.

"Wow. That works too," Alistar said in amazement, his eyes wide. He stepped through the now open doorway, his shoulder brushing the hinges where they were still attached to the door frame.

Surveying the room he saw racks of swords, crossbows, and stands of armor. All of them seemed rusted and beyond repair. Picking up a sword, he slammed it against one of the racks, breaking it in two. He tossed the shattered hilt of the sword to the floor and walked over to the crossbows. "Well, this shit's fucked. The swords are rusted through, and the crossbow strings have rotted, and.." He shook one of the armor stands and the armor fell to the floor in pieces. "The armor looks like it belongs on a skeleton. But this room is totally usable."

"Good. Can we melt down all the metal and use it to make new weapons?" Elzibeth asked.

"Yes, but gods why? This is 2142. We should be able to obtain almost anything we need from surplus resellers on the black market given enough time. Swords, bows, guns. Rocket launchers. Won't be cheap, but we can get it."

"He is right on that part, My Mistress. We can obtain almost anything on the black market. But for now, I believe the children are ready to go, so I shall escort them home and back again," Richter remarked before leaving.

"Very well; what do you need?" Elzibeth asked, stepping up next to Alistar.

Alistar slowly swiveled, observing the room. "Over here in this corner, I see a workbench for fixing gear." He pointed to another corner. "And over here, a reloading bench and a powder cabinet for making various types of ammo." He found a long hallway off the main room. "And if we block this off at the end, we have a built-in shooting range. Add in some racks on the walls for various weapons and an area for crates and storage, and this place will be fully kitted out."

"What? Do you think we are going to raise an army?!" Elzibeth exclaimed after Alistar revealed his grand plan.

"If that's what it takes to make the church think twice about sending anyone else here and keep everyone safe, then yes. I'll train an entire army if I must." Alistar's response was filled with so much conviction that Elzibeth felt taken aback. Alistar looked at her. "Weren't you the one who just a bit ago said something about building a community centered around the castle? I mean, what would you do without me around?" He raised an eyebrow.

"Probably have a much quieter life, but I admit it would be boring," Elzibeth said then smirked. Alistar laughed and started piling swords on the floor so he could take down the racks. Elzibeth helped him, and in under an hour, the racks were broken down for firewood and the swords piled in the barn outside.

Alistar ran the broom across the floor back and forth when Elzibeth gilded back in from taking out the last of the broken-down racks. "Not bad. Maybe I should put you on the cleaning crew," She remarked with a bit of a smile.

Alistar paused. "The church ran the training grounds like a boot camp for the first-year trainees. Cleanliness was put at the top of the list and we were beaten if we didn't pass inspection… I wasn't the best in that area." He started sweeping a little faster, trying to get that memory out of his head.

Elzibeth placed her hand on his arm. "I did not mean any offense or to send you back into a bad memory, Alistar."

Alistar nodded. "It's okay; these moments will happen.

Not your fault. Gotta remember I'm the one with the fucked-up brain."

Elzibeth left her hand on his arm a moment longer then let it fall away. "Anyway, I came to tell you the children are back with their mother, and we could use your help. She is not taking it very well and thinks I will eat her, and the kids."

Alistar leaned the broom against the wall. "Well then, let's go avert a crisis, shall we?" He offered Elzibeth an arm, which she linked with her own, and they walked to the castle entrance.

20

As Alistar and Elzibeth reached the grand hall, they could hear shouting outside. "Hoo, boy, here we go. Let me handle this," Alistar said.

He strolled through the door and into the lit courtyard, his gaze taking in the whole situation. A woman, presumably Marcus's mother, held a knife in her hands, facing off against Richter with Evelyn and Marcus behind her. Alistar noted her being the woman from the inn in Calia who had asked Marcus to fetch the doctor, and though she was thin and frail, she held a fierceness with much fight left in her.Her stringy brown hair hung from under a multicolor knitted cap, and her eyes blazed from a sallow face weathered by age and sickness.

"Mother, no one here is going to hurt any of us. They just want to help," Marcus pleaded, but his mother didn't put down the knife.

"Listen to your son Mrs. Alexandrescu!" Evelyn said, with worry clear on her face as she wrung her hands with uncertainty.

Both of them saw Alistar and Elzibeth step out onto the castle steps.

Alistar sighed. "Elle, whatever happens, don't leave these steps until I call for you, please." Elzibeth nodded and Alistar walked down the steps and across the courtyard toward the woman, a glower on his face. The woman watched him and turned in his direction, slashing with the knife.

Alistar seized her wrist in mid-slash with his right hand and twisted the knife from her grasp with his left, throwing it across the courtyard where it sunk two inches into one of the scrapped weapon's racks. Spinning the woman around, he wrapped her in his arms.

"Look at my left wrist, woman!" he barked. The fierceness of his command momentarily stopped her struggle. Reaching up, she peeled back the black leather glove to reveal his tattoo and she gasped.

"Now, do you think a church Hunter would associate with a dangerous creature? Answer me!" he growled. He needed to keep up the shock and awe so that her emotions calmed down and logic could take over. He let her go a moment later.

He motioned to Elzibeth over his shoulder and she glided down the steps and to his side, bowing to the woman.

"Mrs. Alexandreascu, I welcome you and your children to my castle. The children have told me all that has happened, and I would like to provide the three of you a home where you have no worries or fear from the church, or anyone else. I would like to provide Evelyn and Marcus with employment where they can earn a living and give you a place where perhaps you might get better…"

She fell silent, waiting for the woman's reply.

Shaken from the events, Marcus's mother fainted. Alistar caught her, sweeping her up into his arms. She was still breathing. "She's okay kids, just fainted," he said as Evelyn and Marcus ran over.

"I am sorry, children. I clearly did not anticipate the effect this journey and meeting might have on your mother," Elzibeth said. "Let's get you all inside where you can rest. The dawn is fast approaching. We shall speak to your mother in the evening and, hopefully, she will realize that no one here means her or you any harm."

Both Evelyn and Marcus nodded at Elzibeth's words and headed inside. Elzibeth walked by Alistar's side as he carried the unconscious woman to a spare bedroom and laid her on the bed.

"Elle, I want you to lock your door while you sleep. I don't know how she'll react when she wakes," he said as they closed the door behind them. Richter handed him the woman's knife, which he slid through his belt.

"Alistar—" Elzibeth began.

"No, I wont kill her, no matter what she does. That would break all the trust that Marcus and Evelyn have placed in us."

"What if she stabs you?" Richter asked, and Elzibeth raised her eyebrows in alarm.

"Richter, *if*, and that's a big *if* she can stab me, then she deserves to do so. It wouldn't be the first time I've been stabbed, and it probably won't be the last," Alistar shrugged.

Richter shook his head and walked away. "As you wish."

Elzibeth looked at Alistar, worried. "I do not wish you to get hurt, Alistar."

Alistar smiled. "As I said, it's a very BIG If. The last time I was stabbed, I was fighting a werewolf in Scotland. He was surprisingly good with a rapier. Not so much with his teeth and claws, though. That was about ten years ago." He lifted his shirt to show the small puncture wound going through his right side and out his back. "Pinned me to a tree with one blow. I had to snap the blade and pull myself off. I walked to the pickup point half dead. He ended up getting away. I don't know if he's still out there or not. He would be a fierce ally in this fight if he still is."

Elzibeth touched the scars and frowned. "You really need to stop getting beaten up so much."

"Sometimes I like a little pain, Elle," he replies laughing. "It makes me feel alive. Have a good sleep. I'm going to get in a couple hours of training." He left Elzibeth with her eyebrows raised in surprise.

Elzibeth headed up to her room and closed the door, locking it as Alistar had requested. *Mister Kain, you are still a mystery even now.* She opened the balcony window and saw Alistar entering the courtyard. He started throwing punches and kicks at the air but she could tell it was some sort of combat training. Then, Richter walked over, stopping in front of him. Both men bow to each other. *They are going to train. Interesting.* She watched with rapt attention.

~

Richter and Alistar faced off, each one sizing up the other, looking for a weakness. They placed the backs of their right hands against each other and positioned their right feet forward. In a flash, punches were thrown and blocked in a flurry of motion. Kicks were slowly thrown in as each man tried to down the other.

Alistar backflipped once, twice, and Richter pressed the advantage, moving in, Alistar spun his body, rolling out of the way of a stomp and flipped back up to his feet. His attacks that followed pushed Richter back till he hit the wall.

Alistar threw a punch and Richter ducked, causing Alistar to punch the wall full-strength. Richter however, did not give him time to recover and continued fighting.

Richter connected with a blow that snapped Alistar's head back and caused him to taste blood. Alistar spun, delivering a kick to the side of Richters head, causing the man to hit the ground. Alistar dove and rolled, coming up in a crouch next to Richter with his fist cocked.

Richter knew Alistar had beaten him and he slapped the ground twice. Alistar took his hand and tugged him to his feet. Then they set up and continued to spar, neither man seeming to realize that Elzibeth watched them.

When they completed their training, each man bloodied and bruised, they clapped each other on the back, bowed and Richter headed inside. Alistar looked up at the balcony Elzibeth was on and inclined his head.

He knew I was watching the whole time! She smiled and waved at him. Alistar did likewise before motioning that he, too, was heading inside. As the sun's rays appeared over the horizon, Elzibeth closed the windows and the heavy curtains and lay on her bed, letting sleep take her.

21

Alistar strolled to his room, washed the blood out of his mouth, and tended to his bruises. Afterward, he headed to the room where Marcus' mother lay, encountering Marcus outside about to knock. "Hey kid. Let me talk to her first." He slipped past the boy and stepping inside moved a chair next to the door in the shadows.

"I know you're awake. No one stays in a fainting spell for this long," he said simply.

"What's to happen to me, to my son, and Evelyn?" the woman asked, not looking toward him.

"Nothing. Elzibeth was completely truthful in what she said to you."

"Vampires can't be trusted. The church says so. All they want is our blood!" the woman snapped back.

"Not this one. Pig blood, cow blood, even deer and stag when she can obtain it. But I've never seen her drink from anyone." Alistar did not add, "Except for myself"

"Lies!"

"Really? Would you like to know what Evelyn and Marcus did when they showed up? They admitted that they planned to offer their own blood to Elzibeth if she would do one thing... Save you. Heal you." The woman looked over at Alistar in shock.

"Why? Why would they do that?"

"A son's love for his mother. A son wanting more time with her. And a woman's love for your son." Alistar eyed her from across the room, but she shifted away from his dark, piercing gaze.

"I don't understand. What did your mistress say? And if you are a Hunter, why have you sided with her instead of doing your job and ridding the world of her?" The woman continued staring at the ceiling.

"Elzibeth? She refused their offer. Instead she made a counter. She offered them jobs here at the castle. One thousand leu each per week and basic needs taken care of including room and board. Then she offered to take you in so that you wouldn't be out on the street. She doesn't harm innocents. The only time she's killed since I've known her has been to defend herself, or someone she cares about. Same as any human who's allowed to do if threatened. And that should explain to you why I haven't killed her. Because she's not the monster in this castle."

The woman looks back at him. "If she's not the monster in this castle, and you are implying that there is one, Then who is it?"

Alistar leaned forward till his face could be seen. His eyes glittered in the lamp-light. "That would be me. The monster the church made–, a killer. But then I don't have fangs you can see, or red glowing eyes to show you." He stood and put the chair back. "I'll send your son in to talk to you. I suggest you listen to him." He pivoted to the door. "Oh. Also. Elzibeth offered Marcus one more thing with no strings attached. To use her blood to heal you or at least prolong your life so that your son can get a few more years with his mother."

The woman fell silent but when Alistar reached for the doorknob, she clears her throat. "I shall take your words into consideration, and I will hear my boy out. But if you harm either of them, I will die trying to kill you."

Alistar smiled at the fire in this woman's soul. "I would not expect anything else. Never get between a mother bear and her cubs. However, you have nothing to fear from me either. I only eliminate those who attack the ones I care about, and anyone they care about."

"Those you care about. Does that include Marcus and Evelyn?"

Alistar nodded his head. "I rather like your son. He's a lot like his mother, a lot like mine before she was taken from me." Feeling he had gotten everything he wanted to say out, he opened the door and ushered Marcus inside, stepping past him. Once in the hallway, he closed the door, leaned against the wall and waited for Marcus to reemerge. The boy gently closed the door and looked over at him.

"What's up, kid?"

"Mother says she'll give this a chance. Staying here I mean. She won't take Lady Elzibeth's blood, though. What do I do, Mister Kain?"

"Well kid, your mom's a strong woman. Maybe she'll recover now that she's here in a better place. Elle takes care of those within her walls. And who knows, maybe your mother will change her mind before it's too late. All you can do is have hope."

"Mister Kain? Mother said you told her that Lady Elzibeth wasn't the monster in these walls and that you were, that you were a Hunter who has betrayed the church."

Alistar inclined his head and pulled his left glove down just enough for Marcus to see the tattoo.

"What made you leave? What made you stop being a Hunter?"

Sighing and feeling like this conversation had taken place too many times in the past week, he pushed off from the wall and started walking back towards his room.

"They killed my sister. But I never really stopped being a Hunter, You can't unlearn what you've been taught in life. I did, however, switch sides. Have a good night Marcus."

He did not wait for a reply but turned the corner and wandered through the castle until his meandering brought him to two double doors. Pushing them open he found an old church. Pews were no longer lined up, trash littered the floor, and the cross laid on its side behind the altar. Alistar inspected it for a moment before picking it up and setting it upright in front of a stained glass window of an angel casting down demons. Then, for the first time in many years he knelt and bowed his head.

"Lord, I haven't talked to you in well, a long time. But... I need your help. Am I doing the right thing? Do I have the right to saddle others with the burden that is mine to bear?"

He silently waited for an answer, and as the sun continued to rise, the light streamed through the stained glass to fall upon Alistars kneeling form. The wings of light played out behind him, making it seem like he had flaming wings of fire. He then rose and kissed the altar. Turning, he moved between the wrecked pews and stopped when he noticed a somewhat mostly intact, but burned book. Picking it up he discovered an old version of the Bible, from times beyond the church as he knew it today.

Walking back to his room, he laid the Bible next to his bed, stripped off his clothing, and climbed under the covers, falling fast asleep.

22

The day passed by quickly for those asleep and as the sun set, Elzibeth opened her eyes. Climbing out of bed and picking a new outfit for the evening, she glided down the stairs toward Alistar's room. Knocking softly she called out his name.

"Alistar?" She opened the door a crack to snoring coming from beyond. Opening the door further, she saw him still in bed, his naked body half covered by the sheets and comforter.

He's still asleep. He must have stayed up late. It's no wonder, though. He's had a lot to deal with lately. Slipping through the half-open door, she closed it with care, and not wanting to wake him, sat on the edge of the bed, watching him as he slept. *What a rather handsome man.* She could easily see herself taking him one day to keep him around forever. Leaning down she blew gently in his left ear.

Alistar's right hand shot out and grabbed her around the neck, pulling her close as his eyes snapped open. Instant recognition came across his face as he saw who he held in his grip.

"Well Alistar, you have me. What are you going to do with me?" she asked with a warm smile. For a moment Alistar considered kissing her, but he let go of her neck and his arm fell back to the blankets.

"Good morning, Elle."

Elzibeth was a little disappointed. She had hoped he would have tried to kiss her. But maybe he wasn't ready to admit his feelings. "Good morning, handsome. Or rather good evening." She sat back and he reached for his watch on the side table, then rolled onto his back.

"What time is it?" he asked as he fumbled around.

"It would be shortly after dark. Did you sleep well?" Elzibeth asks, putting her feet on the bed and sitting against the headboard.

Alistar studied the watch and then her words percolated through his brain. "Fuck. No. I didn't. All that moving stuff yesterday and the sparring practice with Richter has left my muscles sore."

Elzibeth smiled. "Where does it hurt?" she asked with compassion.

"Mostly in my back. I think I might have pulled something. That or I have a couple of muscle knots."

"Roll over then." Elzibeth laughed huskily.

"Excuse me?"

"I said roll over, Alistar, or do you not trust me?" Elzibeth pursed her lips with a mischievous glint in her eyes and looked at him through half-closed eyelids.

Alistar raised an eyebrow but then did as she asked. "No, I trust you. So far I have no reason not to."

Elzibeth reached out, her delicate hands deftly moving across Alistar's scarred but well-muscled back, gently feeling for the knots and points of pain. Finding the first knot, she pressed down, hearing his painful hiss. She twisted her thumb as she pressed down, feeling the muscle loosen under her touch, and a sigh of relief from the man under her hands. Her hands lightly caressed the scars again before finding the second knot. Again she pushed down with her thumbs, moving them in small circles until that one loosen as well. Alistar's hiss of pain turned into another sigh of relief. He started to get up, but she put a hand on his back and pushed him back to the mattress.

"I'm not done yet." Leaning over she planted a kiss on the back of his neck and then started to massage his neck, moving to his shoulders. Years of tension drain away under her fingers wherever they touched. From his shoulders she moved to his upper back caressing and kneading, and from there she continued down to his lower back. After a moment more she sat back.

"Feeling better?"

"Gods, yes. You have the touch of an angel, Elle," Alistar said, his voice muffled by the pillow.

"Good. Because I need you to get up. Francois will be here in just a while to measure you all for your new clothes," she said, patting his back and sliding off the bed to stand.

"Understood." Alistar rolled over so he faced her. "I talked with Marcus' mother last night. And then Marcus talked to her. They'll stay here and she'll let Marcus and Evelyn work, but she refused the offer of your blood."

He climbed out of the bed, walking across the room naked to the armoire. *Well this is new.* Elzibeth admired his body.

Alistar stared at Elzibeth in the mirror inside the large wardrobe. Unlike in fiction, vampires in this world casted reflections. "See anything you like Elle?" he grinned.

Elzibeth's eyes caught his in the mirror and she smiled. "Yes… I do." She felt a flush of heat in her face and busied herself with making Alistar's bed.

Alistar chuckled. Finishing getting dressed, he opened the door and held it for Elzibeth. "After you, princess."

"Why thank you kind sir." Elzibeth mock curtsied and she and Alistar broke out laughing. She nudged Alistar in the ribs and he put his arm around her as they walked down the hallway towards the kitchen, which had by now become the defacto meeting place for everyone.

They found Evelyn and Marcus, along with Marcus' mother sitting at the table eating.

"Hey, kids. Mrs. Alexandrescu. Good morning." Alistar nodded and pulled out a chair for Elzibeth, pushing it in after she sat down.

"Elena," Marcus's mother replied.

"Huh?" Alistar paused on his way to get a drink.

"It's Elena. My name."

Alistar nodded in response. "Elena it is then."

He looked around the kitchen. "Is there any coffee in this place?" He started rummaging through cabinets.

"I wouldn't do that, Mister Kain," Marcus piped up.

"Oh? And why not?" Alistar asked. A knife hit the cabinet next to him.

"Mess with my kitchen any further Alistar Kain and I'll have to give you another ass-kicking." Richter said, entering.

Alistar rubbed his jaw and stepped away from the cabinet. "I believe it was me that gave you the ass-kicking last night, Richter, but, hey, I hear you in either case."

Richter wrenched the knife out of the cabinet and pointed it at him. "I have this kitchen organized exactly how I like it and not even Mistress Tepes messes with that. We do indeed have coffee. I just have to grind it. Do me a favor and bring Mistress Tepes her breakfast would you?"

While Richter prepared the coffee, Alistar headed into the next room, poured Elle a chalice of blood, and set it in front of her.

"So the plan for today is to get you all fitted for new

clothes. And then start on your castle training," Elzibeth said as she nodded her thanks to Alistar.

Evelyn and Marcus perked up, excited. But Elena's eyes were on the table, clearly worried.

"Still having doubts about this whole arrangement, Elena?" Alistar asked quietly after walking over to her.

"Yes," Elena responded.

"Well, why don't you try talking to Elle and voicing your concerns. She'll probably listen to you." Richter handed him a tankard of coffee. He took a long draw from the tankard and sighed. "Holy fuck, Richter, I think I might kiss you. This is the best coffee I have tasted in a few years."

Richter looked over with a haughty expression. "It's an old-family recipe, but if you kiss me, I WILL punch you, Kain."

Everyone except for Elena laughed.

Marcus' mother gazed around at the laughter and smiling people. EvenMarcus had a smile. Maybe her son and Evelyn would be happy here. Alistar noticed the look and walked over to the kids.

"Hey, why don't you two join me outside? I think your mom and Miss Elle need to talk." The kids stood and went with him. As he crossed through the doorway, he sent another nod their way.

23

Elzibeth sat quietly and sipped blood from the chalice, waiting for Elena to speak.

Finally, the woman lifted her head. "Your Alistar told me last night everything you offered to Marcus and Evelyn... and me."

"*My* Alistar? He's not mine, although I hope one day he might be," Elzibeth replied with a smile. Leaning forward she held her hand out to Elena. "I meant every word I said. Marcus and Evelyn will have full, happy lives here and be safe within these walls. I will not feed from them nor allow anyone else to do so. You are also welcome here for as long as you like."

Elena hesitated before reaching across the table and taking the offered hand. Elzibeth held it and reached out with her senses. Breathing heavily, her heart struggled to pass blood around her body. She was deathly ill and Elzibeth guessed she only had a couple of months left to live. But she also sensed Elena's only maybe in her early to mid-thirties at most which meant she had Marcus at a young age. She let go of Elena's hand and patted it.

"I have the ability to cure you. My blood could strengthen your body, your heart, your lungs. But…"

"But there is the possibility I could become a creature of the night like you. Never to see the sunlight on my face again. Thirsting for blood, watching my son grow old and die while I remain my age." Elena finishes what Elzibeth started. Elzibeth nods.

"Yes, that is a possibility. I, unfortunately, don't have access to my father's records on how he gave Richter health and long life without turning him."

～

Alistar, Evelyn, and Marcus strolled through the courtyard. "Mother is talking to Miss Elle."

"Yes. She is. They have much to discuss." Marcus, with fists clenched in agitation, kicked a stone in anger. Alistar just watched him.

"It's not fair! Can't Miss Elle just force Mother to take her blood?" Marcus whirled, yelling at Alistar.

"She wouldn't do that." Alistar stayed standing where he was, but Marcus strode up to him.

"She listens to you, yes?"

"So far for the most part, she has."

"Then make her give my mother her blood!"

"I can't do that Marcus." Marcus hit him in the chest and Alistar froze and took it as the boy hit him again.

"Why not?!" Marcus screamed at the man in front of him. "Why…" He punctuated each word with a hit. "not?!" Alistar let him vent his anger.

"Because I, like Miss Elle, believe in free will and not subjugating others," Alistar replied calmly.

Marcus winded up and punched him across the face hard enough to snap his head to the side. Alistar leaned away from

Marcus, holding up his hands as Marcus glared at him and then ran back into the castle. Feeling his jaw with one hand, Alistar moved it back and forth as Evelyn walked over to him.

~

"I know my time is coming. I have done my best to be a good mother to Marcus, and a stand-in one for Evelyn after she lost her parents. But this disease is a wasting one. It makes life more and more difficult each day I wake," Elena said, staring at the table again. She looked up to see Elzibeth watching her.

"Can you promise me that they will be raised right when I'm gone, that they will grow up healthy and wise, with love and respect for others?"

Elzibeth smiled. "I promise they will have the best education I can find IF they wish to broaden their minds. And the best protection while they live here. And I will do my best to teach them proper decorum in the ways of the world."

Elena nodded. "Very well. Then I have everything I could wish for."

Elzibeth nodded back as Marcus ran past the kitchen crying.

"He is taking things pretty hard. I'll go talk to him." Elena said, rising and slowly following her son down the hallway to his room.

~

"I don't suppose you need to work out some anger as well?" Alistar asked as he sat on the castle steps.

"No. Marcus is dealing with this pretty hard, but you didn't deserve that Mister Alistar," Evelyn said sitting beside him. She pulled out the white lace handkerchief

Elle had given her, and dabbed his lip, where a bead of blood formed.

Alistar touched his lip. "Huh. Marcus has a good punch for such a scrappy kid."

Evelyn giggled. "Yes he does, and he's very protective. When we were younger, he always defended me from the village bullies. He didn't always win, but he always got back up." She smiled, remembering those memories.

"*Hmm.* He's a good kid. He'll be alright... And so will you."

A shiny black sports car pulled in through the castle gates, and a thin, tall man with light brown hair emerged.

"I swear, these roads fall more and more into disrepair every year," the man said, looking around. "Well, this place has seen better days since I was last here. I bet Elzibeth still has the same tacky drapes and rugs. I swear, the woman has no taste for decorating."

"It's good to see you again, too, Francois."Alistar looked over his shoulder to see Elzibeth standing right behind him. A smile stretched her face from ear to ear at the sight of her old friend.

"Elzibeth, darling, you must simply do something about your drab castle. It just does not suit someone in your station. Most of your equals are living in mansions, not tucked away in the middle of the Carpathian Mountains." The man flipped his hand.

Elzibeth laughed. "I like my castle, thank you very much. Although I admit maybe it's time to advance the decor and utilities into this century. But then again, that's one of the reasons you are here, Francois."

"Well then, I'm assuming from your message that she's one of the reasons, and he would be the other. Where's the third?" Francois said, striding forward and inspecting Evelyn and Alistar.

"Stand, both of you. Now," he commanded, clapping

his hands.Evelyn quickly rises. But Alistar stayed seated with one eyebrow raised. Elzibeth nudged him with her boot and he slowly stood as well.

"Now turn in a full circle," Francois said. As Evelyn did so he made comments. "Yes, yes, this one has a great figure. We can definitely find something that works."

He moved in front of Alistar. "My, you didn't tell me that Marcus was so tall, or so muscular... Or so old. He looks absolutely delish."

Elzibeth laughed. "Francois, that's not Marcus. That's Alistar."

"Oh him. Well. He certainly is good-looking. I can see why you've taken a liking to him, darling," Francois said with a wave of his hand again.

Alistar looked over at Elzibeth. "Is he?"

Elzibeth grinned. "Very."

"*Hmm.*" Alistar raised an eyebrow and tilted his head to the right in a half shrug.

24

Francois kissed Elzibeth first on one cheek, then the other and hugged her. "Elzibeth, looking as beautiful as ever, but thats one of the benefits of being what you are. You are almost as fabulous as me."

Alistar hadn't seen Elzibeth laugh as much in such a short time as right now.. "Always the charmer, Francois."

"Naturally, darling. Well let's get started then. I'll get the girl's measure first, then come back for this one." Francois said, pointing at Alistar.

Elzibeth placed her hand on Alistar's shoulder. "Are you alright with that, Alistar? We can get you taken care of first if you'd like?" She spotted the blood on his lip and touched it, frowning.

"Marcus is taking things with his mother in a bad way. He needed to work out some anger so I let him."

Elzibeth let her fingers fall away from his face. "Understood. He and I will have a small talk about dealing with grief and anger later, though."

Alistar gave a small shake of his head. "Best let me do that." Elzibeth looked him in the eyes in understanding.

"Very well, as you wish." Turning, she, Francois, and Evelyn headed inside, the girl pausing in the doorway.

"Mister Alistar, would you like me to send Marcus to apologize?"

Alistar shook his head. "No, he'll come around on his own. I know the type. He just needs time."

"Okay." Evelyn said before disappearing inside.

"I saw that hit. You could have moved." Richter said, stopping beside Alistar, before lighting up an old tobacco pipe.

"Yes, but then he would have been even angrier. He just needed something to hit, and it was either me or something solid enough to break every bone in his hand," Alistar replied, holding out his hand.

Richter deposited the pipe in Alistar's hand and he placed the mouthpiece between his lips and inhaled a few puffs before passing it back.

"That's some good tobacco. Solid flavor, not a lot of bite. Where'd you get it?"

"There's a traveling salesman that comes around Calia once a year. Says he gets it from the Balkans. It's not cheap, but it's my one addiction. Granted, Mistress Tepes does not allow me to smoke inside the castle so I come out here for a daily break from my work."

"Well thank you for sharing."

Richter grunted in reply.

Walking back inside, Alistar retrieved the Bible from the bedside table and headed to the castle's small church. Upon stepping inside he saw it was occupied by Marcus and his mother. "My apologies. I didn't know anyone was in here."

"No, it's quite alright Mister Kain. Marcus and I were just praying for forgiveness and for love and peace, among other things. I just wish we had a Bible. I haven't prayed in a while and I've forgotten some of the prayers," Elena said, smiling softly.

Alistar held out the partially burned Bible to her. "Maybe this will help?" Elena's eyes lit up at the offered book, and she took it gingerly from his hand. He turned to leave when she put a hand on his arm.

"Would you stay and pray with us?" After a moment, he sat on the only undamaged pew in the room. Marcus and Elena joined him. Elena opened the book and read.

"Lord, thank you for my beautiful family. It worries me that I cannot protect them from all of the evil in this world. I am on my knees, asking for your help. Please, watch over my family today and in the future when they step out into this world without me. Send an angel to guide them through their days as they grow into strong adults. Amen"

Alistar and Marcus added in their "Amens," and Alistar stood to leave when Elena put a hand on his arm for the second time, making him pause.

"And watch over Mister Kain as he helps to raise my stubborn son in my absence. Let him have patience and understanding with Marcus, and may he teach him how to be a good man... Amen,"

She looked over at Alistar and nodded, and Alistar nodded back. He quickly stood. "I should be getting back. Elle is probably wondering where I am. You may stay here as long as you wish."

"Thank you Mister Kain." Alistar smiled in return and patted her shoulder.

As he walked away, a small tear slipped down his cheek when he reached the door. Opening it he found Elzibeth standing on the other side. She saw the tear and started to speak but he held a finger to his lips, and she fell silent as he closed the door to the church behind him.

"Alistar, what happened?"

"Elena just said a prayer for me, asking the Lord to help me as I raise Marcus in her absence. Even after I told her the other night that I was the monster in this castle, not you," Alistar said a little choked up.

Elzibeth wrapped her arms around him. "You are not a monster, Alistar. You have a heart. I can feel it beating. I have seen your acts of great and terrible violence, and I have seen your acts of great love and kindness. Alistar, look at me. Now tell that negative bitch in your head that if she doesn't stop, I'm going to jump in there and kick her ass."

Alistar chuckled. "Sure thing, Elle. I'll do that right after I serve her papers for back rent owed. You know it doesn't quite work like that. But the hug helps."

Elzibeth smiled brightly. "Good. I have many more where that came from. Now, Francois is ready for you. And money is no object."

Together they walked to a side room. "So there you are. Excellent! Now, off with the clothes, mister."

Alistar's brows bunched together. "I don't think I need to take my clothes off to have you measure me for a suit."

Francois gave Elzibeth a look that said: "Help me with this one."

"Alistar. Clothes off. Now, please," Elzibeth's voice rung out.

Alistar grinned at her, seeing the glint in her eyes. "As you wish."

Francois placed a hand on his chest. "Oh my god, he's seen the princess bride. Elzibeth, I think I may be in love. But seriously darling, I need your clothes off and you on this magical circle so I can design the suit on you, and the under-layer is skin tight. And no, it's not latex. I wouldn't dream of using anything a client might be allergic to."

Alistar shrugged, stripped off his clothes, and stepped into the circle with his hands in front of his privates. Francois positioned himself in front of him, then eyed him up and down. "That's adorable. Look, I'm gay; you're a guy. Think of it like being in the gym locker room. Raise your arms and hold them out at shoulder level."

"Valid point." Alistar did as he was asked.

Elzibeth watched him, her gaze flicking up and down his muscled form. Catching his eye, she smiled, causing him to look at the ceiling as his face reddened slightly.

Francois leaned closer, looking at Alistar's left wrist. "Elzibeth, I feel that you have not told me everything about this man. I see the mark of a high-ranking Hunter on his wrist, and yet he's standing in front of me and not dead by your hands. Why is that?"

"Francois, that's because he is a former Hunter," Elzibeth said while Alistar pinched the bridge of his nose, eyeing her. "and he saved my life on more than one occasion. I have grown quite fond of him. Now get on with it, please."

"Very well." Francois moved his hands and Alistar felt something creeping up his legs. Greenish black fibers weaved their way up the outside of his legs.

What the fuck? Alistar thought as his eyes went wide and he twitched.

"Alistar. Don't. Move," Elzibeth said, catching the look on his face. Alistar closed his eyes as the small tendrils weaved higher. Past his waist, past his chest and back, down his arms, stopping at his wrists and neck.

"Darling, it's done. You can open your eyes now," Francois said from his right. Alistar did so and found his body covered in the strange gray-green fabric that felt cool to the touch.

"What…?"

"Fairy magic, darling. That fabric is living, breathing, and will stop any normal sword or arrow. As long as it's not magical, or silver, nothing will get through it. Oh, and it will keep you cool on the hottest days, and warm on the coldest night" Francois replied with a smile.

Alistar raised an eyebrow and glanced at Elzibeth with an amused questioning look. "No. Alistar, I am not handing you your gun so you can try shooting yourself to test that under-layer." She scolded him with a glare thrown in for good measure.

"You know me well, Elle," Alistar grinned.

"Gun? *Hmm,* I don't know if it will stop a bullet?" A new light shined in Francois' eyes as a grin crossed his face and he looked over at Elzibeth.

"I said no, Francois," she replied turning her glare onto him

"So, umm, how do I take it off?" Alistar asked.

"Well, first, I have to cut the top from the bottom, darling. Then you can take it off just like regular clothes. However, I need to warn you that you will need to lay the under-suit in the sun for at least one full day a week for it to recharge. And, of course it's hand-wash only," Fracois pulled out an organic knife that appeared like it had been grown from a tree.

He slowly cut a line around Alistars waist and where he cut, the material folded back on itself and mended, leaving Alistar in a two piece outfit.

Putting the knife away, Francois pulled out a tailor's tape and started measuring Alistar, writing down numbers in mid-air with his finger. The numbers stayed in the air, hovering like a neon sign on the side of a building.

When he finished, he crossed his arms. "Now that we have the armor part down, what exactly are you looking for in the outer layers?"

"Tactical shirt and pants. Long coat. Lots of pockets and places to mount my equipment." Alistar rattled off his requirements. "Oh, and a belt strong enough to carry my weight and then some. Oh, and in all black."

"Sounds like your standard military or Hunter requirements. How bland. Are you sure you don't want a bit of color? Like some blue or green, or maybe a bit of red?" Francois remarked dryly.

"Pretty sure. I like black."

"Very well, you can step down. I'll make the pants and coat out of stag Leather, and the shirt out of spider-silk cloth. There WILL be a pattern in it. You get no say in the matter. I won't have you running around guarding this one in my clothing without it also looking fashionable."

"I also have regular clothing for him in that bag there," he said to Elzibeth. "Since he clearly has no taste in clothing, I suggest you help him pick out his wardrobe, Elzibeth. I'll start on this custom stuff first, and I should have it done within the week."

Alistar spun around. "Black is a perfectly fine color. It goes with anything."

"Elzibeth, again, help me with this one. I think he's brain damaged!"

"Oh he is not, you damn fairy. He's just lived a cloistered life," Elzibeth said laughing.

Alistar walked over and grabbed the bag. "I'll take this to my room and go through it. You two can deal with Marcus," he said before walking away.

25

Alistar set the bag on his bed and started unpacking the clothes. The articles were way too flamboyant. Elzibeth opened the door to find him with his hands on his hips, staring down at his choices.

"Marcus is being fitted as we speak. Francois wants to put him in a suit. I axed that suggestion for something stylish. He's not a butler, after all."

"Mmmhmm" Alistar replied as he continued to stare at the clothing.

Elzibeth inspected the selection, picking up a shirt and holding it against Alistar's chest. "No." She chose another. "Also, no."

Alistar held up a Hawaiian shirt. "Umm, he does realize this is Romania, and not the islands, right?"

Elzibeth frowned. "Apparently not. What about this?" she asks, holding up a very neon-pink shirt with the words *Tough guys wear pink* on it. She tried to hide her smile because Alistar knew she only teased him.

"I'd rather walk back across the ocean and turn myself

into the church is what I think," Alistar replied in all seriousness.

Elzibeth laughed and tossed the shirt into the no-pile before holding up one made of fine silk with a lovely black and red pattern. "Now this one is nice. Try it on."

Alistar took the shirt and slipped into it, buttoning it up. Tucking her chin into her hand, Elzibeth made a motion for him to turn around with one finger and he did so. *"Hmm."* Then reaching out she undid the top button so a little of Alistar's chest showed.

"I think it makes you look like a tourist... But you pull it off. Keep it."

Alistar saw himself in the mirror. After a second he popped the collar and grinned. "Hey Elle, are there any jeans in that pile of clothes?"

Elzibth found a pair of fashionable skinny jeans and tossed them in his direction. He stared at them for a moment wondering how he would get them over the medical boot around his ankle or how he was going to get the medical boot off his ankle, for that matter.

"Something wrong?" Elzibeth asked, stepping up next to him.

"Yeah. I realize I forgot that these support boots have to be cut off once they're put on."

Kneeling in front of him Elzibeth looked up into his eyes as she wrapped her hands around the device and, in one motion, snapped it in two, pulling it off his leg before standing up again.

"Thank you, Elle.," he said, putting his weight on his ankle.

"So? How is the ankle feeling?"

"It's healing but still hurts. Definitely better, though. Without that boot, I'm not going to be doing any acrobatics anytime soon. I'd say I'm at sixty five, maybe seventy percent." Alistar sat on the bed to put the pants on.

Elzibeth plopped beside him. "You trust me?"

Alistar gave her a look like she was crazy. "I think we've established that fact already, Elle. Why?"

Elzibeth paused and then bit her tongue causing a single drop of blood to well up on its tip. Then leaning over she kissed Alistar, transferring the blood drop to his tongue. The action stunned Alistar and he stiffened, but his composure softened. Breaking the kiss, Elzibeth considered him.

"Swallow." she said, smiling. Warmth suffused his body, traveling throughout his limbs. For a brief second, he felt fire in his leg and then the feeling faded to nothing.

"Try walking." Sliding off the bed, he took a few steps and felt no pain in his ankle.

"Well, shit. Thats fucking amazing. Why didn't we just do that before?" he asked in awe.

Elzibeth stepped up next to him, resting her head onto his shoulder. Unconsciously, he wrapped an arm around her. "Because before, you had not yet trusted me enough, and I was not going to force it on you."

"Huh. Neat. Are there any other benefits?"

"Maybe one or two." Elzibeth's voice issued strongly in his head.

"That's going to be useful," Alistar thought.

"Yes."

"Well, fuck me, we can both send and receive." He shook his head in amazement.

Reaching up he felt his face, and frowned. "I need a shave," he muttered. "I really wish I had a disposable razor."

"I'm sure Richter would let you borrow a spare straight razor." Elzibeth lightly touched his bearded face.

"Yea, that's nice and all. Just one problem, I don't

know how to shave with a straight razor. Never learned. I've just been hacking off the excess length with my combat knife and hoping it looked okay." Alistar laughed.

Elzibeth shook her head. "This won't do. I'll be right back. Go take that chair by the bed into the bathroom, Alistar." She headed out the bedroom door, leaving him alone.

She's not going to shave me is she?

"I am," The reply echoed in his mind along with Elzibeth's mental laugh.

"You know, this whole mental contact thing could get awkward."

"Don't worry; you will quickly pick up on how to shield your thoughts. It does take some time so until then, I will know all your thoughts Alistar Kain." Elzibeth's reply was filled with mental mischievousness.

Oh god. I'm in trouble.

"Yes… you are." He could hear Elzibeth's laughter in his mind.

A few minutes later she arrived with an ornate straight razor. Alistar held out his hand. "Mind if I try it first?" He asked with a patented raised eyebrow.

Elzibeth handed him the razor, smiling, and filled the sink basin with hot water. He stood, staring at his bushy beard in the mirror. Splashing some water on his face he grabbed the razor and started hacking at his beard like he would with his combat knife. The razor being much sharper, easily sliced through the hair and he quickly cut his cheek from too much pressure.

"Shit that stings!" he said, dropping the razor into the basin and putting a hand to his cheek as blood welled up in a line, trailing down his face. Elizbeth wipes his face with a towel. His blood welled up again and, leaning forward, she licked it away, her saliva sterilizing the wound and helping speed up the healing process.

Alistar shuddered at the lick. "Hold still." Elzibeth chided him as she picked up the razor and flicked the water off of it. Her motions were deft and swift, and the hair fell away, revealing more of Alistar's weathered face. She left him a neatly trimmed goatee and soul patch.

"There. I can see more of your face now... I like it." Elzibeth smiled and rinsed off the razor, wiping it dry on a towel.

Alistar dunked his face underwater and then dried it off. "Nicely done with great skill, Elle. Thank you; I probably would have ended up peeling my face off in strips," he said as he looked in the mirror.

"You are welcome. Handsome." Elzibeth reached out and traced the scar that runs down his left eye. The scar traveled from above the eyebrow to below the eye diagonally. "I know about most of your scars, but you have never said anything about this one."

Alistar laughed. "That's probably my only non-hunt related Injury." He threw a towel across one shoulder as Elzibeth reclined in the chair watching him as he cleaned up.

"I told you I'd never ridden horses before the other night but I learned to ride motorcycles at age sixteen, yeah?" He carefully took the razor and started cutting off the longer lengths of hair off his head.

"Yes. So?" Elzibeth remarked, motioning him to continue.

"Well as all young teens like to do, I got in trouble a lot. I was living with my sister when my uncle pissed me off, so I stole his motorcycle and went for a joyride. I ended up crashing it at one hundred miles per hour." He did the quick math in his head. "That's one sixty kilometers per hour for those on this side of the pond. The windshield snapped off and caught me good. So did the authorities. My uncle was so pissed that since my eighteenth birthday was two days away, he kicked me out and handed me over to the church."

"You were a rebel." Elzibeth laughed.

"Nah. I was just some dumb podunk kid pissed off at life. Angry that he lost his parents, and wanted to fight the world." Alistar finished his self-haircut and began cleaning up.

He leaned against the wash basin and crossed his arms over his chest. "And that was the whole incident that led me down the road to today."

Elzibeth stood and again traced the scar. "Then I am glad you did," she said, giving the scar a gentle kiss. Alistar closed his eyes and chuckled and Elzibeth let her hand fall back to her side.

"I must start training Evelyn on castle procedures. And I believe you have an oil stain to get out of my entrance hall rug, mister."

Alistar nodded at her words. "Yes, ma'am. I'll have to go to Brasov to get some cleaning supplies. I doubt you have industrial cleaners here."

"No. I don't think we do, but check with Richter before you go." Elzibeth's threw her response over her shoulder as she walked out, leaving him to get dressed.

26

A week later found Alistar working down in the armory when Elzibeth walked in. "Alistar, why did I wake up to find random men in my castle today unloading large crates?" she asked as she looked around at said wooden crates.

Alistar's head popped up from the workbench. "I didn't know they were arriving today, otherwise, I would have told you."

"Alistar, I found that checklist," Richter said, striding in.

He handed Alistar a list which Elzibeth snatched and started to read.

"What is all this?" she asked, looking at Alistar with a raised eyebrow, clearly annoyed.

Alistar smiled sweetly. "Oh, you know, ammo, firearms, equipment a growing boy needs to defend his home."

Elzibeth frowned. "I don't like that you are starting a war out of my castle."

Alistar crossed his arms defensively. "Elle, I'm just being prepared for when the church comes around again. I want our people to be able to defend themselves if necessary. And besides, you told me to get any supplies I needed."

"True, I did. Fine then. Show me." Elzibeth sighed exasperatedly.

Grabbing a crowbar, Alistar opened the first crate. "Reloading equipment." Walking to the next one he popped the lid. "This is ten AK forty-seven rifles. The crate next to them should have their attachments, sights and stuff."

Elzibeth used her diamond-hard nails and vampiric strength to open the indicated crate and saw that he was correct.

"What is this one?" she asked, pointing to a long black plastic crate.

"Oh, umm, that? Just a toy for my personal collection."

"Again, what is it?"

Yeah, you might be in a bit of trouble, Alistar old boy.

"Maybe. Maybe not. I have yet to make up my mind on the situation." Elzibeth's voice echoed through his mind.

Alistar opened the case to reveal a javelin-guided rocket launcher

"Why would you need that?" Elzibeth looked confused.

"Because if the church sends an actual Godhammer out here, close is not where I want any of us to be."

"Will this kill a Godhammer?" Elzibeth asked with concern.

"Well, considering this thing can take out a tank, I sure hope so. Otherwise we might be fucked."

Elzibeth picked up the launcher. "How do I use it?"

Alistar stepped up behind her. "Well, first, you slide the tube onto the launcher and shoulder it. Then you track your target on the screen here and when you get a long beep, you push the firing stud, and the rocket does the rest. It's rather simple."

Elzibeth leaned back against him. "So I just push this button here?" she asked, grinning mischievously.

"Yes, but don't do it here. I'm not quite ready to die just yet." Alistar pushed her hand away from the firing stud and took the launcher from her, putting it back in its case.

Elzibeth taped her teeth with one long fingernail as she thought. "What's in that case by the workbench?"

"Remember that flash-bang I tossed at the guards chasing us?" Alistar asked with a grin.

"Yes. I remember it being rather effective." Elzibeth stepped over to the crate and picked up one of the small black cylinders.

"Yeah. More of those, but I have to add in the irritant powder to them. I was working on that when you walked in. It's a slow process." Alistar pointed to the grenade sitting disassembled on the workbench.

"What's this for?" She pointed at the wide rolling whiteboard in the corner.

"Ideas and thinking of course," Alistar said, doing a quick rough sketch of Elle in the upper right corner with dry-erase markers.

Elzibeth nodded right as Richter reappeared carrying an old-fashioned letter sealed with wax. "Mistress, we have a situation."

Elzibeth peered at the seal, her eyes going wide, and she slid one nail under the wax, cutting it cleanly free from the paper.

"The council is coming here. They wish to discuss the rise in Hunter activity. Apparently we are not the only ones to see an increase in sightings and attacks. We must get the castle ready for their arrival," she said, laying the letter on Alistar's workbench and rushing out the door followed quickly by Richter.

Alistar picked it up and read it. *"Hmm… two days to prepare. Not much time."*

$\sim$

"We very well could have a problem, Mistress. Evelyn and Marcus will be easy to explain away, and I can spirit Elena to my cabin where no one will find her. But what about him?" Richter asked as he and Elzibeth strode down the hallway.

"If anyone touches him, they will regret it." The chill in Elzibeth's voice could freeze water as her eyes flashed in anger.

"Yes, I'm sure. They touch him, and he stakes them to the wall. Then they all know he's a Hunter and all hell breaks loose inside this castle," Richter bit out a sardonic reply.

"I said I will take care of him, Richter! Go get Evelyn and Marcus and take them to the planning room!" Elzibeth snapped back, her eyes flashing.

"As you wish, My Mistress." Richter bowed and headed upstairs, leaving Elzibeth alone in the hallway.

$\sim$

Alistar stood inside the armory by the door and listened to Richter and Elzibeth argue on the other side. He could easily hear the argument since it echoed down the stone hallway. Upon hearing the conversation end, he stepped out into the hallway.

"How will you take care of me, Elle? What do I need to know?" he asked, his words carrying back down the hallway to Elzibeth's ears.

"The council I'm speaking of is the Council of Elders, the four most powerful vampires in the world. And in two days, they and their entourages will be arriving at our doorstep looking for an audience with me."

She glided back down the hallway towards him and took his hands in hers, looking into his eyes. Alistar could only see fear staring back at him.

"And you're worried they'll find out about me?"

"Yes. If they find out what you are, well, what you were, they will want you dead." Elzibeth laid her head on his chest.

"Wouldn't be the first time this Hunter's become the hunted." He chuckled. Elzibeth pulled away, her eyes flashing in anger.

"This is serious, Alistar!"

Alistar nodded. "I know. I'll behave... mostly."

"Good. See that you do. Please. I don't want anything to happen to you."

"As you wish. But I'm not kissing anyone's ass," Alistar said with a wry boyish smile.

Alistar walked back into the Armory without a second glance and closed the door, leaving Elzibeth worried and confused. *Alistar, what are you planning?*

27

Two days later, after sunset, the castle saw its first visitors. Elzibeth waited on the castle steps in her finest regalia alongside Richter, Evelyn, and Marcus, dressed in their new outfits provided by Francois.

Alistar was nowhere to be seen having left a day ago on the old Ural motorcycle, before the sun set.

Maybe that is for the best, Elzibeth thought.

As vehicles pulled in, people got out with great decorum, greeting each other as they walked up to the castle steps. Standing in front were four assorted vampires and behind them stood four escorts of five servants, standing in order of age and power. Elzibeth was the youngest of every vampire there but due to who her father was, she was the highest on the council, as Dracula's rank had transferred to her when he had disappeared.

Stepping forward, an old Asian male with gray hair, dressed in a fine black suit with red tie, and a cane bowed low to Elzibeth while his entourage knelt on one knee behind him. "Great Lady Tepes, I, Miyamoto Kenji of the Asian lands, greet you."

Elzibeth bowed back but not quite as low. "Greetings

to the chosen of the Kami. You are welcome into my domicile as long as you pledge to follow the Accords of Hospitality. None under my care may be seduced or drank from. The same applies to the townspeople to the north as they are under my protection."

The man nodded at her words and simply replied, "Hai"

Elzibeth waved to indicate that he and his entourage could go inside before she turned her attention to the next vampire.

This one was an Indian Raj, dressed in the finest silks of blue and gold. "Great Lady Tepes, I am Ishani Devi, having recently taken over from my father who saw final death in 2031. I bid you greetings from Sri Lanka." She bowed low and her entourage knelt like before.

"Greetings to you, Lady Devi. Do you pledge to uphold the Accords of Hospitality, observing my rules and harming none under my protection?"

"I do," the Indian vampire ruler pledged. Again Elzibeth motions that the Indian raj and her entourage could step inside.

Next in line is the African Warlord Abdalla Mohammed, dressed simply in jeans and a block shirt with tribal motif down one shoulder and sleeve, and like the others, he bowed and agreed to Elzibeth's terms of entry.

So far this is going well, Elzibeth thought, still wondering and worrying where Alistar is.

The last vampire presented stepped forward, a woman with skin as white as snow and a white dress trimmed in fur to match. "Greetings, Lady Tepes, I am Lydia Siegrist, High Lady of the Swiss Alps, and I bid you greetings. I, like the others, have traveled far and I am famished. Let us dispense with the pleasantries so that we all may dine."

Elzibeth narrowed her eyes. "Decorum WILL be

respected in my domain, Lady Siegrist. Now, do YOU and yours pledge to follow the Accords of Hospitality within my walls and the lands around it and to NOT do any harm to the people I protect?" She glared at the other vampire.

"Yes, yes. I do, as do my servants." The snowy white vampiress waved her hand dismissively.

"Very well, you are welcome in my castle," Elzibeth replied, but she gave Richter a side glance, wordlessly telling him to keep an eye on this one.

After the others entered, Elzibeth walked inside, followed by Richter and then Evelyn and Marcus.

Elzibeth found the others standing around the large wooden table in the planning room waiting for her. She moved to the head of the table and sat. Richter waited by his mistress' side. The rest of the vampires sat only after she had seated herself.

"Evelyn, Marcus, run down and fetch goblets of blood for our guests," she said with a smile.

"Right away, Miss Elzibeth," they reply in unison before heading out the room's side door..

"Elzibeth, surely you don't let your servants call you by first name," the vampire called Lydia said in shock. "It should always be mistress, or Mistress Tepes."

Elzibeth glared around the room. "What I allow my servants to do is none of your concern. You would do well to stay out of my household affairs. My father would not ever allow you to question how he ran his castle, and neither will I!" she snapped, showing a bit of fang.

Lydia bowed her head, properly cowed into submission. "Yes, Great Lady."

~

Alistar sped back along the road from Bucharest. What he found there had him greatly worried. The papers in his pocket that he had taken off a bishop there told of a build up of Hunters and church personnel in the regions of Turkey and Bulgaria. At least two teams of four Hunters were present, along with twice that many support personnel. Something big was happening. He had to warn Elzibeth. The bike screeched around a corner, sailed past a line of four parked vehicles, and stopped next to the stairs. Alistar put the kickstand down.

As he took off his helmet, a man approached him. "Who are you? Identify yourself."

Alistar looked him up and down. "I live here. Who the fuck are you?" The man replied by pulling out a knife. Alistar sighed. *Remember, Accords of Hospitality, no killing.*

~

Evelyn and Marcus arrived with trays full of goblets, each filled to the brim with blood, and carefully passed them out to each vampire, always setting the goblet on the right side before backing away.

"Thank you. You two may leave and take the night off," Elzibeth said, smiling. Her smile dropped as she heard the motorcycle outside and Alistar's mental words to himself. Her eyes glazed over as she saw through his, through their mental bond.

~

As the man moved closer, Alistar whipped his leg over the bike, turning it into a spin, his heel catching the man's chin and knocking him out. "I'm the guardian of Elzibeth Tepes… Anyone else want to fuck with me right now?"

None of the other guards made a move and he took the steps two at a time.

~

Elzibeth's eyes unglazed and she stared at the door knowing Alistar would be joining them shortly. This was no longer off to a good start. Earlier, shen had sensed that Alistar was worried, and if he was worried then she had reason to worry.

~

Alistar caught Evelyn and Marcus in the hallway. "Where's Elle?"

"Mister Alistar, welcome home. She's in the planning room. It's straight down this hall and through the first set of double doors to the left," Evelyn said with a smile, pointing down the hallway. Alistar nodded.

"Thanks."

"Mister Alistar, she has guests!" Evelyn called after him.

"Yep, I know," Alistar threw over his shoulder. Reaching the double doors, he pushed them open with one great shove.

28

The doors to the room opened, and as expected, Alistar sauntered in. The guest vampires seated at the table turned to him, surprised by this interruption.

"Elle, we need to talk. Now." He walked right past the others and up to her.

Elzibeth frowned. "Alistar, I am in a meeting, dear."

"Yeah, well I figure this might have something to do with your little meeting," he replied by pulling the papers from his vest and slapping them onto the table in front of her. He stared her in the eyes.

"You REALLY need to look at these." He tilted his head at the paperwork. Her gaze flickers to the papers and back to him before going back to the papers.

Lydia stepped up behind him and grabbed his left wrist. "This one is insolent. He offers no greeting to the rest of us, and he talks to you like he does and, therefore cannot be allowed to live. Besides, I cannot abide cows' blood, and he looks like an ideal meal." She hissed as her fangs extended.

Elzibeth's eyes turned red and her incisors lengthened

fully. "You touch him and I will stake you out on the roof to see your last sunrise!" She glared daggers at the Swiss vampire.

"Great Lady Tepes. He..." Lydia continued.

"I said he will be left alone! This one and I have an understanding that allows him to speak out of turn if necessary! Now take your hand off of him or I will permit him to take it off himself!" Elzibeth hissed.

"He is but a human. Surely he can't..." Lydia started to say but Elzibeth glanced at Alistar and he spun around in the vampire's grasp, pulling his left hand free, leaving her holding his black glove with a stake firmly planted against her chest.

"You think you can take me? You may test that assumption at your convenience, lady!" Alistar growled low.

Lydia's glance fell on the tattoo on his left wrist and she shrunk back in sudden fear, not of Elzibeth, but of him.

"Hunter!" she screeched in alarm.

Alistar froze and gave Elzibeth a look of apology. *"Sorry love. She yanked my glove off,"* he mentally sent her. He could feel her annoyance at the situation, but also concern and understanding that the glove had been an accident.

Alistar moved closer to Elzibeth and waited for the other vampire to calm down. Thankfully the rest were still seated, just watching him.

"You brought a Hunter in our midst?" Lydia hissed, still not moving back toward her chair.

"No, YOU set this meeting at MY castle where he lives. Now SIT down. If he wanted you all dead, he would have killed you the minute he entered the damn room!" Elzibeth commanded.

Lydia slowly moved back to her seat like a wary animal.

"Great Lady Tepes, I am curious to know how a Hunter came to reside within this castle." Miyamoto's calm, quiet words broke the tension in the room.

"He saved my life on multiple occasions. The first two he had no idea what I was, and even after finding out, he continued to do so twice more." Elzibeth smiled at Alistar and then made eye contact with each vampire in turn.

She glanced down at the papers Alistar had brought. "And it would seem he has possibly saved all of us and brought us much intelligence on the issue of our very discussion. Alistar, how did you come across these papers?" she asked without looking at him.

"I took a trip down to Bucharest since that was the largest city likely to have an established permanent church presence. Once there I found a local bishop and convinced him to give me these papers."

"Is he dead?" Elzibeth's gaze flickered over to him.

"Not at all, but he's gonna have one hell of a hangover in the morning and isn't likely to remember our meeting." Alistar grinned.

Elzibeth passed the papers around the table for the others to see. "It would seem that the situation is worse than we thought."

"We should leave immediately and go into hiding!" Lydia said with great fear. This spurred an argument between the other vampires at the table.

"No, we must fight!" Miyamoto shouted.

"I agree with Lydia. We must hide until this all blows over!" the African vampire, Abdalla exclaimed.

"No, fighting is the only answer!" Ishani shouted back at the others.

Elzibeth continued to sit there, trying to figure out the situation. Seeing her uncertainty, Alistar stepped up.

"Oh sure. Run and hide. That's the usual modus operandi of supernaturals when confronted by the church," Alistar quipped. He already had enough of this bitch.

"Alistar, WHAT are you doing?!"

"Elle, if they don't realize that running is no longer an option, then they get steamrolled when the Church comes through," Alistar replied... Aloud.

"Are you calling us cowards?!" Abdalla asked with incredulity.

"No, not all of you, just you..." Alistars swiveled from him to look at the Swiss vampire, "and her."

"Alistar!" Elizabeth's voice rang out.

"No Elle. They need to realize that running is no longer an option. The church is coming. And now is the time to put up or shut up," Alistar said, looking over at her, a fierceness in his eyes that she had only seen one time before.

He started walking toward the door, then spun around to walk backward. "But what do I know? I only hunted for them for eighteen years, and know all their methods. But, hey, I tell you all what I'm gonna do; I'm gonna go get ready, and when they come knocking, I'm gonna kick some ass to defend my home until they take me out."

He tossed his credentials on the table. "And before you think I'm talking shit, you might want to pass those around. If I'm needed, I'll be in the basement. This meeting's a waste of time." Before anyone could question him, he disappeared through the doors, slamming them behind him.

~

Elzibeth watched him go. She could feel the anger emanating from him. *"Silence!"* Her mental command echoed to everyone in the room, and several sets of eyes swiveled in her direction. "We are taking a break. I need to go check on him."

"You care more for that Hunter than the rest of us!" Lydia said scornfully. Instantly Elzibeth was face to face with her.

"As I said, that HUNTER saved my life... FOUR TIMES within the last two months. What have you or your ilk done for me lately, Lydia? I trust him far more than I trust you," she hissed, causing the other vampire to shrink back. Similarly to Alistar, Elzibeth swept out the doors.

She did not get very far when the doors opened behind her to reveal Ishani and Miyamoto. "We would go with you to talk to your Hunter if you would allow us, Great Lady," Miyamoto said, bowing his head slightly.

"Very well, but your guards stay here." Ishani attempted to speak but Elzibeth raised a hand. "Alistar knows the laws and he chooses to follow them. That's why that bitch, Lydia, isn't dead on my floor."

Miyamoto held out Alistars credentials to her and she took them.

"I knew I had seen his face before. He is the one we call the Ghost of Death." Miyamoto said as they walked.

29

E lzibeth blinked. "Why is that?"

"Eight years ago we had a coven of five young vampires in Japan who refused to listen to rules. They killed who they wanted and attracted the attention of the authorities. We were going to solve the problem ourselves, but a night later, they were dead. We went in and checked the security footage. It showed one man. One man against a coven of five, and on the video he reappears ten minutes, later covered in blood. Without a scratch on him. We tracked him through the city to the airport, where he got on a plane and left. It was then we kept track of him up until five years ago." Miyamoto's cane tapped on the floor with each step.

As they descended the stairs to the lower level, Elzibeth could hear Alistar firing off some sort of weapon at a fast rate and below that loud music. *He does not sound happy.*

When they reached the door, Elzibeth paused, listening to the music. The lyrics speak about being on the wrong side of heaven and the righteous side of hell. It wasn't a song she had heard before. "Let me go first. If you were to enter right now, he might shoot you." Opening the door she peeked around the edge. The music got louder when she did so and flowed out into the hallway.

Alistar huddled over his makeshift gun range with one of the rifles to his shoulder. Each time he pulled the trigger, it barked three times. He continued this way until the weapon clicked empty, then switched to his pistol, and continued firing as he walked down the range toward the target, at one point ejecting a magazine and slamming home another one. Elzibeth waited respectfully by the work bench until he was done. When the bullets ran dry, he holstered his pistol and turned to see Elle.

Taking out his noise-canceling ear plugs, he turned off the music. "Umm, yeah... I probably fucked up back there." He looked sheepishly at Elzibeth and winced.

"Not at all. I actually think you got them deliberating more about a single situation than they have in any meeting I can remember." Elzibeth smiled reassuringly.

"So I'm not in trouble?" Alistar asked, a little surprised.

"No. Just next time warn me so I know what's going to happen." Elzibeth placed a hand on his arm casually as she walked past him.

"Just checking on me, then?" Alistar leaned against the workbench and crossed his arms over his chest.

"Yes and no. Two people from the meeting upstairs wish to hear you out. They are in the hallway." Elzibeth headed to the door and opened it, revealing the two elder vampires.

Miyamoto and Ishani entered the room. Alistar grabbed a crate near them. "Sorry, I don't have any fancy chairs down here, but if you need a drink, the cask room is right across the hall." He pulled out the workbench's stool for Elzibeth.

Near Elzibeth, he leaned against the wall casually,

crossing his arms again as he did so. "So what can I do for you folks?"

"Does he always talk like this?" Ishani asked.

"Yes. He's from what used to be the United States and not well versed in our ways. That's one of the reasons I like him. He tends not to dance around issues he considers important." Elzibeth said from where she perched on her stool.

On a small shelf, Alistar poured himself a cup of beer from a keg. When Elzibeth raised an eyebrow, he smiled. "I might have picked it up in Bucharest when I picked up the papers." He walked over to stand by Elzibeth.

"While the others argue, we see the wisdom of your words young Hunter. So I ask you, what would you have us do?" Miyamoto asked.

Alistar raised an eyebrow. "Well, first off, I don't hunt for the church anymore. I quit five years ago. So, please, stop with the Hunter moniker. It's just Alistar now."

Ishani shook her head. "No… one such as you needs a title. Lady Tepes says you have saved her life four times. So that means you are a protector. In my language, that is *raksha karane vaala.*"

Alistar shrugged. "Hey, if that's what floats your boat, go with it." Elzibeth smacked his arm with the back of her hand.

"Be nice." Alistar nodded at her reprimand.

Alistar cracked his neck and moved to the white board. He started diagramming his idea. "The church exists through fear and the idea that they give the people safety. We need to flip that. Show the people the real face of the church. Show the people the monster the church really is."

Elzibeth rested her chin on one hand, watching him.

"You," his finger swiveled between the three vampires in the room, "need to show the people that you aren't evil creatures. Sure you need blood to live, but other than that, you are God's creatures like anyone else. Win the people over. To do that you build infrastructure. Hospitals, libraries, schools. Give people jobs in companies that you own and pay them well. Make sure they have good health care and education. Take care of the people so they see you as benevolent. This also means policing your own better. Making sure random people aren't getting fed on. Making sure any volunteers are well taken care of, and swiftly punishing any of your own who break those rules. That's gonna take more than a few years, though. You have a lot of indoctrination to overcome. That's the long game." He recapped the marker.

"That seems doable over time. We have vast amounts of money to uplift the people. What is the short game?" Miyamoto asked, stroking his chin.

Near a crate Alistar tossed the old Japanese vampire a rifle. "We fight back, plain and simple. And we do it with everything we can get our hands on. Do you know why the church still uses crossbows, swords, and other archaic weapons against you?" He pulled out his pistol and held it up for them to see.

"I could shoot Elle right now, in the chest and she'd rip me a new asshole before I could pull the trigger a second time. Bullets don't work on you guys unless they're silver, and silver is a soft metal, so you can't use it in an automatic weapon. It jams too easily. That's why when you see a Hunter with a firearm, it's usually a revolver or at most an old semi-auto pistol like this one."

Putting the pistol back in its holster, he continued. "Believe me, if we could have loaded AR-15's and AK-47's with pure silver ammo, we would have wiped you off the map long ago. I should know. I was there when they tried. Dumb-shit got off three rounds and killed two vampires in less than four seconds. Then the damn thing jammed and he was eviscerated."

He paced back and forth, hands grasped behind his back. "Not so for humans, though. You shoot them in the leg or the arms, and they're in trouble. Shoot them in the head and, well, it's all over. Granted, that's the same for any of you as well. Shoot them in the chest and they may or may not end up dead. What I'm saying is that all of you need to join the modern age. Sure it may sound stupid, but it's better than waiting for the church to find you. And believe me, they WILL find you sooner or later. Better to take the fight to them."

He leaned back against the workbench and waited.

Miyamoto pondered Alistars words before speaking. "Very interesting. Modern technology. Going on the attack. That hasn't happened since...."

"My father..." Elzibeth said softly.

"Yes, your father took the fight to the church in his day and beat them back. Maybe it's time to do it again," Miyamoto said with a grim look on his face.

30

Miyamoto stood. "Very well, in my domain, I will implement your long plan. And, I will have my people prepare for the battle to come."

Ishani rose as well. "I, too, shall implement your plan and prepare for war. It will take a while but if it means the reign of the church ends and our people are safe from persecution, then so be it."

Both vampires bowed to Elzibeth. "By your leave, Great Lady. We shall try and talk sense into the others."

Elzibeth nodded and the other two turned and bowed to Alistar. "By your leave, Lord Alistar."

Alistar pressed his lips together in a line and held up a finger, not looking at the two vampires. "I'm no lord. And sure, the door's right there. I don't stand on ceremony."

Ishani smiled. "Not yet, but one day. And if it happens, you might just be the force our world needs to... What are the words... Shake things up?"

The two vampires exited the room, leaving Alistar alone with Elzibeth.

Alistar leaned on the workbench and closed his eyes,

sighing. He could feel the adrenaline beginning to wear off and he started shaking. Elzibeth went towards him but he held up a hand. "I'm okay, Elle. Just need to calm down." When the shaking stopped, he picked up and downed the small cup of beer. "You best get back upstairs before the others tear that room apart with their arguing."

Elzibeth smiled at his words. "And what are you going to do, my *raksha karane vaala?*" She giggled at the words but when Alistar looked at her, his eyes were flat and cold.

"You know you don't want the answer to that question, Elle." He sighed again and turned around. "Theres only one thing in this fucked-up world I am good at." Taking a step forward, he began pacing again. "I'm going to need to lead them away. And..."

"No. You are more than just the lives you take, Alistar." Elzibeth wrapped him in her arms, stopping him in his tracks both physically and mentally. "You are also the lives you save, the lives you don't take. The friendships you make, and the people you stand beside." She paused as a smile crossed her face. "What if there was a way to do this without facing eight hunters?"

Alistar looked her in the eyes. He knew their color, but never really took the time before now to gaze into them. They were liquid storm-clouds of crystalline gray with flecks of blue around the edges. "What?"

"That Seeker you let go. Maybe it's time to call in a favor. She owes you her life. Maybe she can make it seem you are somewhere where you are not and lead them on a wild-goose chase." Elzibeth said.

Alistar chuckled. At the reloading bench, he pulled down a box of ammo and started reloading the two empty magazines for his pistol. "Just so long as it's not Canadian geese. Those feathery fucks are assholes. Yeah, sure, let's try it. After all, there's always option two if that doesn't work."

"Good. I shall get the others settled and tomorrow they will be leaving."

~

Packing a small bag for an overnight trip, Alistar headed outside and soon flew down the road on the back of the old Ural, headed to Brasov. *I just hope that Seeker is still there.* When he had walked upstairs, the elders were still arguing, but he'd heard Elzibeth, Miyamoto, and Ishani taking a solid stand.

Riding into Brasov, he checked the area before heading to the Old Rams Inn. Inside his eyes meet those of the bartender. Being the middle of the morning on a Sunday, the place was dead.

"Not you again," the man said. Alistar tossed a small bag onto the counter. It opened on impact, spilling church gold across the countertop. The bartender's eyes widened.

"I need information. I'm willing to pay."

"I think we can do business. What do you want to know?" The bartender scraped the gold into his hands.

"The Seeker girl. Where is she?" Alistar asked gruffly. The man glanced over to the shadows under the stairs. In a subtle movement, Alistar's quarry broke for the door.

Alistar threw his knife low. It hit the edge of the girl's cloak, pinning it to the floor and causing her to jerk back, falling.

"Owie!" the girl exclaimed. Alistar strode over and she started backing up, pulling on her cloak trying to free it.

"I didn't call anyone! I've been good. I swear!" Leaning down, Alistar tugged his knife free and snatched the girl by the back of her cloak, dragging her across the floor to a table with chairs in the corner.

"Sit," he commanded. The girl scrabbled into the chair next to her and Alistar sat across from her.

"I... I... I..."

Alistar silenced her with a hand. "Calm down. If I wanted you dead, you know you'd be dead. Do you want something to drink?"

The girl's eyes went wide, whether in shock or fear. "What?" Alistar motioned to the bartender. "Get her something to drink. Hot tea with lemon." The bartender nodded and before they could continue their conversation, the girl had a steaming cup of tea between her hands. She sipped it nervously.

"What's your name, girl?" Alistar asked softly.

"It's Adriana." she said shakily above a whisper as her lip trembled, not meeting his eyes.

Alistar sighed and patted Adriana's hand. "I just need a favor, Adriana. You did your job well. You are in no danger from me."

"A favor... from me?" Adriana squeaked out. Her gaze met his, the fear still evident, but now also with a small light of hope.

"Keep your voice down, girl. The walls have ears." Alistar chided her gently as she nervously drank her tea. Scanning the tavern, Alistar rose. "Get up; We're going for a walk. And you'll be safe." Adriana got to her feet and they both headed out the door. "There's a group of Hunters, two teams of four setting up south across the border in Turkey. What do you know about it?"

"It's a new base of operations for the church. The increase of supernatural presence in the general area warranted it," Adriana says as she tried to keep up with his pace. Alistar noticed and slowed.

"No mention of me and my vampire?" he asked, looking around. The weather was crisp and cold. Clouds dotted the sky and occasionally one passed in front of the sun bathing the town in shadow. Off in the distance, a family of birds chirped from a nest atop a light post.

"No. There have been werewolf sightings in Turkey and Syria." Adriana pulled her cloak tight against a sudden cold burst of wind. "I haven't told anyone about you two. I told the church that the Hunter team they sent moved on to the east after dealing with a minor vampiric threat here in Brasov."

Alistar stroked his chin. "Very good of you." This girl is smart. She knew how it all worked. After Hunter teams are done in an area, they move to investigate likely areas of supernatural infestation on their own unless they received specific orders from higher up.

"The information I have says that there's a larger than normal pack of werewolves down south. At least ten strong, led by a powerful alpha. They have been killing the livestock of the farmers down there." She fell silent.

"*Hmm...* hence the need for eight hunters," Alistar mused. "Thanks." He started to walk away but Adriana grabbed his sleeve.

"Wait!"

Alistar paused at her words. "Yes?"

"I want out of this life. I'm done. They treat me like shit. I am given just enough by the church to survive and any hunters who come around beat me for being what I am. Even though I'm a seeker, all they see is a witch with a collar, no better than an animal. One time one of them did worse." She hung her head in shame.

"*Hmm...*" Alistar stopped, thinking of his own sister. Pulling out a pen and piece of paper, he scribbled down some coordinates and shoved it into Adriana's hand. "Meet me there in two days. Come alone, or you know what'll happen." Taking the pack off his back, he dropped it at the girl's feet. "Those supplies should get you there. Plus, that pack has my scent on it so the wolves won't kill you."

"Wolves?" The girl looked scared.

"Yes. They're Elle's pets. They watch over her lands and report back to her... and me. Good luck, Seeker Adriana. If you make it there, you might have a better chance."

31

Two days later, the elders went back to their respective countries, all but the Swiss vampire, Lydia, who eventually agreed to try Alistar's plan. Since then the mood in the castle had improved.

Alistar now got ready for his meeting with the young Seeker. He added a long-range scope to one of the AK's. If she did bring other Hunters with her, he would just shoot them all and leave the bodies in the woods for the wolves. He had no need to get up close and messy. Slowly, one bullet at a time, he started hand-loading two magazines.

Elzibeth walked in. "There's something on your mind, Alistar. I can feel it."

"Yep." Alistar never took his focus from his work.

"Care to share? I have a coin if I must pay." Elzibeth smiled slightly.

Glancing over, Alistar smirked at the coin she had in her hand. "You'd get change back princess. Trust me, my thoughts ain't worth that much."

Sweeping up to him, Elzibeth lowered herself to look him in the eyes, placing her fingertips atop the workbench, trapping him between her outstretched arms. "I think they are worth that and more. This is about that Seeker."

Alistar sighed. "Yeah." He pushed his hair out of his face. "I went and talked to her. The church is setting up a base down in Turkey to deal with a werewolf pack of ten plus an alpha. She told the church about the Hunters that I killed, saying they dealt with a minor vampire threat here and moved east toward Russia. So we have at least a little break before they wander up here again." Finishing with one magazine, he began loading the other one.

"There's more?"

"Yep. She wants out. Wants a better life beyond the abuse of being a Seeker. So I gave her coordinates down to just outside Calia. If she comes alone, I'll be bringing her back here to talk to you."

Elzibeth frowned. "And you couldn't tell me this earlier?"

"We were kinda dealing with four arguing elders upstairs! The castle was in chaos! I figured it probably wasn't the best time, Elle!" He snapped at her. After a moment he sighed heavily. "Sorry. Just stressed. No need to take it out on you."

Elzibeth nodded and brushed her hand across his cheek. "Why do you think I came down here? I could feel your stress all the way up in my room. So what happens if she does not come alone?"

Alistar looked at her but didn't speak. Instead he loaded the full magazine into the base of the AK and racked the charging handle before flicking on the safety and setting the weapon down on the bench.

"I figured as much. You would add more death to your hands to ensure this place is safe," Elzibeth said with concern, touching his hand softly.

"*Mmm.*"

"Why?" Elzibeth's question took Alistar off guard. She

moved next to him, leaning against the workbench and crossing her arms.

"Look around you, Elle. This castle, the kids, you... Hell, even Richter. It's the family I've never had. Someone's gotta protect it." He sighed again, got up, and aimed for the door. Stopping, he glanced back at her. "Oh, and I need to borrow Evelyn so the Seeker can be searched. She's only sixteen, and I'm not going to give her any more bad memories because of me. Not after what she's been through." He sent her a mental picture of what he meant and Elzibeth's eyes changed red with anger.

"Take her. Just bring her home safely. Hopefully you bring them both back. Oh and do send her to me when she gets back." Her words followed him down the hallway.

As he reached the top of the stairs, he ran into Evelyn. "Hey, Evie, put on something black and find me outside. You're going on a mission with me. Elle's given her permission."

"I get to go on a mission?" Evelyn bounced with excitement.

Alistar chuckled. "Yes, you do. Now go get ready."

Eveyln rushed off and Alistar headed outside, hooked up the sidecar to the Ural, and grabbed some bandages, cotton, rubbing alcohol swabs, and a scanning wand. The wand is like the kind used at airports and security checkpoints. Evelyn appeared a moment later in funeral garb. "It's all I had." Alistar eyed her. "Eh. It'll work. Hop in."

He mounted the bike and handed her a small wireless headset as she climbed into the sidecar, and they roared off down the road headed north. A while later, Alistar sat posted up in a tree while Evelyn sat on a tree stump by the road, petting one of Elzibeth's wolves, as a lone figure stumbled ahead, flanked by two more wolves. Alistar could tell the Seeker was getting tired. Thankfully, there were no others with her. The wolves had reported that much back to him.

"Greetings, Seeker." Evelyn said and the girl stopped.

"Do… do I know you?" Her voice showed fear and exhaustion. She took a small step backward.

"No, but I know of you. Mister Alistar told me about you. You're to do as I tell you or Mister Alistar will shoot you. If you try to harm me, he will shoot you. If you run…"

"I understand," Adriana said. Evelyn considered the tree a ways off where Alistar perched.

"Tell her to strip down to her undergarments. Check her clothes for anything out of the ordinary." His voice emitted through the small headset. "Run that wand I gave you over her limbs as well. If it beeps then she has a tracker wherever the beep sounds."

He saw Evelyn nod through the scope. Zooming in on Adriana's face, he waited while the Seeker stripped down. She was cold because of the fog from her breath, and her teeth chattered. He tunes out the fact she was a sixteen-year-old girl. Right now a possible enemy stood before Evelyn. Evelyn ran the wand over the clothing and it stayed silent. Then she ran it over Adriana, and when it reached her wrist, it beeped.

"She has something under her skin," Evelyn said.

"Tracking chip. I expected that. Let her get dressed. I'm coming down."

He slung the AK over his shoulder, jumped from the branch, landing in a crouch, and walked towards the two girls. Adriana was done getting dressed by the time he reached them.

"I'm sorry! I forgot about the tracking chip in my wrist!" she begged, fear evident in her eyes. He held up a hand.

"I knew that one was going to be there." He pulled out

his combat knife, ripping open two of the swabs, and wiped down the blade really well. "Give me your wrist."

Adriana hesitated so he reached out and grasped onto it with his left hand. She trembled as he did so. "Relax. All I'm going to do is take out the tracker. It'll hurt, though. Not gonna lie about that part. I'll try to be quick."

His knife pierced the skin of her wrist and true to his word she only had time to cry out once before the little device fell to the ground. He quickly covered her wrist with cotton and bandages.

Picking up the device he wrapped it up in a small strip of bandage and whistled. A large wolf stepped out of the woods. "Take this far away outside your master's domain and bury it." The wolf grabbed the cloth package in its mouth and ran off to the north.

Alistar turned back to the two girls. "Evie, you'll ride behind me. Adriana, you'll ride in the side-car." He handed her a helmet with a blacked-out face shield. "You will not take that off until you're told to do so. IS that understood?"

The Seeker nodded. "Yes sir."

Alistar pauses. "And please stop with the sir shit. I hate that. It's just Alistar."

32

Less than an hour later, Alistar pulled up to the castle steps with the girls. *"Elle, we're back. I have a couple things I need to do,"* he mentally projected.

"Good. I am in the planning room. Send the girls in here."

"Evelyn, Elzibeth wishes to see that you're okay. Take Seeker Adriana with you. Elle's in the planning room. I have to deal with some stuff so I'll catch you later."

"Yes, Mister Alistar." Evelyn bowed.

Alistar rapped lightly twice on the helmet Adriana wore with his knuckles. "You can take that off."

Adriana removed it and her head tipped backward while she gaped at the large structure before her. "What happens now?" she asked as Evelyn helped her out of the sidecar.

"Now you go see Elzibeth. We shall talk later," Alistar replied as he took the steps two at a time, disappearing into the castle.

Evelyn motioned to Adriana. "Follow me, please."

Adriana does so timidly as they headed into the castle to the planning room.

Elzibeth, at the head of the table, scanned over a large map. She looked up as the girls entered. "Sit. Both of you." Evelyn took a chair near Elzibeth and Adriana sat at the one farthest from her, clearly scared.

"Do I frighten you that much, child?" Elzibeth asked softly with a raised eyebrow, yet amused.

"Umm... Yes, ma'am. I'm sorry. It's just everything I've been taught," Adriana replied meekly, eyes on the table.

"It's quite alright. I promise that no one within these walls will harm you this night, or any night, while you are under this roof. And if you know your lore, you know a vampire's word is their bond." Elzibeth folded her hands in front of her, waiting patiently.

Adriana nodded and, after a moment, shuffled to the chair to Elzibeth's right and sat again.

"There, that's better." Elzibeth smiled. Moving as to not scare the child, she turned the seeker's face so it caught the light, seeing a day's old bruise on her cheek. She frowned. "Who did that?" she asked quietly, but her voice held an edge.

"One of the older kids in town hit me. People around here don't like Seekers much." Adriana hung her head.

"*Hmm...* I may have to send Alistar to deal with that person later then." *Or go deal with it myself.* "What is your name, child?"

"It's Adriana, My Lady."

"Well, Adriana, Alistar says you wish to escape the life of a Seeker."

"Yes, My Lady."

Taking Adriana's wrist, Elzibeth examined the bandages, then gave a questioning look to Evelyn. "She had a tracking chip in her arm under her Seeker tattoo.

Alistar removed it, and I believe one of the wolves is taking it far away from here."

"I see." Elzibeth slowly unwrapped the bandages to inspect the wound. Reaching over she pulled a pin from the map and pricked her finger causing a drop of blood to well up. Carefully she smeared it on the wound.

Adriana's eyes went wide as the wound closed until unblemished skin showed.

"Alistar means well, but he can be a bit blunt and forward when he has to be, dear." Elzibeth patted Adriana's hand.

"You don't seem as scary as the church told us." Adriana blurted out. Elzibeth laughed.

"Dear child, some of my kind would eat you as soon as they saw you, but not me. I don't eat children. And I don't feed on adults unless they attack me or those I care about. So you are safe here, Seeker Adriana."

Adriana took back her arm. "So I can stay?"

"Yes, dear, you can stay. I don't know what we will do with you. I already have a handmaiden in Evelyn, and Marcus helps Richter around the castle. But I am sure we will figure something out."

"Well I'm pretty good with books. Do you happen to have a library here?"

"Why, yes we do as a matter of fact. It's vast, and I bet you could get lost in there for days." Elzibeth smiled brightly.

Adriana perked up. She loved books, but had only been allowed access to certain areas of the Church library. "Would I have access to the entire library?" she asked with a note of excitement.

"Yes, child. Just be careful with reading anything aloud. Some of the books in that library hold great power." Elzibeth fixed a steely gaze upon the girl.

"Yes, ma'am. I'll be careful."

"Good. Then I will put you in charge of the library. It needs a good cleaning and reorganization. Can you do that?" Elizabeth asked, standing.

"Yes, ma'am!" Adriana brightened.

Elzibeth laughed at the girl's bounciness. "Well then former Seeker Adriana, you will be my new Lorekeeper. Come with me. I shall take you to the library."

Adriana followed Elzibeth out the door and down the hallway, where she opened two great big doors to reveal a massive room with bookcase upon bookcase, all filled with scrolls and books. Adriana's eyes lit up.

"Whoa! I get to be in charge of all this?" she asked in a high pitched voice.

"Yes, Lorekeeper, you do. This is all your domain." Elzibeth laughed. *"Alistar dear. I believe our new acquisition is going to be right at home here,"* she mentally sent to Alistar.

"Mmm," he replied in thought.

"Adriana, your room is through those doors. You will find facilities for washing up in another room off it. I need to go have a chat with Alistar. We shall talk later."

Adriana nodded and practically bounced off into the stacks.

That girl is a bit too perky for me. Elzibeth thought to herself as she went in search of Alistar.

"Miss Elle!" Evelyn's voice called out from behind her.

"Yes, Evie, dear."

"Umm, I have a question," Evelyn said, catching up to her.

"Yes?" Elzibeth looked at Evelyn expectantly.

"Is, umm... Is Mister Alistar your boyfriend?"

"My boyfriend?" Elzibeth blinked.

"Umm, sorry, I didn't think. In your terms it might be suitor?"

"No, dear. He's not. It would be nice. I like him, and I get the feeling he likes me. But he has not asked."

"No, Miss Elle, in today's society, some men won't do the asking. They're too afraid of rejection, or I think in Mister Alistar's case, I don't think he even knows how to ask. He doesn't seem like someone who's spent much time around women-folk. He's just kind of awkward like that."

Elzibeth let out a sultry laugh. "So what do you suggest I do?"

"Well, maybe you should try and ask him."

Elzibeth reached out and gently grabbed the bottom of Evelyn's chin. "You are too smart for your own good sometimes. Now scoot. I was just on my way to talk to him." She smiled and booped the girl on the nose with one finger.

"Yes, Miss Elle; thank you Miss Elle." She made it halfway down the hallway before she stopped and turned. "Miss Elle?!"

"Yes, dear?" Elzibeth looked back over her shoulder.

"Good luck!"

Elzibeth chuckled to herself as she walked away. Hearing music coming from outside, Elzibeth headed toward the castle exit.

33

Alistar was training to the left of the castle's entrance, where Elizbeth found him.. The music he trained to had a strong beat and a repeating set of words: "Heavy is the Crown."

She watched as he stood on one leg and slowly extended the other into a slow controlled side kick. He was dressed in long black drawstring pants, a loose black shirt, and wore no shoes. As she watched him, Elzibeth came to one conclusion, he ws grace, and in pure control. Then she noticed the one-inch thick boards set around him in makeshift holders. As the music increased he jumped and spun, breaking three boards one after another in a display of acrobatic martial arts.

Upon landing he slammed his right foot down through four inches of boards, landing in a split. Rolling, he twisted to his feet and spun again to hit the last board. Elzibeth moved into the line of the kick.

Alistar stopped his kick an inch from her face, exerting extreme control, and lowered his leg. "I almost took your head off, Elle." Alistar frowned at her.

Elzibeth's mouth twitched into a smile. "But would

you have really done so? I think not. You have more control than you let on."

Alistar chuckled. "You're right. I could have stopped much closer."

"You sparred with Richter the other day. It's my turn." Elzibeth smiled evilly.

Alistar raised his eyebrows in surprise. "You want to fight me?"

"I do." Alistar's gaze flickered up and down her dressed form. She was in leather riding breeches, knee length boots, and a loose, flowing, red V-neck shirt with frills along the cuffs.

"Why? You've seen what I can do." Alistar scratched his head in confusion.

"I have my reasons, Alistar. Maybe I, too, like to let loose on occasion. Are you afraid?" Elzibeth's eyes glinted mischievously in the torch light of the castle courtyard.

"Well, shit. Now you've done it. Insulted my masculinity. I gotta fight ya now, Elle. I hope you like ending up on your back." He laughed and moved to the center of the courtyard.

"Oh, we will see who ends up on their back," Elzibeth taunted him jokingly before standing across from him.

Alistar swept his foot out in a wide stance. Then like lightning, Elzibeth streaked across the courtyard at him, her arm pulled back with her hand flat like a spear. Reaching him she throats her hand forward toward his throat, nails glistening in the moonlight. Alistar just barely blocked it. He stared into her eyes, whispered "Impressive," then threw a punch in reply.

Elzibeth grabbed his wrist, smiled, and threw him over her shoulder, turning to follow his trajectory as he flew through the air. Alistar transformed the throw into a roll, slapping the ground as he did so, and came up on his feet with his back to her.

Sensing Elzibeth behind him, he backflipped over her head, landing on his feet and spinning around. "You're going to have to do better than that, princess."

"Oh really?" Elzibeth lowered her head a fraction while a wicked grin crossed her face, raising her hand. The wind picked up and torches dimmed as the shadows deepened until Alistar could see only her eyes glittering in the darkness.

"You're playing with me, Elle." Alistar's smile did not seem as confident as before. He followed the darker space that just barely signaled where Elzibeth was amongst the shadows as she circled him.

~

Marcus looked out the window into the courtyard. "Evie, come quick! Alistar and Lady Elzibeth are fighting!"

Evelyn rushed up to his side and looked to where he pointed. "Oh, she's playing with him!" She grinned.

"That's playing? Seems a bit rough to me." Marcus whistled as he watched Elle flip Alistar over her shoulder.

"Trust me, my love, she is most definitely playing with him."

Marcus and Evelyn were disappointed when Elzibeth drew in the shadows, cloaking the courtyard in almost complete darkness.

~

"I just might be." Elzibeth's voice issued from right beside his left ear, so close he could still feel her breath. He threw a backfist trying to tag her but she was no longer there. Her sultry laugh echoed in the dark.

Alistar closed his eyes, listening to the wind. The music overrode the rest of the noise, but he could just make out light footsteps coming from his right. He swept out, his leg going low, and was rewarded with a solid hit to Elzibeth's legs.

"Oof!" He heard her exclaim as she hit the ground. Turning, he searched the shadows for her.

She appeared suddenly in front of him, a finger held against his forehead. She shoved, sending him sprawling back onto his butt. She leapt onto him, pinning him to the ground. "It seems that I win, Mister Kain. "Her eyes glinted in the dark, her mouth half open, her fangs showing slightly. Time slowed before she snickered and rolled off of him.

"That was actually fun."

Alistar rubbed the spot on his forehead as he lay on the courtyard's grass. "That darkness trick was a cheap move. That's what you used back at the inn that night you were outside my window."

"Yes, but I don't understand how you saw me then when you couldn't see me now," Elzibeth replied leaning against him.

"Back then you were motionless, and I could make out the glint of your eyes amongst the shadows. Here, you were near me and then gone again. I couldn't get a proper fix on you except when you came in to attack. I tried using my hearing, but my music messed that up. I did manage to put you flat on your face, though." Alistar poked her in the ribs.

"You did! But still, I was honestly surprised it was that easy to take you down, Alistar. You didn't use your full abilities, did you?" Elzibeth looked at him suspiciously.

"Guilty as charged," Alistar replied, his hands behind his head. The shadows cleared, revealing the night sky, and clouds passed overhead. Elzibeth scooted over to him and laid her head in the crook of his right arm.

"Why not?"

"You weren't trying to kill me. Plus that darkness trick isn't something I've encountered enough to find a good work around for. Not many vampires have that ability." Alistar glanced down at the top of her head.

"Be honest, Alistar. You were worried you'd seriously hurt or kill me by accident."

"Yeah. That too."

Alistar, may I ask you a question?" Elzibeth asked after a moment.

"Yeah. Anything." Alistar took his right hand from behind his head and wrapped it around Elzibeth's shoulders.

"Could you ever see yourself dating a vampire?" Elzibeth's question was soft and full of hope.

"Well, that could be an issue. See, there's this woman I really like, and I honestly haven't had the courage to ask her out yet. She's way out of my league." Alistar ran his fingers through her soft hair, tugging gently, bringing her a bit closer to him.

"Oh? What's she like?" Elzibeth responded to the tug by snuggling a bit further into his side. She wrapped an arm around his, her hand resting above his heart, feeling its strong, slightly racing beat against her palm.

"Well, she's really kind and caring. She's got long black hair, beautiful pale skin, these thin pointed ears, a smile that's to die for, and the most amazing crystalline gray eyes. Oh, and she happens to be a vampire. So… I guess if she asked me out, I'd say yes." Alistar watched the clouds overhead.

Elzibeth lit up inside. "So… is that a yes?"

"Well, if she asked me, then sure."

Raising her upper body, Elzibeth positioned herself to better see him. "I just did."

"Well then, I guess it's a yes." Alistar grinned and Elzibeth leaned in and kissed him. After a few minutes of enjoying the feel of his lips on hers, she suddenly rose, offering him a hand and easily pulling him to his feet. Their eyes met. "Alistar, do you dance?"

Alistar cocked his head to the side. "I have a confession to make. Dancing is not one of my better skills. I know a little, but I never really went to any sort of function. Why do you ask?"

Elzibeth led him to the music player in response. Making her selection she took Alistar's left hand and placed it on the upper left-side of her back, and held his right hand in hers. "I will lead then."

As they moved, "Love Exists" played from the small speaker. Elzibeth guided him expertly, thanks to the hundreds of years of experience in court. What surprised Alistar was when she started singing along with the song, her eyes never leaving his.

34

Marcus and Evelyn watched Alistar and Elzibeth dancing.

"She did it! She asked him! Aww, they're adorable!" Evelyn said, smiling.

"You played matchmaker didn't you?"

"Well duh. I could see how they felt about each other. They just needed the right shove. Couldn't you see it?" Evelyn sighed and took Marcus' hand in hers, pulling him close, wrapping her arms about him.

"I saw it coming miles away," Richter remarked dryly from behind them. "It's about damn time, is all I will say. I was wondering if I would have to lock them in a room together if this went on much longer."

~

Alistar stumbled a few times, but Elzibeth corrected him. After the song is over, she smiled. "Needs work, but you have potential."

Chuckling, Alistar scratched the back of his head.

"Yeah, well, as I said, I didn't get close to many people, and I certainly didn't dance at any gatherings."

Someone cleared their throat and Alistar and Elzibeth turned to see an old man with a walking stick standing at the castle gate.

"Well, hey, there, old timer. Something we can do for you?" Alistar asked.

"I was wondering if this is the castle of Lady Tepes?"

Elzibeth looked at Alistar and then back at the old man, taking in the bent over form, the snow white hair and bushy eyebrows and the weathered face with a serious demeanor. The old man had a pair of bent wire frame spectacles perched upon his nose, and wore threadbare but serviceable clothes and old worn leather shoes. "Yes, it is. I am Elzibeth Tepes."

The old man walked forward into the courtyard, his limbs shaking with age as he used the walking stick to support himself. "My eyesight's not what it used to be, but I remember that voice from long ago. I was but a child lost in these woods, crying and alone, when a pale lady found me, consoled me, and took me home to Calia."

Elzibeth examined the man's wizened face. Even though he was old, she could still see the image of the young, scared boy. "I do remember you. I believe your name is Charles."

"That it is. Now I'm the headmaster of Calia. I oversee the care of the people in my village. Recently new things have been happening. Workers came in and built a new clinic, and homes have been repaired, trees taken down and new fields tilled among other things. And the children have a new school and books, and more food has been brought in from the outside. I assume that was your doing, Lady Tepes?"

"Yes. I am merely taking care of the people under my protection."

Charles smiled, showing missing teeth. "That's what one of the construction workers told me. He said the lady in the castle was paying him to make these improvements to our village. The lives of my fellow villagers have improved and they're happier."

"Well I am glad to hear that. That was my intention, and I am glad to see my plan working."

"It is, and that's why I'm here. The people wish to meet their benefactor. Many of them are scared and confused. They don't understand your benevolent nature. They say you've taken Evelyn and Marcus into your castle." The old man was matter of fact in his statement of local gossip.

"Evelyn and Marcus live here now. I gave them and their mother a home when the church took theirs," Elzibeth said as her gaze flickered to Alistar. He headed inside and a moment later, came back with the children in tow.

"Headmaster Vickers!" Evelyn exclaimed, hugging him.

"Children. It's good to see you. Are you okay?" Charles squinted so his old eyes could see them better.

"We are more than okay. Lady Elle has given us jobs, and a place to live when we had none. The castle is wondrous, and Lady Elle and Alistar are kind. We're not in any danger if that's what you mean." Marcus joined Evelyn and took her hand.

"I'm very glad to hear that." Charles said. Lady Tepes, like I said before, the people wonder about their benefactor, and I came to ask you to come to Calia. To show the people that you're not the scary monster they've heard rumors about. It might do good for them to see that Evelyn and Marcus are healthy and happy here."

Elzibeth tapped a nail against her teeth for a moment, thinking. "Very well, I think that can be arranged. We will need a few minutes to get ready."

Charles nodded and sat on the stool near the chopping block. "Take all the time you need. The night is still young. I'll just rest my weary bones here while I wait."

Less than ten minutes later everyone was ready to go. Alistar was in his usual outfit all decked out with weapons, but Marcus and Elzibeth were in more fanciful outfits, even Evelyn wore a lovely red dress instead of her maid uniform.

"Do you really need all of those weapons, Alistar dear?" Elzibeth tisked as she eyed each weapon, worried he would make the wrong impression.

"I believe, Elle dear, that I'm your *raksha karane vaala*. Therefore my job is to guard you against all threats. Considering we're stepping outside this castle into an unknown situation, I intend to be prepared."

Elzibeth sighed. "Very well, but you are not to place a hand on any weapon unless I specifically say for you to do so, mister."

"I understand."

Richter led out three horses from the stables, including Midnight, Elzibeth's mount.

Elzibeth helped the old man up onto one horse while Marcus knelt so Evelyn could step into his raised hands, allowing her to climb into the saddle of the second horse before he climbed up behind her. Alistar then helped Elzibeth onto Midnight's back where she pulled him up behind her as though he was the same weight as a small child. He settled in awkwardly.

"You know, Alistar, one day we must teach you how to ride." Elzibeth laughed at his awkwardness.

"I like motorcycles, Elle. They don't buck." Midnight turned and nipped at Alistar's hand. "And they don't bite."

"Oh, Alistar, that was just a love bite." Elzibeth laughed again.

35

The horses made good pace and soon the group was on the outskirts of Calia. Alistar tried to dismount, but tumbled onto his rear, hard.

"Fuck me." He rubbed his backside as he climbed to his feet. Elzibeth snickered and handed him the reins.

"Don't bite me." He never took his eyes off Midnight as he grabbed the reins. The ebony horse nickered softly and nudged his shoulder as if to apologize. He walked into Calia leading the horse.

People gathered in the small village square as the horses moved down the main street. Stopping, Alistar helped Elzibeth off Midnight's back and then Marcus, Evelyn, and then Charles off their steeds.

The people whispered and threw furtive nervous glances at each other as Elzibeth stood there taking in everyone assembled. The old man stepped in front of her.

"I've brought our benefactor. She's the reason why our town and our lives have improved… because of her and her actions," Charles said in a clear voice. "And yet you all look at her with fear."

Then a young girl around Evelyn's age moved to the

front of the crowd. "I remember you. It was only a year ago. I was in the woods to the south picking berries in the failing light when a stranger grabbed me. You and your wolves came out of nowhere and saved me.

"I remember, child."

A man with a lad about ten by his side joined them. "You saved my son years ago when he was younger and ran off and got lost. I'm sorry I didn't believe him then. But now, seeing your face, I realize he was telling the truth."

Elzibeth nodded.

One by one more people came forward recounting tales of being saved or knowing someone who had been guided home and watched over by a pale raven-haired lady.

Then a small girl appeared and hugged Elzibeth around the legs. "Thank you, lady." And just like that, the dam broke and people surrounded the group, talking, asking questions, or simply marveling at the sight of the beautiful lady from the castle.

Elzibeth held up her hand and the people fell silent. "Since my father's time, this village has been under protection from the Tepes family, and it will continue to be so far into the future as long as I exist. None of you will ever worry about being fed on or live in fear from anyone in my castle."

"When Marcus and Evelyn told me their story of how you took them and his mother in after what the church did," The old headmaster began. "I didn't believe them at first. But again, and again, they came back every weekend," Elzibeth and Alistar looked at each other, now realizing where Marcus and Evelyn had disappeared to every weekend. Charles continued to speak. "They both seemed happier and healthier. I knew they were being well taken care of. And then the men came and built the new school.

They simply said that the lady in the castle ordered its construction. Same with the new clinic and the repairs on our homes. Always under orders from the lady in the castle."

"Yes. I did indeed tell them to do all that and more." Elzibeth placed her hands on the shoulders of Marcus and Evelyn.

"We encountered Lady Elzibeth and Mister Alistar one night by the lake," Evelyn says with a hint of red in her cheeks. "If they wanted to harm us, they could have done so with ease, but they never touched us. Although we were scared, we simply had a conversation and then they moved on. It was Marcus's idea to offer ourselves to Lady Elzibeth in hopes that she might heal his mother, but Lady Elzibeth refused. Instead she took us in, gave us a home when we had ours ripped away by the church. Yes, we serve her in household fashion, but she's never fed from us. We have enough to eat, and Marcus' mother is well taken care of." Her eyes showed sudden tears of anger. "When the church cast us out, a vampire took us in and showed us kindness."

While Evelyn had spoken, Alistar had moved away from the others, letting them take the attention, his gaze forever watchful. Elzibeth glanced over at him, and he nodded at her as a small child ran up and pulled on her sleeve.

Elzibeth knelt. "Yes, child?"

"Can I see your teef?"

"My teeth? I don't think..."

"Pwease?" The child begged and more children gathered closer.

"Well..." Elzibeth turned her head away for a moment. "Rah!" she said quietly with humor as she twisted back, showing her fangs. The children all scattered except for the original child who reached out and touched a tooth. Elzibeth blinked and picked him up, smiling and tickling him. The boy's mother reached out and laughed as Elzibeth handed back her son.

"My apologies, My Lady. He's very inquisitive." The woman bowed.

"Please, don't bow." Elzibeth took the woman's hands, tugging her upright.

"But, My Lady, are we not your subjects?" another villager asked.

"Maybe in the past, you would be so, but that one," Elzibeth pointed to Alistar. "has taught me that friends and allies are better than subjects, and friends don't bow."

Alistar raised a hand as if to say not to get him involved but Elzibeth reached over and took that hand, tugging him next to her side, continuing to hold it.

He scratched his head. "Look, really, I'm just like Marcus and Evelyn over there. Elzibeth took me in when I broke my ankle and helped me to recuperate. She did all the hard work."

"Wait, he's the one that drove off the bandits!" someone yelled. "I saw him with that gun. He fired it that night and they ran off!"

"Shit," Alistar muttered under his breath.

"Welcome to being a hero, my love," Elzibeth said in his mind. She leaned over and kissed him on the cheek.

"I'm no damn hero."

"Well you are to them, and to me. So deal with it, mister." Her eyes glittered like diamonds, daring him to challenge her.

"If you say so, princess." Alistar glanced over at her with a raised eyebrow.

As the villagers continued to surround them and children ran around, Elzibeth laughed in his mind. *"You are learning."*

36

A week later and everyone's spirits were down. Elena had passed away, and as if in response to her passing, the rain fell as if the very heavens were mourning with their tears.

"It's not fair!" Marcus yelled at Elzibeth. "Why did she have to die?! Why couldn't you just have forced my mother to take your blood?!" Alistar watched from the sidelines, letting Elzibeth handle the distraught child.

Elzibeth sat on a chaise lounge, letting Marcus vent his frustration, knowing the boy was in pain.

"Marcus, I tried multiple times to talk your mother into taking my blood, but she refused, and you know I will not turn a human against their wishes." Her voice was calm and clear but her eyes were sad.

Marcus turned his back on her. "It's not fair." He sobbed. Evelyn stood next to Alistar, her heart breaking for the young man she loved.

Elzibeth rose and placed her hand onto his shoulder. He shrugged it off and spun around, anger flashing in his eyes as he backed away. "Don't touch me! I hate you! You promised!" He ran out of the room and later the front door slammed shut.

"I said I'd try," Elzibeth whispered softly. Evelyn looked from her to Alistar. "Maybe I should go after him."

Alistar shook his head. "No, I'll go. We need to have a man-to-man talk. I've been through this more than once. I know what he's going through."

Evelyn and Elzibeth nodded, and Alistar walked outside into the heavy rain. One of the wolves wandered up to him and pointed its muzzle towards the lake. "Take me"

When he got closer, he could see Marcus tossing rocks into the lake as the rain poured down. Alistar picked one up and chucked it in. "Hey, kid," he said, full of concern.

"You gonna tell me how I was wrong back there?" Marcus grinded his teeth and scrunched his face trying to fight back the sorrow.

"Nope. I've been right where you are. I lost my parents when I was around your age. Then years later, as you know, I lost my sister. We all handle grief in different ways." Alistar handed Marcus another rock.

"What did you do?" Marcus wiped raindrops from his face.

Alistar rolled up his sleeve, showing the horrible scar on his right wrist, just barely visible in the overcast light. "I tried to join them, Marcus. For some reason this world had other plans for me."

"How? How do I handle this, Mister Kain?" Tears now streamed down Marcus's face as he lost the fight with his sorrow.

"I don't know, kid. What I do know is that you've got Evelyn, and Miss Elle to help you through this. They both love you." Alistar placed his hand on Marcus's shoulder, giving it a squeeze.

Marcus looked over at him. "What about you, Mister Kain?"

"Yeah kid, I'm here for you too. I told your mother I'd watch over you. And so did Elle. You're like a kid brother to me now."

"I've never had a brother." Marcus dropped his head to the ground in shame, knowing his words had hurt Elle.

"Yeah, well, I've never had one either, but I'll give it a shot if you will." Alistar smiled.

Marcus turned and buried his face against Alistar's shoulder.

"I got you, kid. I got you." Alistar held the boy tightly.

After a few minutes Marcus stepped back and wiped his face. "Thank you, Mister Kain."

"It's just Alistar, Marcus. No more of this mister stuff, okay?"

"Okay."

"Now, you run back to the castle and talk with Elle, and Evelyn." Alistar motioned with his head back toward the castle, then stared out over the lake.

Marcus started up the path but stopped. "Alistar, does the pain ever go away?"

Alistar looked at the boy. "No, Marcus, but each day it gets a little bit easier to handle. You'll have the occasional day, though where a thought hits you and you get down. When that happens, you come to one of us. We'll help you get through it."

Marcus rocked back and forth a bit, then turned and trudged to the castle. After a few minutes, Alistar tossed one last rock into the lake and followed him.

Elzibeth was waiting at the castle gates, her clothing completely soaked, and hair plastered to her head. "Did Marcus apologize?" Alistar asked her as he examined her disheveled condition.

"No. Not yet." Elzibeth replied, taking his arm.

"He will. He didn't mean…"

"Yes. In that moment he did. But he spoke in anger and grief. Such is the way of many when they hurt. They lash out at those closest to them without thought." Elzibeth sighed and laid her head on Alistar's shoulder. He wrapped one arm around her, pulling her close.

"Yes, but Marcus is a good kid. He'll apologize eventually, when he's ready." Alistar ran a hand through his wet hair.

"When he's ready, he won't need to." Elzibeth looked towards the room where Marcus's mother lay and saw movement in the window.

"I suppose you're right." Alistar followed her gaze. "Where will we bury Elena?"

"I was thinking under the apple tree on the hill. The one that can be seen from the castle. If, of course, Marcus agrees," Elzibeth replied as they walked into the castle.

Alistar raised an eyebrow and regarded the tree Elzibeth spoke of, and nodded. "It's a fitting place."

Marcus was waiting for them at the top of the castle steps, the rain hiding his tears. "I wish to bury my mother."

"Where?" Elzibeth's question was blunt and to the point.

Marcus lifted his arm and pointed to the very tree that Elzibeth had been talking about. "There. Mother liked that tree. I would bring her apples from it every day."

Elzibeth nodded. "Then it shall be so."

Marcus walked past her and grabbed a shovel from a pile of tools next to the woodshed, walking out the gate and trudging up the hill.

"Are you going to let him go alone?" Elzibeth watched Marcus as he started digging.

"I thought about it. All that digging will probably wear him out. But he doesn't need to be alone right now."

Alistar turned and picked up another shovel from the same pile of tools that Marcus had grabbed his from.

"Thank you, my love. Evelyn and I will go prepare Elena's body." A tear falls down Elzibeth's cheek as she makes her way into the castle.

Alistar headed up the hill where Marcus had already started digging.

Neither one of them talked as they dug, they just worked in silence. After three hours they had dug to a sufficient depth, the dirt piled next to them.

"Thank you." Marcus laid the shovel on the pile of dirt and sat down. The rain had stopped and Alistar sat beside him wrapping one arm around the young man.

"Sure." Both looked back towards the castle, knowing what came next. Elzibeth was watching to know when it was time. Hauling the slight woman into her arms, she headed to the tree, dressed now in a flowing black dress that Alistar had never seen before. Elena was wrapped in white linens, shrouded from head to toe.

Alistar withdrew the body from Elzibeth once she was closer, and jumped into the hole, laying Marcus' mother gently at the bottom. He took a moment to reflect on when his own mother had passed away. After a moment he reached up a hand. Elzibeth grasped and pulled him out.

Everyone eyed each other for a minute. Evelyn and Adriana were dressed in black, their faces covered in veils, holding each other as they cried. Richter was in his normal dark outfit, but now his stern countenance was broken by sorrow and he wiped a small tear from his eye as he stood next to Marcus.

"I guess I AM the closest thing to a priest around here." Alistar said, his voice thick with emotion and he choked back a tear. He looked down on the linen wrapped body, silent for a moment before he held out both hands. "I commend you, Elena, to almighty God, and entrust you to your Creator. May you rest in the arms of the Lord who formed you from the dust of the earth. May Holy Mary, the angels and all the saints welcome you now that you have gone forth from this life. May Christ who was crucified for you, bring you freedom and peace. May Christ who died for you admit you into his garden of paradise. May Christ, the true Shepherd, embrace you as one of his flock. May he forgive all your sins, and set you among those he has chosen. May you see your Redeemer face to face, and enjoy the vision of God, forever."

Reaching down he picked up a handful of dirt and tossed it into the hole. Elzibeth also tossed in a handful, and after her Evelyn, Adriana, and Richter did so. Marcus focused on the hole as tears trickled down his face.

"Goodbye Mother." He flung in his own handful. As he cried, the pack of guardian wolves lumbered out of the forest and one by one they howled deep, mournfully, paying their respects.

37

Two days later, a communique arrived via messenger. Richter received it and brought it to Elzibeth. "Mistress Tepes, a letter from Lydia Siegrist of the Swiss Alps."

"What does she want? Is she trying to upset me enough that I stake her out for the sun?" Elzibeth grumbled as she ran a fingernail under the wax seal and opened the letter. Reading it, her brow raised. "Where is Alistar?"

Richter's eyes glazed over, thinking. "I believe he is down in the armory, Mistress."

"Thank you, Richter." Elzibeth swept out of the room, heading down the steps. As she approached the door to the armory she heard Alistar shout, "Fire in the hole!" and then a loud bang.

"Alistar, what are you doing?!" She shoved open the door. Her question was met with coughing and choking as Alistar stumbled out of the armory, followed by Marcus. He and the boy had been spending more time together after the death of Elena.

"Did I... put too much powder... in the grenade, Alistar?" Marcus gasped as tears streamed down his face.

Alistar waved his question away as both were bent over in the hallway coughing and gagging.

"Nope. Just fine." Alistar's tears likewise streamed down his face.

Elzibeth's gaze pivoted between them. "You two need to be supervised. I do not want my castle blown up." The slight smile on her face softened her words.

Alistar straightened. "Hey, Elle... one second." He rushed back into the room and opened the small window to let in some fresh air. Once back in the hallway, a grin pulled up the corners of his mouth.

"What's up?"

Elzibeth handed him the letter and he quickly read it. "Huh. So the bitch decides not to follow the advice I presented to the others, and now she has sixteen Hunters on her turf. That's our problem... how?" He looked up and raised both eyebrows.

Elzibeth started walking in the opposite direction, Alistar and Marcus falling into step beside her. "It is our problem because I am the queen of vampires and so when a vassal or other vampire ruler asks for help, I am required to provide aid, my love."

"Huh. I guess I haven't reached that far in vampire protocol 101 yet. Sorry, teach, but that class bores me. I think you're just gonna have to give me an F." Alistar stifled a laugh.

"Smart ass." Elzibeth chuckled.

"Hey, Marcus, did you hear that? Elle called me smart." The confused half-smile on Marcus' face caused Alistar and then the boy to break out in laughter. Elzibeth rolled her eyes but even she had a smile on her face.

"OK, so all joking aside, how do we handle this situation Elle?" Alistar focused his attention back on Elzibeth as the three of them walked into the planning room.

"We don't; you do. You know Hunters and their

tactics better than any of us. And I have seen you fight. That and the fact you are human means that any authorities in the area will likely ignore you as a single person rather than us all going as a whole group."

Alistar looked at Elzibeth like she was crazy. "You know the bitch hates me and will probably try and eat me the minute I'm in her sight, right?" The confusion in his voice showed clearly in his tone.

Elzibeth held something in her closed fist. "Not if you are wearing this."

Alistar hand shot out and Elzibeth dropped an ornate ring into his palm. "It was my father's. If you wear that, she won't lay a finger on you. That ring symbolizes my claim on you." She pressed her finger against his chest. "You are my human, my suitor, and if she so much as touches you, I will eat her."

Alistar looked at the ring and grinned evilly. He slid it on the ring finger of his right hand.

"You still have to act within the Accords of Hospitality Alistar," she said sternly.

"Oh I will, but that doesn't mean I can't be a certified pain in the ass."

Elzibeth shook her head in exasperation. "Just don't get yourself killed."

~

Hours later found Alistar bundled up against the cold in the back of an old rickety cargo plane. Richter had managed this miracle on short notice with his contacts in the underground. In the back with him was an old snowmobile rigged with a parachute and a bag of weapons and gear. In the seat next to him was another parachute and neatly folded in his pocket was a map of the region.

"Two minutes to jump," an unknown man said to him. "Best get ready."

Alistar gave the man a thumbs up and put on the extra chute.

The cargo bay doors opened as icy cold air rushed in and the noise from the wind increased. Alistar lowered his goggles and put his face mask on. "Ready?!" the man yelled against the howl of the gale.

Alistar gave another thumbs up and hopped onto the snowmobile. "Good luck!" the man shouted then released the locks. The snowmobile and its platform slid down the ramp and into the cold night air. Four small stabilizing chutes opened on the corners of the platform, leveling it as Alistar rode it down. One thousand feet above ground, the automatic deployment device kicked in, opening the main chute.

One minute later the platform touched down and Alistar drove the snowmobile into the fresh powder, the blizzard making it hard to see more than a hundred yards in any direction. He checked his wrist compass, and the glowing indicators told him he was only a few miles east of Lydia's castle.

Revving the engine he navigated west across the forested hills. He raced along and in less than thirty minutes he was met with some company. People on horseback were following him. Breaking into a clearing somewhat protected from the winds, he stopped the snowmobile, leaving the engine running. Moments later ten riders surrounded him.

All were dressed in ornate old-fashioned armor, the cold apparently not bothering them. One rode forward and drew a sword, leveling it at Alistar's throat.

"What business do you have in the lands of Lydia Siegrist, High Lady of the Swiss Alps?!"

"Put that away Thomas. He has an invite." A feminine

voice rang out across the clearing and Lydia, the bitch vampire, strode through the snow dressed in a white gown and a fur cloak until she was mere feet from Alistar. "Greetings Hunter, where is your mistress?" Lydia scowled.

"Elle? She's back at the castle." Alistar removed his face mask.

"Really? I asked for help and all she sends is you?"

"Yep," Alistar replied, watching the vampire.

An evil smile overtook Lydia's face and she ran her hand along his shoulder and across his back. "Human, I could eat you and she would never know." She stopped as Alistar's gloves came off and he held up his right hand showing the ring.

"Yeah, you could, but she'll know, so that's probably a bad idea." His eyes remained forward, not wanting to play her game. "Plus, you would have just eaten your only chance at getting rid of your little problem."

Lydia bared her fangs. "Damn that woman! This must be a joke to her! One man versus sixteen?"

Alistar lowered his hand, putting his gloves back on against the cold and patiently waited as the vampire worked out her anger.

"Look, I'm what she sent you, Lydia of the North. Take it, or leave it. I fucking hate the cold. I hate you and you hate me, and I'd honestly rather be in front of a nice warm fire back in Castle Tepes!" Alistar snapped and Lydia whirled around, her claw-like hands in front of her as though to attack him and mouth wide to show her long sharp canines. If she were human, her face would have been bright red.

Slowly the rage subsided and her fangs and nails retracted. "Fine. Let's head back to my castle and I can show you the maps we have of the movement and attacks of the hunters."

Alistar shook his head. "Not until you say it first."

Lydia scowled at him and then sighed. "Stubborn human. She has trained you well. Alistar Kain, Guardian of Grand Lady Elzibeth Tepes, I grant you the Accords of Hospitality under the Old Laws. Is that better?" The edge in her voice was sharp enough that it could have cut glass.

"Much better, thank you." Alistar gave a slight bow. "Under the old accords, I pledge to do no harm to you or yours while I'm in your domain."

Lydia rudely turned away. "Whatever, I have a room prepared for you in my castle."

"Awesome. I'll sleep in the stables." Alistar gunned the engine, racing off towards the castle, the thought of snow shooting from the back of the snowmobile and onto Lydia was not his concern.

38

Alistar halted at the gates as the others rode up alongside him. Lydia glared daggers at him but redirected her gaze to a man patrolling the top of the castle structure. "Let this one through. He will be staying in the stables."

She rode past him and he sailed the snowmobile inside the open waiting doors of the stable.

Dismounting, Alistar turned to find Lydia standing in front of him. "You are a stubborn ass!" Alistar pursed his lips to one side, running his tongue across his upper teeth, watching her from the corner of his eye as he waited for her to finish. "A bed is waiting for you in that castle and you prefer the horses to the company of myself?!"

"Is that all? It's not that I don't trust you. It's just that I don't fucking trust you."

Turning away he started removing the unused parachute from his back, carefully packing it away. "Men!" He heard the Swiss vampire shriek from behind as she stormed away. "You three! Drag a brazier into the stables so the Hunter will have some warmth! Now!"

Alistar continued to pack away his gear and pulled out a sleeping bag as he heard footsteps behind him. Looking over his shoulder he saw the vampire from the clearing who had pointed the sword at his throat.

"A word of advice, Hunter, do not upset the high lady. Her fuse is short and her anger great."

"Thomas right?" Alistar asked expressionless.

"Yes."

Alistar faced him, crossing his arms across his chest. "Your high lady hates my guts but you notice she won't lay a hand on me because of who my girlfriend is. The ONLY reason I'm here is Elzibeth Tepes asked me to help you all, and I'm the ONLY help you'll be getting. Your high lady knows that. So as great as her temper is, she'll keep it in check for the most part, or I drive straight out those gates never to be seen again, and you all deal with the Hunters on your own."

Three guards dragged in a small brazier and, after adding fuel to it, set it ablaze. "Thank you, gentlemen." Alistar nodded at them. None of them responded. Thomas took one last look at Alistar, then left the stables.

Alistar found a clean stall near the brazier and rolled out the sleeping bag on top of a pile of hay. Then he unfolded the map from his pocket and started identifying local towns and villages. To the east was Arvika and further east was Karlstad. *Where are you fuckers?* The scrape of a boot drew his attention to a woman in a ratty dress and cloak holding a pot of stew and a loaf of bread.

"The high lady demanded I bring you sustenance." She bowed her head, not looking at him.

"Thank you. Just set it on the ground here." Something about the woman's demeanor caused Alistar to really take note of the woman. "How long has it been since you've eaten?"

The woman's eyes showed fear. "My Lord, I ate my one meal this morning."

Alistar scoffed. "One fucking meal in this weather? Jesus fucking Christ. Sit, eat." He pointed to the stew.

"Sl-slaves are provided one me-meal a day and o-one meal only. I-I must go be-before I get in trouble," she said before fleeing.

Alistar saw why the woman had said what she did and then ran off. A guard waited well within earshot.

Shaking his head, Alistar began to eat the food. Though it was mostly chunks of potatoes and some questionable meat in a watery broth, It wasn't bad. Afterward, he picked up the pot and walked to the castle entrance.

"Where do you think you're going?" A guard blocked his path as he made his way to the door.

"I'm bringing back the empty stew pot." Alistar shrugged noncommittally.

"Fine, I will fetch a slave to take it." The guard turned away, dismissing him.

"No, it's fine. I can bring it back myself. No need to involve the staff." *What's the big deal?* He took another step towards the door. The guard pointed his spear at Alistar's chest. Alistar merely looked down at it, unimpressed.

"Let him pass." Lydia stood behind the guard who moved out of his way. "The kitchen is this way, Hunter."

She quickly walked off, but Alistar easily kept up. "So, you've decided to sleep in a bed after all?"

"Nope, just didn't want another of your slaves to have to come out into the cold just to pick up my dirty dishes, and I want to see the maps you mentioned. By the way, keeping people as slaves is the act of an animal and makes you no better than the church." Lydia whirled on him, hand raised to slap him across the face. Her hand paused millimeters from his cheek.

"Yes?" Alistar raised one eyebrow and smiled in amusement. She would not hit him.

Lydia lowered her hand and scowled. Without a word she spun back around and stalked off. "You! Show him to the kitchen!" she said, pointing at the same serving girl from before.

"Yes, High Lady." The servant curtsied. "Right this way, My Lord."

Lydia spun and grabbed the girl by the neck. "You will not speak to him in such a manner. He is undeserving of such respect."

"Lydia of the North! Hold!" Alistar's command brought Lydia's head around.

"Section three of the Accords of Hospitality state that a visiting person accorded hospitality is treated with all rank and respect as that of a noble. That includes calling me My Lord, even though I hate titles. Therefore, your servant is only doing her proper job. Did I get that correct?" His voice held a dangerous edge.

Lydia dropped the girl to the floor. "Yes. It seems you understand our rules better than I thought." With that said she stalked off. Alistar grabbed the woman's arm and helped her to her feet.

"Follow me, My Lord." The woman bowed her head, looking at the floor as she walked. She stopped at a doorway. Through it, the kitchen staff bustled about.

"Thank you. Please wait here." Alistar gave the servant woman a smile. She curtsied to him. "Yes, My Lord."

Alistar saw the washing station and headed over, setting the pot next to the dirty dishes. The servant woman continued to wait for him, her head bowed. "Could you take me to the planning room?"

"Planning room, My Lord?"

"War room, maybe, then?" Alistar lifted an eyebrow. The woman's face lit up. "Yes, My lord."

A short walk later they were standing in front of a nondescript wood door. "Thank you; you may leave." He didn't even listen for the woman's reply before knocking.

"Enter!" Lydia's voice issued from beyond, sounding annoyed.

39

Alistar closed the door behind him. It was opulently furnished compared to Elzibeth's planning room. Blue curtains draped over the windows, and white pine covered the interior. The furniture was likewise carved of white pine with blue crushed velvet fabric on the seat cushions and backs. A large ornate rug spanned across the floor and a fire burned hotly in a fireplace at the other end of the room. "Huh. Nice Digs." Lydia raised her head.

"What did you say, Hunter?"

"I said 'nice digs'. Means nice place, as in I'm complimenting your castle." Alistar stepped to the large map of Switzerland that's spread out on the table.

"Oh. Well, thank you, Hunter." Lydia blinked, momentarily taken aback.

Alistar crossed his arms. "So, what direction are they moving from?"

Lydia pointed. "Here, to the north. I believe they started in Bern and are moving southwest, following the roads. My spies have brought me word that they're slowly going through each town on the way and rooting out witches and the occasional low-level vampire."

"Standard method of operation. Root out information, kill everything not human, and move to the next target. Where were they last spotted?" Alistar leaned over the map as Lydia tapped a fingernail on it.

"Here. Montreux."

"*Hmm.* They are indeed following the old roads, but it does not seem like they are making good time." Alistar scratched his chin.

"From what my spies have told me, they're on horseback. Switzerland as a country has better infrastructure than Romania. Because we stayed out of the war, most countries left us alone, so we retained more of it. Even my castle has electricity. But the roads and areas around them aren't one of the things we maintain very well."

"Huh… I did not know that," he tapped the map with his own finger. "I'm betting they'll head up the valley here and then south again at Sierre. After that, it's straight to your front door up the mountain pass."

"How long?" This was the first time that Lydia had looked worried.

"I'd say two days maybe. Especially if the weather and roads are good. That's taking into account them stopping at each town to source information and supplies." He quietly nodded to himself, contemplating their next move..

Alistar felt a sudden breeze after Lydia opened a window. "I can take care of the weather."

"Ancient forces." She started chanting in some ancient language as her eyes began to glow.
"Hear my call,
create a storm,
a terrible squall.

Snow and ice,
and winds that howl.
Create a blizzard to bring the valley down."

The blizzard picked up and intensified. And gale-force winds screamed past the castle.

When she turned around Alistar's eyes were wide. "The fuck?!"

A high-pitched, silvery laugh expelled from Lydia. "I finally got one over on the great Hunter. Dear man, I was a witch before I was turned so many ages ago. Weather is my specialty. Being turned did nothing to diminish that power and having lived as long as I have, my power has only increased."

Alistar scratched his chin again. "Color me impressed. Fought a few witches in my time, but never a witchy Vamp." He glanced once more at the map before moving to the exit.

"Where do you think you're going?" Lydia's voice held a sharp undertone.

"I'm a human, not a vampire. I need to sleep."

"I haven't dismissed you, Hunter!" Lydia's voice rose behind him. Alistar lifted his right hand and flipped her the bird, still walking away. He switched to the one with the Tepes ring on it just as he got to the door.

"I wouldn't throw that."

It was Lydia's turn to be surprised when she realized Alistar knew she was holding a vase, which she carefully set down. "How?" she started to ask, but Alistar was through the door and heading down the hallway. "Damn that man!" she snarled after him.

Thomas stepped out of the shadows. "I could kill him for you, My Lady."

Lydia glanced over at him as she poured herself a chalice of blood from a carafe. "No. Much as I hate to admit it, we need him. And besides, he's protected. If he dies, we all die. Elzibeth will come down on us like hell itself and nothing of this place or anyone in it will exist when she's done. Do NOT harm him in any way, Thomas. Not that you could. That man is faster than me. He would pin you to a wall before you could blink. Also, I admit he intrigues me."

"Understood My lady." Thomas bowed.

～

The next night Alistar awakened early to find Lydia standing mere feet away, leaning against the wall, staring at him. "Do you always sleep this long, Hunter?"

Alistar checked his watch. "Nope. Usually I'm up at dusk."

"Well it's well past that now and we've lost precious time. What are we doing tonight?!" Lydia snapped.

Alistar climbed out of his sleeping bag and threw on his boots. "Scouting. I want to get an idea of the terrain the hunters will have to go through to get here, see if I can trap them some way and not have to fight them directly."

"You? Outside at this time of night? You must be joking." Lydia lets loose that crystal-clear mocking laugh of hers. Alistar remained deadpan.

"I never joke about something this serious. The moon's out and bright enough to navigate by. I've traveled across the countryside in worse situations than this, using only a flashlight, a compass, and a map. I'll be fine."

"You mean *we* will be fine." Alistar paused in his preparations.

"No, I mean *I* will be fine. I am NOT taking you with me.

"What do you have against me?!!"

Alistar held up a closed fist. "One, you attacked me

without provocation at Elle's castle so I don't trust you." A second finger went up as he ticked off another complaint. "Two, you treat humans as less than human. And three, I am not taking a squad out for your protection. The more people with me, the slower we'll be."

"Then just take me with you."

"What? You'd trust yourself alone with a Hunter who's not exactly fond of you while out in the wilderness where anything could happen?"

"I could say the same to you, Hunter, about being with me. I admit, I don't like you either. But we both know that if my people are to survive, we must work together." Lydia examined the nails on her right hand.

Alistar considered what she had said. "Touche. Fine. You and me, but that's it. Do you have skis? There's only one pair strapped to the snowmobile. Grab what you need and be back here in thirty minutes."

40

Thirty minutes later, Lydia was back with a small pack, and a pair of skis. She was fully dressed for the situation and even had goggles.

Alistar looked her up and down taking in the white Parka with fur lining, white ski boots and goggles perched on her forehead. "Huh. Nice outfit," he remarked as Lydia strapped her skis next to his on the running boards of the snowmobile.

"Why, thank you." Lydia was a little surprised at the compliment.

She went to mount up behind Alistar but he held up a hand. "If you bite me, I will end you."

"I swear neither my fangs nor nails will touch your skin, Hunter."

Alistar nodded at her words and she climbed on behind him, wrapping her arms about his waist, his katana on his back pressed between them. He gunned the engine and the snowmobile took off like a rocket. Guided by the moonlight, Alistar headed north, then west along the mountain ridge.

∾

An hour later, they were high atop a snow covered bluff overlooking the town of Saint-Leonard. The wind was non-existent and the night crystal clear with not a cloud in the sky. The town below displayed a show of lights, lighting up the sky. Certain that he knew the cause but needing confirmation, Alistar positioned his night-vision binoculars and scoped it out. Flames engulfed half the town. The screams of the townsfolk echoed up the valley hills. Without mercy, people were cut down by Hunters.

"This. This is not how the church works." Alistar's voice was full of shock and sorrow.

"Then what is it?" Lydia questioned, her keen eyesight seeing all he saw without the need for a mechanical device.

Alistar lowered the binoculars. "It's a fucking purge. They're not hunting you down specifically. They're just killing your food source. And this is why Elle drinks cow's blood. It keeps down on the whole people-disappearing issue."

"I see your point," Lydia said, her voice filled with anger. "How do we stop this?"

He raised the binoculars. "There's sadly nothing we can do here, but I see a large group of people further east. Must be refugees. Looks like most of the town fled. If the Hunters have transport, they'll easily catch up to them when they're done here."

"We have to stop them from killing those people."

Alistar twisted his upper body around, confusion on his face. "What?" She repeatedly blinked at him, just as confused.

"You just called them people."

"I supposed I did." Lydia fell quiet.

"There might be hope for you yet, Lydia of the North." Alistar dismounted the snowmobile. He unstrapped his skis off the running boards and struggled into them before rummaging in his pack. Pulling out some flash bangs, he clipped them to his vest.

"What are you doing? And what are those?" Lydia looked curiously at the items.

"I'm going to give those people and us extra time by creating a massive avalanche using these six flash-bang grenades. Then... I'm gonna outrace it. I need you to pick me up about two miles east of here." Alistar cracked his neck, releasing some of the tension.

"You're crazy! You'll get yourself killed, and then Grand Lady Elzibeth will kill me for not keeping you safe!" Lydia hissed.

"No... she won't. She knows I know the risks. Now move!" Alistar grinned as he locked into the skis. Taking the poles, he pressed play on his media player and zipped off down-hill as "When Legends Rise" played in his ears.

Lydia watched him take off and she steered the snow-mobile as he tossed the first grenade. "Stupid human!"

The grenade exploded in a blinding flash, and Alistar threw a second one behind him, making a wide turn. With a low rumble, the top few layers of snow collapsed and began sliding down the hill following behind him. Alistar tossed a second grenade and then a third, fourth, and fifth, all while moving down-hill. He crouched low to reduce his drag as the powdery edge started to catch up to him.

The snowmobile burst out of the powder parallel to his course and closed in. Lydia reached out for his wrist. Alistar maneuvered behind the snowmobile and grabbed the back tow handle behind the seat, allowing Lydia to pull him out of the avalanche's path.

They watched as it crashed into the town below, burying it and cutting off access further east.

"Congratulations, Lydia, you just became a hero." Alistar patted her on the shoulder, grinning.

"A hero? All I did was save some people from being mindlessly killed by Hunters." Lydia's voice showed her confusion.

"Yep. And sometimes that's all it takes to be a hero. I don't get it either, but that's the way it is." Alistar shrugged. He motioned for Lydia to head down into the valley.

"Let's go see who's still alive after that."

A few minutes later, they moved on foot among the mostly buried buildings searching for survivors. "Hunter, over here! I found one!" Lydia hissed as Alistar rounded a building to find her standing over a Hunter pinned against a building by debris kicked up by the avalanche.

"Lydia hold. I want information." Alistar said, his voice quiet as the vampire moved in for the kill. She paused at his words.

Alistar knelt next to the wounded Hunter who weakly tried to raise a knife to defend herself. He plucked it from her grasp and slid it into his belt.

"Hey. Hey. Look at me. LOOK at me." He grabbed the woman's face and forced it in his direction. She spit blood at him but he wiped it off.

"Well, she's certainly not friendly," Lydia remarked dryly.

"We fight to the last," Alistar replied.

"Why-why do you... say *we?*" The trapped Hunter's voice was weak, showing she did not have much time left. Alistar pulled back his glove to show his tattoo. "You're... one of us? Why... do you not... kill her?" The woman's head sagged to her chest as she lost consciousness.

"I used to be one of you." Alistar snapped his fingers in front of her face and lightly slapped her cheek, bringing her around. "Hey, wake up." He cracked a smelling salt vial and held it under her nose. "There we go. Welcome back." Alistar smiled grimly.

"You're go-going to torture me?"

"Nah. I don't do that kind of thing in this situation. Your body is broken. You won't survive, so what I'm going to do is ask you some questions, and if you answer to my satisfaction, I'll end it cleanly for you. You answer wrong, and I'm gonna let that one behind me feed on you." Alistar said in all seriousness.

The woman's eyes never wavered. "Ask away."

Alistar nodded. "Why are you purging these people? The church only does that in times of war."

"Remove the source... of food... for the vampires... and they will starve. Make them... come to us," the woman replied, her voice weaker than before. Alistar gave her a small sip of water from a bottle off his belt.

"How do you know where the vampires are?"

"Our... our sources... say there's a castle... to-to the south-east... high on the peak... of Garde de Bordon. That's... that's where the head... the head vampire is... for this region."

Alistar raised an eyebrow at Lydia.

"Actually she's about three feet behind me." Alistar watched the woman's eyes go wide as she reached for a stake. Again he took it from her, holding her hand tightly in his.

"You're in no condition to fight. So stop!" he commanded softly as he inspected her wrist. "A level four. I know there are sixteen of you. What ranks, and how many of each?"

The woman drew in a shaky breath as a trickle of blood ran from the corner of her mouth. "Lydia, do you have a handkerchief?" He held out his hand. Lydia placed the fabric in it and he dabbed the blood off the woman's face.

"Eight... eight level fours. Four le-level threes," she paused to take a deep breath. "two level... twos, and... two se-seekers."

"Last question. How many were still in this town when my avalanche hit?"

The woman's eyes were slowly fading. "Half." Alistar felt her hand go limp, and reaching out, he closed her eyes and stood.

"Why do you offer such kindness to your enemy in a moment like this?"

"Because their fight is done. They're helpless, and the reaper is on her way to claim them. In battle, the decision's have to be made in a split second, and you don't have time to be nice, but in moments like this, anything less than kindness is cruel."

41

"You're a mystery to me Hunter. If I had gotten my claws on you, I would have tried to break you. And then I would have drained you dry," Lydia remarked as they searched through the town for survivors and bodies. The snow had started falling again and visibility was close to zero as white-out conditions moved in.

"That would have been difficult, Lydia. You can't break what's already broken. Got a level three here," Alistar replied, finding another dead hunter.

"You don't look like a man who's been broken." Lydia found a body and checked the wrist. "This one's level three."

"There's a lot about me that you don't know, Lydia."

"Well, why don't you tell me, Hunter. Why don't you make me understand why someone of your rank—"

"Quiet!" Alistar barked softly. Lydia swept up next to him. He pointed and she made out movement up ahead amongst the buildings. "I count four of them."

"Actually, there are five. You missed one Hunter,"

Lydia whispered as she pointed out the lone Hunter away from the others.

"Good catch. Remember what I said about mercy? Now is not the time for that. Be swift; be brutal. Save mercy for later," Alistar whispered back as he drew his katana. He swiftly moved off, weaving his way through the buildings toward the group of four Hunters. Lydia watched him as he all but disappeared like a ghost in the snow. Even her keen eyesight was barely able to track him.

"Maybe Elzibeth was right to send only you," she whispered to herself as she headed toward the lone hunter.

The first Hunter Alistar came upon had only a second to register his presence before Alistar's blade separated his head from his shoulders in a shower of blood. As the others turned at the sound of the body falling, Alistar was among them, his blade flashing. In less than thirty seconds, all four were down with fatal wounds, their crimson blood coating the snow.

Lydia glided over the snow toward her victim, but he was aware of her, and a crossbow bolt streaked through the falling snow, hitting her shoulder, and pinning her to a tree. "Fuck!" she screamed as the silver bolt burned and prevented her from freeing herself.

"Vampire bitch. You think you can sneak up on me, Dimitri Pierce? Nice try," the Hunter said, dropping his crossbow and pulling out his sword. A flicker at the edge of his vision made him turn to find himself staring down the barrel of Alistar's pistol.

"We were always taught to watch our six. Seems like you fell asleep in that class," Alistar's eyes were colder than the snow as he pulled the trigger. The Hunter's head exploded in a shower of blood and brains. Walking over to Lydia, Alistar holstered his pistol, and placing a hand against her chest, yanked out the crossbow bolt with the other.

"Fuck! That hurts!" Lydia yelled. Her eyes reddened and her fangs extended, looking to Alistar with hunger. Alistar held up his hand with the ring and stepped aside.

Lydia hissed, then she leapt upon the body of the fallen Hunter, greedily latching onto the neck and drinking deeply. After a moment she stood and Alistar handed her back the handkerchief she had given him.

"Thank you, Hunter," Lydia said as she wiped her mouth.

Alistar chuckled nervously. "For a second I thought you were going to come after me."

"For a second, I was," Lydia replied, hungrily licking the blood off her fingers.

Alistar raised an eyebrow. "Well it's a good thing you didn't. Cause I ain't got enough bullets for that."

Lydia laughs. "Do you think your bullets can hurt me?"

Alistar looked down at the headless drained corpse of the hunter at Lydia's feet. "I don't know. Why don't you ask him?" Reaching into a pocket he pulled out another magazine. "Those bullets might not have hurt you, but these are another story."

In the flickering light of the fires, Lydia could see silver glinting on the top bullet.

"*Hmm*, point taken. So how many is that?" Lydia pursed her lips in thought.

"That should be eight. Meaning eight more are some-where to the east following that group of refugees." His watch beeped and he checked the time. "However, we don't have time to pursue them. Dawn will be coming soon, and as much as I want to go after them, you can't afford to do so."

He walked back to the snowmobile at a quick pace.

"Then what do we do?" Lydia asked as she fell into step alongside him.

"We will hunt them tomorrow night. For now, though, we race the sun back to your castle."

Reaching the machine, Alistar threw a leg over and sat as Lydia climbed on behind him. "Hang on tight and don't let go," Lydia's arms snaked around his waist and she buried her face in his back next to his katana as he raced across the mountain, the sky just starting to lighten.

An hour later as the sun crested the horizon, the snow-mobile pulled through the courtyard and into the stables. Smoke was coming off Lydia in the dawn's rays, and the servant woman from the night before rushed out with a hooded cloak.

"That one deserves to be treated better. I'll admit that if you treated me like you did her the other night, I would have let you burn. Yet here she is, running out to protect you." Alistar stretched, causing his lean muscled form to show as he climbed off the snowmobile.

Lydia tilted her head in question, then looked at the servant girl waiting nearby with her head bowed with new eyes. "Human, what is your name?"

"It's Lucia, My Lady." The woman bowed further.

"Well, Lucia, you have earned yourself a higher station here. I'm in need of a handmaiden and you have earned the position. Your quarters will be moved closer to mine and you'll receive better treatment. Now go pack your belongings."

Lucia stumbled back in shock and she froze for a moment. "Yes My lady."

"Is that better?" Lydia asked Alistar.

"It's a start."

"Well then, allow me to take another step. Alistar Kain, former Hunter, now protector to my queen, It would be remiss of me to allow you to sleep another night in the stables... Please. I give you my word that you will have the only key to your room while you are here if that makes you feel better." Lydia actually bowed to the man standing in front of her.

Alistar raised an eyebrow at this sudden change. "I suppose a hot bath would be nice after being out in the cold so long. Very well, lead on."

Lydia raised her head. "You do me a great honor."

42

An hour later Alistar was soaking in an in-floor marble tub big enough to host a party when there was a knock at the bedroom door. Grabbing a towel from the floor, he wrapped it about his waist.

"Enter!" he called out, expecting a servant to open the door. Instead he was surprised when Lydia was the one who entered. He glanced at the bed where his things were arranged, including the Tepes ring, and then at Lydia.

Lydia followed his gaze to the bed seeing the ring glinting there. "Fear not, Hunter; I gave you my word. Even I won't go back on that once it's given." Alistar nodded and moved to the bed, turning away and giving her a first look at the scars that decorated his back.

"Did one of my kind do that to you?"

Alistar dropped the towel as he slipped into a pair of pants and Lydia caught a glimpse of what she was not allowed to touch. "Nope. My people did that to me when I left the church."

"Why?" Lydia's question threw him off for a second.

"Why would you care?" He gave her a sideways glance.

Lydia shrugged. "Maybe I do. Maybe I don't, but I am curious, so I'm asking.

Alistar ran a hand through his wet hair and sat on the bed. "Plain and simple? They burned my sister as a witch. I tried to stop them."

"How many did you kill?"

"Five... Five level fours with my bare hands. Then about fifteen of them piled on me and beat the shit outta me. I was tied to a post in the city square and beaten with whips. Then they cauterized the wounds using a torch."

"And how many... non-humans have you killed?"

Alistar's arms crossed on his bare chest. "Fifteen vampires, two witches, and one werewolf pack. By myself. I could probably add on another twenty assorted beings to that list if I include my time as part of a team."

"And what did you feel when you killed each of them?" Lydia asked, mimicking his stance.

Alistar shrugged. "When I was a Hunter, it was just a job. Go in, find the thing preying on the local human population, and eliminate it. You always feel something. There was one, though, when I was working alone—"

"Go on." Lydia quietly sat in a chair, listening with interest.

"I was on a solo mission to western Canada, British Columbia. Rumors were that there was a powerful old vampire living out there. Found a local library to do some research in. Took me a month total and the more research I did told me this vampire didn't attack many humans. From what I could find, it was mostly those who preyed on society. I made friends with the old librarian, who worked the night shift. We'd sit for hours talking and playing checkers. Turns out he was the vampire I was looking for all along. He could have killed me, but when I found him out, he just welcomed death. He didn't fight. He just stood there as I took his head. A five-thousand-year-old vampire, and I dusted him. That was the one that made me second guess if I was doing the right thing." Alistar stared blankly across the room, his eyes unfocused, deep in thought.

"Were there any you let go?"

Alistar nodded slowly. "I tracked down a werewolf in Utah, back in the states. When I caught up to her, it turned out it was just a mother and her two kids. The mother was killing a steer a week to feed her family, and she was the only one infected yet managed not to attack her own children."

"And did you kill them?" Lydia leaned forward.

Alistar shook his head. "I was ready to, but no. They weren't hurting humans, only trying to stay alive. I faced down that mother growling at me with her kids behind her, scared to death, not of *her*, but of *me*. That hit me in my soul. I lowered my weapons and just walked away. Told the farmers that it was just a pack of regular wolves, and that I didn't deal with normal animals. Then I left. Not sure what became of them."

Lydia rose. "Did you ever feel fear during any of these encounters?"

"No. Not really. I've never felt actual fear for myself in any of those situations, but I have felt fear for others." He scratched his chin. "I was once told it was because I was broken. That every man should fear death, and because I didn't, I wasn't normal." He shrugged and put on a shirt.

Hearing a metallic clink behind him, he saw Lydia putting a wrought-iron key on the bedside table. "As promised. I'll request that someone bring you something to eat."

"Thank you." He made a fist and his knuckles cracked. "Do you have a training barracks for your guards?"

Lydia stared at him for a moment. "Yes. You wish to avail yourself of it?"

"Yeah. I need to work out some issues." Alistar cracked his neck, causing Lydia to shudder.

"Very well. If you leave your room and head to the end of the hallway and take a right, at the end of that hallway, you will find it."

"I'll eat later." Donning the Tepes ring, and grabbing his mp3 player and earbuds, he stepped past her and out into the hallway, heading in the direction she had indicated. Inside the room were vampire soldiers talking amongst themselves as they trained. They all fell silent, their eyes following him around the room.

"Are you lost, Hunter?" Thomas asked before him.

"Nope. This is exactly where I need to be right now," Alistar scowled at the vampire.

"Are you sure? You are standing in a room full of vampires. We might get hungry," Thomas joked, showing a hint of fang as he laughed.

Alistar looked around. "I see six of you and one of me. I call that fair odds. You *might* take me down."

Thomas' eyebrows rose in astonishment. "Surely you must be joking."

"I'm perfectly serious. But I don't think your mistress would want me breaking her toys."

All the vampires laughed. "You will regret those words Hunter. Pick your weapon," one of them said with scorn.

43

"Commander Thomas, we are under orders to not lay a hand on him!" a vampire whispered frantically as Alistar walked over to the weapon racks on the walls.

"This is a simple training exercise among allies. If he happens to get hurt, we'll just have to patch him up." Thomas grinned evilly.

"And who's going to patch you up when I'm done?" Alistar asked, his back still turned away as he picked out a heavy shafted spear used for boar hunting. He pulled off the head leaving himself with a six-foot long, three and a half-inch thick staff.

Walking over to the training ring, he positioned himself in the inner circle.

"What's going on here?!" Lydia's voice rang out.

"High Lady, the Hunter was just going to join us in some training exercises as a cross-bonding experience," Thomas said.

"Is this true, Hunter?"

Alistar shrugged. "They threw down the gauntlet. I'm just picking it up."

Lydia nodded. "Very well, Thomas. Do not bite him, and do not kill him. And Hunter? Do not break my men."

Alistar chuckled. "I make no promises on that. But they'll be alive when I'm done."

One of the vampires rushed him and Alistar spun, swinging the staff as hard as he could. The staff impacted the vampire across the chest, sending him flying across the room and into the wall. Alistar twisted to face the others as Lydia watched.

Every other vampire looked shocked. Alistar cracked his neck. "Get him!" Thomas yelled. Three vampires grabbed swords and rushed Alistar.

Spinning the staff again, Alistar blocked the first swing, and then the second. His return swing knocked the blades from both men's hands. He followed up with another smashing blow to their midsections, sending them flying out of the ring as the staff shattered in his hands. Sliding across the floor on his knees, he picked up the dropped blades and parried the swings of the third vampire as he slid past him, letting the slide carry him back to his feet.

Lydia grinned. "Thomas, I think your men are outmatched."

"He is but one human, High Lady," Thomas replied sharply.

"Well I watched that human take out five hunters earlier tonight, and just now, he beat three of your men in two attacks." The third vampire hit the floor behind Thomas. "Make that four of your men. Maybe I should get a Hunter of my own instead of you all."

Thomas donned on his helmet and whirled around. "Everyone else get back! I'll handle him on my own!" Grabbing a sword off the rack, he squared off with Alistar, who tossed away one of his blades.

Alistar bowed to Thomas. "You will not shame me in

my house Hunter!" Instead of bowing he attacked. Alistar blocked and returned blow after blow, both men spinning and tumbling trying to gain advantage. In their final move, they ended up swinging so hard their blades shatter upon each other, leaving the men with broken hilts.

Both men dropped their broken weapons and began throwing punches and kicks, neither wanting to give up the fight.

Thomans managed to get close enough and Alistar felt his nose break. He returned the favor, punching in the nose guard on Thomas's helmet. The sixth vampire snuck up on Alistar and grabbed him in a headlock.

"That's enough!" Lydia's voice rang out, freezing everyone in their tracks. The anger on her face was evident. "Thomas. Since when do my men cheat in a friendly sparring match? And didn't I tell you NOT to break him?!"

"Hi-High Lady, I-I." Thomas' body subtly shook in fear at his mistress's rage, his eyes wide.

Alistar tossed the man over his head and stepped out of the ring. He hauled the downed soldiers to their feet, patting them on their backs, before doing the same to Thomas.

"Good fight." Thomas nodded in stunned reply as Alistar walked past him and Lydia and headed back to his room, not wanting to listen to Lydia chew out her people.

Staring into the bathroom mirror, he placed his palms on either side of his nose and applied swift pressure. With a snap, the sharp spike of pain causes his eyes to water.

Three sharp raps sounded against his bedroom door, followed by one more a second later. "Come in Lydia!" he yelled, and Lydia stalked inside.

"Three of my men have broken ribs, and Thomas's pride is wounded. I asked you not to break my men." She sent a glare his way.

"They'll heal with some blood. And that's only a taste of what they'll face should those other Hunters make it up here."

Lydia stalked over to him and grabbed his chin, turning his face back and forth. She placed both thumbs on either side of his nose and squeezed. There was another pop and Alistar's eyes watered again.

"There. I can't send you back to Elzibeth in a damaged state."

"Thanks… I couldn't quite get it."

"You're welcome. Now I'm headed to sleep. You're welcome to join me, oh guardian of the queen." A single finger caressed his jaw and she lifted a seductive eyebrow.

"Right. I may not fear death, but even I'm not that stupid." Alistar laughed.

"*Hmmm…* I wonder about that. In any case, good night." Lydia bowed to him.

"Good night Lydia of the North. This is one man who will NOT be joining you in your bed tonight, or any night."

Lydia let loose her crystal laugh. "Oh, I do look forward to the day Grand Lady Elzibeth gets you in her bed. In the old days, she would have devoured a man like you." On that note, she glided through the doorway, closing the door behind her.

Alistar stretched out on the bed. *Hmm… Could be fun.*

44

The beeping of his watch and the emptiness of his stomach woke Alistar from a deep sleep. His nose hurt as well, but that was the least of his worries. Sliding out of bed, he padded over to the mirror in the bathroom and lifted his shirt exposing bruises across his body.

Damn, those are going to be hard to explain to Elle. Near the bed he quickly dressed in his armor-layer body sleeve, the one made by Francois. He threw on the white outer winter layer on top before grabbing the rest of his things.

Two vampire guards standing on either side of his door snapped to attention. "Good Morning My Lord!" they said in unison, then bowed.

"My Lord? Since when do you guys call me My Lord?"

"Since we heard you almost whipped the captain of the guard, one on one."

"Not so loud. He might hear you!" the other guard hissed.

Alistar chuckled. "Alright, you two are with me for the night." He headed down to the war room. Lydia was already at the table, pacing back and forth. She glanced at the two guards behind Alistar and they stopped.

"Apparently after last night, either I have a fan club, or you put these two at my door," Alistar said to the vampire before him.

Lydia leaned against the table. "A little of both. You impressed them, and Thomas is a sore loser, and I don't trust him not to try and kill you in your sleep." She gestured with a head tilt to the two vampires behind Alistar to enter, and they headed over to the table, examining the map.

Alistar glanced down at the map. He grabbed a pin and shoved it into the town from the other night. "So we were here. After last night's fight, the Hunters know we know they're in the area." He scratched his head as Lydia appeared beside him. "They'll hold up somewhere defensible to plan their next move." Alistar's fingers ran over the map. He tapped a location. "Here. Unfortunately I'm not capable of properly pronouncing the name. Little rusty on my French, and by a little, I mean I don't know any."

Lydia leaned over Alistar's shoulder. *Chateau des Nobles.* It's the Chateau of Nobles. It's a small castle just south of Sierre. It guards the bridge from here to Sierre itself and overlooks the river that flows into Sierre."

Alistar bent closer and stared at the map. "It's a control point. That's where they'll be heading if they're not already there." He whirled toward the door.

"And just where do you think you're going?"

"I'd like to get back to my vampire so I'm gonna go do what I do best."

"What's that? Be an annoying asshole?" Lydia laughed.

"Exactly."

"Not without me, you're not." Lydia said sternly.

"Look, I'm the only asshole around here. The world would implode if you start being one as well, Lydia."

"You're asking me, the queen of the north, to admit you're higher rank than I?"

Alistar couldn't hold back a laugh. "Please, I'm a master of my class. You can't even begin to reach my level of skill, bitch."

Lydia's eyes flashed in annoyance, but there was a smile on her lips as they bantered. "You may be a master, but I've had more experience, human."

"You may be old, but this is a young man's game now. Let the younger generation handle it, grandma."

Lydia snapped her jaws, her eyes flashing at Alistar's dig at her age, which actually got to her.

"Umm, should we really be arguing at this point? I thought we were planning the next move," one of the two guards said with uncertainty.

Alistar glanced over at the two soldiers. "Umm, yeah. For a minute I totally forgot you two were here. Sorry about that. You're coming as well. This mission will require a small team. What are your names, by the way? I can't just call you Thing One and Thing Two."

"I'm Conrad." The vampire who spoke had sandy blond hair, a beard with a chiseled jaw, and a muscular physique.

"Julian" The other was lean and slender with dark brown hair, green eyes, and a clean babyish face.

~

The group found themselves huddled together and sneaking up on the small castle. It consisted of a tower with a courtyard and a wall surrounding it all, really just an outpost. Light flickered inside at the highest level. "Here's the game plan. Anyone who attacks you is fair game. If they drop their weapons, subdue them. If they try to run, subdue them. Other than that, I don't care what you do. Fangs, claws, it's all legal against anyone who attacks you. Take the tower and we'll sort it all out later."

He started to stand. "Oh, and if I tell you to get out, get out fast." He rushed to the base of the courtyard wall and knelt, holding out his hands. The three vampires race past him and leap the wall. "Right. Vampires. Sure wish I could jump a ten-foot wall in a single bound," he muttered. Conrad and Julian leaned over the wall holding out their hands. "Thanks for coming back for me."

Both vampires grabbed a wrist and pulled him up. Surveying the scene, Alistar dropped into the small court-yard and ran over to the tower wall, where Lydia was waiting in the shadows.

"Now what?" Her voice was just loud enough for the others to hear.

Alistar set down his pack and pulled out the wrist-mounted grapple launcher. "Now we go up. This reel has one hundred feet of high tensile five-fifty cable." "How much do you weigh, Lydia?"

"Hunter, that's not a question you ask a woman." Lydia said peevishly, glaring.

"Normally, no, but I need to know if this will carry us both."

In response, Lydia placed her hands against the wall and climbed, sticking to the wall like a spider. She looks down at him. "Coming?"

Alistar chided himself mentally for again forgetting these vampires were not normal people. He was getting too comfortable around them. Conrad and Julian followed their mistress up the wall and he waited in the shadows of the battlements.

Aiming the launcher he fired, the grapple arcing high in the air and landing on the battlements with a small metallic clank. A lone Hunter standing by the parapet turned to check on the noise and Julian reached out, grabbing the man by the front of his outfit, and pulled him over the wall. He ripped his throat open with his nails, dropping the body to the courtyard below. The rushing river behind the tower covered the sound of the body's thud as it hit the ground.

Hitting the retraction button, Alistar let the launcher pull him up the wall to the battlements where he climbed onto the parapet and moved deeper into the shadows. Looking through the window, he could make out seven shadows moving.

Alistar pointed to his eyes and held up seven fingers. The three vampires nodded. "Someone go swap out with Marius," a voice from inside suddenly issued forth. "His shift is done. Tomorrow we hit the castle at Garde de Bordon."

The group listened to the footsteps as they made their way over to the door ten feet away before it slowly opened.

45

A young Hunter exited out and after mostly shutting the door behind him, lit up a smoke. Breathing it in he exhaled. "Marius?"

The cold steel of Alistar's blade touched his throat. "Nasty habit you got there. It'll get you killed one day." Alistar's voice was a sinister whisper as he stepped out from behind the man into full view.

"Yeah, so? You might kill me right now." The kid sounded tough but Alistar noticed his hands shaking.

Alistar nodded his head slightly, watching the kid's eyes. Those were key. The eyes told all. The kid's head tilted downwards towards his own waist where Alistar noticed a knife in a sheath. "Don't, or I WILL kill you." The kid's head snapped back up. Alistar could see the tell-tale signs of serum abuse in the blue-colored veins on his face.

"What now?" he asked. Alistar slugged him across the face, hard, tweaking his neck and knocking him out. Catching the unconscious body he lowered it to the floor and checked the kid's wrist. This hunter was only a level two.

"Might be your lucky night, kid. You get one chance at redemption," he whispered as he tied the kid up and gagged him. Lydia padded over, her fangs extended. "No. This one is no longer a threat." He searched the man and found three vials, two full of the blue liquid and one empty. He tossed them to the courtyard below. "Nasty stuff."

Lydia looked at him curiously and opened her mouth. "I'll tell you after we're done with this mission," Alistar said, not even looking at her.

Alistar pointed to the old leaded-glass windows on three sides of the tower. "Lydia, take that one. Conrad that one, and Julian; you know what to do. In ten seconds, I kick in the door. You three come through the windows."

Moving in front of the door, he silently counted down and when he reached zero,they moved on to their step. The door slammed open on recently greased hinges, revealing five very surprised Hunters. However due to their training, they quickly recovered, going for their weapons.

The glass of the windows shattered as the three vampires crashed through with weapons drawn. Well, two of them had weapons. Alistar noticed that Lydia preferred to use her nails and teeth.

Four Hunters attacked Conrad and Julian, two on each vampire, while the fifth one went after Lydia. Alistar watched as Lydia ripped his throat out with her nails and buried her face in the fountain of blood, slaking her thirst.

Conrad likewise dispatched one of his attackers with a deep stab to the stomach. Twisting the blade, he pulled it out in time to block a sword attack from his second attacker before spinning around and decapitating the man in one blow.

Julian was having a bit more trouble dealing with his attackers. One shot him in the knee with a bolt and his face was a grimace of pain as he favored the other leg. Alistar pulled his pistol and shot the man in the back twice, leaving Julian to finish his remaining attacker. With only one to deal with he quickly got the job done.

"Well that was an absolutely delicious encounter," Lydia said as Alistar starts counting bodies.

"Hey, Lydia? Weren't there supposed to be eight hunters left after the avalanche?"

"Yes. Why?" Lydia responded, wiping her mouth with a torn piece of shirt from her victim.

Dust rained down in front of Alistar from above. "Aww shi—" he barely got out before the Hunter hidden in the rafters swung down and kicked him out the door with both feet.

Alistar plummeted toward the cold rushing river below. Julian had the Hunter backed against the parapet. *Only got one shot.* In a matter of seconds, Alistar extended his left arm and sighted along it, pressing the firing stud on the grapple launcher. The bolt whistled out and snagged on the Hunter's shoulder as Alistar yanked on the line, momentarily halting his fall before his plummeting continued, pulling the Hunter over the edge with him.

"If I'm going, I'm taking you with me, asshole!" Alistar growled as the line reeled in, wrenching the Hunter closer. The man threw a punch at Alistar, one which Alistar returned twofold as they fell the thousand feet toward the river below.

Alistar grabbed the man's shoulders and twisted, turning them so the man was on the bottom. "Tell your brothers that Alistar Kain sent you!"

Both men hit the ice of the river, smashing through it. The fact that the Hunter was on bottom when they hit gave Alistar no comfort. The freezing water covered his head and the shock forced out a gasp, causing him to take in a lungful of cold river water as it swept them away.

Alistar grabbed for a boulder on the icy river bank and barely managed to hold on. The cold quickly sapped his strength and his fingers slipped as the weight of the Hunter still attached to the grapple, and his own soaked clothes pulled him off the rock and deeper into the water.

So this is how I die. Huh. Kinda peaceful. Alistar felt his body go completely numb and the outer edge of his vision blackened. Vaguely, he was aware of a pale figure with white hair swimming toward him in a white outfit.

As his eyes closed he was aware of an arm snaking around his neck.

~

Alistar came to in the snow coughing up river water. "Fuck that burns," he gasped as he inhaled.

Lydia placed her hand on his shoulder. "Breathe! I didn't just give you the kiss of life for you to stop breathing on me again!" Alistar struggled to breathe, and Lydia helped him roll over, coughing up more water, and gasping until he could get an easier breath.

He fell back, repeatedly blinking to clear any water from his eyes even as it froze in his hair and eyelashes. "You... you gave me... mouth to mouth... Why? You could have let me get swept away and been at no fault with Elzibeth."

"Yes... well... I no longer don't like you." Lydia examined her nails as she spoke.

"So... so you like me."

"More like I am indifferent now, and I honestly want to see what trouble you get into next," Lydia replied, flashing her fangs.

"Ye-yeah, well, th-that may end up be-being sooner ra-rather than later," Alistar said, now shivering.

Conrad appeared along the bank. "I found the

remaining Hunter and dispatched him, My Lady," he said as Alistar's shivering increased, his teeth now snapping together.

"Well, this won't do. We simply must get you out of these wet clothes," Lydia said with an evil leer.

Alistar reached for his pistol with a shaky hand only to find it missing from its holster.

"I'm joking. Don't be such a prude," Lydia chided him.

46

Back at Lydia's castle, Alistar began packing his things when a knock sounded on the open door to his room. He knew who it was from the pattern of the knock. "Yes, Lydia?" The door opened.

"I want to thank you, Alistar, for helping... me."

Alistar shrugged and crossed his arms, leaning against the bedpost. "It's what I do. I kill shit, and I know things. Elle knew I was the best person for the job."

"How very astute of her," Lydia said, a smile crossing her face. "And by doing so, she knew that at the end of it all, I would owe you a favor in return."

"Well, she didn't say anything about favors. But since you brought it up, I lost my pistol when I was kicked into the river. If anyone happens to find it, I'd like it back. But if you can't, I'll think of another favor." Alistar returned to packing.

Lydia nodded. "If we find it, I shall make sure it is returned to you. But tell me, what will you do without your iconic sidearm?"

Again Alistar shrugged. "Go back to the old ways I

guess." He pulled out his knife and twirled it before sliding it back into its sheath.

Lydia laughed. "Woe be to those who end up finding out how deadly you are with that." She sat on the bed. "I have a request."

Alistar waved his hand nonchalantly. "Ask away."

"Conrad and Julian, I'd like you to take them back with you and train them in your ways. They have taken a liking to you for some reason."

" I suppose I can do that. And in return, I'd like you to treat the humans of your domain better."

Lydia rose to open the window, allowing a strong breeze to whirl into the room, blowing the curtains aside and ruffling her hair. Alistar heard voices from the court-yard below. "Take a look for yourself."

Alistar joins her to see a long line of humans coming in through the gate. Vampire soldiers stood in the court-yard passing out food, drinks, and clothing, and Lydia's servants, clearly in better clothing than their stations would warrant, were directing the refugees on where they could go to find beds.

"Impressive. Not a food source I take?" Alistar asked, raising his eyebrows in slight surprise.

"Not a food source. That one there..." Lydia pointed at the doorway and Alistar turned his head to see Lucia. "Has found a way to make cow blood palatable. Don't get me wrong; it doesn't even begin to compare to a fine-aged vintage, but it's better than another group of Hunters coming here. By the way, you said you would explain those vials of blue liquid you found."

Alistar ran his hand through his hair. "The serum is what gives Hunters the edge when fighting supernaturals. They inject it before an encounter. The benefit is increased speed, strength, and sense. Basically all the base abilities you have except they can't cling to surfaces, fly, or control the weather. It's an enhancement drug, and like all drugs, it's very addictive. You can get hooked on it from the first go. I should know."

"You've taken it then?"

"Yeah. In my first few years I used it a lot. It gives you this rush, this feeling of power, like you're unstoppable."

"I also get the understanding that you've dealt with the downside of using it," Lydia said, closing the window.

"Yep. I'm one of a few who got addicted quickly. Soon I was taking it every day, even when not on a mission. I took far more than my share until my mentor caught me. He wasn't happy." Alistar sighed.

"What did he do?" Lydia was surprised that such a strong man could be an addict.

"He tied me to a bed for two weeks while I detoxed. Let me tell you, coming off that stuff is worse than any drug imaginable. Every day I would scream for more, just for some relief from the body-wracking pain... Which is what's going to happen to the young Hunter in your jail."

"Yes well I don't quite know what to do about him yet, but I don't think I'll kill him. Turn him, maybe. Bed him... certainly... If I can ever get that close. He's rather good looking." Lydia stared at the closed window deep in thought.

Alistar hoisted his bag onto his back. "Well, on that note of too much information, I believe it's time for me to hit the road. I've got a long way to travel to get back to Elle and the others."

"No, you don't."

Alistar's forehead furrowed in confusion and Lydia laughed.

"I have my own private jet, and an airfield to go with it. How do you think I made my way to Castle Tepes for the initial meeting, by horse and carriage? Please, Alistar, we elders might be old, but some of us have adapted to the times."

"You mean you let me fly here and para-jump into the frozen wilderness when I could have landed at an airfield and taken a vehicle up here? You really are a bitch, Lydia."

Lydia again laughed that crystal laugh. "I'll take that as a compliment, Alistar Kain."

~

Sometime later, Alistar was sitting on a lavishly furnished private jet across from Conrad and Julian as the plane headed south towards Romania. He marveled at the rich white leather seats, the dark blue carpeted floor, and the mini bar, which was unfortunately filled with bottles of blood and not booze.

"Lord Alistar, it is a great honor to be under your tutelage," Conrad said.

Alistar held up a hand. "I'm not lord anything. It's just Alistar. I hate titles. I hate being called sir. Get that in your heads right now... please."

"As you request... Alistar."

"You know, you two don't sound Swiss. I have you pegged for Russian," Alistar remarked nonchalantly.

"That's because we are. Both of us are from Moscow. We immigrated to Switzerland before the war," Conrad replied, smiling, just a hint of one fang poking out under his top lip.

The plane touched down at Brasov International Airport. The landing was extremely bumpy due to the lack of upkeep.

"Fuck, my back. Damn, in a few more years this place will be completely useless," Alistar grunted, holding a hand to his back. Julian moved behind him, wrapped him in a bear hug, and pulled upwards. Alistar felt every bit of his spine crack in quick succession and then great relief. Julian quickly stepped back out of blade range.

"OK, you can certainly stay. How in the fuck did you learn how to do that?"

"Even vampires get out of whack sometimes," Julian said with a fanged grin, his fangs just slightly longer than the rest of his teeth.

"Nice. Just next time warn a guy." Alistar said seriously but then smiled.

"Yes, sir… I mean, yes, Alistar."

The three men disembarked and climbed into the limo that was unloaded from the cargo area. As it took off, Alistar sunk into the seat with a sigh. "We have got to get Elle into this century."

"In a few more years, this too will be unable to function. Then it will be back to horses and carriages around here," Conrad remarked.

Alistar face palmed. "Don't remind me. I hate horses. They smell. They kick… they bite."

"Must be Midnight." Conrad grinned.

Alistar peeked at the man from between his fingers. "You know about Elle's horse?"

"Oh, yes, that horse belonged to her father and has a matching temper."

Alistar rolled his eyes. "Well, that explains that. So how old are you two exactly?"

Conrad was the first to speak up. "One-hundred and eighty."

"Fifty-seven," Julian replied.

"Fuck, you're both still kids by vampire terms. Julian, you're practically still in diapers.

"Fuck you, Alistar," Julian said crossing his arms.

Alistar kicked him slightly. "Hey. It was a joke. You acquitted yourself fairly well back at the tower." He grinned. It was an infectious grin and soon the other two were grinning as well.

47

When the limo pulled into the courtyard, Elzibeth was standing on the steps. As Alistar climbed out of the vehicle, she rushed down and embraced him. "Welcome home, my love." Alistar grunted in pain from all the bruises and wounds he had taken, and she quickly let him go and lifted his shirt.

"Alistar Kain, did…?"

"No, Lydia didn't do any of this. Her men did during a friendly sparring match." A red overtook Elzibeth's eyes and he rested a hand on her arm. "Relax, Elle. I gave as good as I got. Put four of them in intensive care. Lydia stopped the match when Thomas and the remaining one cheated."

Elizabeth's eyes stayed red for a moment then cooled to their normal crystalline gray. "Very well. Let's get you inside to a hot bath and some rest."

"Umm yeah, about that," Alistar said as Conrad and Julian appeared behind him. Elzibeth was in front of them in a split second, fangs extended and hands around their throats. Alistar could feel the sudden anger in Elzibeth's mind at the intrusion of other vampires into her domain without invitation or advanced notice.

"Elle, no!" Alistar barked out two words and Elzibeth's head pivoted to him. "Meet my new recruits, Conrad and Julian."

"Why?" Elzibeth asked.

"Lydia's changing. Taken in human refuges that the Hunters displaced from their homes, Treating her staff better. Drinking cow's blood instead of feeding off humans."

Elzibeth's hands released of their own accord.

"She even saved my life. Pulled me from an icy river. In return I agreed to take these two on and train them so that they could protect her domain and her people. And... I kinda like them." Alistar gave a lopsided grin.

Elzibeth looked at the two vampires and then back to Alistar. "Did they participate in this sparring match?" Her fangs shone in the moonlight.

"No. But they heard about it, and well, now I have a fan club."

Elzibeth's anger cooled and she relaxed, her fangs retracting. "If they so much as touch the children, I will kill them."

"Grand Lady—" Conrad started to say but Elzibeth cut him off.

"Silence." Her glare did more to silence him than her words.

Alistar intertwined his arm with hers. "Elle, if they touch Marcus or Evelyn, or Adriana, I will handle it myself. Is that understood, Conrad? Julian?"

They nodded "Yes Lord Alistar!"

"*Lord* Alistar?"

"Don't ask Elle. Just don't. It's something I plan to beat out of them if I have to."

Elzibeth laughed suddenly. "Oh, no you won't! I like it."

"Oh, for fucks sake," Alistar said as he facepalmed. After a second, he looked over at Conrad and Julian. "You two, inside. Now. Barracks are in the basement level. Start cleaning."

"Yes, Lord Alistar!" Both vampires grinned.

"Okay, that's it, I'm gonna—" Alistar growled as he moved toward them. Elzibeth wrapped her arms about him, keeping him where he was.

"You two know the Accords of Hospitality. Go. I'll keep him here long enough for him to cool off."

"Yes, Grand Lady!" Both vampires replied, quickly grabbing their few belongings, and rushing into the castle.

Once she sensed that he had calmed, Elzibeth let Alistar go and he sighed. "I better go help them clean the barracks. "First rule of being a leader is don't make your men do what you yourself are not willing to do."

"Your men?"

Alistar rolled his eyes. "It seems I've gone from sole protector to command of the royal guard. So, yes, my men. At least until I send them back to Lydia."

Elzibeth slung her arm around his back. "Lord Alistar, it has a nice ring to it."

"Oh don't you start on that!" Alistar grumped at her. A deep, husky laugh exploded from Elzibeth's mouth, before she laid her head on his shoulder as they headed inside.

Hours later after the barracks were cleaned and Conrad and Julian are settled in, Alistar found himself in a hot bath, brooding as Elzibeth sat on the edge. "So, what happened in Switzerland?" she asked, cleaning his bruises and cuts

"The church is changing their methods. They weren't just hunting vampires. It was a full-on purge. They burned a whole town and slaughtered a lot of the people. I barely managed to stop their pursuit of the survivors."

"Oh? How did you do that my love?"

"I brought the fucking mountain down on their heads, burying them in an avalanche. Lydia and I cleaned up the survivors of that team."

"Typical you. Always over-doing things."

"There's an old saying I was taught as a Hunter. There's no kill, like overkill." Alistar chuckled.

"What happened after that?" Elzibeth ran the sponge down his back and over the scars.

"The next night we tracked the rest of them to a tower where they were holed up. I got careless. The last Hunter was hiding up in the rafters and kicked me off the parapet into the river below. Lydia dove in, pulled me out, and revived me."

Elzibeth tensed. "Look Elle, I was half dead, and that water was well below freezing. She resuscitated me. She didn't bite me, didn't give me blood, nothing like that. Just chest compressions and air until I started breathing on my own. Relax."

Elzibeth's muscles slackened. "The idea of her mouth on yours makes me angry."

"Yeah, well, it was that or I was dead. I'm no super-hero. I probably swallowed half the damn river," Alistar replied leaning back in the water.

"Then I guess I shall be thankful. I don't want you to die," Elzibeth said softly after a moment.

Alistar reached over and took her hand. "Everything dies, Elle. One day I will, one day you will. It's inevitable. I accepted it a long time ago, and when I do finally pass, I'll greet the devil with a grin on my face and open arms."

He climbed out of the bath and enveloped himself in a towel, padding into the bedroom

"Mister Kain, I am keeping you around as long as I can." Elzibeth whispered under her breath. "And when you do die, I'm walking into hell and telling the devil that he can either give you back, or I'm kicking his ass and taking his throne."

48

Alistar woke with a start, realizing he was not alone in his bed as a pale and very feminine arm snaked around his chest.

Did we? Embarrassment flooded Alistar, not remembering what had happened earlier in the night.

"No, we did not. By the time I cleaned up the bathroom, you were passed out, and it was close to dawn so I slept here," Elzibeth murmured as she snuggled closer to him and put her head onto his shoulder.

Alistar lay his head back on the pillow. "This is nice. I could get used to this."

Elzibeth peeked at him through sleepy slitted eyes. "So could I."

"Well I hate to be the bearer of bad news, princess, but I gotta go wake up the boys and put them through their paces."

Elzibeth rolled over as he climbed out of the bed and dressed. "Go back to sleep love. It's not yet fully dusk."

Alistar found the largest cooking pot and spoon in the kitchen. "I'm just gonna borrow this, Richter as we don't have trash cans here."

Richter, who was sitting at the table, pointed a knife at him. "You will bring that back when you are done or we will have words, Alistar. That's my favorite pot and spoon."

"I got it!" Alistar headed downstairs to the barracks. Slowly opening the door, he steps inside and sets the timer on his watch. He banged on the pot rapidly with the spoon, the noise echoing in the room and startling the two vampires awake. "To arms! To arms! The castle is under attack! Gear on and toe the line!"

Conrad and Julian scrambled to get their gear on. After a full two minutes, they were standing in front of him and he pushed the stop button on his watch.

"Congratulations boys, you're dead because you were too fucking slow! Gentlemen, it is oh dark thirty! Welcome to training! From this point forward until I send you back to your high lady, your asses belong to me!"

"But, but, Lord Alistar!" Julian stammered.

"Dead men don't talk! They run until I get tired! Around the castle, full laps, Go!"

Conrad and Julian sent each other questioning looks and raced out the door. Alistar turned, seeing Marcus standing in the doorway.

"Hey, kid, what's up?"

Alistar, I want to learn to fight. Will... will you train me too? Make me like you?"

Alistar pulled out two chairs at the only table in the room. "Sit." Marcus followed Alistar and sat in the other chair, resting his elbows on his knees.

"Why? Why do you want me to train you? You wanna kill? Because I'll tell you, it's not easy to do. Each death steals a piece of you, makes you a little less human." His voice was soft and he waited for Marcus' reply.

"No. I want to be able to defend Evelyn, and Miss Elle, and..."

"And what Marcus? Spit it out."

"And you. Maybe if I knew how to fight, you wouldn't have to protect us so much." Marcus fell quiet, waiting.

"Very well Marcus. I'll train you to fight."

"Thank you. So, umm, when do I learn how to use a sword and guns like you?"

"Not for a while. You must first learn how to use this." Alistar pointed to Marcus's head. "And this." He moved his finger down to Marcus's chest. "Before you ever draw a weapon, you'll learn to fight with your head and your heart before you choose violence. You must learn to show mercy to an enemy when they're down, and you must know when to be quick, decisive, and if necessary, merciless. And you need to tell which situation requires which decision."

"Yes, Alistar, I will!" Marcus's face beamed.

"Good. Now, you have two vampires to catch up to. You'll do laps around the castle until I tell you to stop. Now go." Alistar grinned and lightly punched Marcus in the arm. Marcus raced out of the room and down the hall past Elzibeth.

"My, what has gotten into him?!" She laughed from the doorway as he ran down the hallway.

Alistar stood, chuckling. "He asked me to train him like I'm doing with Conrad and Julian.

Elzibeth frowned. "Are you sure that's safe?"

"Nothing is ever safe, Elle, but he wants to be able to defend his loved ones… including you, including me. But for the most part it's safe. He ain't touching a weapon until I say so. However, I need to get out there and start running with them."

"Train with them? Why would you train with them?"

"Because a team trains together. Bonds together. It makes them more cohesive and stronger." Alistar grins.

"Oh really? Interesting. Very well. Run along my raksha karanevaala."

❧

Conrad and Julian passed the castle's front gate and surprisingly only a minute later, Marcus ran by. Putting his fingers in his mouth, Alistar let out an ear-piercing whistle, startling all three of them, and drew a line in the dirt with his boot. "Fall in! Toe the line!"

All three men ran over to the line. "Look to your left! Now look to your right! These are your brothers! There is no human; there is no vampire! There's—" Elzibeth appeared on the line next to the others.

"Elle, what in the fuck are you doing?!!!"

"You said a team that trains together, bonds together and becomes stronger. Are you and I not a team?" Elzibeth challenged.

Pressing his lips together, Alistar got up in her face, holding up a finger.

"Yes?" Elzibeth asked sweetly..

"Fuck! Should have seen that coming." Alistar agreed, pinching the bridge of his nose. After a second he sighed. "Yeah. We are."

The other three laughed and Alistar whirled, glaring at them. "Push-ups, now! Count them out!"

Conrad, Julian, and Marcus dropped to the dirt and started doing push-ups. When he turned around again, Elzibeth was on the ground doing push-ups as well. "Are you joining us, Lord Alistar?" Her smile was mischievous.

Laughing, Alistar dropped to the ground face to face with her and started hammering up push-ups faster than any of them.

49

A week passed and Alistar had everyone running more laps in addition to climbing the short but rocky cliff near the castle. He was honestly impressed as Julian, Conrad and Elle climbed using only their ability to stick to surfaces. They quickly learned how to leap frog up the face, and every so often one of them grabbed Marcus and tossed him up to a waiting teammate who caught him and gave him a moment to set a spike before moving on. And one of them always stayed with the boy, making sure he didn't fall. It was rather efficient.

A few feet away from Elle, Alistar climbed with them, using only his skill. Still he kept up without help, until at one point a loose rock gave way, and Elzibeth's hand clamped onto his wrist, halting his fall.

"I have you," she said, holding him while he found his footing again. He ended up beside her and nodded in thanks before continuing his climb.

"I think Conrad and Julian have taken a liking to Marcus." He chuckled as they climbed side by side.

"I agree. He's their little brother now," Elzibeth replied

as she leapt and stuck to the cliff further up. She held out her hand and Alistar caught it.

"I think..." Alistar said, jumping for a hand hold a bit further up. "I'll start them off on some basic self-defense techniques today." He got a firm hold on the outcropping he was on and then held out his hand for Elle.

They continued this back and forth.

"Marcus will enjoy that... and so will I." Elzibeth smiled and leapt, grabbing the top of the cliff and pulling herself up. Alistar scrambled up next to her a moment later. Conrad, Julian, and Marcus were sitting on the grass waiting for them.

"You're late," Conrad joked.

"Yeah, well, some of us... are old... and out of shape. And... and I don't mean her," Alistar said, catching his breath.

Everyone else laughed. "You are NOT old, Alistar."

"Yeah, tell that to my back." Alistar groaned.

Elzibeth was by his side. "I'll help you with that later, my love."

"Oh, geez, get a room you two." Marcus rolled his eyes.

"Marcus, do you like swimming in an ice-cold lake at midnight?" Elzibeth said, her face suddenly a blank slate.

"Umm, no, Miss Elle." Marcus replied, suddenly deciding to admire the clouds.

"Then I suggest you remember I can easily hear the things you and Evelyn do in your free time in my castle. Perhaps we should soundproof your room?" Elzibeth smiled as Marcus's face changed red from embarrassment.

"Alright, folks, that's enough of the banter. Let's get back to the castle and then we can start the fun stuff. Double time. Move!" The three men ran down the hill leading to the castle. "That means you too Elle."

"Yes Lord Alistar." She took off at a run, looking back over her shoulder.

"Oh, I'm so gonna!" Alistar shouted, taking off after her.

A few minutes later they were all standing in the courtyard. "Conrad! Front and center!"

"Yes, Lord Alistar!" Conrad stoped in front of him.

"Seriously? Y'all gotta stop with this lord shit. Now, grab my throat with your right hand."

"Umm, sir?"

"Did I stutter? Grab. My. Throat." Alistar's expression went deadpan and Conrad put his hand around Alistar's throat.

"Thank you. Now, you all think I'm pretty much fucked at this point. Not so." Reaching up with his right hand, Alistar found the pressure point in the vampire's wrist and squeezed, easily pulling Conrad's hand away from his throat.

"Vampires have more muscle and speed than the average human, but still have the same body build. Which means nerves and pressure points. Granted, their nerves transmit information from their brains to their extremities faster than an untrained human." He held up Conrad's wrist showing where the spot was and with his left hand flicked the nerve deadened fingers.

"Squeeze a pressure point in the wrist like I'm doing, and the extremities it's feeding information to go dead. By the way, the same thing applies to humans." He twisted Conrad's wrist, forcing the vampire to the ground. "If you control certain points, you can control a situation." Letting Conrad go, he nodded. "Thank you. Back to your post. Everyone pick a partner. Elle, you are with Marcus. Don't eat him."

"I would never!" Alistar grinned.

"Alistar, dear, you are starting to annoy me!" Elzibeth hissed.

"Am I now? Okay, never mind, you're with me."

"I shall partner with Conrad," Richter said. "Julian can partner with Marcus."

"Fantastic idea Richter. Thanks for the help. Everyone practice this nerve block fifty times. Then we move on."

Elzibeth grabbed Alistar's throat. "What are you going to do now, my love?"

Smiling, Alistar slowly reached up, his hand going to grab her wrist, and stepped in fast, quickly turning his back to her front while holding higher up on her arm. A second later he twisted and threw her forward over his shoulder so she ended up on the ground on her back.

Everyone else froze. Elzibeth gasped up at Alistar as he held out his hand.

"What was that?"

"Simple tendon lock like I showed them combined with a two-handed shoulder throw," Alistar replied as Elzibeth took his hand and he pulled her to her feet.

"How often is it effective?"

"Eh." Alistar shrugged. "It's situational. On a vampire like yourself, not as much as I like. Human to human though, pretty damn effective."

Elzibeth's gaze flickered over to the others. "Teach them. All of it. And it's my turn."

Her eyes held a mischievousness that had Alistar hesitating.

Oh, I'm in trouble.

"Yes my love, you are." Elzibeth's eyes sparkled.

50

"Oof!" Alistar hit the ground hard on his back after Elzibeth had tossed him. It had been three weeks since everyone started training and now they were a cohesive team. Alistar flipped back up to his feet as Marcus closed in for the attack.

Alistar blocked Marcus' punch and tossed him into Julian who caught him and whirled the boy around, setting him back on his feet. As one both man and vampire closed in for the attack as "How Did You Love" played in the background on the new player that Elzibeth had bought Alistar after his old one ended up waterlogged by the fall into the river.

Elzibeth snuck up behind him, catching him in a headlock. As Marcus and Julian closed in from one side, Conrad moved in from the other. Elzibeth nipped his ear. "You got careless, my love, and for that, you lost this battle." she whispered in his ear.

Alistar could see she was right and he reached up and patted her left arm twice, tapping out. She released him and everyone else stopped.

"Good session everyone." Alistar walked over to a crate

and flipped up the lid revealing the AK-47's. "Now for something different." He pulled out a rifle.

"This is an AK-47. Standard issue of the old world Russian military back before the war. It has one job. To put holes in whatever it's pointed at." He racked the charging handle and aimed it across the courtyard at a target Richter had set up earlier. He fired, putting a hole in the center of the target's head. He dropped the mag and racked the handle again, catching the unspent bullet as it flew out of the gun before setting it on the crate.

"That." he said, pointing at the target. "Will end any human. It can also end any of you." Julian and Conrad talked with Marcus and he stalked over to them.

"Gentlemen, am I boring you? Because if so, you can teach this class and I'll sit and learn what new insight you might be able to bring to the table."

All three looked up guiltily. "Bullets don't hurt vampires." Conrad said.

"Really? Care to test that, Conrad? Go on. Stand up there. Now."

Conrad slowly rose and drew Elzibeth's attention. *"Alistar, you are not going to shoot him,"* She mentally said.

"Yes, actually I am. He's gotta learn the hard way." Alistar loaded the single bullet he had back in the rifle. Taking aim he lowered his sights to Conrad's right knee and fired.

Conrad's knee exploded. "Fuck!" Conrad fell. Turning, Alistar grabbed a canteen and tossed it to the vampire. "Drink. You'll heal."

He again held up the rifle. "Sure, vampires can heal from anything given enough blood, but I don't have to kill you with this. Take out a knee and you're twenty five percent less effective, and you're also on the ground where I can finish you off with a blade much easier. Hunters will do the exact same thing with a crossbow." Walking over he helped Conrad up. "You alright?"

"Yes Lord Alistar. My apologies." Embarrassment coated Conrad's face as he met Alistar's gaze.

"At least you can heal quickly. I saw a recruit get shot in the knee by a crossbow when he wasn't paying attention during training. He was out for weeks." Alistar clapped the vampire on the back. "Luckily, after the war, many weapons like this fell into disrepair and are now hard to come by. I have no fucking clue how Richter got his hands on this crate and the ammo to go with it. The man is magic is all I will say."

"Don't sweet talk me, Alistar. I still won't spoon with you." Richter sat on the parapet eating an apple.

Everyone laughed. "Yeah, well you ain't my type anyway, Richter." Alistar grinned at the friendly exchange.

Walking over, he picked up another magazine and held up a round from it. "This is a marker round. It's filled with paint. When it hits," he said, squeezing the tip, then crushing it, and getting red paint on his fingers. "You know you've been hit. Back in the old days military forces would use this to practice engagements with."

Setting the rifle down, he continued. "Sadly, even Richter is having trouble finding these kinds of rounds. So we can't really do much training with them. However what I can do is let you each take a turn with the weapon and get a feel for it on that target down there." He loaded a magazine full and slapped it into the AK. "Conrad, you're up first."

Conrad stepped forward and took the rifle. "Put the stock against your shoulder just like a crossbow. Aim down these sights and line them up on the target. Slowly squeeze the trigger; don't jerk it. It's not your dick."

Conrad was rewarded with a neat hole in the paper target. He fired off a few more rounds, landing each one next to the other. "Nice grouping," Alistar said, taking the weapon back.

The others took their turns. Marcus was last and Alistar put in a fresh magazine and before handing the boy the weapon. "Now it's gonna buck hard, kid. Hold on tight." Marcus fumbled the weapon a bit but finally managed to finally hold it properly.

"Miss Elle! Miss Elle!" Adrianna ran from the castle and stepped into the line of fire. Just as Marcus pulled the trigger, Alistar moved in front of the rifle, grabbing the barrel.

The rifle barked and Alistar staggered back. Elzibeth was by his side as Conrad pulled the rifle out of Marcus's grip.

Alistar held up his hand. "I'm okay but that's gonna leave a mark." He lifted his shirt and a squashed round clattered to the courtyard's cobblestone. "Well, I'd say this undersuit of Francois's works against bullets."

He sat as Adriana greeted them, unaware of how much danger she had just been in.

51

Marcus backed away shocked and bumped into Julian, who held him. "Little brother, everything is okay. Lord Alistar is fine."

"Yeah, kid, I'm fine, see?" He drew in a breath and winced. "Okay, maybe you cracked a rib. But everything is fine."

"Gee, did I cause that?" Adriana asked, moving closer. "I'm sorry! But I did find out some news that Miss Elle needs to know!"

"We are waiting, Lorekeeper," Elzibeth said, more than a little annoyed with the girl.

"Oh, right! Well, I was examining a vial of Hunter serum I found in the armory, and it turns out that it's distilled from vampire blood!"

"Huh, that means the barrack's rumors were true." Alistar scratched his chin.

"What rumors?" Elzibeth asked sharply. He answered quickly so as not to annoy her further.

"Back when I was a fledgling Hunter, there were rumors that the serum was made from the blood of captured werewolves and vampires. Every so often a high-level team would be sent out with gear that was obviously designed to capture and not kill. They'd always come back with a hooded figure bound in manacles. That could have been why they were sent after Lydia."

"I thought you said they were purging the people."

"No one said someone can't do two things at once."

Elzibeth moved over to him. "And just what do you know of these capture missions, Alistar?"

Alistar raised an eyebrow and gave a half shrug. "I've been on two. But the higher-ups never told us why we were capturing anyone or anything, just that our targets were needed alive. And when I say high-level Hunters, I mean fours and fives. And the group that hunted Lydia and her people had eight level fours."

Elzibeth squinted at him. "And just how do they know how many of a given class of Hunter to send after a specific target?"

"Oh that's easy! They have supernatural's classified as well," Adriana piped up perkily.

Elzibeth rounded on her. "Lorekeeper, you have been holding out on me."

"Umm, in my defense Miss Elle, you never asked me that question, and I kind of figured Mister Alistar told you already."

Elzibeth gave Alistar the same questioning look.

Alistar coughed. "Umm yeah, never asked me that either, Elle." He scratched his head, looking anywhere but at her. "I mean it's not like we have a Hunter's handbook. At least *I* don't. I threw mine away after year one."

"I have one in my belongings." Adriana said. "I took it off one of the Hunters at the tavern the day you killed them rescuing Miss Elle."

"Go get it please." Marcus had appeared by Alistar's

side while she talked. "And bring it to the planning room. I would like to read it," Elzibeth said with an edge to her voice.

"Are you really okay? I could have killed you," Marcus asked, his voice quivering as his hands shook slightly, betraying the worry he was feeling.

"Yeah, kid, it's nothing Elle can't fix. Besides, I was gonna test that suit myself at some point. And, hell, I've broken more bones than I care to admit." He put an arm around Marcus and in a small one-armed hug.

"Speaking of you, Alistar. Inside the castle. Now!" Elzibeth growled, as she watched Adriana run back inside.

Alistar coughed again. "Richter, would you be kind enough to take Marcus through more training on the rifle today? I have a feeling Elle is going to want me on my back for a while."

He dodged a backhanded smack from Elzibeth and grinned. "Mister Kain, you have thirty seconds before I drag you into that bedroom!"

"Yes ma'am!" Alistar said with a snappy salute. He moved quickly into the castle, leaving Elzibeth standing in the courtyard with the others.

"Most days I want to kiss him." She rolled her eyes.

"And other days you want to bite him?" Julian joked.

"Yes... That. Exactly that," Elzibeth muttered as she followed Alistar inside.

Behind her Richter began teaching Marcus the finer points of using a rifle.

~

Alistar was in his room taking off his shirt As Elzibeth strode in.

"That was stupid! You were stupid! You could have died!" Elzibeth's eyes flashed as she slammed the door.

"Oh come on Elle, you know I was gonna try it myself at some point. Besides, if I didn't step in the way, Adriana would be dead right now, and even you can't bring someone back from having their head blown off!"

"What if the undersuit did not work?!" Elzibeth yelled, getting right up in his face.

"Well then I guess you would have had to turn me! It's my fucking job to protect you and everyone else in this damn castle!"

"You... I..." Elzibeth felt flustered for maybe only the fifth time in her life. She fell silent for over a minute. "Is that all we are to you? A job?" she whispered, closing her eyes.

Alistar wrapped his arms around her from behind, pulling her close. When he next spoke, his voice was quiet. "No. You are my reason for living. When you first encountered me, I was looking for a way to die. I had nothing left to live for. I tried Elle; I tried. That scar on my right arm, the one running down the inside from elbow to wrist. That wasn't a vampire, werewolf, or a thug with a knife. That was me in my darkest hour."

Elzibeth traced her fingers down the long ugly scar. "I knew as much when I heard the songs after I took your player, and I vowed to never let you die. You scared me out there in the courtyard tonight."

"I know, and I'm sorry for that. But it was not the first time I was that close to death, and it probably won't be the last. This world is full of danger and death, and she follows me wherever I go." Alistar released her.

Elzibeth turned in his grip. "Promise me you won't die?"

"I can't do that Elle, You know that. But I promise you I'll always do my best to come back to you. The good news is you're pretty good at healing me from whatever life throws at me," Alistar said softly, looking into her eyes.

Leaning in Elzibeth kissed him deeply, biting her tongue as she did so, giving him a bit of her blood. When they broke the kiss, he swallowed automatically, then sat on the bed feeling his ribs knit and the bruises fade.

"For you, I'll fight."

52

One week later found Alistar in Japan standing in front of Kenji Miyamoto. "Miyamoto Sama, Konichiwa." Alistar said bowing low. Dressed in a black suit with red shirt and black tie, Miyamoto sat upon a throne made of polished blackened wood. Red crushed velvet made up the cushions. Behind him hung red banners marked with a chrysanthemum, the Japanese imperial seal..

"Gurandokuīn no gādian e no go aisatsu."

"Please correct me if I am wrong, Miyamoto Sama, but I believe you just said, 'Greetings to you protector of the grand queen' Am I correct?"

"Hai," Miyamoto said, inclining his head. "However, for your sake, we will continue all conversations in English."

"I appreciate that. My Japanese is a bit… incomplete."

Miyamoto made his way down the steps leading from his throne and shook Alistar's hand. "Come. I called you here to show you all I have done for the humans of Japan so far, and to ask for your advice on certain matters."

Alistar followed Miyamoto through the massive

mansion in Osaka. Guards stood at every hallway dressed in black armored uniforms with red accents, looking like modern day samurai. "Master Miyamoto, I have prepared the room for Lord Kain as requested," a healthy manservant wearing a suit said, bowing.

"Excellent. Thank you, Shinji," The servant bowed and turned to leave.

"Wait. Shinji, is it? How does Lord Miyamoto treat you and the other servants?"

Shinji glanced at Miyamoto. "Tell him the truth, Shinji,"

"He treats us well, Lord Kain. A month ago, I was a man on the street, homeless and without purpose. Master Miyamoto found me and instead of killing me, offered me a job and a position in his household. He has done so for many of the less fortunate," Shinji said, then bowed low to Alistar.

"And does he and his kind feed off you and the other servants?" Alistar motioned for the man to walk with them.

"No. Every kyūketsuki or vampire as you call them, including Lord Miyamoto derives sustenance from the blood banks they own."

"I'm impressed," Alistar said.

"Any rogues are swiftly dealt with harshly." Alistar's attention was drawn back to Miyamoto. "There are clubs where my kind can drink from willing humans and I, myself have made use of such facilities. The willing participants are always well compensated. Some even make half of their living off being willing donors."

"Lord Miyamoto has set up work education programs, schools, hospitals. Our medical system was almost back to pre-war status but under the watch and care of the *Kyūketsuki* like Lord Miyamoto, it has grown considerably. We have even captured a few Hunters."

At this last statement, a look of annoyance crossed Miyamoto's face, and Shinji bowed, taking notice of his master.. "Forgive me, My Lord. I speak too much."

Miyamoto waved the man's apology away. "I would have shown him that soon enough, Shinji. Worry not."

"You captured an entire team?"

"Hai. Four lower-level ones came to Japan though they will not tell us why."

Alistar's gaze flickered between the two men. "And where are they right now?"

"Just down this hall. They have tried escaping more than once but my men are well trained and easily subdue them each time. None of them have been harmed other than minor injuries incurred during the initial capture and each time they try to escape. My people tend to their wounds and put them back into their room. One of them is the reason I called you here. He has been granted certain liberties such as being allowed to walk the grounds with an escort but he never tries to escape. He seems to have honor. His name is Vance."

"I'd like to see them." At Alistar's request Miyamoto pointed to a door ten feet away. Nodding, Alistar removed all his weapons, handing them to Shinji.

"Will you not need those?"

"No. I'll be fine."

"And where is your famous handgun?" Miyamoto asked, noticing the lack of the weapon among Allstar's things.

"Lost it... saving Lydia's ass. As far as I know, it's at the bottom of a very cold river," Alistar grumbled.

"I heard about that incident. It would seem your actions changed the white witch's opinion of humans." Miyamoto smiled.

"Yeah, well, one step at a time and all that. But I did love that gun." Alistar sighed. "Okay, here I go."

"Good luck," Miyamoto said as Alistar stepped through the door. It closed behind him, leaving him in an antechamber.

"Stand still for scanning," a voice issued from a speaker in the ceiling. Alistar did as told and a few moments later, the voice spoke again. "You're clean." The inner doors opened and he stepped inside.

The attack came from the left as a woman launched herself at him. Ducking, he flipped her over his back and onto the nearby bed. Then a man to his right threw a haymaker. Alistar caught his fist and squeezed hard, dropping the man to his knees.

The room's other two occupants stayed where they were sitting on their beds. "If we can dispense with the greetings, I've come to talk." He glowered at the four Hunters in the room as his attackers moved back with the other two.

"Talk, and why would we talk to a blood sucker such as yourself?" the woman snapped.

"Me? vampire? Hardly. I'm as human as the rest of you." Alistar replied, looking around the room. It was sparsely furnished with four very comfortable-looking beds, and a utilitarian metal table with four chairs. The floor was black marble and the walls painted gray.

"With reflexes such as that, I'd warrant not." One of the Hunters sitting down stated.

Alistar pulled down his glove, showing the mark on his wrist.

"Well fuck me. It's a rescue. About fucking time!"

"Not quite. I'm retired. I don't hunt anymore," Alistar remarked, amused at the woman's words.

"Bullshit. Hunters don't stop hunting until they're dead." The man who had attacked him stated, his voice dripping with disdain. Alistar grabbed a chair and dragged it over to the wall next to the door where he sat.

"The church would like you to think that. The truth is many Hunters walk off the job to simpler lives."

"Yeah, sure, but not one of your rank. Lifers like you don't just walk!" the woman snapped again sullenly.

"They do if the church burns their sister at the stake for being a witch instead of helping her develop her powers to become a Seeker." Alistar's voice was flat and devoid of emotion.

"Fuck... You're him, aren't you? You're Alistar Kain, the Traitor." The woman said. Her eyes widened and she shrank away from him, almost seeming like a smaller version of herself, acting like a prey animal not wishing to be noticed by a predator.

53

A listar let a moment of silence pass as the Hunters looked at each other.

"So that's it; you've come to kill us then, do your master's dirty work?" Alistar wondered if this woman was the leader of the group.

Alistar smiled at her stupidity. "I have no master, and IF the vampire outside this room wanted you dead, he wouldn't need me to do the job for him. No, I'm here for an entirely different reason."

The Hunters all sat forward except for one sitting cross-legged on his bunk and seems to be meditating. "Oh? And just what would that reason be?" the woman asked.

"Isn't it obvious, Caroline? He came to make us an offer." The meditating Hunter uncrossed his legs and opened his eyes.

"Got it in one. Very observant, Mister…?"

"Vance. You can call me Vance," the man stated, standing before sitting at the small metal table to play chess by himself.

"Ah, so you're the one with the right to walk around." Vance nodded.

"I am. Since I've put up no resistance or made any attempt to escape, Miyamoto offered me more freedom in exchange for my word that I wouldn't try anything. For a vampire, he seems to have honor and dignity and despite the attempts of the others to escape, he's surprisingly continued to do so."

Alistar rubbed his chin. "That's because he IS a being of honor. Tell me, when you arrived here, what did you see out in the city, Vance?"

Vance paused in a move. "I saw.. I saw people happy, and healthy. I saw better infrastructure than people have back in the States. Are you saying that's his doing?" Vance moved a knight to its position on the board. He looked up at Alistar. "Do you play?"

"No, I'm a checkers man myself. And, yes, that is what Miyamoto's doing, at my suggestion."

Vance cleared the board and pulled out a set of checkers. "Bullshit," Carline said. "Vampires don't take advice from humans!"

Walking over, Alistar sat opposite Vance and began to play. "They do when the human in question happens to be the suitor of their queen." He let that little fact settle in as he moved his first piece, watching for Vance's moves.

"You're the suck boy of the queen of—" Alistar's gaze flickered to her and she quieted.

"I'm thirsty. Is anyone else thirsty?" he asked, repositioning his next piece. He did not wait for a reply, instead glanced over to the door. "Can we get some drinks in here, please, for these fine folks and myself?" He turned back to his game. "I'm not her suck boy. I'm her boyfriend. While she *has* drank my blood when I've offered it, she hasn't bitten me without my permission, and hasn't tried to turn me. She doesn't even drink human blood unless she's attacked first and she must do so to survive." Alistar followed Vance's move with his own.

"Why does she keep you around then? The only purpose of a human to vampires is food or slavery." Caroline snapped again as Shinji tentatively carried a platter weighed down with teacups and a teapot. He served Alistar first, then Vance, leaving the pot and the other cups on the table, not wishing to approach the others.

"Thank you, Shinji." Alistar said with a nod before looking over at Caroline as he picked up his cup and took a sip. "And who told you that? The church? Have you actually explored the world without being on their leash with them telling you what to do and how to think? Tell me, Caroline, how have you been treated here? And by that I mean, I know you're held in this room against your will, but have you been fed on, have you been forced to work? Because where I'm sitting, this room is pretty nice. Certainly better than the Hunter barracks and their rickety cots and threadbare sheets. That's unless things have changed back home and conditions have gotten better?"

Caroline remained silent as did everyone else as Vance moved. "King me."

Alistar looked down. "*Mmm.*" He placed another piece on top of the one along the board's edge. "I'll take your silence as a no. It's true that some vampires are ravenous monsters who indiscriminately prey on the local population, but for the most part, I've found they're just like us. They want to live, and they'll do what's needed to ensure their survival... Including taking care of everyone around them." He pushed back his chair. "Let's go for a walk shall we?" Vance stood with him.

"I meant everyone. You all could use some time outside," Alistar looked at the camera in the corner of the room and waited for the inner doors to open. Alistar walked into the antechamber followed by Vance. Slowly the other three joined them. Miyamoto and sixteen guards waited in the hallway. The guards, armed and ready, surrounded them as an escort. Shinji handed Alistar back his equipment.

Alistar turned and faced the Hunters. "If any of you try anything, I'll be on you before these guards can even move, and I WILL put you down... hard." The look in his eyes told them he was not lying.

"Just what are you trying to do here, Kain?" Vance asked, stepping up next to Alistar and Miyamoto as they began down the hallway.

"I'm trying to foster peace. Supernaturals were here long before they were discovered and the church took power, and they'll be here long after the church falls."

"I was there, you know. Five years ago, when your sister burned. I saw how you fought. I saw the pain in your eyes," Vance whispered.

"And? What was your opinion on the situation?" Alistar asked as they stepped outside into the large Japanese courtyard garden with cherry blossom trees and koi ponds. Children played and people lounged in the moonlight. The guards moved away, giving the Hunters their distance.

Vance thought for a minute. "It didn't sit well with me. I have a little brother. Hell, everyone on this team has at least one family member." He looked at the others. "Don't deny that you've thought about what you'd do if one of your family was found out to be a witch, or was turned. You all know what the church would do." Their eyes locked in a shared understanding, someone finally verbalizing those unspoken words, which could result in punishment or death.

Alistar sat on a stone bench next to Miyamoto. "Go talk to these people. Ask them questions. Find out what life is like under the so-called vampire tyrant at my side. But do them no harm." He watched as the Hunters walked out into the courtyard doing just as he had asked.

A young boy ran up to him and smiled, revealing fangs. "And who might you be, little man?"

The boy bowed. "I am Ryu Miyamoto, Kainsama," he said before running off again. Alistar looked over at Miyamoto who chuckled.

"He is my grandson, Kainsan. He was born into this life as one of us."

"His parents?"

"Dead. His mother was human. She sadly did not survive his birth. She was one of my servants. After her death, his father went into the blackness of his mind and stepped out into the sunlight to join her. I now take care of Ryu in their stead. I try to raise him right, teach him to be respectful of the humans and other beings around him, so that one day he may reign as a fair and compassionate leader when my time passes."

"Well it seems you're doing a pretty good job." Alistar watched as the boy ran up to Caroline and tossed a ball at her. She caught it, threw it back and the two played catch for a bit.

After an hour the four Hunters came back to him.

"What have you all learned?" he asked softly.

Vance stepped forward. "Might I borrow a knife?"

Alistar slowly pulled a knife out and handed it hilt first to the Hunter, holding it and the man's eyes for a few seconds before letting go. The guards around them all tensed up. Vance cut into his wrist beside the tattoo and a small clink followed as the tracker fell to the flagstones. He passed the knife to the next Hunter, who in turn, passed it to the third, each one cutting out their tracking chip until it reached Caroline, who held it, unsure.

"Want me to do it?" Alistar asked. Caroline nodded

and he took the knife, digging it in with expert precision and soon her chip, too, was lying on the ground. Shinji stepped in and bandaged their wrists and then collected the trackers.

"So now what? You just expect us to join you on your crusade?" Caroline asked.

Alistar shook his head. "No, my war is just that, *my war*. It's my burden to bear, no one else's unless they want to. All I've done is opened your eyes to the truth. What you do with that truth is your decision. You can help, or you can disappear into the world, have families, live a life other than what the church has set for you."

"I think I'd like to sit out here for a while longer if that's okay?" Caroline asked. Miyamoto nodded and motioned for her to do so.

Vance sat next to Alistar. "We're young. Would this have been so easy if you had been talking to a group of level fours?"

"No. Admittedly not. By that rank, the indoctrination is pretty much ingrained, and only a tragedy like I experienced would give me the chance to open such eyes," Alistar remarked, watching as Caroline continued to play ball with young Ryu.

"Tell me, Alistar, what's your vampire like?" Vance asked.

"She's a kind, caring woman who took in a stray ex-hunter and helped him find his humanity again. She gave me a reason to live, a reason to fight. She—"

"Alistar! Hunters!" Elzibeth's telepathic cry echoed in his brain. "She's in trouble!" Alistar finished as he stood up suddenly.

54

"Good job little brother!" Julian yelled as Marcus managed to score a hit on Conrad with his wooden sword.

"Yeah, Marcus, good job!" Conrad said, returning the attack that Marcus actually blocked.

Both vampires paused. "Incoming!" Conrad shouted, diving to cover Marcus as an explosion rocked the castle. Arrows pelted the courtyard as both vampires picked up the boy and rushed him inside.

Elzibeth met them in the main hall. "What is going on?!" Conrad and Julian barricaded the doors with a heavy wooden beam. Another explosion rocked the castle.

"We're under attack Lady Elzibeth!" Conrad said as they grabbed shields off the walls.

"I can see that, but by whom?"

Just then Adriana ran down the hallway. "It's Hunters! I managed to get an old radio in the castle basement working. Their chatter is all across the airwaves!" Her voice quavered and was filled with fear.

"Conrad! Julian! Get Evelyn, Adriana, and Marcus

into the armory. God knows Alistar fortified that room most of all!" Elzibeth commanded.

Richter came running up just as the large glass window above the door shattered in and five Hunters dropped into the room. Richter was on them in an instant, showing over seven hundred years of skill and training. In less than a minute, all five were down with knives stuck in their necks.

"Mistress Tepes, we must flee!"

"No Richter, this is my castle, MY Home, and I will make them pay for every inch they destroy!" Elzibeth's eyes flashed and red took over, her fangs and nails lengthening.

Ten more Hunters rappelled into the room and opened fire with crossbows. "Go, Grand Lady!" Conrad yelled as he ran a Hunter through and ripped another's throat open with his talon-like nails.

Elzibeth didn't listen as she flashed across the room, a blur of speed and nails, eviscerating three Hunters on her own.

~

"Miyamoto, Elle is in trouble! Hunters are attacking the castle! I need a favor from you. Now!" Alistar rounded on Vance, grabbing the man by the front of his shirt. "What do you know of this?! Tell me now!"

"Nothing! I swear! We're all just level ones! You know they don't tell us anything at this rank!" Vance yelled back. Alistar dropped him and started pacing.

"Kainsan!" Alistar looked over at Miyamoto's sharp words. "Compose yourself! Then follow me."

~

As more Hunters arrived through the smashed window, the defending vampires and humans pushed down the hallway as the castle doors blew off their hinges.

Marcus arrived with an AK- 47 and started laying down fire, but even he was driven back by the hail of arrows, many of which Conrad and Julian's shields blocked.

"Go! To the armory!" Elzibeth yelled.

"Eveyln! She's upstairs!" Marcus yelled back.

"I will get her, Marcus! Go with Julian and Conrad!" When the boy hesitated, Conrad and Julian grabbed him by the arms and started dragging him down the hallway, still blocking arrows with their shields.

Elzibeth ran up the stairs of the north tower. Shouts and more explosions sounded from below as she burst into her room where Evelyn lay unconscious from a blow to the head. Two Hunters stood over the girl.

Elzibeth stiffened and dropped, writhing to the floor in pain as she felt electricity course through her body.

Alistar closed his eyes and drew in a long breath, centering himself. Both men then moved at a frantic pace back into the mansion. An elevator took them to a lower level where they stepped out into a large armory. Racks upon racks lined the walls, covered with swords and other weapons of warfare.

"Take what you need, *Kainsan*. I shall send out word to the other elders that their queen needs them and their forces. We shall all meet here."

Alistar shuffled through the weapons, picking out a Howa-type- twenty assault rifle, a second katana, and an assault vest. He shoved magazines of ammo into the pouches until he had two in each pocket. Vampires and humans alike dressed in the red and black of Miyamoto's colors streamed into the room around him, likewise gearing up for war. None of them spoke.

Looking over, Alistar saw an old M72 LAW, a light anti-tank weapon, on the wall and grabbed it. "I'm just gonna take this!" He growled. No one stopped him.

Taking the elevator back up he encountered a guard. "Kainsama, I am ordered to take you to High Lord Miyamoto." Alistar followed him to a single door which slid aside to reveal a war room out of the late 1900s.

Old electronics lined the walls, and centered across from the door an electronic map showed the world. Miyamoto stood in front of an old computer console, typing in a message and sending it out.

"Now we wait. It will take a few hours for them to get here," Miyamoto said solemnly.

"Elle may not have a few hours! I need transport to Castle Tepes now!"

"You will do the queen no good by rushing in, *Kainsan*." Miyamoto's voice remained calm.

Alistar closed his eyes and, then spinning, punched out a nearby computer monitor. Deep down he agreed with Miyamoto. He knew the Hunters wouldn't kill Elle. If they were assaulting the castle, they wanted to capture her, not kill. Still, if they took her and left, what did that mean for the others?

No, Conrad, and Julian would make sure Richter, Evelyn, Adriana, and Marcus got out even if they couldn't stop Elle from being taken. Alistar knew this because he had ordered them to do so before he had left on this trip should something happen while he was gone.

He sighed. "Sorry about the computer."

"We have more in storage. They are easy to replace."

"Is this the one?" a Hunter asked about Elzibeth as she writhed on the ground.

"Yes. That's her. Wrap her up," their leader replied as he dropped a device on the floor.

The Hunters wrapped Elzibeth in a fine mesh net stronger than rope and interlaced with silver. The silver burned her skin and she screamed in pain.

"What about the girl?" one of the Hunters asked their leader.

"Leave her." The leader looked down at Evelyn. "She is of no consequence. Probably just a slave."

~

Marcus fired between the shields of Conrad and Julian as the three continued backing down the hallway. Richter had been surrounded and killed by the swarm of Hunters, though he sold his life to stall them, letting the others get away.

Marcus ran out of ammo and went for a mag swap. A Hunter took careful aim and sent a bolt flying in his direction. Seeing it, Julian leapt in front of Marcus.

Marcus watched as time seemed to slow. The bolt hit Julian in the chest, right in the heart, a bolt meant for him. "NOOOOOOOO!!!!!" he screamed as Conrad pulled him into the armory, and struggled to close the old single-person vault door, which someone had recovered from a bank. Three-inch-thick plate steel lined the walls at Alistar's request. Conrad knew that once that door closed, the Hunters had no chance at entry. Marcus screamed with rage and bolted through the gap of the closing door, two AK's in his hands.

"Marcus no!" Conrad shouted, but it didn't matter. The door closed and the latches slammed shut. Conrad heard full automatic gunfire, and the screams of rage from Marcus.

~

Eleven hours later, three vampires strode into the halls of Miyamoto's mansion.

"Ishani of the Desert Sands answers the call of the *raksha karanevaala!*" the Indian Raj said, bowing low to Alistar.

"Abdalla of the African Tribes answers the call of the protector of the queen!" the African warlord said, going down on one knee.

"Lydia of the North answers the call of the suitor of the queen!"

55

"I put your name on the summons, *Kainsan*," Miyamoto said. "We follow you, for as the suitor to our queen, you are her right hand. Your word is her law."

"This is bullshit. You follow a human. Vampires don't bow to humans," Thomas said, but Lydia, grabbed him by the neck with lightning speed. "You will bow to, Lord Kain, Thomas, or I will end you here and now! You may not like him, but you WILL respect him." she hissed before smiling at Alistar.

Thomas slowly lowered to one knee. "Rise, all of you," Alistar said and the four vampires stood.

"What is the situation, Alistar?" Lydia asked.

"Hunters have attacked Castle Tepes, just like they attempted to do to you. Fuckers waited until I was gone, Lyd. They took my girl. I need your help getting her back. I would owe you all favors if you help me." He marched over to Thomas, ensuring the vampire understood the situation. "Even one to you, Thomas, much as it pains me to say. Please."

Thomas broke eye contact with Alistar's intense gaze.

"That won't be necessary, Kain. I'm beholden to Lydia, and therefore to our queen. But if you're offering, I wish for a rematch when this is all said and done."

"Then it shall be so."

"Lord Alistar, we each have brought the five strongest warriors we have," Lydia said.

"Miyamotosama, please tell me you have a mode of transport that is swift."

"*Hai*. I have an experimental CX-27 cargo transport in my fleet. It was the only one ever invented before the war. It can fly at Mach one."

"Lord Miyamoto, why not use the corridors we just came through?" Lydia asked.

Alistar raised an eyebrow at her question.

"We do not know if Great Lady Tepes kept the mirror intact on her end. If that is the case, we would all die."

"Mirror? What do these mirrors look like?" Alistar asked.

"Large, inlaid with gold leaf. Probably fifteen feet tall by eight feet wide. Kinda gaudy actually," Lydia replied. Alistar grinned at her description.

"Oh, she has one. I saw it in a back room in the castle's lower levels one day. It's covered by a drop cloth. The only question being: Is it still intact?"

Lydia grabbed his hand and whirled. "This way. Now." They ran down the corridors to a room with a single large mirror exactly how Lydia had described.

Placing her hand on the mirror, Lydia concentrated. "Castle Tepes," She muttered. The mirror shifted and rippled but stayed dark. "I am sorry, Alistar, but it appears the mirror on her end has been shattered." Lydia hung her head.

Alistar sighed, but then after a moment noticed a ripple down in the mirror's lower corner. "No. It hasn't. It's just still covered. Look!"

Lydia too notices the ripple. "Then there is hope."

"How fast—"

"Less than an hour to travel through the corridors, then an hour of rest. The corridors are useful, but they drain the energy of any being that passes through them," Lydia replied as the other vampires entered the room.

"Then let's do it. We've already lost enough time."

"*Kainsan*, there is something you should know about the corridors. They have a far worse reaction on humans than they do on our kind," Miyamoto said.

"What kind of reactions?"

"For every hour spent within them, you will age a year. The effect is less so on our kind, but still, that is why we don't normally use them. Only Great Lord Dracula himself could use them without ill effect, seeing as how he invented them."

"No fucks given. I have to save her," Alistar whispered, stepping through the mirror. His world shifted and twisted and he felt like he would puke. Then a moment later, as if no time had passed, he found himself covered by the large drop cloth and brushing it aside. Falling to his knees, he retched violently, almost puking as he reached behind him and pulled down the drop cloth the rest of the way. Slowly one by one, the four elders wandered into the dark room.

Unable to see very well, Alistar felt a hand on his arm. "I have you Alistar. Give it a moment; the feeling will pass." Lydia's voice came from one side and as his vision adapted to the darkness, he barely saw her face next to his.

"Bring the troops," he growled before doubling over and puking. With an empty stomach he stood on shaky legs. "Let's not do that again any time soon."

Someone pressed a bottle of water to his lips and he drank deeply, then checked his watch. It was still night out according to the device. The troops of the four vampire lords poured through the mirror. The vampires remained relatively unaffected, but the human guardians fell to their knees, puking.

"Fan out, search the place," Alistar said as he walked to the door and pushed on it. It remained closed.

"Allow me, protector." Abdalla pushed him aside. Grabbing the door, he flexed his vampiric muscles and pulled. The door creaked and groaned, and with the wrenching squeal of metal, he pulled the door and frame from the wall. "After you."

"Thanks." Alistar stood in one of the lower level corridors. Smoke and dust hung in the air but Alistar knew where to go. Standing in front of the armory door, he grasped his knife and used the hilt to rap the first five notes of "Shave and a Haircut." He was rewarded by the last two knocks. Clanking sounded as the latches were thrown back, revealing Conrad and, behind him, Adriana.

"Mister Alistar! The Hunters are after Miss Elle! I think they took her!" Adriana cried, running into his arms.

"I know, Adriana. I know. I'm gonna get her back." He met Conrad's eyes. "Who's still alive?"

"Adriana and me. Richter is dead. He fought to the last. Julian gave his life for Marcus," Conrad said, a pained look on his face.

"And Marcus?" Alistar asked softly.

"He ran out the door as I was closing it, carrying two rifles. The time lock engaged and, after that, all I heard was gunfire and then silence."

Alistar pivoted at the vampire's words and headed down the corridor. "Marcus! Marcus!" Up ahead he heard sobbing and, turning the corner, he found Marcus cradling the body of Julian. Next to him Evelyn knelt, her arms wrapped around him, a large bruise on her forehead.

Around them lay the bodies of ten Hunters, all shot in the chest.

"Alistar, he needs blood!" Marcus cried out seeing him. Alistar went to a knee next to the boy and placed a hand onto his shoulder. "It's too late, kid. He's been dead too long. I'm sorry."

56

"Did… did Marcus do this?" Lydia asked, taken aback. Alistar shifted his feet.

"Yeah. Julian gave his life for him." He looked at the ground, his heart breaking for the man on the floor.

"They took my brother," Marcus said from where he sat with a look of haunted anger. "I made them pay. Every single one of them." His words drew a pained expression from Alistar.

Lydia attempted to help but Alistar placed a hand on her shoulder. "Not now, Lyd. He needs time."

Lydia nodded. "The rest of the place is clear, but it's in bad shape. The Hunters used some sort of cannon to bombard the castle. We also found another survivor."

Like a ghost, Richter appeared in the hallway and Marcus blinked in confusion. "I saw you fall. You died!"

"Contrary to popular belief, rumors of my demise are highly overrated," Richter said grimly. "The Hunters headed south, I assume to that new facility in Turkey. They had motorcycles and off-road vehicles. There's at least eighty of them."

Alistar sighed. "Richter, we need transport that will carry twenty-six."

"Twenty-seven. I'm going with you," Marcus growled, struggling to his feet.

"The fuck you are, kid." Alistar whipped around. Marcus glared defiantly at him. "I love you like a son, but I will knock your ass out if I have to and tie you to a bed. Evelyn needs you right now. You're all she's got. You both are staying here under guard. Go on, argue with me. I dare you." Alistar's own glare made Marcus's head lower.

"Yes sir." Alistar swept him into a hug. "Marcus, this isn't a situation of defense anymore. I'm going to war. That's not something I want you to be a part of."

"Alistar?"

"Yeah?"

"Make them pay for me then," Marcus cried, burying his face in Alistar's shirt with a sob.

"Oh you bet I will. Today, the Hunters become the hunted." Some of Miyamoto's human servants entered the hallway and started tending to Evelyn.

"I will have Evelyn and Marcus taken to my mansion, *Kainsan*. All of you can stay there until such time as you rebuild this place," Miyamoto said from behind them.

"Good. I need a few items from my armory before we go." Alistar let go of Marcus, allowing the servants to tend to the boy. Richter and Lydia followed at his side.

"How the fuck did you survive, old man? Both Marcus and Conrad saw you fall. And don't give me any of your *just lucky* bullshit!"

"Lord Tepes made me immortal using alchemy. If I die, I come back to life a few minutes later with all my wounds healed," Richter replied before heading past the armory and down another hallway.

"Huh. I have inside me the blood of kings," Alistar

murmured, quoting a line from an old movie he had once seen. Stepping into the armory, he opened a small black case. Inside contained the vials of serum he had collected from the Hunters he had killed. Lydia drew in a sharp breath.

"You can't be serious Alistar. You told me what this stuff does to you. You can't be considering this!"

Alistar glared at her. "Eighty Hunters, Lydia! Eighty! We can't take on that many in a fortified location without an edge!" His glare made her take a step back. Alistar scooped up three vials and pocketed them.

"Through my contacts," Richter began. "I have acquired the use of an old Russian Mil Mi-26 cargo helicopter. It will be here within the hour with pilots provided."

"Excellent. Everyone rest up. When that chopper arrives, we move out." Alistar strode out of the armory and up the stairs to the north tower, entering Elzibeth's bedroom. Sitting on the foot of the bed, he examined himself in the wall's small mirror. His hair had taken on more gray thanks to the trip through the corridors.

A knock at the door made him look up to find Lydia standing there. She walked inside without an invitation and sat next to him. "Are you sure you want to do this?"

"What? Rescue Elle? What kind of question is that, Lyd?"

Lydia touched the pouch that held the serum. "No, I mean this."

Alistar closed his eyes. "I have to. Whatever the risk, I'll take it... for her." He pulled out a vial and saw the glowing blue liquid, then slid it back in the pouch.

"I understand." They sat quietly for a while. "You know that Hunter we captured back at the tower is doing rather well. Although I admit, he's almost as infuriating as you."

"Shit. I didn't think anyone could be an asshole of my level."

"Not quite, but there are some days I just want to bite him and put him out of my misery."

"Then why don't you?"

"I find myself rather liking him and want to keep him around a while longer." Lydia smiled.

Alistar laughed. "I think Elle and her way of picking up strays has rubbed off on you, Lyd."

"Perhaps it has, Alistar. Perhaps it has. Or I may just be saving him for a midnight snack." Lydia patted his leg. "Plus, unlike you, he actually sleeps in my bed."

Alistar snorted in reply. "Typical male. Thinking with the lower brain every time."

"That would imply you men have one to begin with," Lydia joked.

"I'll have you know I have a brain… I just don't use it all the time. Thank you very much."

"I think you use yours more than you care to admit. You've brought great changes to our world." She wandered over to the window as her vampiric hearing picked up the sounds of a helicopter.

"Did the great Lydia of the North just give this human a compliment?" Alistar asked, looking at her.

"Indeed, I did… human, Don't let it go to your head, though. I wouldn't want you to get a swollen ego."

Alistar's hearing finally picked up what she heard. "This might actually be the beginning of a beautiful friendship, Lyd."

Lydia snorted. "Don't take it that far, Alistar. I just have more respect for you now than I did when we first met. Now get ready. It's time."

57

A few minutes later, Alistar sat in the helicopter surrounded by vampire soldiers. Next to him sat Lydia and the other three elders.

Lydia nudged him. "What are you thinking about, Alistar?"

Alistar's gaze flickered over to her, then back down to the floor. "The people I'm about to kill. What they might be doing to Elle. How many innocents might be caught in the middle. How many of us will make it back alive. If I'll lose control down there. Those sort of things," He said, rolling a vial of Serum around in one hand.

Lydia blinked in surprise. "Well considering there's only two humans here, I would think that two will make it back alive," she joked. When the joke fell flat, she tapped the vial of Serum in his hands lightly with a fingernail. "Well, do you have to use that right away?"

"There's at least eighty Hunters down in that facility, Lyd. You KNOW the answer to that question. They get ONE chance to give her up. After that, any that get in my way die."

"Except for the Seekers, right Mister Alistar?" Adriana asked from a few seats away.

"What? Oh… yes, except for the Seekers."

"Five minutes to drop." The pilot's voice came across the intercom and Alistar stood, shrugging into a parachute.

"*Kainsan*. A gift for you," Miyamoto said, holding out a heavily inlaid wooden box. Opening it, Alistar found twin high-tech .45 pistols.

"I had them custom-made as a gift for you after seeing your plan become so successful. You will find they fire much faster than your old one, which may serve you well in this coming battle."

"Umm, thank you Miyamotosama. And thank you for taking care of Evelyn and Marcus." Alistar said, bowing slightly.

Miyamoto held out a set of twin leg holsters with pouches for three magazines each. "Well, shoot, I have my hands full. Lydia, would you?"

Lydia's eyes closed to slits and one side of her mouth tilted upward in a wicked smile. "My pleasure." She buckled the holsters around his legs and attached them to his belt, copping a feel in the process, and then slapped his ass.

"That was your one freebie, Lydia. Enjoy it." Lydia just grinned at him flashing her fangs.

"One last thing, *Kainsan*." Miyamoto held out an ear piece. Alistar took it. Every vampire in the chopper put one in as well and he heard, "Squad one check, Squad two check. Squad three check, Squad four check."

"Ancients check," the elders said before turning to him.

After a moment of thought, he spoke. "Ghost check," Miyamoto nods.

A red light came on inside the chopper and the door

man opened the back ramp. Alistar dove out into the cool night air, dropping at a rapid pace. The ground rushed up and he pulled the ripcord at the last second. The chute fully opened at the right moment to cushion his fall, allowing him to roll with it.

He cut away the chute and dropped it behind him as he strode toward the Hunter base. Popping the top off a serum vial, and sliding it into an injector, he slammed the needle into his upper left arm. A spotlight hit him. "Halt! State your business!" a guard's voice sounded out across the wasted tundra.

"I'm Alistar Kain. I've come for my vampire! You have two minutes to bring her out, or I won't regret my next actions!" His voice rang clearly in the quiet night.

Laughter rang out from the wall. After a moment, the large gate opened and four hunters walked toward him with crossbows pointed at his chest. Their leader eyed him. "You are but one man. What can you do alone? Even if you were *the traitor* you couldn't possibly take all of us. And you don't even look like him."

"Yeah, I heard he was taller," another Hunter said.

"Alistar checked his watch. "Ten seconds, boys."

"Yeah, big man? What happens in ten seconds?" a third Hunter asked.

The watch beeped and Alistar looked up, his eyes glowing blue. "Death," he says simply. He moved faster than the wind and the Hunters tumbled to the ground in less than a second with their throats slashed so deeply that their heads looked like Pez dispensers.

The elders fluttered to the ground near him as their subordinates made a circle, leaving the elders in the middle, none of them having needed the parachute like him.

Lydia handed him the M79 Law and he sighted it at the doors. There was no joke, no witty remark, he just silently pushed the button, a look of sad determination on his face. The rocket roared across the space, and blew one of the doors off its hinges. When an alarm began to wail the vampire soldiers ran toward the fortress. Even though they ran fast, Alistar ran faster still, weaving in and out among them as he closed in on the entrance.

The elders watched him in surprise.

"I've seen him fight, been at his side, but never before have I seen him like this," Lydia remarked in amazement.

"That man is a force of nature," Miyamoto said beside her. "and the heavens help anyone who gets in his way."

Hunters rushed out of the gates to man the walls. Hundreds of crossbow bolts rained down among the vampire forces from automatic crossbows, and a heavy machine gun opened fire from up on the wall.

Alistar stopped, taking aim with his rifle, and fired, sending tracer rounds back towards the Hunters manning the heavy machine gun. They fell, but two more quickly took their place. Alistar aimed at the gun itself and held down the trigger, controlling the rifle with strength born of the serum he had injected. In seconds, only an unusable wreck remained of the gun emplacement.

When the Howe 20 jammed, Alistar worked to remove the old brass in the firing chamber. A bolt hit him in the chest, but his undersuit protected him.

"Fuck!" he cursed, throwing the rifle and running into the compound.

Vampires fought Hunters all around him. Some had their hearts run through, while others had limbs cut off in flashes of blades and claws. A group of fifteen Hunters ran up and took aim, firing crossbows at a furious pace. Vampires fell in the volley of bolts.

Pulling his katanas, Alistar weaved among them, and as he passed by, bodies dropped to the ground as he cleared the way for the others.

More Hunters rained bolts down from the walls even as vampire forces attacked them, and throats were slashed open, hearts ripped out. Still, Alistar knew the Hunters led the battle. Even though they had greater skill, there was only so much could be said for that, and eventually numbers would win out if he didn't step up his game.

"No!" he growled, pulling out his second vial of serum. Sliding it into the injector, he emptied it into his body. Power rushed through him, and time seemed to stand still.

He leaped up to the wall and ran along it, his blade bringing death where he went. The Hunters had less than a second to register his presence, and some even took a half step before their heads rolled from their shoulders as he passed by.

Six Hunters beset Lydia. She held her own but barely. Alistar leapt, landing in front of her, his blades flashing as he spun and kicked. One hunter dropped back losing an arm, another had his chest crushed in by a spinning side kick and then thrown across the courtyard. The third and fourth had their necks cut as he continued to spin. They bled out as they fell, their life force draining to seep into the soil between the paving stones. The last two turned to run but they didn't get far. Dropping his katanas, he picked up the first man, slamming him down across his knee. Bones cracked in the man's back breaking it and Alistar threw him away like how someone might casually toss a wadded-up piece of paper. Grabbing the other one by the back of his vest, he threw him to Lydia, her fangs sinking into the Hunters neck, healing the wounds she had incurred.

58

The Hunters retreated from the open courtyard, heading into the main building and giving the vampires a brief respite. Glowing blue eyes met anyone who dared to look at Alistar. Only fifteen vampires remained, including the elders.

His breath came out hard and heavy as the blood pulsed in his ears. He sunk to one knee for a moment.

"*Kainsan*, are you all right?" Miyamoto asked.

"I'll be fine. Just need... a moment," Alistar responded, his head swimming. Standing back up he marched towards the main doors of the Hunter's headquarters. Steam rose from his body as his metabolism jumped into overdrive from the effects of the serum. Blue glowing veins popped out all over his face and neck.

"I said... give me back my vampire!" He yelled, kicking the doors. They held fast. "Fine. You want to play it that way? Then so be it."

Pulling out the last vial of serum he loaded it into the injector. "Look at you, Alistar! Look at what the serum is doing to you!" Lydia said, her voice filled with concern.

She placed her hand on his arm before taking it away.

He was burning hot to the touch. Sweat dripped down his flushed, red face.

Lydia grabbed for the injector in his hand, trying to stop him. "This one could kill you! Do you think Elle wants that?!"

"Lydia... Get. Out. Of. My. Way!"

"No! I won't let you throw your life away like this because it will kill Elle to lose you!" She went toe to toe with him, her face inches from his, eyes red and fangs out.

Alistar's gaze flickered to the side and in the blink of an eye his hand held a pistol. It barked three times and the Hunter preparing to shoot Lydia in the back, fell out of a window. Putting the pistol away, Alistar grabbed Lydia by the throat and threw her behind him as more bolts rained down. He used his body to block the shots but one arrow got through the mystical fabric, burying itself in his side. He snapped it off, leaving the head in his body and moved the door, slamming the last vial of serum into his arm.

Lydia watched as the vial's contents disappeared.

"Blow the fucking doors!" he commanded. Four vampires placed explosives on the hinges and detonated them. The doors pitched outward with a loud crash and lots of smoke.

"Fire!" a voice said up ahead and crossbow bolts pelted him. Using his arms to shield his head, Alistar rushed towards the Hunters. Reaching the first one, he snapped the man's neck one-handed. The next Hunter had his arm broken cleanly in two, the elbow bent in the opposite direction. The third, fourth and fifth Hunters all have their chests crushed in-ward by powerful blows. Reaching the last one, he seized the man's throat and pulled, ripping out his trachea.

Vampires streamed into the building around him, moving down hallways to do room-by-room searches. Adriana stepped up next to him, followed by her escort.

"Mister Alistar, according to maps of other compounds I have seen, the Seekers will be kept in the barracks room in the northwest corner."

Alistar nodded and signaled to her escort. "Go with her. Get them out any way you can. Some of them may fight in fear. Subdue them if you must but don't kill them or drink from them." The vampires started to move. "Do not let the Lore-Keeper die, or Elzibeth will be most displeased."

The five vampires darted off with Adriana. "How many have we killed?" Alistar asked Lydia, waiting beside him.

"Roughly fifty out in the courtyard, plus the six here, so fifty six, give or take two."

Halfway down the hallway, Alistar arms himself with his pistols. A Hunter steps out into the corridor and his head explodes. The body slumps against the wall. Whirling around Alistar finds himself pointing a pistol at Lydia.

"Where do you think you're going?"

"With you. You'll have to kill me to stop me," Lydia replied, her eyes flashing in defiance.

Alistar lowered the pistol, then brought it back up, shooting the Hunter behind him without looking. "Fine."

"Alistar!" The weak mental cry of Elzibeth reached his mind. Lydia's eyes grew wide, signaling that she, too, had heard it.

Alistar tugged a map from his back pocket. Adriana had crudely drawn it up, but everything was mostly in its place. "Holding cells are this way." Down other hall-ways, Vampires and Hunters killed each other to the sounds of gunfire and the *twangs* of crossbows.

"When you are done with your individual missions, clear out. I'll take it from here," Alistar said over the radio and received confirmations.

~

Elzibeth, her mouth gagged, struggled weakly against the titanium chains coated in silver that bound her to the small cell's wall. They had burned her wrists and tears streamed down her cheeks, soaking the gag in blood.

She opened her eyes as an explosion rocked the building and men shouted as gunfire erupted somewhere in the building beyond her cell. *"Alistar!"* she cried weakly, sending out the call along their mental connection.

More gunfire erupted, getting closer with each passing moment until finally a thud hit the door. A moment later the door creaked open and a man entered, his eyes glowing vivid blue. Blue glowing veins pulsed along his sweat-covered face and neck. For a second she felt fear until he stepped into the almost non-existent light of the cell revealing the face of her beloved.

"Hey there, gorgeous. You look a little tied up at the moment." He smiled that boyish smile and began untying the gag from her mouth. His breath hitched and he let loose a moan when his lips met hers. Her teeth grazed his bottom lip but she didn't draw blood. "Save that for the bedroom, princess." He placed his forehead against hers.

Backing away, he glared at the chains that bound her. "Lydia, key." He held up his hand and Lydia placed a key into it, which she had gotten off the door guard outside. Unlocking the chains he caught Elzibeth.

"Alistar, I need blood." Lydia dragged the door guard inside.

"Feed, My Queen. Your suitor needs all his own blood inside his body for now."

59

Elzibeth took a minute to feed, quickly draining the body of its entire supply of blood. Standing she touched Alistar's face, feeling the heat emanating from it. "Alistar, what have you done?"

"What I must, Elle. And my work is not done yet," Alistar replied as he turned away from her, letting her hand slide from his cheek. Elzibeth glanced over at Lydia with a worried expression.

"We will talk about this when we get out of here, Lydia. You can be assured of that," Elzibeth said.

Lydia bowed her head. "Yes, My Queen." Both vampires followed Alistar out of the cell. Surprise filled them when they realized he did not head for the entrance, instead going up the stairs to the second level. He stumbled but caught himself.

Not now! Just a little longer. Destroy this place and get them out of here. Then you can die, Alistar, he thought to himself, forgetting to block his thoughts from Elzibeth.

"What did he do Lydia?

"He took three serum vials. And… I think it's killing him. All he could think about was saving you. He told me what the serum does, Elle. It makes a Hunter as fast and as strong as one of us. But in a rare few such as him, it's also addictive and dangerous," Lydia whispered.

Elzibeth's eyebrows disappeared into her hairline. She rushed up the stairs after Alistar, who disappeared down a hallway, followed closely by Lydia.

The sounds of battle died down as the teams cleared out of the fortress.

Alistar stumbled again and punched the wall, his vision swimming. Pulling himself to his feet, he leaned against the wall and headed toward a door marked *Bishop Clarendon*. A Hunter stepped out of an office up ahead and Alistar's hand shook when he raised his gun and fired. Three bullets stitched holes across the man's chest.

He limped past the dead body, blood pooling around it.

Crashing through the bishop's office door, he found the man facing him with a cross in his hand.

"Back foul creature of the night!" the bishop screamed in terror. Alistar staggered towards the desk, leaning on it with one hand. "I said back!"

Alistar drew himself up to his full height, summoning his last reserves of inner strength. "Got yourself a little problem there, holy boy. I'm as human as you are." He grasped the man by the front of his vestments, pulling him across the desk.

His fist connected with the man's face but he had pulled it enough so he didn't kill him. He hit him again and again and again, over and over as his rage built, until only a blood ruin remained of the man's face. "Leave my friends alone! Leave my FAMILY alone! LEAVE.. MY... VAMPIRE... ALONE!" The final punch snapped the man's head around, breaking his neck.

Alistar slumped against the desk, his head pounding

and vision swimming further as he passed in and out of consciousness.

Elzibeth and Lydia entered the office and Elzibeth rushed to Alistar's side. "My love. What have you done?"

"Safe... now..." Alistar said before his breathing stopped. He dropped flat to the floor, eyes rolling back into his head, his body shaking.

"Lydia!" Elzibeth cried, unsure of how to help him. Lydia held him down. After a moment his seizing stopped and his breathing returned.

The scrape of a boot signaled someone had entered and they saw a grizzled man with many facial scars standing in the doorway. In his right hand was a bright shining blade, and in his left was a pistol much like the one Alistar used to carry.

"You will not take him!" Elzibeth hissed and tugged Alistar closer, holding him protectively. Lydia crouched on all fours, her fangs exposed, ready to attack.

"Interesting. And why would one of your kind protect one of mine?" the man asked, his voice gruff and gravelly. The two vampires saw the mark of a level-five hunter on his wrist.

"I... I love him," Elzibeth answered back automatically. The man paused for a second, pondering the situation, then put his pistol away and pulled out a small vial containing black, purplish liquid. He tossed it to Elzibeth.

"If you love him, you will give him that immediately. Inject it directly into his heart."

"What is it?" Lydia asked.

"Essence of Nightshade," the man replied as his steely gaze flickered to her.

"That will kill him!" Elzibeth exclaimed.

"Normally, yes, but in someone who's undergoing serum addiction and withdrawal, it will neutralize the serum and allow them to detox. Now if you truly love him, you WILL give him that injection."

Elzibeth looked at the vial in her hand then pulled the injector from Alistar's vest pouch. Sliding the vial into it, she kissed Alistar's lips. "I'm sorry, my love." Then she slammed the needle into his chest and watched the liquid enter his body.

Slowly, the blue glow faded from the veins in his face and neck and his eyes appeared normal.

The Hunter turned away.

"Wait! Why would you help us?" Elzibeth asked.

"I'm not helping you; I'm helping him."

"Why?" Lydia asked. The man paused. Reaching into his pocket, he pulled out a bullet on a chain and tossed it to her. "I made a grave mistake in our past, and someone he loved died because of it. Maybe my actions tonight will atone for that misdeed. When he awakens, give him that, and tell him all debts are paid in full. When I see him again, and I WILL see him again, we are enemies."

He studied the two vampires and the man on the floor for a moment longer. "Wherever you are going, you will want to tie him to a bed. He's in for a rough two weeks or more, I reckon."

"How do you know that?" Lydia asked as she stood up.

"Because I've been through this once before with him." The man closed the door behind him. Lydia gasped.

"They killed the bishop and ran this way! Follow me!" Pounding feet moved past the door as people followed the man, but it remained closed

60

An hour later Elzibeth was sitting on Miyamoto's private plane headed back to Japan. Next to her Alistar lay strapped to a gurney. Lydia sat across from her. At the other end of the plane sat Miyamoto and Adriana. Alistar's head tossed back and forth, caught in the throes of some feverish nightmare.

Reaching over Elzibeth grasped his hot hand in her cool one.

"After seeing what he did this night, I truly believe that Alistar will walk through Hell for you, Elle." Lydia rolled the large bullet around in her hands that the other hunter had given her, deep in thought.

"I know he will. Yet I do not wish that for him. After the life he's lived, he deserves peace," Elzibeth replied as she changed the now dry compress on Alistar's forehead.

Sitting back down she looked at Lydia. "You gasped when that Hunter said he's been through this with Alistar before. What do you know about this?"

Lydia focused out the window. "Alistar told me about the serum, and what it does to the Hunters who take it. He also told me about his past addiction to it. How he took too much, and how his mentor caught him and forced him off it by tying him to a bed for two weeks."

"You mean we just met Alistar's mentor?"

"I believe so, yes," Lydia said as Adriana walked up and glanced at Alistar. Elzibeth's gaze flicked over to her.

"Good evening, Lore-Keeper." She nodded at the girl.

"Good evening, Lady Elle. I'm sorry for interrupting, but I heard you and Lady Lydia talking. I thought I could shed some light on the situation." Reaching over, Lydia unlocked one of the seats, and spun it around for the girl. "Sit, Lore-Keeper." She said, patting the chair.

Both vampires watched the girl expectantly.

"I need some more information to know for sure if it was who I think it is. What kind of weapons did he use? Did you see his mark?" Adriana asked after a moment.

"He was a rank five like Alistar. And like Alistar he carried a longsword and a pistol. The sword had a blade so bright it hurt to look at," Lydia replied.

"There's only one Hunter I've heard of besides Alistar who carries a pistol and a sword with a shining blade. If I'm right, his name is Mikhail Bransen. He's the church's top Hunter. You two should be dead right now. It's said he's never lost a fight."

"He let us live and distracted the other Hunters with him so that we could get away," Elzibeth replied softly.

"He also gave Elle a vial of Essence of Nightshade for Alistar."

"That's for detoxing Hunters who overdose on the serum." She glanced over at the twitching man strapped to the gurney. "I'll need to check the records we obtained while rescuing those other Seekers, but I'm sure it was him. How much of the vial did you use?"

"All of it," Lydia replied.

"What do you know about the side effects of the serum?" Elzibeth asked.

Adriana sighed. "I know that Mister Alistar is going through the toughest fight of his life right now. He may not make it through this as who he was before."

"What do you mean?" Lydia asked.

"One of the Seeker roles is to be a medic to the team they're attached to. Serum affects the body by making the nervous system fire faster than it should. Information is sent from the brain faster and the limbs respond faster. The downside is that the body can't handle that stress for long before it tears itself apart and wastes away. Muscle damage can be irreparable and some Hunters end up wheelchair-bound after a few years of constant use. Most die before then. After each fight, Seekers give small injections of Essence of Nightshade to counteract the serum."

Adriana fell silent and again looked over at Alistar. "All we can do is pray he pulls through. If he took that much serum that he needed a whole vial of Essence of Nightshade, he may not wake up at all. All I know is that the coming days will be much worse."

She rose and went back to her seat as Elzibeth and Lydia's eyes met, concern on their faces.

Lydia placed her hand on Elzibeth's arm. "Elle, he's strong. IF anyone can come out of this in one piece, it's him."

"I know. Lydia, what happened to us? We were friends for such a long time."

"Sisters even. I remember many months being fostered at Castle Tepes. If I remember correctly, it was over a human boy we both liked, and wanted. Cassius."

Elzibeth leaned back in her seat. "Cassius. He was easy on the eyes and we were just young vampires and absolutely smitten with him even though he was a servant."

"Your father forbade association with him other than that of servant and master because he was just a human.

He had that other vampire lined up for you. What was his name?" Lydia thought.

"James. He was such an idiot. Always trying to impress my father and woo me. I could not stand him." Elzibeth rolled her eyes at the memory.

"Well I wouldn't exactly call Alistar smart either." Elzibeth's eyes flashed and Lydia held up a hand. "Alistar is an idiot in a different way. Always putting himself in danger for you. Always pushing himself beyond his limits. He's not flashy for the sake of being flashy. He just is."

"It is his way. Always fighting, always in harm's way for what he believes in. From what he has told me, it is the only thing he knows. He even once told me he has never known love," Elzibeth said, closing her eyes.

"He was one of those Hunters. Always fighting. Explains a lot actually," Lydia remarked, then Elzibeth's words hit her. "Wait, are you saying he's a virgin?" She raised an eyebrow.

"That's exactly what I am saying, dear sister." Elzibeth chuckled, opening her eyes.

"Oh, geez, Elle, you really need to just bed him. Maybe enough wild sex will temper the fire he has within." Lydia laughed. Alistar moaned on the gurney and this time Lydia changed the compress on his fevered brow.

"No, I think I am going to take my time with this one. He is worth it. And I honestly doubt any wild sex will tame him," Elzibeth said.

61

Alistar jolted awake. A cool hand lay on his arm. "Elle?" he asked weakly, his mouth dry.

Lydia removed her hand from his arm and lifted her head from its resting spot near the window, turning on a light by the bed. "She's asleep in the next room. I made her get some rest," she said, sitting back in her chair.

Alistar tried to move but found himself restrained. "*Hmm.* I appear to be a bit tied up at the moment. My mouth is also a bit dry." Lydia held a straw to his lips and he drank, feeling the rush of cool water across his tongue and down his throat. Drinking too much resulted in a short coughing fit.

"Take it easy, Alistar. Elle and I didn't nurse you back to health these past two weeks for you to die by choking on a simple glass of water."

She felt his forehead. "Your fever has broken. How do you feel?"

"Like hammered shit." He tested the bindings but they held firm. "I don't suppose you could..." He directed his gaze to his restraints.

"Only if you aren't going to hit me again."

Alistar looked away. "I'm sorry that happened."

Lydia placed her hand back on his arm. "You weren't yourself, Alistar. You were fully in the grip of the serum detox. Elzibeth had to throw herself on top of you and hold you down while we got the restraints on you. Even then it took two more vampires to help hold you in place. That serum is dangerous stuff."

One by one she undid the restraints and helped him sit up.

"So what happened while I was out? How *long* was I out?"

"Oh, you know, lots of yelling and moaning, mostly from you. Some flailing about. Your heart stopped twice. Miyamoto's people had to shock you back both times. And to answer your second question, two weeks." Lydia smiled.

Elzibeth swept into the room and over to the bed to sit beside him.

"Hey, princess." Alistar croaked.

Silently Elzibeth brushed a strand of hair back from his face. "Hey yourself handsome."

"Elle, I…" Elzibeth held a finger to his lips.

"Hush, my love. I know. I'm just glad you are back." A knock came from the door. "Enter," Elzibeth said.

The door slid open revealing Evelyn and Marcus with Miyamoto standing behind them. "These two wanted to check on you, *Kainsan.* I hope you are feeling better."

"I'm alive, so that's a plus."

Evelyn stalked over to the bed and slapped him hard across the face. "That's for making Miss Elle worry!" Then she hugged him. "That's for coming back alive."

Alistar gave her a questioning look and rubbed the side of his face. "Ow."

Lydia laughed. "You know you deserved that one, Alistar. I've wanted to do it myself more than once."

Marcus stepped forward. "Hey, kid, what's up?" Without a word, Marcus bent forward and hugged him.

"I thought I'd lost another brother," he whispered. Alistar hugged him back.

"I'm not that easy to kill, Marcus." he replied, ruffling the kids' hair.

"Yeah, he's a stubborn ass," Lydia remarked.

"You bitch!" Alistar grumped at her.

Lydia rolled her eyes. "He's going to be fine, Elle."

Elzibeth smirked. "Yes, he is, considering I'm not letting him out of this bed until he can stand on his own without help."

"On that note…" Alistar remarked, throwing back the covers. He recovered himself a second later. "I'm gonna stay right here. Elle… I know my clothes are missing, but who undressed me?" he asked, hoping it had been her.

"I did, of course. Lydia and I may be friends, but there's no way I'm letting her get her hands on you," Elzibeth replied smiling.

"Good."

"Oh, come on, it's not like I'd strip him naked and have my way with him."

"Oh, you damn well know you would, Lydia, and I know it too." Elzibeth laughed.

"Drat! I need to stop being so transparent!"

"Umm, Miss Elle, Alistar, I have something to say and to ask before Marcus and I head back to our room," Evelyn said.

"I'm… umm… late," She mumbled

"I don't know about that. You managed to make it here in time to slap the shit outta me."

"Really, Alistar?" Elzibeth questioned.

"She's saying she's with child, you dumbass," Lydia retorted, her voice filled with sarcasm.

"Oh… Oooohhhh." He looked over at Marcus. "Marcus, did you knock up my girl here?"

Marcus looked sheepish. "Guilty as charged."

"Well, damn. I didn't even get the chance to talk with you yet. I was gonna throw a bullet at you and say they move faster after eleven. Welp, there goes my plans for today." Alistar threw up his hands in mock annoyance. Everyone else laughed. "No, but seriously, congratulations, you two."

Evelyn wrung her hands. "My question is for Lydia."

Lydia perked up and lifted her eyebrows. "Yes, Evie?"

"Well, Marcus and I were talking and if the child is a boy, we'd like to name him Julian. If it's a girl, Juliana."

"I think he would be honored," Lydia said, placing her hand on Evelyn's shoulder.

"We would like Elzibeth and Alistar to be the grandparents since, you know, ours aren't around anymore."

"I would be honored to be grandmother to your child my dear." Elzibeth looked over at Alistar.

"Sure. I can teach him how to hunt, fish, and ride a motorcycle. Lydia can be the crazy aunt who drinks too much and is a pain in the neck," Alistar said grinning.

"Elle, let me bite him just once!" Lydia growled, her eyes flashing. "I'm not good with children. This is a bad idea from the king of bad ideas."

"Well, actually, we were going to ask you to be Auntie Lydia," Marcus said, scratching his head.

"Well shit. You two are lucky I like you. Fine. I'll be the child's aunt, but I won't change diapers." Lydia said with slight annoyance.

62

"Then it is settled," Elzibeth said, turning to Marcus. "You will marry Evelyn before the baby comes, yes?"

"That was the plan. I just didn't have money for a ring, or someone to officiate."

"I have both of those covered, Marcus."

"Well, that's good because I left all my money back at the castle," Marcus chuckled.

Snoring interrupted further conversation. Alistar had passed out. Elzibeth's gaze flickered to the others. "We shall discuss this a little later," she ushered Evelyn and Marcus out the door.

Lydia headed to the other room. "Now that you're up, I'm going to sleep. I've been at it for three days straight. Oh, and don't let him know how long you were up."

"Oh, he will never know. At least not from me," Elzibeth replied, smiling. The door closed behind Lydia, leaving Elzibeth alone with Alistar.

He muttered as she lay him flat and then crawled in next to him, wrapping herself protectively about him. In a moment she was fast asleep to the rumble coming from his chest.

~

Alistar woke a few hours later in the cool embrace of Elzibeth. "I can get used to this," he muttered, gently moving her arm and leg off himself. He slid out of bed and with shaky, weak steps padded to the open bathroom door. After using the facilities he leaned against the door. A cool hand slid up his arm.

"You should have woken me," Elzibeth said softly.

"Yeah well, you looked so darn cute lying there, and it was only like ten feet."

"Uh-huh. Back to bed, mister," Elzibeth chided while tucking him in. Again she crawled in next to him and lay there, her eyes glowing in the dark.

Alistar stared at the ceiling. "Elle, I know the only way to save me was Essence of Nightshade. How…"

"A Hunter gave it to us." She dangled the bullet on the chain above him. He could barely see it in the dark. Reaching up he felt the familiar shape and closed his eyes in recognition.

"Fuck."

"Who is he?" Elzibeth asked, already knowing the answer.

"Mikhail Bransen. He was my mentor for five years and, after that, my partner in the hunt. We used to be close friends but not after that day." His mind flashed back to the different hunts, the time spent at bars and seedy motels in different towns and cities.

"I don't know how you and Lydia are still alive. He's a class five, just like me. Almost everything I know is because of him. He should have killed you."

Elzibeth gave a one-armed shrug. "He gave me the

Nightshade, and said he was helping you, not me. Then he tossed us the bullet. He said you'd know what it meant."

Alistar sighed. "Yeah, I do. It means the next time I see him, I will kill him, or he will kill me."

"Why?"

"It's just the way it is, Elle. It's the way it has to be."

~

A week later found Alistar healing a little day by day, but with that healing came withdrawal and agitation.

"Fuck!" Alistar muttered as he shakily stumbled while walking.

"Let me help you, my love."

"I'm fine, Elle. I'm not an invalid," Alistar replied with an edge to his voice.

"You are not fine. You push yourself every day to heal faster than you should. You did the same thing when you broke your ankle."In a gentle yet firm hold, she took his arm..

"I said I'm fine, Elle. Now back off!" The vampires and humans surrounding them gave a wide berth.

Elzibeth's expression remained serene.

"Sorry. I... It's frustrating."

"Miss Elle!" Adriana came running up to them. "I've been researching the serum more and I think I'm on to something." In her hands she held a vial of the blue glowing liquid.

Alistar's gaze locked on to it. He reached out with a shaky hand. Seeing this, Elzibeth covered his hand with her own. "No. Alistar."

"Please. Just a little. Just enough to take the edge off. Help me with my strength," Elzibeth saw the need and hunger in his eyes and felt it inside his mind.

"I said no. That is the last thing you need right now.

Adriana, take that and lock it away. Do NOT let him anywhere near it. Do you understand?" Her voice held a slight edge to it and more than a bit of concern.

Adriana moved back out of Alistar's reach and pocketed the vial. "Oh, gosh! I'm so sorry. I didn't think."

Alistar lunged. "Give me the damn serum!" Elzibeth grabbed him around the waist and held fast, her vampiric strength and his still-weak body keeping him away from Adriana. He struggled and shook in her grasp.

"Go, Adriana. NOW. He can not be near that stuff!" The Lore-Keeper turned and ran away. Alistar broke down, crying. He sunk to the floor, dragging Elzibeth with him.

Passing vampires and humans looked upon him with pity and Elzibeth glared at them. "Leave us!" They quickly vacated the area.

"Need a hand with him, Elle?" Lydia's voice came softly from behind her.

"Yes, please." Lydia stepped around her and helped pick Alistar up. Then she slapped him… hard, his head going to the side.

"Snap out of it Alistar!" When his head swiveled around, he growled, his eyes changing from their usual dark brown to a yellow shade, fangs showing when he raised his upper lip.

Lydia stepped back suddenly. "Umm, Elle… we have a problem here."

Alistar went limp in Elibeth's grasp. "Look at his eyes, Elle. Look at his mouth." Lydia held him up for Elzibeth's inspection.

Elzibeth opened his eyelids one by one and lifted his upper lip. She drew in a sharp breath. "I'm taking him back to our room. Bring the doctor immediately."

She picked up Alistar in her arms, like one would carry a child and quickly walked back to their room, laying him on the bed.

A few moments later, a young man barely out of his teens and dressed in a cream colored suit, walked in. In actuality, he was a vampire nearly as old as she was. Making his way to the bed he lifted Alistar's upper lip and then shined a light into his eyes. Placing a hand on Alistar's forehead, he concentrated.

"I can-not read his thoughts. Something is blocking me. He is fully catatonic."

Alistar's eyes snapped open revealing a golden sheen that faded back to their normal brown. "Elle."

Elzibeth clasped his hand in hers. "I'm here."

"What's happening to me?

63

The doctor removed Alistar's hand from Elzibeth's and checked his pulse. "Well, he *was* catatonic. Welcome back to the land of the living, young man." He checked Alistar's breathing.

"I'm going to need some blood for tests."

Alistar held out his trembling wrist. "Yeah, sure."

Drawing blood up into the syringe, the doctor injected it into a vial containing anticoagulant. "This will take an hour or so to process. Until then, he stays in bed."

"I'll be right here, doc. Not that she'd let me leave even if I didn't feel like I've been drained dry. Think it would be okay if I had something to eat?"

"I think food would be okay. Nothing heavy. Maybe some miso soup and some sushi," the doctor replied.

"I'll send a message to the kitchen. I'm feeling rather hungry, myself," Elzibeth stated before she called the kitchen on the intercom and the doctor left them alone.

She walked back over and helped Alistar sit up. Perching on the edge of the bed, she looked into his eyes, brushing a strand of hair back from his face. "You should not have taken the serum."

Alistar glowered at her. "It's not like I wanted to take it, Elle. I did what I had to do to save you."

"That look has no effect on me, my love."

Alistar closed his eyes looking even more weary and tired than he was. "Elle. It's too bright in here. My eyes hurt."

Elzibeth blinked. The lights were low. Reaching over she turned them down until barely any light shined out. "Is that better?"

Alistar squinted his eyes. "Yes, thank you." Elzibeth turned his face toward her to see his eyes glowing again.

"Elle, what's wrong?"

Standing, Elzibeth walked to the closet door and opened it wide enough so Alistar could see himself in the mirror. Alistar's jaw dropped. After a second, he reached up and touched his teeth. "Well, that's new."

Elzibeth sat on the side of the bed. "Have you ever heard of this happening in Hunters taking serum before?"

"No. A normal Hunter just gets faster and stronger. They certainly don't end up with glowing yellow eyes..." His fingers sensed sharper teeth. "Or fangs. I mean while they're under the effects of the serum, their eyes do glow blue, but that wears off after the detox." He dropped his hand.

"Then again, when have I ever been normal? My whole life has been anything but normal. How many people do you know who have broken away from the church after eighteen years as the church's bitch only to end up with a vampire girlfriend?"

Elzibeth made a show of thinking about it for a moment. "Well, there's you. And Lydia has Brady. So I guess that would be two?"

"Brady, right. I give him six months before she eats him."

"*Mmm...* I do not think so. She has changed. She

actually feels gratitude to you for that." Elzibeth rested her chin in her hand.

"Never thought the ice queen would ever feel gratitude, but I've been wrong about many things before."

The door chimed. "Enter." Elzibeth called. It slid open and a dark skinned human male with a soft jawline and even softer eyes, dressed in chef's whites entered pushing a rolling cart. "Your food, Grand Lady."

"Thank you. Please bring it over here, and then you can go." He rolled it to where she wanted and turned to leave. Taking the lids off the plates Elzibeth sets them aside. Not hearing the door open and close, she looked over to see the staff member still standing there. "Is there anything else?"

"No, Grand Lady. I'm sorry. I have just never seen eyes like his," the human replied, bowing his head.

"They are unusual. But they may be a side effect of his overdose. Now... Please leave." The staff member bowed. "YesGrand Lady."

Picking up the bowl of steaming soup and a spoon, Elzibeth turned back toward Alistar.

"You aren't gonna feed me." Alistar rolled his eyes at her.

"I am. And you will eat," Elzibeth smiled, taking a spoonful of soup and blowing on it.

～

An hour later the doctor walked back in. "I have the test results."

"And?" Elzibeth asked.

"He is still human, but he has one extra genome in his DNA. This has allowed the vampiric cells in the Serum to bind with his cells, making him different."

"What does that mean?" Elzibeth raised an eyebrow.

"It means that on him, and any others like him, with enough doses of the serum, it could cause them to turn."

"Wait, so I'm a vampire now?"

"Not quite. By binding with your cells, the serum effects, while not as potent, have made you faster and stronger than a normal human, but not quite as fast as a vampire," the doctor replied, leaning against the wall by the door.

Alistar looked at Elzibeth. "You want to tell him, or should I?"

"Tell me what?" The doctor's head swiveled between them both, amused.

"Alistar is possibly faster than Lydia even without the serum." Elzibeth said offhandedly, stroking Alistar's hair.

"Well, this is interesting. This means he may be as fast as you. When he's healed, I would like to do more tests."

"When he's healed. And only IF he agrees."

"As you wish." The doctor bowed and walked out of the room.

"Umm, Elle, does this mean I'm gonna start craving blood?"

She grabbed her chalice from the table and held it to his lips. He took a deep sniff. "Nope. I think I might puke. Take it away."

"I would say that is a no." Elzibeth smiled before taking a sip.

"Well, that's a relief," He said, then yawned. "I... I don't think I could eat babies."

Elzibeth slapped his arm. "I don't eat babies and you know it.

"Ow. I was talking about Lydia. Lay off the invalid." Alistar rubbed his arm.

"Oh, so now you are an invalid. Mister Kain, if you were not in recovery, I'd kick your ass around this room,"

Elzibeth growled, her eyes flashing. Even still, the smile never left her face.

"Were I... feeling better, Elle... I might... just let you do that. Sounds... like fun." Alistar's voice betrayed his sleepiness. He sunk under the covers and was fast asleep.

64

Two days later, Elzibeth escorted Alistar into a room with four chairs.

"Umm, Elle, what's going on?" Alistar asked, confused.

A short, Japanese woman walked in from another door. She wore a black woman's power suit top with a knee length black skirt. "Good evening, I'm doctor Kim Miyamoto. I'll be heading up your therapy sessions."

Alistar raised an eyebrow and turned toward the door. "Nope. I don't do shrinks." He stopped as Elzibeth's hand clamped down on his wrist.

"Elle, let go. I don't do shrinks." Alistar tugged at his wrist but Elzibeth's grasp remained firm. Her gaze flickered between him and the chair.

"Fine." Alistar sighed and made a move toward one of the chairs. Elzibeth let his wrist go and sat next to him.

"Seriously? Vampires have shrinks?"

"Of course we do, Alistar. Newly turned vampires need guidance in their new lives. And even older ones occasionally need someone to talk to," Kim said, sitting and crossing her legs, then opening a folding clipboard to look at the papers within. "So, tell me about your life, Alistar."

Alistar sighed again and his eyes lost focus while aimed at the floor. "Not a whole lot to talk about. Parents, dead in a house fire. Sister, burned at the stake for being a witch. Then there's me."

"And what about you, Alistar?" Doctor Kim asked.

Alistar chuckles. "I'm a whole lot of fucked up. But that's of no consequence; I manage."

"Everything has a consequence and meaning, Alistar. Please continue." Doctor Kim gave him a level stare.

Alistar ran his hand through his hair and sighed irritably. "Aunt and uncle took in my sister and me, but that didn't last. I got kicked to the church when I hit the age of eighteen. From then on it was training, fighting, and hunting."

Doctor Kim scribbled something in her clipboard. "And when did you first use the serum?"

"I think it was on my third or fourth hunt during my second year."

Hours later Elzibeth and Alistar walked out of the therapy session and outside into the courtyard of Miyamoto's mansion. "Feel better?" Elzibeth asked him.

"Honestly? A little. I still don't like shrinks," Alistar said, shrugging.

"Well I like her. She's good." Elzibeth took his hand and smiled as they strolled down the path in the courtyard.

"Yeah, well, I tend to... How did she put it? Compartmentalize things? And then I usually hit the gym." Alistar stumbled but Elzibeth kept him standing with her firm yet gentle grasp.

"The gym? That is good. Because you have physical therapy next. And you are going even if I need to have Lydia tie you up so I can carry you. She's very good with ropes," Elzibeth said with an evil smile.

"Umm, no, I'll go. She might enjoy that a little too much."

"Enjoy what?" Lydia said as she stepped out of a nearby door.

"Helping me help Alistar with his physical therapy. I need to borrow a car from Miyamoto. Watch him."

She strode off toward the garage of the compound as Alistar plopped onto a bench.

"So, how did the psych session go?" Lydia asked.

"It, umm... was revealing. Apparently I'm more fucked up in the head than I thought."

"Anyone who can do what you do and just turn the switch off is obviously fucked in the head as you put it. It's not healthy."

Alistar pulled a pack of smokes from his jacket pocket and lit one up. He breathed in, then exhaled, coughing.

"And just where did you get those?"

"One of the staff members got them for me. Why?"

"Well, you better share. Those are clove cigarettes, and I haven't had one in a long time." Lydia said, sitting to his right.

Alistar held the pack and lighter out to her. "These are so bad for your health."

"Yeah, well, it's this or booze, or the serum again." Alistar said, his hand shaking slightly.

Lydia shoved the pack and lighter back in his jacket pocket. "Oh, hell, no. Even I don't want to see you go through that again."

"Was I that scary during the battle?"

"Scary doesn't even begin to cover what you were. I

haven't seen savagery like that since Elle's father was around." Lydia took another drag on her smoke.

"Did he really impale hundreds of people?" Alistar asked, likewise popping the cigarette back into his mouth. A billow of smoke exploded with a cough.

Lydia waited a moment before speaking. "Oh, yes. He wasn't big on having his authority challenged. The only ones who could even mention he might be wrong on something were his wife Anna, Elle, and Richter. Anyone else was likely to die if they didn't phrase things properly. But the battle wasn't why you scared the fuck out of everyone around you. It was what happened to you after we got you home."

Alistar raised his eyebrows. "The man, the myth, the legend." He stubbed out his smoke in the palm of his hand.

"You dumbass. There's a butt container right to your left," Lydia said, watching him. He held his hand out in the moonlight, and they watched as the burn healed.

"Huh. That would normally take a week to heal."

"That's the kind of shit I'm talking about. The glowing eyes, the fact I personally pulled that arrow out of your side and watched you heal. As I said, it took four of us to hold you down to get the restraints on, such was your strength." Lydia leaned over him and dropped her butt into the container.

"The rooms have cameras. Did they record it?"

"Yes. Some of the others are using it as evidence as to why we need to find the source of the serum and destroy it."

Alistar pulled out the pack again and lit up another smoke. Lydia reached over and snagged another one as well. "I think that's a good idea, Lydia. As soon as I'm better, and we find the lab's location, I'll lead the charge."

Lydia gave him a sideways glance. "You're a special

kind of stupid, Alistar. Did it ever once occur to you that you don't have to do any of this alone anymore? You have friends willing to go with you on this little crusade of yours."

Alistar chuckled. "Friends, huh? Never thought I'd find more comradeship with a bunch of vamps than with my own kind. Does that include you, Lyd?"

"Listen here, mister. The elders don't just answer a call from anyone. We did it because even though some of us don't like you, we respect you."

Alistar gave her the side-eye. "Even you, Lyd?"

"Yeah, well, you've grown on me, you asshole."

"Bitch." Alistar grinned and they both laughed. A horn honked outside the gates and, a moment later, a car drove in.

"Come on hero, let's get you better. Oh, and a word of advice, if you EVER take that stuff again, I'll kill you. I won't let you put Elle through that hell again."

"I quit once before, so I can do it again. Scouts honor," Alistar said, holding up three fingers and rising.

"I highly doubt you were a boy scout, Alistar."

65

"Push, Alistar. One more." Elzibeth coached him as he sat on the weight bench using the leg-lift attachment. He lifted the weights one more time, then released them.

"Well, Mister Kain, how do you feel?" the physical therapist asked, walking over to check on him. She was a small but fit twenty something human woman with red hair. She was dressed like many of the people in the gym, in shorts and a t-shirt and her hair was tied back in a ponytail.

"Like my legs are rubber." Alistar stood up from the machine, taking Elzibeth's hand to steady himself.

"Well they should. You just did one hundred leg lifts of two-hundred and twenty-six kilograms. That's a vast improvement over your weight of fifty at the start of the week."

Walking over to the weight rack, he picked up the twenty-five kilogram dumbbells, lifted them to his chest and pushed them out in a one-two punch combo.

"He is improving at a fast rate. Far faster than I would

expect from an ordinary human. Have you been giving him blood?" the therapist asked Elzibeth.

"He is not ordinary, but, yes, I have, a little each night."

"Not sure I approve of that." Elzibeth's gaze flickered from Alistar to her.

"I was treating wounded soldiers and patients at hospitals with my blood long before you were even born. My years of medical experience vastly outnumber yours."

Alistar ignored their argument and popped in his earbuds before heading to the punching bag.

Pressing play he hit the bag as a song called "Footsteps" started. Throwing punch after punch he zoned out, not realizing the bag had broken under his onslaught. He kicked it with a spinning back-heel kick. The chains snapped and the bag flew from its stand, right past Lydia when she walked through the doors.

Alistar paused as everyone else turned to him. "Umm, whoops. Guess I don't quite have a feel for my own strength yet."

Elzibeth smiled. "Three more weeks and he will be back to his full ability."

"Yeah, and after seeing that, I'm more than a little bit scared, Elle. I shouldn't need body armor and a riot shield to walk into this place," Lydia said.

Alistar moved to the speed bag and started into a slow rhythm. His fists pounded faster and faster until the bag became a blur. Closing his eyes he slowed the speed of his punches, managing not to destroy the bag.

"I think that's enough therapy for the night," the therapist said. Alistar prised out a smoke and lit it up, inhaling. Elzibeth scowled.

"There is no way you are kissing me after having that in your mouth, Alistar."

"You heard her, bitch boy. Hand them over." Lydia grinned.

Sighing, Alistar handed her the pack and she tugged one out and lit it as Alistar crushed out the one he was smoking. Elzibeth's gaze flicked to her.

"That's not going to work on me Elle, I don't plan on kissing you," Lydia said, taking a long drag and savoring the flavor.

"Alistar, dear, would you please throw Lydia in the car trunk and lock it?" Elzibeth asked sweetly.

Alistar made a move toward Lydia, grinning.

"You might be my sister, Elle, but sometimes you are such a bitch," Lydia rolled her eyes.

~

The next night Alistar stood in front of a pool in a pair of black swim trunks. "So, umm…. Yeah… I should probably mention at this point that I can't swim."

"You have got to be kidding me. You fell two hundred feet into an ice cold river and lived. How in the fuck can you not swim?" Lydia asked in surprise.

Alistar whirled on her, now facing away from the pool. "Only because YOU saved me. There are three things I can't do. I can't dance, I can't play billiards worth a damn, and… I don't know how to swim." Water splashed behind him.

"Time to get wet Alistar." Lydia shoved him hard, sending him flying back into the pool. He hit the water with a large splash and came up sputtering.

Strong arms wrapped around his waist. "I have you." Elzibeth's voice sounded next to his right ear.

"You better, Elle, because when I get out of here, I'm gonna kill her!" Alistar coughed, struggling to breathe.

Elzibeth held him back and he glared at Lydia as she

dove into the pool, wearing a white two piece bathing suit. Swimming over she flicked him on the nose.

"To kill me, you're going to have to catch me first, and believe me, I'm the better swimmer. But if you need a pair of water wings, just ask." Gracefully back flipping, she swam away.

"Some days I really hate her!" Alistar growled.

"I know dear. I'll talk to her." Elzibeth kissed his ear.

"Nah. You're my girlfriend, not my mother. I'll just get her back later."

"Very well. Now, tread water, like this." Elzibeth let go of his neck and he turned around, still holding onto one of her hands. Elzibeth wore a black one piece. Alistar eyed as much of her as possible as she treaded water.

"Stepping into the modern-age fashion there, Elle?" He raised an eyebrow.

"You like it?" she asked, moving closer till their noses almost touched.

"I do."

"Good." Smiling, she pulled him through the water, showing him the different swimming strokes. The physical therapist joined them in a red lifeguard suit and helped in his therapy.

"This is the side stroke."

"That's not the stroke he should be doing with you, Elle! Show him the breaststroke!" Lydia shouted from across the pool, laughing.

"Shut it, Lydia, or I will have words with you later!" Elzibeth's eyes flashed.

By the end of the swim session, Alistar had managed to swim on his own. No Olympic awards had his name on them, but he wouldn't drown in the right conditions either.

66

Three weeks later Alistar had just finished up fifty laps in the pool after a hard day's worth of therapy. He climbed out and picked up a towel from next to Elizbeth, in her lounge chair reading an old book. As he toweled himself off, her eyes stayed glued to him.

Sitting in the chair next to her, he leaned over to glance at the back cover. "Huh... "Bill the Vampire" by Rick Gualtieri. Never heard of it, or him. Also never figured you'd be reading a vampire novel, Elle."

"It's comedy and crude humor. I happen to like it." Elzibeth swatted his arm with the book.

Alistar held up both hands in surrender. "Hey, if that's what you like, I'm not gonna stop ya."

"Don't you read books?"

Alistar paused while putting on his socks. "The last major book I fully read was the Bible... and that was only because we were required to do so. Granted, it was changed by the church to fit their beliefs and agenda, I'm sure. I've never actually taken the time to read an old one. Other than that it's mostly been target documents and information on the regions where I was hunting."

"Such a shame. Books allow us to escape reality," Elzibeth replied, sitting up and placing in a bookmark.

"Shit, Elle, my whole life could be a book. Think about it. Crazy ex-hunter meets the daughter of Dracula and falls in love? Sounds like a sitcom, only I'm living it as we speak." He ran his hand through his hair and flicked the water off onto the pool deck.

"Maybe you should start writing."

"Maybe I should…" Alistar paused and then shook his head. "Nah,"

Elzibeth laughed and swatted his arm again. "Get dressed, handsome. We are going out tonight."

"Oh? Where to?" Alistar covered his head with the towel and rubbed it back and forth.

"Just a meeting outside the castle."

The towel dropped away and Alistar narrowed his eyes at her. "Uh-Huh. Something's up, Elle."

"Very well, there are some lower-ranking vampires in the city who have eluded Miyamoto for some time, and he thought maybe you could pay them a little visit and scare some sense into them. We don't need more Hunters coming to Tokyo."

Alistar stared at her for a minute. "Right, I'll get my things."

Turning away he packed up the gym bag he had brought with him. Behind his back Elzibeth smirked.

~

The car pulled up to an old, dilapidated warehouse on the edge of Osaka's Sakai province.

"Huh. Doesn't look like much," Alistar remarked.

"Yes, well, looks can be deceiving," Lydia said from opposite him.

"True that, Lyd." Alistar press checked both pistols before sliding them back into their holsters.

"Why do you still feel the need to bring those things, Alistar? You know bullets don't kill our kind," Lydia rolled her eyes.

"Yep. But be it vampire, werewolf, or human, your knee-caps explode all the same. Would you like a demonstration?" Alistar did not even look at her.

"You are a truly sadistic asshole, Alistar."

"Yeah and you're still a stuck-up bitch but we're still friends," Alistar replied, grinning as he clambered out of the vehicle.

"You say the sweetest things." Lyda emerged after him and blew him a kiss.

Turning, Alistar took Elzibeth's hand, helping her out of the car. "Thank you, my love." She planted a kiss on his cheek.

They made their way toward the building with Elzibeth on his right and Lydia on his left. "So, how are we gonna do this? I could kick down the door."

"How about you try knocking instead of going in guns blazing," Lydia retorted sarcastically as Alistar bent down to examine the motorcycles parked outside the door.

"Huh. That's an old Kawasaki Ninja. Nice"

"Hello. Did you even hear a word I said?"

Pulling out one of his pistols, Alistar knocked on the metal door and stepped to the side. "I might be an idiot from time to time, but I'm not deaf, Lydia. Of course I heard you."

"Stop it, both of you!" Elzibeth snapped. A small sliding window opened. She flashed her eyes and teeth and heard the door unlock from the inside.

Alistar swung around the door frame, cutting the corner. "Clear," he whispered. The hallway beyond was dark, so dark he could barely see.

"Fuck, I forgot my flashlight." He checked the two doors on the left and the right but found them locked. Posting at the end of the hallway he scanned out into the main room, just barely making out the shapes of tables.

"Why the fuck does this feel like a trap?" he asked.

"That's because it is," Lydia said. Suddenly the lights snapped on, blinding him momentarily.

"Surprise!" Multiple voices shouted. As his vision cleared he saw a handmade banner strung from a balcony that said *"Happy 40th Birthday!"* on it. And under it stood all the vampires and people he knew.

"Happy birthday!"

Rounding on Elzibeth he lifted a finger. "You—"

"Happy birthday, my love." Elzibeth smiled, kissing him before he finished the sentence.

"Are pure evil," he finished once she broke the kiss.

"I know, but you can't hide secrets from me, especially not one this important." Elzibeth's smile changed to a grin and even Lydia wore the same expression.

Alistar rounded on her. "And just what hand did you play in this?"

Lydia held up his creds. "I had to snatch your creds so we could hack them to find out your birthday."

"You, bitch!" Alistar glowered at her and she grinned even wider, showing fang. "Welcome to the family, Alistar."

"Elle, I DON'T do birthdays. I stopped a long time ago," Alistar said through their mental link.

Elzibeth took his arm in hers. *"Well, you are doing this one, and many more to come."*

67

Alistar sat at a table with Elzibeth, Lydia, and Miyamoto as folks milled about the place.

"So, just how long has it been since you celebrated your birthday, Alistar?" Lydia asked before taking a sip of blood from a wine glass.

"Twenty-three years ago," Alistar replied, downing half his soda in one gulp.

Lydia blinked. "So seventeen? That's kinda sad actually."

"Yeah, well, on my eighteenth birthday I got pissed off at my uncle, stole his motorcycle, crashed it, and was immediately sent to the church. They're not big on birthdays," Alistar replied, crossing his arms and leaning back in his chair.

"Why the fuck not?" Evelyn asked, sitting next to him.

"Evie, dear, don't curse. It's not becoming of a lady." Elzibeth chided her.

"Because our life expectancy was supposedly equal to that of a snowball in a blast furnace. In our first year of actual hunting, we were given two months. If we survived longer than that, it was a miracle." Alistar looked over at the stage where speakers were being set up along with a microphone stand.

"And if you survived longer than a year?" Elzibeth asked softly.

"At that point we learned to create our own miracles. By all rights, I'm a statistical anomaly." He chuckled.

"I would say you most certainly are, *Kainsan*. To survive eighteen years against all odds is a work of the *Kami* indeed. They were watching over you." Miyamoto grinned.

Alistar laughed and shook his head. "Yeah, something is watching over me. Whatever it is, I'm pretty sure it needs therapy by now after dealing with me all this time."

"Well, I sure know I would if I had to deal with you for that long," Lydia scoffed, half joking.

"Well, Lyd, I'm not going anywhere anytime soon, so you might want to sign up with a good doctor now. Or I'm sure we could find you a nice hug-me jacket and a padded room." Alistar's deadpan expression broke into a slow smile.

"Alistar!" On unsteady feet Marcus stumbled over and enclosed Alistar in a hug. "I just wanted to say I love you, man! Happy birthday!" Marcus put more weight on Alistar's shoulders, not releasing him.

"Okay, there, kid, I love you too, but you gotta slow down on the sauce," Alistar said, pulling over a chair for Marcus.

He sent Elzibeth a mental message: *"He's hammered."*

"So what's with the mic and speakers?" he asked, pointing at the stage.

"We have a traditional way of fun during a celebration. Karaoke," Miyamoto replied.

Everyone looked at Alistar grinning. "Uh-uh. I don't sing."

"Why not? Everyone is drunk. Even us vampires. No

one will care how bad you might sound. It's all in fun. Also, happy birthday." Kim Miyamoto said, walking up.

"She's right, Alistar. You should sing." Evelyn said.

Alistar thought for a moment. "Okay. I'll do it... but only if Elzibeth and Lydia sing at some point."

"You think that's a challenge?" Lydia rolled her eyes. "I used to sing opera. Give me a harder Challenge."

"It could be fun. I will try it," Elzibeth said.

Slapping his knees, Alistar stood. "Okay then I guess I'll go first." He scanned through the song list. "Crap. Crap. Crap. That's crap." *Hmm... that might work.* He thought to himself.

Stepping up to the mic, he tapped it three times. "*Umm* ... yeah. Thank you all for this surprise. And, yeah, you all got me good. When you do what I did in the past, you didn't celebrate these things because you didn't have time. So I'm not at all used to having one again. Anyway, this is supposedly tradition around here so as they say when in Rome and all that, or Japan as it may be."

The introduction of "Life after You" played and he started singing, not even looking at the lyrics on the screen. The spiked liquor washed over him and Alistar seemed to come alive. His voice and tone matched the singer's perfectly. When he finished, silence met him..

"What?" He blinked in shock, looking around.

"Holy fuck, that was amazing! Do another one!" Lydia shouted. Everyone clapped and agreed so he found another song from the list.

This time he went with "If I Ever Lose My Faith in You" by a band called Disturbed. He closed his eyes, his body moving slowly with the music. As the music hit its crescendo, he broke out into the heavier tones. And when it ended, he paused to catch his breath, his face red.

Miyamoto stood up and Alistar held the microphone out to him. The old vampire shook his head. "No. Tradition states that the one being celebrated must do three songs and then others may sing."

"Don't lie, Miyamotosama. You just made that up, didn't you?"

"But I am the lord of this land. I can change tradition as I see fit."

Elzibeth laughed from where she sat, enjoying Alistar's singing. *"One more, my love, then I will be up there,"* she mentally sent him.

"For you, okay." Alistar smiled at her. "This next one goes out to a very special vampire who took in a wayward former Hunter and taught him hope and love. And for that, he is forever grateful." In a sedate manner, he broke into "Heaven" by Drew Jacobs and David Garcia. His eye's remained locked on Elzibeth's throughout the song.

Resting her chin in her hands on the table, Elzibeth stared back at her human.

With the end of his final song, he put the mic back on its stand and bowed to a round of cheering and applause.

Walking up on stage, Elzibeth kissed him as they passed each other.

She took the mic after finding the right song, and started singing. "I'll Keep Your Secrets." By Trans Siberian Orchestra. Alistar stared in slack-jawed amazement at her haunting voice.

"Oh, you've got it bad, Alistar," Lydia said, poking him in the arm with a finger from behind. So engrossed as he was with Elzibeth's singing that he did not notice Lydia move closer to him.

"Huh? What were you saying, Lydia?"

Lydia just chuckled evilly in reply.

68

"So I have a question. You mentioned that even the vampires here were drunk… How?" Alistar asked Miyamoto.

He paused and his gaze flicked to Lydia expecting some sarcastic retort. "What? It's your birthday. I'm not going to give you shit right now."

Miyamoto leaned forward. "For special occasions, we get the animals drunk before we bleed them. The alcohol infuses the blood and we can actually get drunk. It's a rather simple process."

"Huh. Forty years alive and this is the first time I'm hearing about it." Alistar reached over and stole a smoke from Lydia. He was just about to light it up when Elzibeth stole it from him and handed it back to her.

"Hey! I wanted that!"

A sweet smile caressed Elzibeth's face. "I know, but no," she said, tapping him on the nose.

Alistar rolled his eyes and sighed. "So, which one of you spiked my drink? Don't think I didn't notice."

"Guilty as charged," Lydia bragged. "Can't have the

birthday boy sober while everyone else is having a good time."

Alistar side-eyed her. "Yeah, well given the direction this conversation has gone, I was thinking I was about to be the main course."

"No, we do that on your fiftieth birthday." Lydia waited a minute, then laughed. "I'm joking!"

Alistar shook his head and chuckled as they watched Evelyn and Marcus get up on stage and take their turn. Evelyn had a beautiful voice, but Marcus couldn't carry a tune. After their song finished, they headed back toward the table.

∼

As the night winded down, Alistar left the club holding on to Lydia's arm with Elzibeth on her other side, helping the white-haired vampire. *"Jeez, when she goes all out, she really goes all out,"* he mentally sent Elzibeth.

"Lydia has always been a party girl. I told her to go easy," Elzibeth replied in annoyance. As they walked and chatted, neither noticed the man creeping out of the shadows until it was too late, their senses dulled by the booze.

"Die, vampire!" Alistar's head whipped around as a crossbow *twanged.* He shoved Lydia and Elzibeth out of the way as the arrow passed under his arm. The man dropped the crossbow and took off down the street.

"Is everyone okay?" Alistar asked, helping Elzibeth and Lydia up off the street.

"*Alistar!*" Marcus' shout caused Alistar's head to change directions where he found Marcus cradling Evelyn in his arms, an arrow sticking out of her chest. Alistar was at her side in a second, adrenaline pumping through his body.

"No. No. No. No. Come on, Evie." He pulled out his

knife and cut her shirt off. "There's too much blood. Marcus, give me your shirt. Now!" Evie gasped for breath, her eyes full of fear.

Elzibeth prodded Alistar aside but his focus remained on Evelyn. "Alistar, let me take care of this. I was a nurse. *Alistar!*" she screamed mentally. His head whipped around, his eyes large saucers of uncertainty. "I have this. Get *him*. Bring him back alive. I want my shot. Do *not* kill him."

"Yes, dear," Alistar replied before running in the Hunter's direction.. *Where are you, you bastard?* He thought to himself.

Footsteps down an alley to the right caught his attention and he just barely glimpsed the man as he turned a corner. *I don't think so,* he thought and pushed himself faster.

The man cut down another alley and then another, always managing to keep just a little ahead of Alistar, but his lead would come to an end. Rounding a corner, Alistar put on a burst of speed and tackled the man, slamming him into a wall.

"You son of a bitch!" Alistar yelled, flipping the man over and punching him hard in the nose. He smashed him against a wall before advancing. The man unsheathed a knife and Alistar reached out, sliding his hand down the blade impaling himself through the palm to grab the man's fist. He squeezed hard and the man dropped to his knees in pain.

Alistar dislodged the blade from his hand, tossing it down the alleyway. "I would kill you right here, right now, if I didn't have orders not to!" Alistar growled, punching the man hard enough to tweak his neck, causing him to black out. He tied the man's hands behind his back and headed to the main street, dragging the man behind him.

A large group of people had congregated around Evelyn. He stopped when he got about twenty feet away.

Pulling the man up, he slapped him. Again. And again. "Wake the fuck up, asshole."

The man blinked a few times before coming back to consciousness. Alistar had him face the crowd, throwing him to his knees. "Look!"

His eyes remained on the street. Alistar yanked his hair back while pulling out a pistol and placing it against the back of the man's skull. "Look at her!" he growled, forcing the man to look at Evelyn lying on the ground with Elzibeth and the others taking care of her.

"That was my daughter... and my grandchild. And they might die. If they die, you die."

"I'm not afraid of death," the man replied.

Alistar leaned in close. "I never said I'd let you die easy... or quick!" The man headbutted, him causing blood to spurt from his nose. Alistar blinked, then proceeded to beat the shit out of the man in uncontrolled rage as tears flowed from his face.

Arms encircled him. "Alistar. Alistar!" He whirled on the person, his eyes unfocused and, for a moment, he almost attacked. He saw Elzibeth's covered in blood.

"Is she?" he choked out.

"No, but I had to give her a lot of my blood to heal her. The arrow hit her heart. She may end up turning. For now she is thankfully unconscious."

"And the kiddo?" Alistar askd, closing his eyes.

"I don't know. I've never given a pregnant woman this much blood."

69

Alistar paced and watched through the window as Elzibeth and Lydia interrogated the man. His keen hearing made out what they were saying.

"Why do you attack my family? We have done nothing wrong to you. Yet you and your kind keep coming after us." Elzibeth's voice was sickly sweet and on edge at the same time.

"You're monsters. That's a good enough reason." The man spit in her face. Lydia leapt across the table and knocked him to the ground, still in the chair.

"Was that girl a monster?!" she screamed, standing over the man.

"I wasn't aiming at her: I was aiming at you. If your servant didn't push you out of the way, she would be fine, and you'd be dead." Blood streamed from his busted lip.

Lydia pointed at Elzibeth. "My servant?! That MAN... is HER suitor, and that girl's adoptive father! She is with child! An innocent! Not yet born, and unable to even take sides in this stupid war of yours!" Her voice came out as an angry hiss.

"Lydia!" Elzibeth's sharp word instantly snapped the

other vampire back into coherency. Reaching down she uprighted the chair with the man still in it.

A nurse walked into the room behind Alistar. "Yes?" he asked without taking his eyes off the scene in the next room.

"Evie is awake, Lord Alistar. She's asking for you, Elzibeth, and Lydia."

Alistar turned at her words. "Four guards in here now, and a medic. I want him kept alive."

"Yes, my lord." The nurse nodded and stepped back into the hallway motioning to four armed vampires. The five entered as Alistar walked into the next one.

Elzibeth's and Lydia's attention turned to the door when it opened. "She's awake and wants all of us," Alistar said.

Lydia glared at the man strapped to the chair. "You get to live a while longer."

The vampires followed Alistar to Evie's recovery room.

A light filled Evie's eyes when she saw them. "Hey, girlie," Alistar said softly before kissing her forehead. He noted her forehead felt cool under his lips.

"How are you feeling, Evie?" Elzibeth asked as Lydia hugged the girl.

"I hurt a little but other than that, I feel okay. The lights do hurt my eyes, though."

Alistar, Lydia and Elzibeth exchanged glaces and Alistar silently mouthed "Cold skin" to Elzibeth. Lydia nodded at his words.

"Evie, dear, you were injured so badly that I, as you know, had to use my blood to heal you. Quite a bit in fact. This may have an adverse reaction to your body," Elzibeth said with concern.

"You mean I might turn into a vampire. I know. The doctor already filled me in on the outcomes," Evie replied with a slight smile, not meeting their eyes. Worry had settled on her face. "What will happen to the baby?"

Elzibeth clasped her hand. "We honestly do not know, dear. A naturally born vampire such as myself can have children. And so can turned vampires. But in your case where the baby is a fetus during the turning of the parent, there is a chance the placental barrier effect will happen."

"What does that mean?" Evie asked.

"It means that one of three outcomes will happen. You and your baby both become vampires;, just you become a vampire, and your baby is perfectly human; or…" Lydia said but fell into silence.

"Or what, Lydia? Tell me." Evie grabbed the white-haired vampire by the arm and held fast.

"You could have a miscarriage and lose the child." Lydia gently placed her hand on top of Evie's.

The door slid open to allow the doctor entry. "Luckily, Miss Evelyn, you have the best doctors that vampire society can provide, so we will do everything we can to make sure you and the baby come out of this happy and healthy."

He checked the chart and stepped over to the bed, checking Evelyn's vitals. He shined a light in her eyes and she flinched away. "Miss Evelyn, you look good. However, it does look like Grand Lady Elzibeth's blood is indeed overwhelming your system, and though the change is slow, eventually, you will become one of us. You of course will need to take education in being a vampire, the do's and don'ts, and things like that."

"I will personally oversee her education," Elzibeth said.

"Hey, you all talk; I gotta go do some things," Alistar said, backing away.

"And just where are you going?" Elzibeth raised a finely shaped eyebrow.

Alistar shrugged. "I'm just gonna go have a nice talk with our new friend."

Elzibeth held his gaze for a moment. "Don't kill him."

Alistar bowed. "As you wish, my love."

Out in the hall, he found Richter heading his way. "Hey, Richter, I need a favor. Need you to pick up some supplies." Alistar tugged out a small notepad and stubby pencil and scribbled down a small list. He handed it to the other man who read it.

"I can get all of this in a half hour. Most of it we should have here in Miyamoto's compound. How is Evie?"

"She's gonna be a vampire. As far as the baby, no one knows for sure yet." Alistar shrugged. "Anyway, I need those supplies as fast as possible." Alistar patted the other man's shoulder and walked past him.

Back in the outer room, he stared at the man in the chair through the one-way glass. About thirty minutes later, Richter came in pulling an oxyacetylene torch, and carrying a plastic bag.

"Everything you requested. Although I do not know what you need these for."

70

Richter followed Alistar into the room.

"So, you've come to kill me?" The man watched Alistar unplugged the camera and closed a sliding curtain across the window.

"No." Alistar's voice was a growl. "That's not for me to decide." He blindfolded the man and then brought in the things Richter had brought him. He locked the door last.

The door to Evelyn's room shot open and Kim Miyamoto entered. "You need to get back to the holding room now." Concern filled her eyes as she looked at Elzibeth and Lydia.

The three women walked quickly down the hallway, and as they entered the observation room, they could hear screaming and loud rock music.

"Dear God, he's torturing the man!" Elzibeth tried the door.

"He's locked it. That door is designed to keep one of

our kind in or out. And don't bother with the glass; it's five inches of bullet-proof polycarbonate. We can't get into the room. The camera is disabled as well, and the curtain pulled." Kim jiggled the door handle.

"What's that smell?" Lydia wrinkled her nose.

Elzibeth sniffed the air. "It smells like meat cooking." She shuddered as the man in the other room continued to scream over the music.

"Alistar, WHAT are you doing?!" Elzibeth asked him through their mental link. But she got no reply.

A few minutes later, the door opened and Alistar came out, his eyes haunted but hard set.

"Alistar, you didn't," Elzibeth breathed.

"He's physically unharmed. I'm an asshole, but I'm not a monster."

"Yes, you are! That was a perfectly good steak you've ruined!" Richter complained, walking out behind him.

"Steak? What steak? Why are your gloves sticky if that man is unharmed?" Lydia looked confused.

"See for yourself, Lydia." Alistar stepped out of her way, stripped off the rubber gloves, and pulled his signature black glove over his left hand so it covered his Hunter tattoo.

Lydia peeked into the other room. The man still sat, bound to the chair. Sticky red fluid dripped down his back. On a nearby rolling table, a charred steak waited and next to it the torch still attached to the oxy acetylene tank, its tip still glowing. Walking over, she touched the sticky red fluid, sniffed it, and then licked it.

"Cherry?" Putting two and two together, she found Alistar leaning against the observation room's wall, eating a red popsicle.

"What did you do?"

"I blindfolded him, and charred the steak with the

torch while jabbing him in the back with the popsicle and telling him I was burning the fat off his back." Alistar smiled evilly. "The cold of the popsicle numbed the skin and made him believe I burned so deeply that the nerves in his back were dead. The melted popsicle made him think blood was running down his back."

"Where did you learn to do that?"

"Saw it in an old movie once." Alistar shrugged. He tossed the wooden popsicle stick in the trashcan next to the door.

"And did it work?" Elzibeth asked.

"The serum storage facility is in Rome. Which also happens to be the local headquarters for the church on this side of the world. Also, someone needs to talk to Vance. This guy was his team lead. I'm going out. I need time to think."

Alistar pushed off the wall and headed out the door.

"I am worried about him. I think tonight he crossed a line that he has never crossed before." Elzibeth said to Lydia and Kim.

"I agree. I will go with him," Kim said. "He missed a therapy session the other day, and I'd like the chance to talk to him." Kim gave Elzibeth a pointed look before leaving.

~

Alistar walked out of Miyamoto's compound and into the night. The roar of a motorcycle behind him had him pause and the bike pulled up beside him.

Kim lifted the helmet's visor. "Get on. I'll take you anywhere you want to go, but in exchange, we will talk."

"Fine, but I drive." Kim scooted back and handed him a spare helmet before Alistar mounted the bike.

"Where are we going?" She wiggled around finding a comfortable position against his back.

"Where's the nearest fight club?"

"I know a werewolf club that holds fights, but why would you want to go there?"

"Therapy." Alistar gunned the bike and roared off down the street.

Thirty minutes later they arrived in front of a seedy warehouse turned bar. The bouncer at the door grinned. "Kim Miyamoto, you just can't stay away."

"Oh, come on, Brandt. I just like seeing you get your ass kicked in the ring." Kim kissed him.

Alistar raised his eyebrows but stayed silent.

"Did you bring this one to watch?" Brandt glanced over Kim's shoulder to the man behind her. "We have guests from afar, and currently they're ruling the ring, and the race track."

Alistar cracked his neck. "No, I came to participate."

Kim spun, shock evident on her face.. "You said you wanted to come here for therapy!"

"Yep. I did." Alistar pushed past her and Brandt, stepping inside to loud pulsing music and the sounds of fighting. He breathed in the musky scent of werewolves and body sweat. In the open center of the warehouse sat a massive steel octagonal ring where two werewolves currently fought.

Kim frowned and sent a text message along with their address before stepping inside.

Alistar motioned to the bartender.

"What will you have?" the burley, bald, tattooed bartender asked.

"Water, and information on how I get in there." Alistar motioned to the ring behind him.

The bartender slid him a dirty glass of water and

Alistar slammed it back. "You don't smell like ulfur faeddur."

"I'm not wolf born, I'm something else."

"If you want in the ring, you'll have to race me, and beat me, mannlegur," a feminine voice with an Icelandic note said from behind him.

71

Alistar put his back against the bar and looked at the tough, tall woman. She had red hair braided with beads, extremely muscled physique, and was dressed in leather. After a moment, her male counterpart arrived and put his arm around her.

"*Ja*, my mate has beaten everyone on the track so far, and everyone in the ring as well."

Alistar cocked his head. "That's gonna be an issue. My bike is all the way in Romania. I'm just here visiting a friend."

"Oh, too bad then. Can't race without a bike. You can't race; you can't fight." The woman laughed, her eyes sparkling as she kissed the man beside her.

Kim sighed behind Alistar. *I'm going to regret this,* she thought to herself. "He can use mine."

"Well then, we have a race!" The man laughed as he and the woman walked away.

Kim turned to Alistar. "If you break my bike, I'm gonna be pissed. And just what in the fuck are you doing?"

Alistar eyed the short Japanese vampire. "Giving my

pound of flesh." With that said he took the keys out of her hand, headed out front, and grabbed the bike, pushing it to the track in back of the building.

A run down old stretch of road with a partially caved-in bridge in the middle described the track. It opened above a long drop into a spillway for a flood-overflow basin. Kim walked alongside him as he pushed the bike to its starting position. "Your pound of flesh? You can't be serious. What happened to Evelyn was NOT your fault, Alistar."

Alistar rounded on her. "IF I were faster, if I was NOT drunk, she would be okay! So yes.. It IS!" The anger in his eyes made the small vampire take a step back and he straddled the bike before he looked over to the other woman mounted on a red Venom x22R.

"The rules are simple, *Ja*. "Three times down, three times back. You must jump the bridge. You win? You can fight," the woman said before lowering her visor. She revved the engine and peeled out. Alistar took off after her.

Both racers sped down the stretch of road. Alistar hugged low to the bike, decreasing his wind resistance. He watched as the were-woman rocketed over the opening in the bridge milliseconds ahead of him. His bike launched into the air and for a microsecond, Alistar experienced free-fall. Then the bike hit the pavement.

Both riders completed the first and second lap with Alistar on the were-woman's tail. On the third return lap the were-woman's bike started smoking before she reached the bridge. She wouldn't make it across. Her bike would go off the edge even if she slowed.

He lowered and pulled up alongside the woman. "Give me your hand!" he shouted. She peered at him, at his hand, and back to him. Reaching out she grabbed it and he pulled as she jumped. She landed on the seat behind him right before he hit the bridge and they sailed across.

Come on. Come on! Alistar thought as the bike flew through the air. The front wheel touched down but the back wheel caught on the edge, sending the bike out of control.

Both riders hit the pavement hard and rolled as the bike skidded on its side down the strip.

Alistar lay on his back breathing hard. His smashed helmet had saved his skull. "Hey, are you... alive over there?" he groaned.

"*Ja.* I am alive, thanks to you. I am wondering if that may change, though, considering what is on your wrist." The were-woman's eyes were locked on Alistar's left wrist..

Alistar looked over, seeing the glove on his left hand peeled back and his tattoo showing. He chuckled. "Former Hunter. I don't do that stuff anymore."

"So you get your thrills saving random women from certain death then?"

"Yeah... something like that." Alistar rolled over. "So neither of us finished. What's that mean?"

"I think I let you have this one. Since you saved me and all." The were-woman showed no fear in her eyes.

"Cool." Alistar repositioned his glove as Kim and the were-woman's mate showed up.

"Dammit! That was a new bike, Kain!" Kim cursed. She helped him up while the man helped his mate. "Good save though, I'll admit that." They all sauntered back toward the bar.

"I have to agree, Mister..." The male werewolf stared at Alistar, perhaps judging him.

"Kain, Alistar Kain," Alistar replied without thinking.

The other man stopped. "You are the Nightbane. The boogeyman that werewolves tell their children about."

Alistar looked over at the other man coolly. "Yeah, I

used to be called that back in the day, but that was long ago. As I told your mate here, I don't do that anymore."

"Is true. He did say that." The were-woman shrugged.

"I can confirm. Instead he protects Grand Lady Elzibeth Tepes, and he is her suitor," Kim said.

Alistar nudged her in the ribs.

"What? Elzibeth will be here at some point so they'll find out that part soon enough. As for that damn tattoo, I'm surprised you didn't just cut it off."

"Tried. Can't. It's mystical."

"Well, I guess you did save Ingrid. So you can't be all bad. Still… I would keep that hidden around the others." The man smiled fiercely.

"Duly noted. I'll do my best." Alistar paused by the building. "Give me one second." He slammed his shoulder against it.

"What are you doing, Alistar?" Kim asked.

"I dislocated my shoulder, pulling Lady Ingrid off her bike." He looked over at the little vampire.

"Oh, is that all? Allow me." Kim grabbed his arm. There was a pop as she gave it a swift yank.

Alistar just grunted and then nodded. "Thanks."

72

A listar stepped into the building alongside the two werewolves, and Kim Miyamoto.

"I am Randolph by the way. So why do you want to fight?" Ingrid's mate asked, holding out his hand.

Alistar considered it for a moment then clasped it in a firm handshake.

"I wish to undergo your right of Yfirbót." Alistar replied solemnly.

Ingrid's eyes widened. "You know what you ask?"

Alistar nodded. "Yep. I do."

"You are either brave, or stupid," Randolph remarked.

"Or both," Kim retorted. Alistar stripped off his jacket and then his shirt, revealing the scars across his well-muscled body. He left on his boots, pants and the glove on his left hand. The bar quieted at the sight of him and people started whispering.

Alistar walked through the open door to the fighting ring and turned around to face Ingrid, Randolph, and Kim.

"I'm not one of you, but I have my own pack, my own family. Tonight, I failed them. Let one of them get hurt and almost killed. I'm their guardian, their protector, and I failed them. I invoke the ritual of *Yfirbót*."

Randolph sighed. "Well, now he's done it. Once invoked, ritual cannot be taken back and must be seen through."

"This man has invoked *Yfirbót!*" Ingrid said beside him. "He wishes to pay for his transgressions with the ritual of combat! Who will answer his request?!"

Two younger werewolves stepped forward, one had shaggy, sandy locks that fell about his face, and the other, short black hair cut in a neat military fashion. "If the human wants his ass beat, we shall happily do this for him," one of them said, grinning."

Randolph nodded. "So it shall be. Trial by combat. BUT. I am giving him a second so you do not kill him, *Ja*."

The two werewolves shrugged. "If you say it is to be, *Alfa*, then it is to be."

"I do it. I owe him life debt," Ingrid said from within the ring. "So you don't get killed before you are ready." Ingrid's look dared him to say no.

The two werewolves climbed into the ring. "Pick your weapons, human."

"I choose fists." Alistar cracked his knuckles.

Suddenly a third werewolf jumped in, this one had three slashes down the side of his face, and was missing an eye. The door closed and locked shut.

"Look at his wrist! He's a Hunter! Tonight you die." The third werewolf transformed and grabbed Ingrid from behind in a bear hug. "And you will not interfere, *Voru Kona*." The were-woman struggled against the one holding her.

Until now, Alistar had not realized the damage done to his glove after the race. Now that it was out of order, he had no way of hiding his tattoo.

"Human Alistar, if you do not fight, you die! These three have no honor!" Ingrid shouted.

"Dammit, Kain! Elzibeth is gonna kill me!" Kim watched, panic in her eyes.

"What is going on here?!" A familiar voice rang out over the rumble and roar of the crowd. Silence fell and everyone turned to see Elzibeth, Lydia, and Miyamoto standing by the door.

Elzibeth flowed through the room until she was standing at the cage. "It looks like you are challenging my boyfriend to an unfair fight." Her eyes flashed in anger and her voice edged with steel.

"You were supposed to watch him and keep him out of trouble."

Kim looked down at the floor. "I tried, My Queen. He is headstrong."

"Yes, he is."

"Grand Lady Tepes," Randolph said, "your suitor has invoked *Yfirbót*. Once invoked, it cannot be rescinded."

"He wants to get the shit beat out of him?" Lydia said in shock. "Hell, I would have done that for free and had fun doing it." Elzibeth silenced her with a look before stepping over to the cage.

"When we get home, you and I will speak, Alistar Kain. I do not agree with why you are doing this. Evelyn is fine. Her child WILL be fine. She would not wish you to do this, and neither do I."

"That's enough talk, vampire!" one of the younger wolves yelled at her before swinging on Alistar.

The punch rocked Alistar's head back. He tasted blood but did not fight back. The werewolf hammered him with a left hook, snapping his head around. A tooth flew out of his mouth, landing in front of Elzibeth, and he dropped to his knees facing her, blood dripping out of his mouth.

"Look at him. He's just gonna let us kill him!" One of the werewolves shouted with joy.

Elzibeth knew why he was doing this but still she hated it. "Fight back, my love."

The werewolf grabbed him by his hair, dragged him away from the cage wall, and put him in a headlock. The other werewolf closed in, hammering Alistar's stomach with a powerful blow. Alistar closed his eyes, falling to his knees as the first werewolf let him go, but then he climbed back to his feet.

"You both hit like bitches. Come on, if you're gonna hit me, fucking HIT ME!" Alistar roared.

The first werewolf spun him around and punched him hard in the face. His right orbital socket broke.

"Shit. My vampire hits harder than that, you wimp. Try again."

The werewolf's second blow snapped his nose.

"Oh, yeah, now we're talking! But you can do better. Come on, one more shot. Make me feel it!"

"Dear God, I think he's punch-drunk," Lydia whispered.

"Once we're done with you, we're going out there to fuck all three of your vampire friends."

Alistar's eyes snapped open in fiery rage, at the werewolf's threat.

"Uh, oh. Wrong thing to say," Lydia said.

"Why is that?" Randolph asked.

"Alistar doesn't care about himself. Man has a death wish or something, but mess with those he loves, and he'll kill you. I personally watched him take on an entire compound of Hunters just to rescue Elle over there. He killed at least twenty on his own."

"Really? Well, then, those pups are going to learn a lesson tonight," Randolph said grinning.

Alistar kicked out, his boot crushing and shoving the

knee of the werewolf behind him backward. The man fell to the ring howling in pain as Alistar vaulted over him. It would not last long considering most werewolves' healing factor.

"Hey, wolf-girl. Do me a favor," he said, his deadly calm voice carrying over the crowd.

"*Ja?*" Ingrid asked as she struggled in the grasp of the werewolf behind her.

"Spread your legs."

"What?" Ingrid looked shocked, thinking the man was clearly insane. *"Is he propositioning me?"* she thought to herself.

Alistar looked at his right foot then back up to her. Realization dawned on the were-woman's face.

Alistar raced across the ring and Ingrid reached behind her, seized the werewolf holding her by his neck and lifted herself, going into a split in mid-air. Alistar's boot flew up and connected with the werewolf's lower regions, lifting the werewolf off the ring floor by three inches. He dropped Ingrid and grabbed at himself, howling in pain.

Alistar spun, his heel smashing the face of the were-wolf coming up behind him.

"If you fucks kept it between us, I wouldn't have fought back. But you just had to bring my family into it!" He growled. Ingrid turned and haymakered the werewolf behind her, knocking him out. She transformed and roared

The other two werewolves backed away. "No. You don't get off so easily, guys," Alistar said. He jumped to the side of the cage, pushing off and elbow-smashing the were-wolf closest to him in the face with his full weight.

Ingrid grabbed the other werewolf, hammering his head against one of the metal posts repeatedly until unconsciousness welcomed him. Then she and Alistar turned to the last werewolf.

"I submit," he said, going down on his knees. Alistar chuckled with a bloody grin, even with the pain throughout his body.

Ingrid howled in triumph. Alistar's body seemed to struggle to stay upright next to her, blood dripping from his nose and mouth onto the floor of the ring, his one eye fully swollen shut.

73

The cage door clunked open, loud in the quiet bar.

"Ladies first," Alistar said, motioning to Ingrid. The were-woman bowed to him and transformed back into her human form.

As Alistar stepped out of the ring, every werewolf in the place bowed. "Umm, what's going on?"

Randolph stood. "You won your *Yfirbót*. We pay honor to that."

"Oh... cool, I guess."

"Jesus, you look like shit," Lydia said nearby

Alistar smiled, showing bloody teeth. "I might look like shit, but I feel.. better. Really needed to release some frustration."

"Well, maybe next time, you should try running instead." Lydia laughed.

Elzibeth swept up to him, lightly touching his face. After a moment, she sighed, kissed his cheek instead of saying anything, then stood by his side, their arms entwined.

Randolph pushed a drink into Alistar's hands and

clinked his own against it. "We celebrate!" Alistar looked at the drink, handed it off to Lydia who passed it off to a random person and walked over to the bar.

"You don't wish to celebrate?" Ingrid asked.

Alistar ran his hand through his hair. "Yeah, celebration is good, but I'm gonna lay off the booze for a while. It, ummm... disagrees with me. You might say it got me into this mess."

Lydia handed him a glass of dirty water, then smacked him upside the back of the head. "Dumbass," she muttered.

He rounded on her, anger flashing in his eyes but Elzibeth placed her hand on his chest and he fell silent. After a minute he clinked his glass against Randolph's again and drained it in one go.

Randolph and Ingrid observed the interaction with interest.

"Alcohol was the start of the situation that brought you here?" Ingrid asked.

Alistar nodded at the were-woman's words.

Randolph's head swiveled between them, listening. "I get it. So does Ingrid. We are descended from vikings and carry many of their traditions. Including the more celebratorious ones."

"Randolph means we like to party, and we party hard," Ingrid added in. "But after the party, things can happen."

"Yeah, well, no more parties for me for a while, and no more booze." Alistar chuckled. His watch beeped. "Well, that's the sunrise warning. We'd best be going."

Alistar lounged in the back of the limo across from Elzibeth, Lydia, and Kim.

"It's not Evie I'm worried about," Alistar finally said.

"We know. We're all worried about the fetus," Lydia replied. Elzibeth just watched him.

Alistar looked out the window as the lights of Osaka flashed past in the predawn light. "I am supposed to be the Nightbane to werebeings, the Ghost of Death to vampires, the raksha karanevaala to the queen, and supposed guardian to my family. Yet tonight I don't know what I am except for a man who nearly lost a daughter, and possibly a grandchild. And even though you would think I should be used to it by now with all I've lost, it scared me to my core. I felt so helpless." He paused, putting a hand against his chest as a sharp pain hit. Lydia and Elzibeth watched him closely with concern. "I'm fine. Too much exertion I guess."

Elzibeth reached across the space between them and placed her cool hand on his warm one. "Sometimes due to my age, I forget what being afraid is like. When you got shot by Marcus, I was scared. Back in the Hunter compound when you collapsed after saving me, I was scared. I thought I was going to lose you both of those times, and again tonight, seeing you in that fighting cage with those werewolves..." She stroked his face lightly. "I thought I might lose you again."

Alistar closed his eyes. "Yeah, I thought I might be done for as well honestly. But then..."

His eyes popped open. "They brought you into it, and I wasn't having that."

"Sorry about the bike, Kim," he said to the small spunky Japanese vampire.

Kim waved away his apology. "It's just a bike, and honestly what you did may have opened inroads with the werewolves of Japan. Most certainly with Randolph and Ingrid's pack, though they are visitors."

"So, Alistar, is this your normal method of operation?" Lydia questioned.

"You mean get myself beat to hell and back whenever I feel like I've done something wrong? Yeah. Pretty much."

"That needs to stop," Elzibeth said. Alistar closes his eyes again and a wistful smile appeared.

"Not gonna happen, Elle. There's something in the pain, in the fight. A rush that makes everything better, that reminds me I'm not dead inside."

"Why don't you just fight us?" Kim Asked.

"Right, and end up killing you. Like I want THAT on my ticket!"

"What makes you think you would kill us? You didn't kill Richter, or Elle?" Lydia asked.

Alistar tapped the side of his head with his right index finger. "That was then, before I overdosed. I'm not sure I'm even human anymore. The voices up here are pretty convincing. If I get into the fight too much, I might lose control. I can't let that happen with anyone I care about."

"So instead you go into a wolfborn bar to get the shit kicked out of you? That's fucking stupid," Lydia snorted.

"Yeah, well, I never said I was intelligent." Alistar rolled his eyes.

Lydia laughed. Elzibeth glared at her. Then she used one finger to turn Alistar's face to her.

"The next time you need to fight to release whatever is inside you, you come to me. You will not say no... to me. I will find a safer way for you to do so." She did not use her ability to force her will against him, her words were simply words.

She held Alistar's gaze a moment longer. "Okay. I will." His gaze fell to the floor.

"Good. Now, don't be upset, but Evelyn has decided to let the Hunter who shot her go."

"Is she stupid?!"

"No, she's following your example. I, however, agree with you. I think he should be drained and his body thrown into the ocean," Lydia's voice was full of annoyance.

74

The limo stopped in front of Miyamoto's compound. Evelyn appeared and hugged him, then examined his face.

"You... you jerk. You had all of us worried!" She punched him in the chest. It actually hurt.

"Ow! Evie, I was okay! Ow!" Alistar held up his hands.

"No, you were not. Don't lie to her." Elzibeth said.

Evelyn hit him again and he backed away. "Hey!" He grabbed her wrist and pulled her close, hugging her as she struggled. "Evie, I'm okay. I mean I have three broken ribs, a cracked orbital socket, I'm missing a tooth, and am bruised as all get out, but I'm okay."

Evelyn stilled at his words. His shirt became wet as she cried. "I can't lose another parent."

Alistar knelt painfully as bruised muscles moved and pulled. "Hey. I'm not gonna say I'll be here forever, but I can tell you that I'll always try to come back, Hell or high water."

He wiped her tears away. Then she hugged him back. "You better!" Alistar stood as the sun rose over the horizon.

"Well, sun's up. Time to get under cover and for all good vampires to go to bed." He smiled.

～

Alistar lay in bed, Elzibeth curled around him, running her finger across his chest.

"Your injuries look painful, my love."

"They are," Alistar replied, gazing at the ceiling.

"I can heal you." Elzibeth put her finger in her mouth.

"No. I'll heal these the old-fashioned way and deal with the pain." Alistar said, turning his head and looking her in the eyes. Elzibeth pulled her finger from her mouth and placed her hand on his chest. "Okay."

～

Six months later, Alistar finished packing his bags. Miyamoto had started work months ago on getting Castle Tepes repaired and rebuilt, and now it was finally finished and everyone could go home.

They stepped through the mirror gate, and into the now rebuilt gate room. On the other walls hung three identical mirrors.

Miyamoto spun around, walking backward. "Your castle has been rebuilt as you can see. The walls might still look like stone, but on the inside two-inch-thick steel plates have been mounted and covered with stone veneer. The amenities have been upgraded to more modern standards."

He opened a door to reveal the war room. The room's insides appeared much the same as before, but along one wall an electronic map like that which resided at Miyamoto's mansion had been installed.

"The windows might look the same but they are now made out of four-inch-thick bulletproof polycarbonate. And of course there are cameras mounted all over the place."

"Oh, great, Lydia can perv on me when I'm taking a bath!" Alistar joked.

"As if. I wouldn't perv on your ugly ass if I was paid! Besides, I've already seen you naked. I helped Elzibeth undress you after the serum incident."

Elzibeth smiled at him. "She did."

Alistar face-palmed as everyone else laughs. "Oh, Jesus, Elle, you said you were the one to undress me."

"She only took off your outerwear. I did the rest," Elzibeth said, giving him a kiss on the cheek.

Miyamoto continued the castle tour, taking them into the newly improved kitchen, and then up to the second floor where the bedrooms for the castle personnel were located. Alistar decided to leave his things in a room when Elzibeth took his hand.

"No, my love, this is not your room." She smiled slyly as she snuck him away from the group and led him up to the tower. Opening the door at the top, she pulled him inside. "This is your room."

"But this is your room, princess." Alistar gazed at her with a quiet smile. Elzibeth placed a finger against his lips.

"It's your room now as well, Mister Kain."

Alistar pulled her to him. "Is it now? I thought no one was allowed up here." He gave a boyish grin.

Elzibeth looked in his eyes and then kissed him. "Yes. Except that was then, and this is now."

She bit her lower lip in thought. Closing the door behind them, she locked it and shoved him back onto the bed, climbing on top.

∽

A week later found Alistar in the war room pouring over maps. "These maps are good but they don't show patrol routes."

Lydia shoved some pictures under his nose. Alistar blinked a few times at her in question. "We have human agents in many cities, including Rome." She chuckled.

He grabbed the pictures from her and drew on the map of Rome with time stamps. "How's…"

"Evie and the child are both fine, though the baby is growing slightly faster than normal. I would say in another month or so Evie is gonna be ready to pop." Lydia said.

"So does that mean we're literally going to have an ankle biter crawling around the place?" Alistar asked with a slight smile.

"Baby fangs do not come in till three to six months old. So until then the child will look like a normal human baby and feed the same, so we will not know until we run tests," Elzibeth replied while looking at the maps with him.

"Duly noted. I'll make sure to baby proof the castle after this last mission." Richter quipped as he stepped into the room, carrying two chalices of blood for Elzibeth and Lydia and a cup of tea for Alistar.

"Thanks, old man," Alistar said, taking the tea and sipping it. Richter grunted in reply as Elzibeth and Lydia took their drinks.

Alistar circled a building, then shuffled through a stack of maps until he found the interior layout of said building. Silence ensued while he jotted notes and symbols with a grease pencil. Elzibeth and Lydia watched him closely. He chewed on the end of the pencil in thought until Elzibeth extracted it from his mouth. After a moment more he snagged it back then jotted down more notes.

"Well, it's gonna be tough, but it's doable. Ideally we

would need to get an agent inside but that's not happening. So I guess we go with plan B."

"And what is plan B?" Elzibth asked.

"One team of six sneaks into the city under the cover of darkness. Then six teams of ten post outside the city proper and launch an attack a few hours later as a distraction. The initial six infiltrate the main compound while the Hunters are busy dealing with those outside. Scratch that, make it ten teams of ten." Alistar crossed his arms and tapped the pencil against his left shoulder.

"Who is the team of six?" Lydia asked.

"Well, myself, Elzibeth, since she won't allow me to go anywhere alone anymore..."

"You better believe that, Mister Kain," Elzibeth muttered loud enough so Alistar knew she meant business.

"Richter of course, and you," Alistar finished as he pointed at Lydia with the pencil.

"That's only four," Richter remarked.

"Yeah, well, I haven't thought quite that far ahead yet!" Alistar snapped before pacing the room in thought.

"Alistar. Alistar!" Lydia snapped him out of it.

"Umm, yes... Lydia?"

"What about those werewolves we met? One of them still owes you a life debt, and they all love to fight."

"Lydia, I could kiss you. I won't because Elle would kill us both, but I could." An evil grin consumed Alistar's face..

Elzibeth moved out of the way. "Just this once, I will not."

Alistar flashed over to Lydia, flowing more like a vampire than an enhanced human. Taking her arm he tugged her to him and bent her backward, kissing her. The signal of annoyance in his mind from Elzibeth told him when to break the kiss. He then straightened her.

"Damn. You're so lucky you got to him first, Elle." Lydia said in shock.

75

Five nights later, Alistar watched a pack of twenty-two werewolves ride up to the castle on motorcycles and various off-road vehicles. A distinctive Venom RX motorcycle led the pack.

Pulling through the gates, the werewoman removed her helmet and shook out her hair, with a bright smile. "Well this is certainly a nice place you have, *Ja?*"

Randolph parked beside her as Alistar came walking down the castle steps. "Kain! *Ulfor Brodir!*" When Alistar stuck out his hand to shake, Randolph instead clasped it forearm to forearm.

"I see you all made the trip with no issues?" Alistar asked as the man pulled him into an unexpected hug.

"*Ja.* We did, thank you." Ingrid says, clasping his arm like Randolph had.

Elzibeth swept down the steps and Randolph pulled her into a bear hug. "Ah, Alistar's better half!" Elzibeth stiffened for a second before realizing she was not in fact under attack, then laughed.

"Randolph Sigurdson! You put that poor woman down right now or so help me! She does not need you crushing her in one of your famous hugs!" Ingrid scolded her mate then gave Elzibeth a much gentler hug.

"Rather huggy, aren't they?" he muttered to Lydia.

"*Ja*. We *Ulfur Faeddur* are all about friends and family. We hug those we like," Ingrid replieed, smiling with a lot of teeth.

"So what happens to those you don't like?" Alistar asked, raising an eyebrow.

"We fight them and then we are friends if they wish. If they do not wish, we kill them." Ingrid shrugged.

"Well, that's a simple outlook on life." Alistar laughed.

"*Ja*. Simple life is best for sure." With a broad smile Randolph advanced on Lydia.

"Don't you dare, wolf boy!" Lydia backed away, snarling, trying to look fierce and not laugh.

"Randolph Sigurdson! Heel!" Ingrid commanded. Her mate appeared dejected and came to stand by her side.

Alistar shakes his head. "Nope. Not gonna say it." He chuckled.

Ingrid rounded on him with narrowed eyes, then she grinned. "*Ja*. In *Ulf Faeddur* society, the males may lead the pack, but females are really in charge. Otherwise their mates might not get any for a while."

Alistar doubled over in laughter but found Elzibeth peering at him. *"The same thing could be said for you, my love,"* she mentally said with a slight smile and a knowing raised eyebrow.

"Umm, yes, dear." she heard in her mind. "Well, let me show you all inside. Is this your entire pack?"

"Ja, and then some." Ingrid's gaze located three very familiar werewolves among the rest of her pack. They stepped forward with heads bowed.

Alistar frowned. He knew these werewolves well because they had tried to kill him in a cage match.

Elzibeth flowed over to his side, her arm protectively entwining with his. "And what are these three doing here?"

The one with three claw marks on his face and one eye scratched his head. Ingrid nudged him with her booted foot. "We wish to atone for our... umm... unwarranted attempt at trying to kill your mate, Grand Lady Tepes." Whether being respectful or just scared, she did not know because he kept his eyes on the ground.

Elzibeth scrutinized him with a cold gaze for a full thirty seconds. "Very well..."

~

Alistar stood around the map table with Elzibeth, Lydia, Richter, Ingrid, and Randolph.

"I suggest we put the pack outside the town. Two *ulfur faeddur* with each team of vampires. That will bring your teams up to twelve strong each and give them more of a punch."

Alistar tilted his head to the right and raised both eyebrows. "That's gonna give the church fits. Let's do it."

"*Ja'* but you mention this infiltration team of six. I see four here. Who are the other two?" Ingrid asked. Alistar tossed her and Randolph each a communication earbud.

"Welcome to the alpha team. We're the vanguard. Each of your werewolves WILL follow the orders of their team leader; make sure they know that."

"Aye, they will know, or I will personally kick the shit out of them if they survive!" Randolph growled.

"Excellent. Let's get geared up." Alistar turned and paused. "One more thing. This city has innocents in it. Our fight isn't with them. They'll be scared, and some may even attack. Subdue and restrain them. We have to show that we are NOT the bad guys."

"But there are always casualties in war. It can not be helped." Ingrid looked in amazement at his suggestion.

"Not this time," Alistar said with a leveled gaze.

~

Alistar's group reached near the center of town and stopped in an alley. "Everybody check their makeup," Alistar whispered over the comms. Lydia and Elzibeth popped open mirrors and, in the slight moonlight, checked to make sure the foundation was still covering their pale flesh. If no one got too close to see their ears, they just pass for humans.

"Alright, we're going in," he continued before stepping out of the alley, through the door of the nearest building, and into a tavern. The others followed him inside.

Alistar's gaze flickered quickly around the room, noticing its lack of patrons. "Alright, we'll rest here for now." He met the bartender at the bar.

The man glanced at Alistar and his group, all dressed in black leather with hooded cloaks. Alistar showed his tattoo and the man relaxed thinking they were all Hunters.

"You folks come in for a drink?" he asked as he polished a glass.

"I'll have a cup of tea. Bring the others two glasses of wine, and three beers." Alistar tossed the church-marked gold coins on the counter as he played up his guise of Hunter team lead. The man snatched the coins.

A bar-maid brought out the drinks and set them in front of the others while the bartender placed a steaming hot cup of tea in front of Alistar.

The door behind him slowly opened, the night's chill air rushing in, quickly filling the bar.

76

Everyone in the room froze when Mikhail Branson entered, scanned the interior, and stepped over to the bar next to Alistar. Four Hunters followed him inside.

"You have a lot of nerve coming here, Kain," Mikhail said gruffly. He glanced at the bartender, knowing Alistar's love for tea. "I'll have what he's having."

Ingrid and Randolph started to stand but Alistar stopped them with one word. "Don't."

"How'd you find us, Mikhail?" Alistar whispered, before blowing on his tea and having a sip.

"Nothing goes on in this city without my knowing. You should know that. I've been tracking you all since you entered." Mikhail then likewise took a sip of his own tea.

"We gonna fight?" Alistar asked calmly as he took another sip.

"Yes, but not here in this fine establishment. You and I alone would wreck this place." Mikhail chuckled.

Elzibeth stood and Mikhail looked over at her. "I'd sit back down if I were you, vampire. At this moment I mean him no harm. Just two old friends having some tea together."

The bartender gaped back and forth between the two groups, then beat a retreat

"But, Master Bransen," One of the Hunters said. "You're standing next to the traitor, and there are vampires over at that table!"

Mikhail Branson fixed the younger Hunter with a baleful glare. "You are barely out of diapers, kid. The man standing next to me would kill all four of you in less than two seconds if you so much as touch that vampire over there. So, Sit. The fuck. Down. That goes for the rest of you."

The young Hunters perched on seats at a table across the tavern from Alistar's group and Mikhail turned his attention back to Alistar. "What are you doing here, Kain?"

"Oh, the usual. pissing off the church in the best way possible, old friend." Alistar sipped his tea again.

"If you think you can get to the serum facility, you are wrong. You can't take the place with only six of you, even if one of them is yourself."

Alistar raised an eyebrow. "Who said I only have six? For all you know, I could have a whole army."

"Kain, if you have a whole army, I'd know about it." Mikhail growls. Then he sighs. "Look, if you all leave right now, I will make sure the church never messes with you or yours ever again.

Alistar's eyes flashed with anger. "Don't make promises you know you can't keep, old man. You already did that once before and it led us to this."

A look of shame passed across Mikhail Bransen's face. "We all make mistakes we regret, kid."

Alistar tipped the tea back, draining the cup. "Yeah,

well, I'm fixing mine. You could join us. Fight for the right side for once."

"There is no right side in war, only killing," Mikhail responded. He finished his tea and turned away. "You know what happens next time we meet."

"Yeah. I do."

An air raid siren blared and Mikhail looked out the window, then back at Alistar.

"How many?"

Alistar raised an eyebrow. "Over one hundred."

Mikhail shook his head. "Damn you, Kain. You were the best I trained. But the one thing you always had was that damn charisma, even when you were being a little shit. I shouldn't be surprised you raised an army of one hundred vampires."

"Lets not forget the twenty werewolves," Lydia said.

Mikhail flashed a shocked expression to her, then aimed for the door. "Let's go. We are needed on the front lines. I will deal with this group later if they make it inside."

With those words, he rushed out the door. The four Hunters with him seemed uncertain and Alistar proceeded toward them, making their minds up for them, and they followed their leader out the door.

"Bartender! One more!" Alistar yelled, holding his hand back behind him. After a moment he felt a shaking mug pushed into his hand. He downed it in one gulp and flipped a coin back over his shoulder, hearing it clink on the counter as he walked away. "All teams check-in."

"Bravo here. Charlie here. Delta here..." It continued down the line until he heard "Kilo here."

"Alright, folks, listen up. Remember, innocents are not to be harmed. If they're in harm's way, you WILL save them and move them to a safer place. If a Hunter surrenders, detain them. Push through the city toward the facility. We'll lead the way. Alpha out."

He threw off his cloak. "Let's go knock on their door."

He and his team flowed out the door and into the streets. People ran about in panic at the sirens. A team of seven Hunters appeared facing them. Alistar snapped the staff off his left gauntlet and spun it, snapping the ends out into place. Then without warning he found himself among them: a knee smashed, a helmet crushed in, arms broken, and pelvises shattered. But when he finished, they still lived. Behind him on the edges of town, gunfire and the faint sounds of fighting could be heard.

"Be smart and stay down, boys and girls," he said glaring at them before heading down the street. As another group of Hunters, fifteen strong, rounded a corner, he leapt off the side of the building and landed, spinning like a whirling tornado as Elzibeth, Lydia, and the others joined him, all careful not to kill.

Running around another corner, he stopped as twenty Hunters aimed crossbows at him. He roared and charged as bolts flew, then he found himself back in the fray, pulling weapons from their hands and punching and kicking the Hunters so hard they flew back and hit the walls where they lay unconscious.

A mother and children ran out into the street and Lydia and Elzibeth went for them, ushering the scared, confused family back in-doors. Alistar smiled at this.

"Let's go!" He motioned for the others to follow him. The closer they got to the facility, the more Hunters they encountered and the more Hunters they had to kill. By this time Alistar had switched to his pistols and showed off an impressive gun-kata routine.

He spun, shot one Hunter in the kneecap, another in the neck, more spinning, and then a burst took out three more. Leaping high into the air, he flipped almost into a headstand and he rained down lead on the Hunters before landing between them and shooting four more, left, right, front, and back. His guns clicked empty as he aimed at the last Hunter. Pushing the eject button, he let the mag fall, and he spun kicked it into the Hunter's face, breaking the man's nose. Seconds later Elzibeth found a hunter and bit deep, her eyes fully blood red and glowing. As she fed, Alistar reloaded both pistols.

Two more encounters went similarly before they reached the armored doors of the serum production facility.

77

Alistar bolted toward the doors and leapt, kicking them with the full force of his weight. The doors shuddered noticeably and bent inward a little, shocking everyone else. He steped back and got ready to make another go at it.

"Kain, let us open it," Randolph said as he and Ingrid transformed. They wedged their claws into the crack between both door halves, then strained and pulled, and after a few seconds, the door halves peeled back like tin foil.

"I knew you two would be useful. Big furry can openers," Alistar joked.

Ingrid's big, furry, wedge-shaped wolfen head snorted, the movement of her breath making his hair move.

Alistar turned to his friends and family. "I really should do this alone from here on out."

Everyone stared blankly. "Not on your fucking life," Elzibeth stated with a bit of anger.

"You really are a dumbass if you think I'm gonna let a friend walk into this Hell alone," Lydia piped in.

"I've grown to like you, Kain," Richter said. "so you are not getting rid of me that easily."

Alistar shrugged. "Heh. Figures." He chuckled.

He turned back to the hallway's darkness. Flashing red emergency lights were the only navigation. The place seemed deserted until they rounded a corner and found five Hunters kneeling.

Alistar paused and five pairs of glowing blue eyes appeared in the darkness. The Hunters lifted their heads, their faces covered in glowing blue veins.

"Shit. I knew this was too easy. Move fast; go for the kill. These guys are all level four. And they are juiced," Alistar said, as he brought up his pistols and unleashed a barrage of shots. The bullets streaked down the hallway.

He watched as the Hunters rose and deflected all the bullets.

"Don't feed on them! Their blood is poison!" he yelled, slamming his pistols back into their holsters and pulling his twin katanas. He swung the first blade and the Hunter nearest him blocked it but couldn't stop the second blow as Alistar spun around, cutting the man in half with his backswing.

Ingrid and Randolph jumped over his head pouncing on the two nearest Hunters, slashing with claws and biting with ferocious jaws, even as the Hunters slashed and stabbed them. Blood covered the two werewolves, the Hunters and their own. Elzibeth and Lydia swept in from the sides with elegant ornate swords drawn. They moved like quicksilver, their blades flashing. Richter sent knives flying into the fray, striking two Hunters who took the hits and remained standing. Alistar focused on the next Hunter, his flurry of blows backing the man against the wall and tearing great rents in the uniform and skin beneath.

Dropping one of his katanas, Alistar pulled his combat

knife. He flipped it in his hand and pivoted, slamming it backhanded through the man's right shoulder, pinning him to the wall as the other hunters fell to his allies.

As one, the others stepped up behind him and he stared at the pinned hunter struggling to get free. As the man grew weaker, Alistar reached out and took his security badge. Then with lightning-fast speed he snapped the man's neck one-handed.

With his katana back in hand, he retrieved his combat knife, letting the now dead body slump to the floor. "Bags," he said. At the one word, Richter and the vampires opened backpacks, revealing explosives within.

"Richter, Ingrid, Randolph, you three start planting the explosives on any structural support you can find. Set the timers for ten minutes and then get out. DO NOT. I Repeat, DO NOT wait for me." He fixed them all with a stern glare.

He paused at the door feeling the presence of Elzibeth and Lydia behind him. "You two should probably leave as well. I don't know what's behind this door."

"Did we not have this conversation just a few minutes ago, my love? My place is by your side no matter the outcome." Her face showed determination and love.

"And where she goes, I go. You don't get to make friends and then think we won't stick by you until the end," Lydia chimed in.

Alistar shook his head and sighed. "Fine."

"The lab where they make the serum is through this room," Alistar said as he scanned the badge and hit the button to open the doors. The doors slid open to reveal Mikhail standing on the other side of the room, cigarette in his mouth.

Alistar stopped dead in his tracks. "Mikhail!"

"You knew it would come to this, kid. I told you in that bar it would be a fight to the death the next time we meet," Mikhail took a long slow drag from the smoke in his mouth.

"It doesn't have to be, Mikhail. Join us. Help us change the world for both humans and supernaturals."

"I can't do that kid. One of our paths will end here tonight. I can't just let you walk in and destroy everything. Hunters need the serum this place produces to have an edge against the enemy." Mikhail flicked the cigarette away and removed his long coat, revealing tattooed arms. One of the tattoos' on his arm said *Brothers Forever*. He lit up another smoke.

"Come on, kid. Show me that the training I taught you is still somewhere in that head of yours. Old rules. No guns. No throwing knives. Just us, one on one."

"I don't want to do this, Mikhail."

"We have to, Alistar. We are soldiers, and this is war. One side wins, and one side loses. That's the way these things work."

Elzibeth stepped through the door, watching the two men. "Alistar, we don't have time for this." Lydia looked past her, concern on her face.

"Stay back, you two," he said, glancing over his shoulder at the woman he loved. "He WILL kill you if you interfere."

"We know. We have met before, afterall," Elzibeth replied.

"If you interfere, vampire, your life is forfeit. However if you don't, then I promise you will walk out of here to see another night." Mikhail glared at her.

Alistar pulled out his guns and ejected the magazines, throwing them behind him. Mikhail removed five throwing knives and tossed them aside. Alistar ejected the rounds in each chamber of his pistols. The rounds *pinged* as they hit the floor and he used his foot to slide the pistols away. A tear fell from his cheek, knowing what he had to do.

Mikhail nodded as Alistar took off his long coat, revealing a similar tattoo to the man across from him. Elzibeth had seen this tattoo before, but now she understood the connection. *Oh, Alistar!* she thought to herself. This wasn't just honor. This was a fight between family.

Alistar drew one of his katanas, and Mikhail drew his own sword, a bright shining longsword. Alistar knew it well. The mystical blade Redemption, was said to be able to cut those with a pure heart.

78

The two men eyed each other for a moment longer, and Mikhail let the cigarette drop from his lips. It seemed to float towards the floor, tumbling in the air before it hit in a shower of sparks. Both men flashed across the room toward each other.

Alistar pushed himself to his limits and beyond, his blade flashing in the room's lights. As fast as he was, Mikhail kept up with him, Redemption easily blocking the blow.

He came back at Mikhail from behind, bringing his blade down in an overhand swing. Mikhail calmly maneuvered his blade up, blocking the katana.

The blades sparked with each clash as Lydia and Elzibeth watched.

Alistar and Mikhail spun and parried, dodged and thrusted, each trying to get the upper-hand. Alistar threw a punch and nailed Mikhail in the face, and Mikhail kicked him in the ribs in return, shoving him back. Alistar changed tactics when he realized they were evenly matched.

What was it you taught me, old man? Sometimes you

have to take the sacrifice to win one for the team? he thought to himself, but he had forgotten to shield his thoughts. Over by the door, Elzibeth's eyes widened.

"Alistar!" she shouted the instant Alistar ran himself onto the tip of Redemption. He felt no pain until he saw his former friend impaled on his own blade, blood leaking out of the man's mouth.

Mikhail fell and Alistar caught him, lowering him to the ground. He held his dying friend in his arms. "Dammit, Mikhail! You could have dodged that blow and you know it!"

Mikhail chuckled, coughing up blood. "So could you, kid. Damn. I guess maybe I was on the wrong side after all. You still have a good heart. Maybe you can make this peace thing work with the help of your vampire."

The bright shining blade still impaled Alistar's chest but caused him no harm. He pulled it free, laying it on Mikhail's chest.

Elzibeth knelt next to the dying man, taking his hand in hers. "I can save you if you let me. There is still a chance for you to join us."

Mikhail smiled. "That's kind of you, little lady, but no. I'm old, and long in the tooth. Well past my prime. There's no place in this world for an old-war dog like me. I'm tired of it all. Now *him*? He's got the spirit for the fight ahead."

Another fit of coughing wracked his body and he clutched Elizabeth's hand tighter. "You listen to me, vampire. You keep him close and you hold on tight. He's got no one else in this world now. I always thought he would be the best Hunter this world needed, but I was wrong. He's going to be the savior it needs, but he can't do it alone."

He handed Alistar his sword. "Take her, kid. She's yours now. Use her well. I've always been proud of you.

When you meet her, remember... she's not your sister anymore." His hand went limp and slid from Elzibeth's grasp.

Alistar stood and closed his eyes as tears of rage and anguish poured down his face. The pain in his heart reached its breaking point, and something in him snapped. He screamed. The scream echoed, growing louder until the room's windows shattered in a hail of glass.

When he next opened them, the red irises had glowing yellow centers, and tears of blood poured down his face. Elzibeth could sense another presence in his mind. She stepped over and hugged him from behind, weeping for the man she loved.

The doors at the far end of the room slammed inward under a fierce blow, and through the wreckage walked a woman, flames engulfing her, claws marking her fingertips. Black flaming wings sprouted from her back. She streaked across the room in a split second, now face to face with Alistar.

"Hello, brother!" she sneered. Alistar's eyes widened in shock and confusion.

"You're dead," he choked out as a small trickle of blood flowed out of his mouth.

"No, *you're* dead." Elzibeth felt a sudden moisture coat the front of her uniform and when she looked down, she saw the woman's arm sticking out of Alistar's back, his still beating heart clutched in the woman's palm. The heart continued to beat, spurting blood.

"Run!" Alistar choked out. When Elzibeth hesitated, Alistar's gaze wandered over to Lydia with scared, frantic eyes, and the vampire moved, grabbing Elzibeth and dragging her out of the room at full vampiric speed.

"Alistar!!!!" Elzibeth's scream faded down the hallway. The Godhammer that was his sister used one claw to turn his face to look at her. "You could have been my vessel instead of this girl, but HE got to you first. Since then, you have been a thorn in my side. That ends today."

"So-sophia." Alistar wheezed, feeling his life-force fading.

"Oh, she's still here. Trapped, her body mine to do with as I please." The Godhammer tapped the side of her head with one claw in emphasis, scanning the room. "Was that your girlfriend? Figures my big brother would fall for a fang. You always did have an eye for the pretty ones. It's a pity you didn't stay with the church. We could have had such fun, you and I," she said, kissing him before dropping him to the floor.

"Don't worry; I'll make sure she and the others join you soon in hell." With those words, the creature that was his sister sauntered down the same hallway that Lydia and Elzibeth had taken, leaving Alistar lying on the floor in a pool of blood.

79

Alistar lay there, his life draining upon the floor, when a tall pale man extravagantly dressed in ancient regalia stepped into his view.

"Huh. I must say you've impressed me."

"Dracula? How can you be here?" The world seemed slower to him for some reason.

"I'm not actually. My body is in the next room in a glass tube being drained to make that blasted serum of theirs. But…" He reached down and pulled Alistar to his feet. Alistar felt light and he could see his body lying on the floor next to him.

"I'm also… in here." He tapped the side of Alistar's head.

"Am I dead?"

"Not yet. We are in your mind where time has no meaning," Dracula responded.

"Are you the HE my sister mentioned?"

"I am." Dracula gave a slight fanged smile, his red eyes twinkling in amusement.

"How? How are you in my mind?"

"The serum, boy. When you took too much of it the first time, years ago it allowed me to make a bond with you. Since then, I've transferred my consciousness into your mind, hiding in the shadows where you wouldn't notice me. The body in the next room is now a shell. Do you really think you developed all those magnificent abilities on your own?" Dracula chuckled before he continued.

"No, dear boy. I gave you those abilities, and helped you to become better. Helped you be the warrior you are today. You are you... because of me."

"I don't understand." Alistar's voice betrayed the confusion on his face.

Dracula sighed in annoyance. "Mortals. Never understanding the true nature of power. I gave you part of my power and the knowledge that goes with it. I made you the monster you are, slowly changing your body over the years, preparing it for my inhabitation." He waited for that to sink in. "But... I admit, there was one thing I did not count on."

Lydia and Elzibeth fled from the building and into the streets. The outer wall blasted out and the Godhammer flew into the night sky.

"Where are you? Come out and I promise I will make your deaths quick and painless," the creature that was Sophia said, landing lightly on the ground and furling her wings behind her. A werewolf leapt at her from the shadows. She caught it one-handed, easily holding the snarling beast off the ground. With a swift motion, she snapped its neck and dropped the body before sauntering down the streets.

"I did not count on you and my daughter meeting... or falling in love," Dracula finished.

Alistar actually held up his hand and Dracula looked at him. "Yes?"

"Elle. I have to save her. I can't let her die."

Dracula nodded. "I do not wish to see her dead either. She IS my daughter, after all. Therefore, I have a proposition for you. I will give you ALL my abilities, ALL my powers, and the knowledge on how to use them. BUT... you must do me TWO favors."

"What are they?" Alistar asked with uncertainty.

"I'll be honest with you mortal, I am tired of this world. I wish for release. My daughter won't do it, but I know if I ask, you as an honorable man, will. The time of MY reign is over."

Alistar nodded slowly. "And what is the second favor?"

"You will protect my daughter above all else," Dracula replied, turning away. "You will keep her safe, and you will reign at her side, a just and fair ruler of my people until the day you both pass."

"I love Elle more than life itself... But I am no ruler. I wouldn't know how."

Dracula revealed a knowing smile. "Do you think being a good ruler is something you just know? It took me years to learn that lesson. Why in my mortal existence, my savagery would make what you have done pale in comparison. But as I aged, time tempered my rage and I learned to be a fair ruler to all under my domain."

"I can't promise I'll be any good at it, but I'll at least give it the old college try."

"You will have my daughter at your side. She will guide you until you can rule on your own." Dracula said dismissively.

"No." Dracula looked at him in rage.

"What do you mean no?"

"I mean I won't rule alone. She and I will rule together. As for the other thing, I promise you it will be done," Alistar declared with resolve.

"*Hmm.*" Dracula tapped his bottom lip with one pointed nail. "It would seem you are wiser than I thought. That's surprising, considering most mortals are complete fools. Consider me impressed. Very well." He walked away from Alistar, fading as he did so.

Inside Alistar's body, blood and flesh began to knit, forming into a heart. The heart started beating as bone grew back and skin healed. The hole in his chest came together until only a patch of blood and a ragged, bloody hole in his under armor was left.

Alistar's eyes snapped open and he gasped for breath. "*Remember your promise... Alistar Kain,*" Dracula's voice sounded in his mind as he rose to his feet, going from horizontal on the floor to vertical, without getting up.

"Okay, that's kinda cool." he muttered, walking into the room beyond. There in a great glass tube filled with liquid and wires and tubes attached to it floated the body of Vlad Tepes. Walking over to the computer nearby, he started flipping switches and the machinery around him began to shut down until the last fan turned off. The tube slid open, spilling both the liquid in it and the body onto the floor.

Alistar crouched next to the ancient vampire, cradling the man's head in his lap. Dracula's eyes opened slowly. "I knew I chose well, when I chose you, mortal. Now do your task."

"Elle is going to be upset." Alistar smiled wistfully.

"She will, but I will always be up here should she... or you, need my council. I however will not answer unless I deem it necessary to do so. I can't give you all the answers.

Some things you will have to figure out for yourselves." He tapped the side of Alistar's head. "Now... do it. Release me."

80

Alistar closed his eyes, and pulling his silver-coated combat knife out, shoved it through the side of Dracula's head, giving it one swift twist. He watched as the light in the vampire lord's eyes faded.

A rush of power flowed through his body and his eyes snapped open, blazing with a great light. All the memories of Vlad Tepes swam through his mind and then of Dracula like a split-second replay.

Standing, Alistar cracked his neck. "Let's go save our girl." He said in a deep hollow voice, a blend of his own and the great vampire who now resided inside him. Closing his eyes he located Elzibeth's mind, pinpointing her exact location in the city and viewed the situation through her eyes. After taking the coat off the body and donning it, he disappeared in a flash of darkness.

~

Lydia and Elzibeth ran down an alleyway with the Godhammer fast on their heels. They stopped as they reached a dead end, turning, fangs bared ready to fight for their lives.

The Godhammer that was Sophia Kain strutted towards them. "The chase is over, little vampires. Now you die." Holding up her hand she gestured and a fireball formed between her fingers. She threw it and Elzibeth and Lydia braced for the impact, closing their eyes, both women wondering what it would feel like to be immolated in Hellfire… But the pain and fire never came.

Opening their eyes, they saw a man standing in front of them, holding the ball of fire at bay with one outstretched hand. The man flung it away where it hit a wall and dribbled to the flagstone, setting everything in its path on fire.

"Did you miss me?" Alistar's soft voice floated back to the two vampires.

"I killed you!" the creature in front of him shrieked.

"Yeah, you did… but a stronger power brought me back." Alistar turned to the thing that he once knew as his baby sister, his eyes blazing.

The Godhammer shrunk back in fear. "You!"

"Yes, me. This one is mine; we are one." The voice that issued from Alistar's mouth was that of Vlad Tepes.

"Father?!"

Through Alistar's body, Dracula turned his head. "Hello my dear child. Forgive my prolonged absence. Please leave the city now, as it may not be standing when we are done with this demon."

He paused and tilted his head to the side as if listening to something. "Alistar said that you should make sure to evacuate all the innocents you can, while you can."

He disappeared in another flash of black smoke but reappeared in front of the Godhammer, launching the creature into the sky with a vicious uppercut before disappearing again. In front of the creature again, he grabbed her, slammed her face first through several floors of a nearby building and stepped back.

"Release this one from your grip, demon!" Dracula ordered.

The creature pushed free from the rubble, rising into the air. "But we've become so attached. If you want her, you will have to take her from me," she said, forming another fireball and throwing it at the man below her.

Dracula let it wash over him and stepped through the flames unharmed. "You think you have mastery of Hell-fire, demon?! Let me show you true power. Inferno!"

Hellish flames flashed up from the street below, washing over the creature burning her. She screamed in pain. "How?!"

"I am the most powerful vampire in existence! I have had millennia to study the dark arts and master them!" Dracula replied as he raised his hands. Behind the demon a dark portal formed. "It's time for you to go back where you came from!"

The demon looked back. "No! I won't go back! I—" it screamed before Dracula's hand grabbed its throat, cutting off its words. He floated toward the black portal holding the creature at arm's length.

Blackened hands reached from the portal, grabbing hungrily at the creature, not flesh, but the spirit of the creature inside the body. "No! You can't!" the creature choked out before being pulled from the body. As it left, Sophia screamed in pain. She went limp in Dracula's grasp, and once the demon vanished, the portal closed.

Dracula brought Sophia to his chest and floated to the ground, holding her out across his arms. Slowly she opened her eyes. "Big... bro...?" she said weakly. Dracula faded into the background of Alistar's mind, giving him full control.

"I'm here, Squirt."

"So tired. So much... pain," Sophia replied weakly.

Dracula? What's wrong with her?! Alistar's panicked thought flashed through his mind.

"The demon's inhabitation of her body has destroyed it, and her soul. She does not have long to live," Dracula replied with a bit of sorrow in his tone.

How? How do I save her?! I've lost her once! I can't lose her again!

He became aware of another presence and looked up to find a woman in a black cloak standing next to him.

"I have come for this one." Alistar knew immediately who she was thanks to the knowledge Dracula had given him... *Death.*

"You can't have her! You won't take her!"

Sorrow filled Death's face. "I must. It is my job in this world and others to convey those who have passed into the next world."

"I don't give a fuck! I won't let you take my sister!" His eyes narrowed. *Come on man, you gotta—*

"Turn her." Dracula's reply was short and simple.

I don't know how. Alistar said in his mind.

"Alistar, she will no longer know pain, sickness, or hardship," Death said.

"You now possess my powers, those of the only vampire capable of turning a mortal with but only a bite if he so wishes," Dracula replied after a sigh.

Alistar paused, thinking for a moment. Closing his eyes he opened his mouth, his fangs lengthening, and as a tear fell, he sunk his teeth into his sister's throat, feeling her blood rush down his own.

Turn, damn you! Turn!

EPILOGUE

A month has passed since the attack on Rome, and Alistar stood in front of the full-body mirror, holding up opulent outfits against his chest, looking at and rejecting each one. "Why in the fuck do I have to dress up for this damn dog and pony show? Can't we just elope? I hate ceremonies," he grumbled.

Elzibeth kissed him on the cheek. "It's an important event and you must dress accordingly for it. And we Are NOT eloping," she replied walking into the bathroom to paint her lips, the elegant white dress flowing behind her.

Alistar sighed. "Yes, dear." He dug through the old wardrobe finding an old red and black cloak and outfit. The black cloak had a red interior while the knee length, long coat came with full-length sleeves and four-inch cuffs emblazoned in red with dragon motifs. A long turned-down Napoleon style collar with red motifs decorated the front of the coat. White edging complimented the black shirt and came with a red four-inch-wide sash.

"*Hmm...*" Alistar thought as he put it on. Then he looked down at his waist, trying to figure out the sash. Elzibeth stepped out of the bathroom.

"Now where did you find that old thing?" she asked, laughing.

"In the back of the wardrobe, with everything else." Alistar replied, his gaze flicking to her. "I just can't figure out this damn sash."

Elzibeth smirked and wrapped the sash about his waist three times before tucking it on itself, cinching it in place. "That's it?" Alistar asked.

"Yes, my love, that is it." Elzibeth replied, inspecting him and tapping her teeth in thought. She stopped, picked up the cloak, and wrapped it around his shoulders, fastening it in place about his neck. Stepping back again she motioned for him to turn around.

Alistar spun in place, making the cloak twirl about him. "It might be old, but for some reason it fits you." Elzibeth smiled sweetly.

Alistar popped the collar and looked at himself in the mirror. "I kinda like it."

Elzibeth fixed the collar back in place. "You look better like this." She leaned her head on his shoulder. "Alistar?"

He lifted an eyebrow. "*Hmm?*"

"Is my father still in there?" she asked, her gaze flicking up to his face.

"I can't feel him. Maybe he's on a vacation?" Alistar tilted his head to the side, shrugging.

Elzibeth and Alistar ambled down the carpet of the throne room. People from Calia, various vampires and even a few werewolves filled the room. All bowed as the two passed by. Stepping up to the throne, they paused, facing Richter.

"Ladies and beings of various creature types, we are

gathered here today to recognize the union between Grand Lady Elzibeth Tepes and Alistar Kain," he began solemnly.

Elzibeth faced Alistar, taking his hands in hers.

"Born of two different worlds, fate brought them together to change this world, and each other."

Alistar motioned to Marcus who carried a ring on a pillow. Alistar removed the Tepes ring, placing it on the pillow next to the one that looked like a silver dragon mimicking his own, but in reality was made of titanium. Blue sapphires dotted the dragon's eyes with a small diamond inside the mouth. Elzibeth smiled at the boy dressed in a fine suit looking rather dapper.

"Alistar Kain, do you take Elzibeth Tepes to be your wife? To guard and protect her, cherish and keep her, and rule by her side over the creatures of this world as long as you both may live?"

Alistar looked deep into Elzibeth's eyes. "I do."

"Elzibeth Tepes, Daughter of the Great High Lord Dracula, and Grand Lady of Vampires, do you take Alistar Kain to be your husband? To walk with him in darkness, and hardship? To rule fairly at his side?"

Elzibeth paused for a few seconds, studying the man in front of her. "Yes... I do."

After a moment of silence, Richter continued. "These rings represent the union between these two, forever showing their love and commitment to each other." He looked at Alistar, who nodded and picked up the ring. Taking Elizibeth's hand, he slid it onto the ring finger on her left hand.

Elzibeth took the Tepes ring and slid it likewise onto the ring finger of Alistar's left hand.

"What has come about, let it not be rent asunder. May this union in these times shine a light in the darkness. May it be a beacon of hope to all creatures on this planet to show that coexistence is possible."

Leaning forward Alistar kissed Elzibeth deeply and then together, they stepped up to the thrones they stood before and carefully sat.

"Elle, this throne makes me uncomfortable," Alistar said in her mind.

"Get used to it my love." Elzibeth replied in a whisper only he could hear.

"Ladies, gentlemen, and various creatures of this world, I give you Grand Lord and Lady, Alistar and Elzibeth Tepes-Kain. May their dynasty rule with peace and love. May their watch over this world help heal it and mend the brokenness that has befallen it," Richter finished.

The room erupted in clapping and more than a few wet eyes. Evelyn sobbed in the corner with tears of happiness.

"That's my big brother up there! Hi, fuck face!" a feminine voice shouted out from off to the side.

From his throne, Alistar looked over at his now much paler sister and smiled, his eyes glowing a red tinge with centers of gold. Elzibeth laughed at the girl's comment.

"We have a long road ahead of us, Elle," Alistar whispered. She reached over and clasped his hand. "I know, my love, but together, we will weather the coming storm."

ABOUT THE AUTHOR

Andreaus Whitefyre was raised and lives in Southern Indiana. 40 years old, he's a geek that loves Scifi, Fantasy, Vampires, Werewolves, and anything supernatural. An avid gamer since his early teens, he is a veteran of many pen and paper RPG's.

Andreaus loves writing about what he loves and is currently working on a Scifi Novel called Starbound, and a modern day bodyguard novel with a supernatural twist called Angel's Howl. All of his novels incorporate action and adventure, along with a little bit of romance and plenty of comedy and crude humor.

Dracula's Daughter is his first foray into the world of Authorship.

To find his Author page on FB, go to:
https://www.facebook.com/profile.php?id=
100090056087999

BOOKS BY THIS AUTHOR

Dracula's Daughter

Alistar Kain is a man running from his past. He is a broken man seeking an end to his pain. When he saves a beautiful Vampire Queen all that changes and as a friendship forms between them, Alistar finds there may be a life still worth living in this world. When the Church comes hunting them both down Alistar will find that he must reawaken old skills long put to sleep to defend his family and friends he now has. He's willing to go to any lengths to erase the mistakes of his past and protect those he loves including dying for them. Will it be enough to save him when his vampire and their friends step in? Will they succeed in saving him? If they do, he may just find the redemption he seeks in… Dracula's Daughter.

Angel's Howl (WIP)

Starbound (WIP)